Joy Dettman was bo

Melbourne.

Joy, a mother of four, is a full-time writer and a published author of several award-winning stories and the highly acclaimed novels *Mallawindy* and *Jacaranda Blue*.

Also by Joy Dettman

MALLAWINDY

JACARANDA BLUE

goose girl

JOY DETTMAN

PAN
Pan Macmillan Australia

First published 2000 in Macmillan by Pan Macmillan Australia Pty Limited
This Pan edition published 2001 by Pan Macmillan Australia Pty Limited
St Martins Tower, 31 Market Street, Sydney

Reprinted 2003,2005

National Library of Australia
cataloguing-in-publication data:

Dettman, Joy.
Goose girl.

ISBN 0 330 36264 X (pbk.).

1. Domestic fiction. I. Title.

A823.3

Printed in Australia by McPherson's Printing Group

For Don, my expert on all things mechanical,
and for Karli, too far away.

prologue

Too much of her life had been wrapped in newsprint; she rarely looked at newspapers these days, but her face was in them again.

'I look like Kermit the frog in this one,' she said. 'That photographer should aim his camera one more time, then go and shoot himself.' She'd put on a couple of kilos since she'd tossed away the cigarettes, and she'd been proud of herself, but the photographer had captured every gram.

'It comes with the territory,' he said. 'It's a great interview.'

'Who's got time to read the interviews? They'll take one look at that photograph, then turn the page.'

'Then turn the page. It's easy. Take your thumb, give it a big lick, and flip.'

She did, with a theatrical lick and an elegant sweep of her hand, then she pushed the paper from her and looked out at the Melbourne skyline. It was hazy today, smog shrouded, but smog smoothed out the harsh lines of tall buildings, softening the city.

Old Melbourne town, chock-full of memories. She didn't want to remember the last time she'd been here. Bad days, those. Hadn't wanted to come back here.

'I'm scared stiff,' she said. 'I'm scared silly.'

He placed a cup of strong black coffee before her and he kissed her, then offered a stale motel biscuit. 'What's to be scared of? Apart from motel biscuits.'

'Newspapers. They'll crucify me tomorrow.'

'Crucify Kermit the frog? Never. Everyone loves him. An entire generation was raised on Kermit. I used to be in love with Miss Piggy.'

She tossed the newspaper at his head and the pages flew. Kermit landed in her coffee. A good place for him too.

'It's not easy being green,' she sang. 'Anyway, I didn't like the Muppets when I was a kid. Shane and I were raised on Humphrey B Bear. For a while we were, and then –'

'No looking backwards. Today will be yesterday tomorrow, so let's make it a good one.'

'I had that dream again last night. I was driving along the freeway in the old Datsun, and there was this pea-soup fog; I couldn't see a thing, but I wasn't worried because I knew you were somewhere up ahead. Then suddenly it wasn't fog – it was smoke. And . . . and there was this huge red moon ahead, racing towards me down the centre of the road and it was setting the bitumen on fire.

'I tried to put on the brakes but they didn't work, so I kept on going, straight ahead – into the flames –'

that moon

1978

They had to drive Mummy to her bookings because she couldn't drive the car, and the man making the party only paid for a taxi home. The taxi cost lots of money and Daddy didn't have lots of money left over, and that was because of the repayments. Sally knew all about the repayments.

Most Saturdays, they bought takeaway for dinner, because mostly Mummy sang on Saturdays, and she didn't get time to cook dinner. She had to do her hair and look after the boys and fit in all her practising.

Tonight the booking was nearly thirty kilometres from Geelong, at a birthday party on a farm. Daddy showed Sally where it was in the map book, but they didn't have to get there till half-past eight o'clock, so they were having dinner very late tonight.

Daddy stopped at their favourite fish'n'chip shop and he bought a huge big parcel of fish and chips and potato cakes, and Shane said he wanted to go to McDonald's, like he always did. But Sally and Shane and Robby and Nicky were in their pyjamas and Mummy was in her cowgirl clothes and boots, so they couldn't get out of the car and go to McDonald's. The people would think, what a nutty family, Daddy said.

Everybody laughed. Even Nicky laughed his pretty baby laugh, and he clapped his tiny hands and ate some chips that Sally made sure weren't too hot for his mouth.

She just loved Nicky. He was all fat and cuddle and he smelt so good when he had a bath, and his hair was like white thistledown, and Daddy said he was going to be blond like Sally, because she had white thistledown when she was a baby.

And they ate everything, all the chips and all the fish and potato cakes, and it was like having a picnic in the car with Mummy feeding Daddy as he drove.

Mummy had to get all dressed up when she sang, because her costume helped her to put it across, which was sort of like hiding that she was really a mummy, not a nearly famous singer. Her guitar and cowgirl hat were in the back of the station wagon. It was a very expensive guitar and nearly brand-new.

When they finished their car picnic, they all wiped their hands on the wet sponge Daddy brought in a plastic bag, and Sally had to wipe Nicky's face and his hands while Mummy fixed her lipstick.

Then they got to the booking, which was way out down a dark road, and Mummy kissed everyone with big smacky kisses so she didn't spoil her lipstick, while Daddy got out to get the guitar and hat from the back and talk to the man making the party.

Then Nicky started to cry. It was way past his bedtime and he was teething and he wanted Mummy, and Daddy knew that the best way to stop Nicky from crying was to drive the car, so he got back in very fast, and because Sally was the biggest, she got to ride in Mummy's seat, in the front with Daddy.

Nicky went fast asleep in his little car seat just as soon as the car got going, and Robby was sleepy too, so he just sat there, all quiet and sleepy-eyed and noddy.

Shane wasn't sleepy. He was only just one year less than

Sally, and he was being the usual silly sausage, Daddy said. He was pulling Sally's ponytail because she was in the front and he wanted to ride in front.

'Daddy, make him stop it,' she said, but Daddy couldn't make him stop because he had to look at the road and drive carefully because he had a car full of precious cargo. That's what he said, and then he said, 'Just laugh at him, Sally-gal. He'll get tired of tormenting, the silly sausage.'

So she did laugh, and Shane stopped pulling her hair but he started trying to pinch her Teddy bear from over her shoulder.

She wouldn't let him get Teddy. He was very special. Sally got him from Grandma and Papa for a birthday present and he went everywhere that Sally went, except to school, but he even went to school on special days when it was show-and-tell time about your favourite toy.

Mummy said that Sally was too big to take Teddy everywhere, but that was just because poor Mummy was so busy with four children and getting so many bookings since she went on *New Faces*. Sally had watched her sing on the television that night, and it was, like, very special that her own mother was on the television. Like she was a very famous person.

Raelene from next door saw her, even. And Raelene's mother, who was Mrs Mason, said that Mummy should have won the prize money from *New Faces*, she was just so good. But it didn't matter that she didn't win the prize money, because everyone still wanted her to sing for them at their parties. She got lots and lots of bookings, which she had to write down in her diary.

Sometimes Sally and Shane went to bed late on Mummy's working nights, and they got to drink milk and eat bickies when Mummy came home – if the taxi wasn't too late and if they stayed awake. They loved having a little party with Mummy and Daddy and feeling very grown up and special, and they had lots of laughing and Mummy sang just for them, and if Nicky was awake, Daddy jiggled him on his knee and fed him a bottle while

Nicky's foot sort of kicked with the rhythm. Daddy said Nicky was going to be a singer too, and soon Glenda Jean De Rooze would have her own homegrown quartet.

That was Mummy's proper name, Glenda Jean De Rooze. People rang up and asked for Glenda Jean, and sometimes Sally was allowed to pick up the telephone, but Shane wasn't, because he didn't say 'Hello' properly. He just made silly noises, and giggled. Even Mummy knew that!

Sally didn't giggle; she was Daddy's little secretary; she always said 'Hello' very nicely, and then she called Mummy, and Mummy would take the phone and put on her special telephone voice and talk like an important lady, and she'd write down her booking in her diary that Daddy bought for her. She made some money from her singing and it helped to pay for the house and saved the bank getting interested.

They had a beautiful house that the building man built just for them. It had poppies in the front near the lawn and it had little trees, that would grow into big trees, and Daddy and Sally had planted some passionfruit vines near the fence and they put up a really tall trellis and Sally helped hold it for Daddy and then she helped to paint it green, and that was years ago when she was little. Now the fence was all green with the passionfruit leaves and it got beautiful flowers on it, and if the boys didn't pick them off the flowers grew into purple fruit, and this year Daddy said they would have heaps of purple passionfruit.

And they were driving home to their beautiful house that night. They had left the light on, so burglars would think there was someone home so they wouldn't rob them, and Sally knew that their house would look all bright and welcome in the dark street, like it was waiting just for them and for nobody else.

She was thinking that Mummy wouldn't be late tonight, and she was thinking about the packet of chocolate biscuits. Because she was Daddy's big girl, and his helper, while he put Nicky and Robby to bed she would make the party ready. She'd put the chocolate biscuits on a special plate and she'd get Mummy and Daddy's cups out and the little mugs for her and Shane – if he stayed awake. She wasn't even a little bit sleepy yet.

The moon started coming up as they were driving and it was big and fat and so bright. They were on the very dark road and not back in Geelong yet, so they could watch the moon coming up over the trees ... and ... and it was like round fire.

'Just look at that magic moon,' Daddy said, and Sally was looking over the trees to this giant moon and she'd never seen one as big before, then suddenly they were driving into a world of moonlight that lit up the narrow road, and she was looking at the silver trees running by so fast and thinking it was a magic night, like a fairies-dancing-beneath-the-trees night, and Daddy was telling about why the moon looked so big when it first got born.

Then Shane tricked her. He said, 'Hey, look at the big owl in the tree, Sally,' and while she was looking where he pointed, with his other hand he snatched Teddy and he threw him way over the back seat, and he giggled a cheeky Shane giggle because he'd tricked her.

'Daddy. He's got my Teddy. Make him give it back.'

'Daddy's driving, Sally-gal. Teddy will have to ride home in the back tonight.'

'But he's lonely. Can I get him? Please, Daddy. I'll be very careful,' Sally said.

'All right, but don't tread on the boys,' he said.

And she undid her seatbelt and she climbed over the seat, and gave Shane an elbow in the tummy as she tumbled over the back.

'Kangaroo, Daddy,' Shane yelled, and it was like another Shane trick. Sally thought it was a trick.

Then it wasn't a trick any more.

It was like ...

Thump!

And like the biggest BANG! in all of the whole world.

And it was like a bumpy ride at the show.

And it was like fast and flying and then the car was upside-down and Sally wasn't in it. She was on the wet grass, and ... and ... and Shane was upside down in the car and he was screaming.

'Daddy! Daddy! Daddy!'

He screamed, and he screamed.

And the flames came out small ... and ... and too fast, like *Whoooooosh*! And the car was all flames.

'Daddy! Daddy! Daddy!'

And Shane screamed, and he screamed while the car burned.

melted away

Sally couldn't help Daddy and the boys. She was only eight, and eight wasn't really big. Daddy just said she was his big girl. Even the man in the truck couldn't help. He didn't find Sally but she watched him try to put out the flames with his fire extinguisher.

No one found her until the fire engine came screaming, and the ambulance and the lights and all the men and noises came, and one of them yelled out, 'Hey! There's a little kid over here!'

The policeman sat beside Sally on the wet grass. She was sucking her thumb and reaching for the yellow balloon moon, wanting to ride up with the yellow balloon to the sky and all the stars and go with Daddy and the boys to God's heaven.

That's where people went when they got dead. She knew all about getting dead, because of Grandma and Aunty Bernice; they were bright stars in God's heaven.

The policeman wrapped Sally in a blanket because he thought she was cold. She wasn't cold at all, just shivering, and then he picked her up and put her in a car and drove away from Daddy and the boys.

At the hospital she told him about home, at Number 29 Carter Street, and she told them about Mummy at the farm playing Glenda Jean, and her singing while the car and everybody got burned. And metal shouldn't get burned. It shouldn't. And she told about a taxi coming at eleven o'clock. Later, Mummy came running into the hospital room still wearing her funny cowgirl clothes and Sally was wearing funny pyjamas.

Everyone would think, what a nutty family.

She tried to tell Mummy about the fire, like it was just a dream and if she told about it, then it would go away. She tried to tell.

'Silly Shane, well, he threw my Teddy over the back seat, Mummy, and Teddy was lonely, and I undid my seatbelt and climbed over the seat and over the boys and into the back, and I didn't tread on them, and –'

Mummy yelled at her to stop, but Sally couldn't stop. She wanted to talk all the bad-dream pictures and the bad-dream smell out so she could stop shivering.

'Daddy said I could get Teddy, Mummy, and I nearly got him in my hands, and I was near the back window, and then Shane said about the kangaroo, and it was an immense big one.'

Then Mummy did her bad screaming thing, so Sally didn't talk any more, like Daddy never talked any more when Mummy did that screaming.

She'd really wanted to tell about the kangaroo that just jumped on the car, and about how she thought it was a Shane trick when he said kangaroo, like with the owl. Maybe Daddy thought it was a Shane trick, too. She wanted to tell about the big tree, and the giant Bang! And about . . . like flying . . . like being a fairy, flying away between the moonlit trees, and the slippery slide on the long grass, but more than wanting to tell, she didn't want Mummy to do that screaming again, so she didn't talk any more.

She wasn't hurt at all. That was the baddest, baddest part. She should have got hurt bad, like broken arms and legs, and Mummy might kiss her better.

It was after a while that Sally and Mummy went home to the beautiful house but there wasn't anybody in it. Except people who came. Lots of sad things happened then, like funerals and pictures in the newspapers, and there was school again and after a bit the pictures in Sally's head got all hard, like the old newspaper when you mixed up glue with it and you made things with it, then left it in the sun till it dried and got stiff, and even if the news words and pictures were all still locked in there, you couldn't get them out because they were all stuck together.

That's when the fire dreams started. They came into her bedroom every night and she couldn't scream about them either.

Other strangers started walking through their beautiful house a bit later, and one family came in with a fat girl. They poked into everything, even the wardrobes and cupboards, and the lady and the girl talked too loud and they turned up their noses at everything. Sally saw them do it, and she heard the man who was trying to help Mummy sell the house.

'Desperate to sell,' he said to the fat girl's father. 'Nice big rooms,' he said.

'No garage,' the man said.

That was because Daddy didn't get time to get the garage. That was for next year and now there wasn't going to be next year.

The man took the people and the fat girl with the glasses into the boys' room. The bunk beds in there were painted blue. Then the man took the strangers to Sally's room, Sally's very own beautiful room, and she hated them looking in her wardrobe. They looked at her quilt that was made of swan's-down, its cover sprinkled with pink flowers, and they looked at her curtains, and they pulled at them, and turned up their noses again. They didn't even like the pink wallpaper that Sally had picked for herself.

'We'll strip and paint it, Carol, and build some shelves for your toys.'

Sally didn't want Carol Rigg's toys in there, didn't want her Teddy put on the bed. Sally's Teddy used to sleep there. No more Teddy with his nodding head and his bright bead eyes. He'd gone to be a star with Daddy and the boys.

They were not under the marble blanket in the cemetery that she saw every time she went there with Mummy. They were not down there and she wouldn't let them be down there. Nicky would get his asthma, and Robby always had to have a night-light, and Sally just would not go back to that stupid place again. Not ever again. She would not. She hated the cherubs Mummy had ordered for the boys. The stupid things made her get so mad, because she knew that Shane would have hated them. He would have wanted a Superman tombstone instead of three stupid naked babies with potbellies. Sally didn't like Daddy's tombstone either, because it had Mummy's name already on it, under his.

Glenda Jean De Rooze. United in death. 1950–19–

'One day I'll sleep here with him,' Mummy said.

There was no Sally name on the stones. How come Mummy hadn't bought four cherubs and stuck Sally's name on the boys' stone with number 1970–19–?

How come, anyway?

But she hadn't. It was like there was no place for Sally any more. Like there was no room left anywhere for her. Like a rubbish tin will do for Sally when she gets dead because she was Daddy's girl and Mummy had just hated that.

Mummy liked putting things in rubbish tins. Even good things she just . . . just threw them in the rubbish.

After that day, Sally stayed next door with Raelene on Mummy's cemetery days, and at Raelene's place they still had nice food smells and laughing time. Laughing was good. It squeezed all of the hurt from out of her tummy and made her think happy thoughts of Daddy, because he'd made a lot of laughing time. Sally helped mix the Christmas cake, and she got to lick the bowl, and she got sandwiches too, and a banana and also a huge handful of sultanas from Raelene's mother.

Mummy didn't buy sultanas, or anything, and she didn't even

make Christmas that year. She cried all the time and went to look at the dumb tombstones. And when she wasn't doing that, she was wrapping up things, packing up the house so the bank could give it to fat Carol Rigg.

Sally helped her with wrapping up, but she was pretending that she was wrapping up Christmas presents for Daddy and the boys. She wrapped the goose girl very well. It was beautiful, but very heavy for her hands, so she had to be careful. She helped wrap Daddy's photograph and the one of the three boys in their sailor suits, but not any of her pictures.

There were only four more sleeps until Santa came. Before that bad night, she'd asked Santa for a bike. She really wanted a bike and she wondered if Santa knew about the fire, and about them moving to another house on the tenth of January in 1979.

He didn't give her a bike. She just got a plastic doll from Kmart, because Santa didn't care about her either now that Daddy and the boys were dead, so she threw the stupid hard old doll straight in the rubbish bin, and Mummy saw her do it and there was screaming and . . . and more sad things.

Some people had to empty their beautiful house on the tenth of January and all their furniture had to get put in storage in Raelene's father's double garage next door because with all the screaming, Mummy broke down and went to hospital. Sally got put in storage too, at a stranger lady's house.

After a bit, the lady took Sally to the hospital to visit Mummy, but Mummy didn't want to see her. She just screamed, 'Take her away. Get her away from me.'

She screamed other stuff too, so half the world could hear her, and she didn't have to tell everybody about that. She didn't have to tell.

Sally just sucked her thumb until the lady picked her up and carried her away. Someone was always picking her up, just like the rubbish collectors picked up the bins, like she was just rubbish too. The lady told Sally a thousand times not to take any notice of what Mummy said, that it was only because

Mummy broke down and she didn't know what she was saying, and that the doctor was giving her medicine to make her better.

But Mummy knew what she was saying. She knew exactly what she was saying because she'd said it thousands of times before. But not when people were listening.

The lady didn't take Sally to the hospital again, not for ages, and when she did, Mummy said, 'My precious little girl,' and everyone was happy with her and she could come home.

Their first flat was in Geelong and it wasn't far away from the beautiful house, so Sally still went to the same school and that fat Carol Rigg girl was there too, and every day after school she went home to Sally's beautiful house and to Sally's bedroom and to Raelene next door, and Sally went home to a flat without any cooking smells but plenty of mouse smells.

Mummy liked the mice. She thought the noise they made was Daddy and the boys' ghosts come out of the ground to talk to her. She'd stand in the little lounge room and talk to the mice, just as if she was talking to Daddy and Shane. She wouldn't do anything else, though. She wouldn't wash things and get food in the fridge and she wouldn't unpack things, so Sally unwrapped all the ornaments and she played pretend. She had to pretend that the hard pictures of the fire were all gone away, because she had to make Mummy stop sleeping and crying and start singing again. Just play pretend until Mummy's breakdown was better and then the pretend could be over.

But they didn't have a phone at the flat, so there was no phone to ring for Glenda Jean. Mummy never sang again, except for sad songs at night, and she'd wake Sally in the night to say sad things like, shouldn't have, shouldn't have, shouldn't have. And it got so Sally didn't like to sleep in case she got woken up for more shouldn't haves, and when she did go to sleep the fire dreams came, and if she screamed, she woke Mummy, who could scream even worse.

Sally learnt about the counting in that first flat, learnt about counting the fire dreams all away. She'd just count and have, like, magic numbers, so when she got to a special number, she could make a bit more bad dream go away. Sometimes she had to count to thousands until all the dream pictures were gone.

Then one day a man came to their place and Mummy hid under the bed and Sally hid with her, because he was a very bad man, Mummy said, and Sally couldn't go to school for all the week, and when she did go to school, the bad man came back and Mummy did her screaming so the lady from next door got the doctor and he gave Mummy some more pills.

It was because of the man in the green car that they had to move from that flat. There was the packing up again and a junky old house and a different school, and the house was smelly and its cupboards were full of cockroaches.

Mummy was much better though, with her pills. Well, she was better if she took pills, so Sally made sure she took them. She brought them to her with a glass of water and she wouldn't go away even if Mummy threw the pills and did her crazy-lady screams. Sally just kept picking up the pills and standing there with the glass of water. Just staring at Mummy and nodding her head until the pills went down.

Mummy was still going to the cemetery, and staying there all day while Sally just watched television. She was nine when the doctor told Mummy that it would be better if they moved right away from Geelong, or the child welfare department might make Sally live with another family.

Only that doctor listened to Mummy's crying now; most people were sick of listening to it because she'd got a monster amount of insurance money for Daddy and the boys. They had to get a house, the doctor said, and he helped buy the house in Ballarat, and he got people to move the furniture; he got a lady to help Mummy clean the house and help with shopping so there was food in the fridge, which was good.

It was a redbrick, middle-aged house and not so bad, and Sally went to another new school. She didn't tell anyone about her father and her brothers, or about the welfare ladies. She just wanted to be all new again and stay in the Ballarat house with the happy doorbell forever.

But Mummy had some new people to tell. She told the mailman about her three boys. She told the people at the shops. She howled in the street, in the supermarket, because she once went to Ballarat with Daddy on her honeymoon.

'Oh, you poor dear, Mrs De Rooze,' the people all said. 'You poor, poor dear.'

Sympathy was a bit like the bread from the supermarket. It got stale very fast and it went mouldy so you couldn't eat it or you got poisoned.

After a bit the lady got sick of all the crying and all the house cleaning, so the not-so-bad house got turned into a terrible house because Mummy broke things when she did her mad bit. After a while that house got sold too, and they packed up the china and Grandma's dining room suite and they moved to a motel somewhere.

Moving. Moving. Always moving. Always some stupid excuse.

The shops were too far, or that green car was following them, or they had to hide under the bed because someone was knocking at their door, and it was probably only the welfare again; they were always knocking at the door, because people told tales on Mummy and serve her right.

Got to move again. Got to pack up your life in newspaper and go, Sally De Rooze.

The insurance money, that was going to buy them another house, got wasted paying for motels where they lived for weeks, and it paid for the caravan parks and for the storage place to store the empty fridge and Grandma's dining room suite and all the other junk.

That's when Sally found out that all Mummy wanted to do was to carve her numbers on Daddy's tombstone in Geelong.

Sally was eleven. They caught the train to Geelong and booked into another motel for two weeks. At least they were using the insurance money for something good this time. She could visit Raelene and maybe go to the old beach where they used to go with Daddy.

Mummy liked motels because they made her breakfast and she didn't have to make her bed. She was very happy and singing all the time at the motel. She'd brought her guitar with her and one day Sally was playing it when Mummy came back from the cemetery, and Mummy snatched it.

'Shane would have been the singer. He could sing when he was a year old. You sound like a crow with a sore throat,' she said.

They didn't go to the beach, or to visit Raelene.

'Too many memories,' Mummy said, and after that she took her guitar to the cemetery and Sally stayed at the motel watching television.

But one night, she got clever. She went out for the fish and chips and she didn't put the change back in Mummy's purse, and the next day, when Mummy's taxi left for the cemetery, Sally telephoned her own taxi and she got the man to take her to Raelene's. She had enough money to pay him too, and enough left for the ride back. She kept taking money from Mummy's purse after that, and she rang the taxi three times.

Then the two weeks were gone.

That last night at the motel Mummy was so happy. They sat up watching television, and later she sang and even let Sally play the guitar, and she taught her some more chords. Then she said they didn't have to leave Geelong, ever. Wasn't that good? Wasn't that so good?

'It's good,' Sally said, but she knew it wasn't good. Mummy's happy wasn't good; it wasn't safe.

Mummy laughed and made two big drinks of chocolate milk. But she never ever made food or special drinks, and her eyes looked too bright and starey, like the wicked witch when she offered Snow White the poisoned apple.

She turned into a witch too, and she got mean as a meat axe

when Sally tasted the drink and said it was yucky. Mummy said, 'Drink it!' and other old stuff, but Sally still wouldn't drink the chocolate milk, so Mummy drank both drinks herself.

The next morning when the breakfast trays came, Sally couldn't wake her, but she found an empty bubble pack in the bathroom rubbish bin. It should have been full of pills. That's when she knew. She ran to the motel office and got the lady to ring the doctor.

The motel lady and man were scared stiff. They ran back to the room and Sally just left them fussing while she telephoned the taxi man, then she scraped the two breakfasts onto one plate and took them outside, and ate everything while she waited for the taxi to come. And when he did, she left her plate on the fence and left Mummy waiting for the ambulance with a whole heap of people running around like chooks with their heads cut off.

She told Raelene's mother the truth. Mostly. Not about the double chocolate drink though, because that was bad. She had to tell her a bit because someone had to pay the taxi and Sally didn't have any money. Raelene's mother paid, and she said, 'You poor little kid.' Sally got to stay there, got to sleep in Raelene's room, got to live there for a whole week.

It was like she had died and gone to food heaven. She ate huge dinners every day, like three sausages and mashed potatoes and pumpkin and green peas. And they had sweets too, ice cream and peaches, or steamed pudding and custard, and she was allowed to drink as much milk and orange juice as she wanted.

But Mummy wasn't getting any better and she got sent to Melbourne and Mr Mason was getting sick of being stuck with Sally. Also . . . also, Sally just got to hate having that Carol Rigg living in her house next door, and swinging all day on that swing-set.

Squeak-squawk. Squeak-squawk, all day long.

Squeak-squawk. Squeak-squawk.

carol rigg

1981

Sally had watched the house at 29 Carter Street being built. She could remember it when its walls were only frames, and the lawn was only mud; she could remember Grandma and Papa had come one day and they'd all had a picnic of bought cakes and tea in a thermos, then they'd all walked around the house and talked about the rooms. Rotten Carol Rigg might live in this house but it did not belong to her and it never would – not the swing-set, or the fences, and certainly not the passionfruit vines.

Sally picked a green passionfruit and she hammered it on the top of the fence until it broke in half. It had a few pale yellow seeds in it which she licked out, but they tasted like yuck.

The vine was loaded this year. Hundreds, maybe thousands of passionfruit, and all for fat Carol Rigg. Even on this side of the fence there were dozens, so the vine must have been extra loaded on the other side where the roots were. Sally knew exactly where they were. She'd helped plant them when she was four, and she'd helped Daddy put up the trellis so the vines could climb high. Then she'd helped to paint the trellis green.

And Mummy had sold everything. 'Too full of sad memories, my precious girl.'

What else was there but the memories? They carried them around like Grandma's dining room suite and her ornaments, packing them and filling up all the empty spaces with old sad memories so there was no space for making new happy ones. Daddy and the boys had been dead for three horrible years, but for Mummy it was like they'd died yesterday.

The green paint on the trellis was nearly all gone now. Sally stood on the fence rail and reached high, picking at a flake of green still held safe between the wood where it crossed over. She picked with her fingernail until she got it. It was only a little bit, but still good and green, and she held the flake in her palm because it was precious, like a diamond, or an emerald – even more precious than that because Daddy's hand had painted it there.

Her jeans kept slipping down; they were Raelene's jeans and Raelene was heaps bigger than Sally. So was Carol Rigg. Everyone who was eleven was bigger than her. Everyone who was nine was bigger because they didn't get starved half of their lives and picked on for the other half.

Squeak-squawk. Squeak-squawk.

That swing noise sounded so sad today. It made her feel so sick-sad in her heart and in her head. Carol Rigg didn't care. She kept on swinging, doing it on purpose, just to torment, like she said Sally's mother was in a nuthouse, just to torment.

It wasn't a nuthouse. It was a hospital for people with nervous breakdowns.

Saturday. What a horrible, rotten day. Raelene was at a birthday party. That was half the reason why Sally was feeling sick-sad, and all curled up inside like a slater bug. If she still lived at 29 Carter Street, and if she still went to Raelene's school, then she would have got an invitation to the party too. They'd always got invitations to the same parties when she'd lived next door. But she didn't live next door. Rotten Carol Rigg did.

She couldn't see over the wall of vine, so she climbed up the fence and onto the trellis. Pieces of it broke away as she placed her weight on them, but she found safe footholds and made it up to the garage roof. If Raelene's father had been at home he would have banged on a window and roared like a bull, but he wasn't home. He played golf on Saturdays.

She liked it up on the roof; she could see right inside the kitchen window next door, and she could see in her old bedroom window, where the Riggs had put up new curtains. They'd tossed away Sally's pink ones with the flowers. Probably tossed them in the rubbish bin. Quickly she looked away from that window and back to the kitchen, where Carol Rigg's mother was working at the sink, washing dishes or something.

'I'm going to tell on you. You're not allowed to get up there. Mr Mason said so,' Carol Rigg said.

Sally ignored her. Carol was just pure jealous; she couldn't have climbed on a roof even if she'd been game to try. She was as fat as a pig, and she wore dresses with frills and flowers on them. And glasses, stupid blue ones that slid down her fat nose because it wasn't long enough and was always sweaty. Yesterday, she'd got red-faced jealous when Raelene wouldn't go over to play, and she went inside sulking, then came out with two ice creams, and she called Raelene over to the fence and gave her one. Then she whispered something, and Sally knew she'd been whispering about Mummy and the nuthouse even if Raelene wouldn't say so.

'You'll just get mad at me,' Raelene kept saying and letting the ice cream drip. 'I don't like these much,' she said – which was a lie and Sally knew it. 'You have it, Sally.'

'It's probably poison.'

That's when things started getting sad and mad and bad in her head, so she'd walked up to the shop on the corner and she'd nicked a chocolate bar. It wasn't the first time either. She was good at nicking things.

Squeak-squawk. Squeak-squawk.

That was yesterday, and the mad and the bad had got worse in the night.

On her stomach now, stretched out flat on the roof, the roofing iron warm beneath her, she was reaching down to pick green passionfruit, which she threw at Carol Rigg. She didn't miss either, and Carol screamed out to her mother, who screamed out at Sally, but the swing kept on squeak-squawking.

Then it came to her, a really funny idea. It was her special pretend trick to make the sad go away. She thought about stupid things that made her laugh, and after a while the game got like it was real and she laughed so hard that it killed the sad. Just like Daddy always used to say, 'Laugh and the world laughs with you, Sall, my precious gal.'

The world was really laughing with her as she climbed down, and almost choking with giggling when she got the hose with its orange spray thing on the end. She turned the tap on full bore, but with the spray turned off, and she tied the hose around her. It wasn't easy climbing back up, the hose trying to pull her down, but she could do anything she wanted to do, and she wanted to get the hose up on the roof. And she got it up there.

Squeak-squawk. Squeak-squawk.

Daddy used to put grease on the parts that made that noise, because that sound used to drive Mummy crazy; even way back then she was a bit crazy, and the swing had always made its squeak-squawking, right from the Christmas Day when it was put up, when she was four and Shane was three and there wasn't any Robby or Nicky. For a long time there had only been Sally and Shane.

She shook that thought away and pointed the spray down the roof like a gun aimed at Carol's head and she waited for her to look up. She never spoke to her. Never once. Carol Rigg was a house thief, that's why.

Then the house thief pushed her glasses up and she lifted her head and squinted up at the garage roof, looking all bug-eyed and open-mouthed, like *Oooo*. That's when Sally turned on the spray and let her have it, right up her fat nose.

Her glasses went flying and she nearly fell off the swing, then when she did get off, she fell over, and she looked like a screaming turtle on its back. Sally kept hosing her until she got up and went yelling and slipping to the back door with the water following her.

Her mother tried to come out. She was yelling like crazy too, so Sally gave her something to yell about.

Then Raelene's mother came out with little Jamey. She was tall and fat and slow. She looked around, sort of slow, like she always had a million hours of time to do things. She looked slowly at the fence, then over the fence. For a while she didn't know what was the matter; she couldn't see Sally on the garage roof. She looked up at the water, sort of surprised, like she thought there was a cloudburst, but not properly burst, just sprung a leak, and it was leaking all over next door. It wasn't until she looked up that she saw where the leak was coming from.

A lot later, around dinnertime, Carol and her mother had changed into dry frilly dresses and Mr Rigg had come home and he'd found the blue glasses, which were back on Carol's nose. Raelene's father was home from golf so they were all standing together at the fence. Half of the neighbours were out with their sticky noses, but Sally was a bird on her perch, watching everything, hearing everything and busting to go to the loo.

'She's a social welfare problem.'

'What can you expect? The poor little kid. I mean, dragged around from pillar to post, like she's been. She doesn't know who she is any more.'

'I'd call the welfare. That little terror isn't going to come down.'

'Come on, sweetie. You can't sit up there all night. We've got crumbed sausages for dinner.'

Sally really liked Raelene's mother, and she loved her crumbed sausages, but she didn't get down, not even for sausages. She kept picking and throwing passionfruit at Carol Rigg's roof and watching them roll into the guttering, hoping they were blocking it.

Mr Rigg and Raelene's father got the ladder out; they climbed up, but Sally dodged them all over the big roof, praying for it to get dark in a hurry so she could pee into the next-door yard.

That's what dogs did. They peed on things to mark them, like saying this is my place, stay away you other dogs. It didn't matter what everybody in the whole world thought, that house still belonged to Sally.

Then the welfare people drove up with a police lady. They spoke for a while before the man climbed up the ladder at the front of the garage.

He thought that he made Sally come down, but he didn't. It was just because of the loo. She jumped from the back of the garage to the lawn, and it was like flying, like wind in her face flying away from everyone and everything, sort of free – until she hit the lawn and all of her air was pushed out. But she got some in when the police lady ran around the back. Sally dodged her behind the peach tree until she could make a break for the house, where she locked herself in the loo.

They took the door off with a screwdriver and she had to go to some other place because Raelene's father said he'd taken her in out of the goodness of his own heart, even if everyone knew he didn't have one. And Raelene's mother said, 'We feel that sorry for the poor little kid, but as Jim says –'

Then Raelene's father butted in. 'That sort of behaviour can rub off on our girl.'

'Who cares?' Sally said. 'I don't care where I go.' She walked to the big white car as if she didn't care one little bit, then another lady drove up with a car full of kids and balloons and Raelene got out crying and she ran to the car.

'Write to me, Sally.'

'I don't care,' Sally told her and all of them, and she sat in the back of the car as if it was her own car, as if she didn't care, and she opened the window and did up her seatbelt, and even when the man wound up the window, Sally just opened it again and sat there, not looking at anyone, and not even waving to Raelene.

But she counted. She counted to a hundred maybe a hundred times before they got where they were going, to some lady who had a house full of beds and enough kids to fill them. She pretended she was kind and she tried to give Sally a cuddle. It wasn't like Raelene's mother's slow, soft, chesty cuddle, it was a hard, fast, stiff-handed cuddle.

'Your mummy is very sick, dear,' she said.

'If the dog bites the postman, that's not news,' Sally said.

'This will be your home until Mummy is well again.'

'As if I care,' Sally said.

For days she said it. 'Get stuffed,' she said. 'As if I care. Leave me alone. I don't care about anything.'

But she did care. God, how she cared.

the guitar

1983–1986

Sally had learnt a lot in the two months she lived with the lady and the ten other kids. She'd learnt to say the F word and to smoke, learnt a lot of other stuff before the doctors had let Mummy out to play the same old games, over and over and over.

Wrap up the china, Mummy's half-sane. Pack it up, Sall, she's off again.

Another motel. Another caravan park. Another rented flat. Another town.

And another bloody school!

'My precious girl,' Mummy's mouth said when someone was listening in, but her eyes never said it.

Sally was six months away from fourteen. Most of the insurance money had been wasted, so they were on the full pension when a housing ministry flat became available in Lakeside. It wasn't old, and the rent was cheap. Someone organised the move.

It was a weird little town; the bus had to drive around the mountains and down into it, and there was no way out of this place, except the way in. No train out, and if you wanted to get to Geelong, you had to get a bus to Bacchus Marsh then a train to Melbourne and another one to Geelong.

That was good. That was very good.

Daddy and the boys had been dead for over five years, and it was like they hadn't ever been real anyway. Just pictures in some kids' book; Sally was too old now for fairy tales. She owned a really good book, *Gone with the Wind*, which had come from some library somewhere; Mummy had been hauled off to the nuthouse before the book was due back, so now it belonged to Sally. She loved it. She loved the title and tough Scarlett, and she read it over and over.

These days she didn't even look at Daddy and the boys' photographs, though she was an expert at wrapping them up in newspaper. She was an expert at washing floors too, and killing cockroaches, and lining mouldy cupboards and frying sausages, which she did in Lakeside. After a bit, life got to be about as normal as it ever got.

But they stayed there too long and she started liking it, and liking places wasn't a good idea.

The town was so old and sort of interesting, locked in safe, away from the world, mountains and forests all around. And it had a beautiful lake that looked more blue than the sky some days. You could swim in it too, like in the ocean at Geelong. And they had an old gold mine, like in Ballarat, and the flat was a bit like one of the houses they'd lived in some place, with the same front door and how you walked through the laundry to get to the back door. It was weird, as if here in Lakeside, everything was trying to come back together. Like with a broken ornament she was trying to repair with glue, Sally kept finding the broken bits and fitting them into place.

Even the school was like the one in . . . in some place. It only went up to Year Ten, then you had to take a bus over the hills to do Eleven and Twelve – if you were smart enough to stay at school. She wasn't. She was in Year Seven, a year behind her age group, but no-one noticed because she was smaller than the other kids.

They wanted to be friendly, like, Oh, new face in town. And they all wanted to know her business. She didn't tell them – just made up stories – but she actually did get to know their names. Jen Larkin was sex mad. Deb Davis was smart. Gina Marvin was a snob. Karen Matthews was six foot tall and a dork. Away from Mummy was better than with her, so after a bit Sally refused to miss school; it didn't matter what stunt Mummy pulled, she went to school anyway.

And she learnt a bit. When you went every day the work wasn't too hard. Bits were actually interesting. Maths was always okay, music was ace, and she loved drama, loved pretending to be someone she wasn't. Putting words on paper was rotten. All the words she'd let clog up in her head ages ago never seemed to come out right. It was a case of squeezing the words out like you'd squeeze out a pimple, but she kept squeezing them out; everything was going okay.

Until that bloody music teacher.

He found out she could play the guitar, only because she was mucking around with one she shouldn't have been, and singing mad songs, making Deb and Gina laugh. Anyway, the teacher didn't get mad. He just said something about 'pitch and stuff' and he said it would be great if Sally could have her own guitar, and would it be possible for her parents to buy her one.

He didn't know about how things were at home, and Sally sure as hell didn't tell anyone. She told him that she had a guitar, though, and he said to bring it to school.

Mummy's guitar was on top of her wardrobe in its case and Sally wasn't allowed to touch it of course, but Mummy never touched it either these days, so as long as its case was there, she wouldn't know if it went missing, would she?

Sally waited for her chance, waited until Mummy was flaked out on the couch asleep, the television laughing, then silent as a robber she crept into the bedroom, carefully took the guitar from its case, put the case back, old newspapers on top. Easy.

God, she loved that guitar; still so new, so shiny. She was going to leave it with Mrs Jenner in the back flat until tomorrow, so she crept down there. But she couldn't keep her hands off it. She sat for a while softly playing it, soft strumming, soft singing 'Old Shep', which she used to sing for Daddy.

Then out came Mummy, tanked to the eyebrows. She bought bottles of port every pension day, which wasn't as bad as it sounded because she was better when she was tanked up – sleepy, but better. Except that day she wasn't better. She snatched the guitar and did the usual *killed'em* song and dance, then smashed the guitar against Mrs Jenner's wall. Just smashed and smashed it, wishing the guitar was Sally's head.

The next day she did her old, *Don't you go to school or I'll be dead when you come back* bit.

Sally was still as mad as hell, sick and sore and mad as hell, and so coal-black angry. It had been a beautiful guitar, expensive, and much better than the ones the other kids at school had.

'I'm sick and tired of living with your crazy fucking head, Mummy. I wish I'd killed you instead of Daddy.'

That's what she'd yelled. Shouldn't have said it, shouldn't have said the F word. Shouldn't have, because . . . because, when she came home at four o'clock . . . when she came home from school at four o'clock she found Mummy sitting in a bath full of pink water. She'd cut her wrists with a kitchen knife.

Mrs Jenner called Dr Sleiman. He sewed up the cuts while Sally walked around the little hospital for the first time, sort of wondering why Mummy had left it so late when she could have cut herself at nine o'clock that morning.

She spoke her thoughts out loud later. Spoke them to the doctor when he came to tell her that he was sending Mummy over the mountains to a Melbourne hospital. He was young and small, and his fingers on her shoulder were worms crawling there. She pulled away from him, and her question had come out because his hand had made her feel goosebumpy scared.

He was a yuck. His hair was thin and white-blond and it fell in a long half-fringe almost to his left ear. And he had buck-teeth and yellow pop-eyes, as if the bones of his face didn't like his eyes much so they were trying to push them out. And green trousers. Who ever wore green trousers?

She had her back to the wall, ready to dodge to the left or the right if he came at her again with his worm hands. She'd had to dodge a few creeps at the homes and she knew all about them.

'Yeah. Yeah, well, what I want to know is why she waited until I got home from school to do it. If she thinks she's hurting me by hurting herself, then she's got another think coming.'

The creepy sleaze didn't say anything else. Probably thought, what a rotten kid – and who cared? Anyway, as soon as Mummy was conscious he packed her off to the psychiatric hospital in Melbourne.

Sally was three weeks away from fourteen, and fourteen year olds weren't supposed to stay in flats by themselves, but she sure as hell wasn't going to be dragged off to another emergency care place. She'd take off for Melbourne, live on the streets, if they tried to drag her away again.

Mrs Jenner gave her a really good dinner that first night, vegetables and meat and gravy. Sally felt a bit bad when she told her that she'd telephoned her grandmother and she'd be coming down from Melbourne tomorrow. Mrs Jenner looked at her a bit funny. She probably already knew Mummy's life history, but she didn't say anything, except, 'Would you like some apple pie and cream, dear?'

Anyhow, who did everyone think had been looking after Mummy since Daddy died? And as sure as hell, it would be a damn sight easier just looking after herself and not having to dodge flying port bottles.

She stayed away from Mrs Jenner after that, but she went to school every day. She cleaned up the flat, put the rubbish out on Wednesday, watered the garden. It was okay too – until Mrs Jenner contacted the school. Then everyone got into the act.

Mrs Bertram, who taught art and sewing, asked Sally if she'd like to go to her place for dinner that night. She and her son had a farm.

Sally said, 'I'm okay. My grandmother is coming tomorrow. She got held up, but she's definitely coming tomorrow.'

But Mrs Bertram knew from the school records that Sally only had Mrs Jenner's name as the emergency number to ring. She also knew Sally had holes in her shoes and that she'd had no school lunch for a week, and she probably knew that she'd nicked a chocolate bar from the canteen. Karen Matthews had seen her do it and Karen was a lanky goody-goody dobber dork.

'Come out for dinner and have a look at us. You might decide you'd like to stay for a few days, Sally,' Mrs Bertram said.

So she went. Just for dinner, though, because she was massively hungry and any port in a storm.

Mrs Bertram's son, Ross, looked like a man. Sally was wary of him. But he wasn't really a man, just a giant-sized eighteen year old, and already a footballer. He ate heaps that first night and she couldn't help but stare at his plate, which he kept on filling up. Then they had farm cream in a sponge cake and he tried to make Sally eat as many pieces as he did. She ate three pieces. All she'd had since that first night was cereal for breakfast and pancakes for dinner and a couple of chocolate bars. The fridge and her mother's purse were empty.

'Stay the night, and we'll talk about it tomorrow,' Mrs Bertram said.

So Sally stayed in the sleep-out bedroom and Mrs Bertram found her a T-shirt for a nightie, and there was porridge and thick cream for breakfast and so much toast and homemade jam and milk from a cow, and they were so sort of laid-back friendly that she told Mrs Bertram that she'd lied about her grandmother.

'She died when I was about three, so unless she does a Jesus and rises from the grave she won't be coming to look after me. Right?'

Mrs Bertram tried not to laugh. Ross started it, then Mrs

Bertram joined in and they bellowed with laughter. Sally just sat there, wanting to laugh but refusing to give them the satisfaction. Stickybeaking busybodies. She'd known too many of their type, but the food was good and there was acres of room at the farm. She wouldn't have to see too much of them except at meal times.

The only trouble with that was that they weren't really the true do-gooder types. Mrs Bertram was big and fat, a bit like Raelene's mother, but a reddish blonde with a huge face and a snub nose. Ross was the living image of her except his hair was only short blond spikes about half a centimetre long. And also, they knew about losing people, because when Mrs Bertram drove Sally to the flat to pick up some clothes, she said how Ross had lost his father when he was twelve.

Sally showed her the photograph of Daddy, which was face-down on the cabinet. 'He died when I was eight.'

'You don't look like him. Do you look like your mum?'

'Yeah, worse luck. I'm going to have my face fixed when I stop growing.' She offered the second photograph. 'That's Shane and Robby and Nicky. They're dead too. Shane looked like Daddy. So Mummy says. I don't remember any of them.'

'You poor little girl,' Mrs Bertram said, and she kissed Sally's cheek.

Sally drew back, all hot and embarrassed. But Mrs Bertram put her arms right around her and she gave her one of those soft squishy hugs like Raelene's mother used to give, and she kissed her again.

It was like . . . like . . . like deep-sigh, little-kid safe, like being held in Daddy's arms and him making the hurt all better. Sally's thumb went to her mouth and tried to get in. But she snatched it away, then stepped away. Fast. It wouldn't last. If you didn't have anything, then no-one could take it away from you, and the taking away was worse than the not having and she wasn't going to let anyone take anything else away from her. Mrs Bertram would pack her off soon to someplace, or they'd let

Mummy out and she'd start packing the ornaments.

But she was still in the nuthouse when Sally had her fourteenth birthday. No-one knew it was her birthday and she didn't tell them, but that night she decided to give herself a present and she went to Davis's pharmacy with Mrs Bertram after school and got herself a bottle of nail polish, which she palmed then slipped into her uniform pocket. That night she painted her nails black, because she felt black.

'You've got beautifully shaped nails,' Mrs Bertram said. 'I always wanted to have beautiful nails.' She picked up the bottle of polish and looked at it, then she took five dollars from her purse. 'If I were you, Sally love, I'd give that to Mrs Davis tomorrow, and I'd tell her I was very sorry.'

'I'm not sorry, am I?' Sally put the money in her pocket and gave her nails another careful coat of varnish.

'That's your decision, my love.' Mrs Bertram placed a ten-dollar note on the table, and Sally wouldn't look at it. 'It's yours. Put it in your pocket.'

'I don't want it, and I don't want your pity either. And you don't know anything about me.' She took the five-dollar note out of her pocket and tossed it to the floor.

'I know that you're a frightened and angry little girl.'

'Who cares?'

'I care.' She didn't say anything else, just started cooking dinner. Then Ross came in and he saw the ten dollars on the table and the crumpled five-dollar note at his feet and he started talking about the bull and Sally sat there, tears trickling. And when they still wouldn't look at her, she swiped the ten-dollar note to the floor too.

They just kept on talking about bulls and heifers and ignoring the money, just walking over it, so Sally stood up and yelled, 'It's my fucking birthday today,' and she ran into the sleep-out and wouldn't come out for dinner. They didn't care that she was starving either. She could hear them scraping their plates and talking, probably laughing about her starving.

The next morning she thought they'd pack her off somewhere, but it was like nothing had happened.

'Oh, Sally love, I was just thinking. Would you like to invite a couple of your friends out for a barbecue and a sleep-over on Saturday night?'

'I don't need your . . . a party.'

'I like parties. But it's up to you.'

'No-one would come, anyway.'

'They certainly won't come if you don't ask them,' Mrs Bertram said.

'Ask who?'

'Some of the girls in your class.'

So, just to be rotten, Sally asked all the girls in Year Seven, and nearly all of them said yes, and it seemed like a good joke too, but by the end of the day it had started to feel like a bad joke, and she got too scared to tell Mrs Bertram.

She told her at the dinner table and she waited for her to scream or something, but all she said was, 'Did you tell them to bring their sleeping bags?'

On the Saturday morning Ross found an old tent full of dust and spiders and Sally helped him put it up in the back yard, and by six o'clock no-one was there. She knew they wouldn't come, that they'd been making fun of her.

Then suddenly the cars started driving up, and everyone brought sleeping bags and presents and they played games and ate heaps and drank bottles of Coke and when Ross and Mrs Bertram went to bed the girls talked about boys for half the night, and then Deb Davis said she was having a party the next weekend and could Sally come.

That night Sally fell in love with Mrs Bertram and she prayed her first prayer in five years. Please, God. Let me stay with her forever. And please, God, let me have Ross for a brother forever, amen.

He was a brilliant football player. She hadn't known a thing about football before the Bertrams, but most Saturdays she and

Mrs Bertram drove to Melbourne to watch him play, and to call in on Mummy – if she was receiving visitors.

All the way to Melbourne Mrs Bertram talked and asked questions. Sally told a bit about the crash and how, if the window had been open, Shane could have got out. And how she should have found a bit of wood or something and broken the window.

'You were an eight-year-old baby, my love. There was nothing you could have done.'

There was nothing you could have done. Words offered like a lake full of clean, warm water, and she dived deep into them, and it put out the fire dream. Just like that.

The next Saturday when Mrs Bertram was driving to Melbourne, Sally wound up the car window, which was good because it was winter and the rain had been blowing in. She still held tight to her seatbelt, her hands ready to open it, and she still watched the road for kangaroos, she watched the trucks and trams in the city, but when they got to the football she learnt to yell as loud as Mrs Bertram, 'Come on, Ross. Kick it, Ross.'

The yelling was good, too. It let out all of the hard old hurting, like all the years of locked-in screaming had found a safe way to come out.

Lakeside had been invented by God, and he put the Bertrams there, just for Sally, but so she wouldn't start thinking the town was actually heaven, he invented Sleimans.

They owned about half the land beside the lake and when one got married they built another mansion. It looked like an exclusive holiday resort with a tennis court, a swimming pool and a razor-wire fence. And one Sleiman was Mummy's doctor.

He met them at the Melbourne hospital one Saturday and he said Mummy could go home next week, and Sally didn't want her to go home. That was being honest, like Mrs Bertram said that people should always be honest. Not that she'd want to hear that much honesty. But no more farm, no more laughter?

Please, God, I don't want to play watchdog again, be the local garbage again. Please, God, don't make me go back to Mummy and I won't nick things from the shops ever. Please, God, don't make me leave Mrs Bertram.

Prayers didn't work; she gave up religion the day they let Mummy out, and it was back to purple carpet and Grandma's dining room suite and two new packets of pills.

But she didn't lose Ross and Mrs Bertram so she only nicked things from the shop people she didn't like, not from the ones where the Bertrams did their shopping.

Mrs Bertram sort of adopted Mummy, and Sally watched how she treated her. She discovered that if she treated Mummy exactly like Mrs Bertram did, Mummy thrived on it. Sally gave her Bertram hugs, and patted her back when she cried. And when she did the old *killed 'em* song and dance routine, Sally didn't scream, she said Bertram things like: 'Gee your hair looks nice when it's first washed, Mummy.' Or, 'I love the colour of that jumper on you.'

It worked too. It worked well for the longest time. For two whole years, life was almost good.

It wasn't real, though. Sally still wanted to scream that she was sick of living with a crazy nutcase. Deep inside she still planned to pack her bags and get on a bus, go to Melbourne and stow away on a plane and get as far away from Mummy as a plane could take her. Then get her face fixed.

She was the image of Mummy. Everyone said it. Her hands, feet and hair were like Mummy's, even her fingernails, so how could the inside of her head be any different? And keeping all the mad and bad and the angry inside was like Mrs Bertram's pressure cooker when the steam hole got blocked with rice. The whole thing could blow.

Sally hated the inside of her head; she could hide it from Mrs Bertram and Ross, but she couldn't hide it from herself. Sometimes the pressure of un-screamed words got so bad that the only way she could hold the scream in was to hide in her room, crawl under her old bed and pull a blanket over her head. Hide there in the dark and suck her thumb, just as she had when she and

Mummy had hidden beneath the bed when the man came knocking on the door.

She was hiding there one day when Mummy went off her lid again, and all because Sally wanted to go on a school camp for two nights. Just two lousy nights. Mummy wouldn't sign the papers, even though Mrs Bertram said she could stay those two nights at the farm so she wouldn't be alone.

No way. That wasn't what she wanted and one way or another Mummy always got what she wanted. Always had. Always would. She popped half a packet of pills and ended up in the psychiatric hospital again and Sally got to go back to Mrs Bertram and Ross.

Hallelujah! Oh, Hallelujah!

She was sixteen and a bit, and the football season was almost over so Ross had to go to a posh dinner in Melbourne. First he wasn't going because he didn't have a suit, and then he was going. He'd hire a suit. Not worth buying one. But he'd feel a fool going by himself when he'd be sitting at a table with all the other players and their girlfriends, so he wasn't going after all. Then he didn't know what he wanted. He was standing there, rubbing his mouth and looking at Sally.

'For goodness sake, Ross. Ask her.'

'No', he said. 'I'm not going.'

'Ask her, you great big galoot. She's a young lady now.'

Ross blushed and rubbed his mouth. Sally was looking at him, hoping they were talking about what she thought they were talking about.

'Would you like to go to the footy dinner with him, Sally love?' Mrs Bertram said.

Radical. Like wow! She didn't get to go to the school camp but she was going out to a big footy dinner in Melbourne. She ran at Ross and bear hugged him, then she raced outside to the back garden and she screamed, 'Yippee!' And the dogs all barked yippee too.

Mrs Bertram made her an after-five dress. It was a dusty

peach pink. 'Perfect for a girl just bursting out into bloom,' she said. 'And what a bloomer you are going to be, my Sally De Rooze with those big navy-blue eyes. They're like the lake in spring. Men are going to drown in those eyes before you're much older.'

Tiny Sally in peach pink. Big Ross, popping out of his hired suit. So proud, so protective of his date.

What a pair.

What an incongruous pair.

sunsets and sex

1988–1998

It took two years for Ross to get up the nerve to kiss her. It took Mrs Bertram's funeral. That big, beautiful decision-maker, matchmaker, dressmaker, life-remaker, was dead in the top paddock with a tonne of tractor on her when Ross came home from football training one cold winter night.

Like *Jaws*. Like, just when you think it's safe to get back in the water.

Like . . . like black, wipe-out desolation.

Emptiness.

And bloody Mummy acting up, screaming out for attention as if she was the one who had lost everything. She'd lost her little yellow taxi and its patient driver. That's all she'd lost. She'd lost two willing ears. That's all she'd lost.

Ross had lost everything. But there he was working and walking around, white as a ghost and shaking, his mouth, his eyes, his hands; just shaking and doing what had to be done. Driving sheep, penning steers. Just doing and shaking.

And –

God! God! God! It wasn't fair.

Sally wanted to run away. Head for the hills and keep on running to some place where there was magic and nobody ever died. And she could now. She'd been working at the supermarket for eighteen months and saving hard. She had eight hundred dollars in the bank. That would be enough to run on.

Couldn't run, though. Couldn't leave Ross to get through the funeral alone. She'd wait for a week, then pack a bag and run, just go and never, never, never look back.

Half of Lakeside was at the funeral. People from the school, schoolkids forming a guard of honour. Even old Mrs Sleiman and her daughters-in-law were there.

Sally sat with Ross in the front pew. She was still crying buckets of tears, couldn't make them stop. Ross wasn't crying, though his big hands were shaking so hard today she thought they'd shake off. And she couldn't stand watching them, so she took them in her own hands and held them tight. After that he wouldn't let her hand go, like he'd found something to hang on to. Then at the cemetery, he asked her to go home with him, help him clean out his mother's room. That's what he and his mother had done when his father died, so he had to do it for his mother.

'That's what she would have wanted us to do,' he said. 'She always said that life was for the living. That's what she said when Dad died. He wouldn't have wanted us to crawl into the coffin with him, she said when he died.' He kept talking, talking, afraid that if he ever stopped talking, he'd howl.

Sally left Mummy at home, going bananas, and she went with Ross to the farm where she cried more tears, cried for all of the things Mrs Bertram had taught her, and for all the things she'd had no time to teach. She'd learnt to cook in her kitchen, but she still couldn't make the light fairy sponges. She'd helped Mrs Bertram crochet a bedspread during long winter nights beside the open fire, but she'd never learnt to follow a knitting pattern. She'd learnt to hand-stitch hems, but not how to use a sewing machine.

What had she learnt from Mummy? Just fear and tears and guilt and how to pack china, squash cockroaches and clean up mouse dirt. And cry.

Standing at Mrs Bertram's bedroom window, wiping her eyes, she was looking at the land and at the last sunset. Mrs Bertram had loved the sunsets. Often she'd called Sally and Ross to this window to watch the sun setting behind the distant hills. And God must have known how Mrs Bertram loved his sunsets because he'd painted a super special red one for her tonight. It was like he had the world's heart bleeding for her, and there was this huge drop of red-hot metal, perched on a hill.

She had been thinking of hot metal, thinking of the burning car, when Ross came in. He picked up his mother's old slippers, just left where she'd last kicked them off, and he held them to his chest and he wept for the first time. Finally his hands stopped shaking.

But, God, he was ashamed of his tears. 'Stupid,' he said. 'I'm sorry. A man is a weak, blubbering fool. He's making a complete fool of himself. I'm sorry, love.'

He'd never called her love, but his mother had. 'Sally, love,' she used to say.

'You're allowed to cry for her, Ross. I'd think you were a fool if you didn't cry for her,' Sally said, and she took the old slippers, tugged them from his hands, and placed them in a plastic bag. Then she put her arms around him, like Mrs Bertram would have if she'd been alive, and she held him close before the window, comforting him, and herself. She told him to look at the last sunset. Still holding each other and crying, they watched the sun all melt away until the bloody sky faded to purple. 'Soon she'll be a star in heaven,' she said. 'She'll be up there with Daddy and the boys, and every night we can wave to her and blow her a kiss, Ross.'

The room became dark and somehow they were sitting on his mother's bed, close to her, smelling her scent on the crocheted bedspread. Sally was still holding him, comforting him, giving something back, and he was holding on to her like he wasn't ever going to let her go.

Then he kissed her. Kissed her mouth. And it got him all breathless, and he did it again, did it until it got like desperate kissing. He'd found something to turn off his brain and stop the hurt for a little while, and she wasn't going to stop him. She didn't want to stop him either, because it was washing some of the pain out of her heart.

They held each other tight, and then there was more than kissing. He was touching her breasts and it made her stop thinking of Daddy and death, and of how everyone around her seemed to die. She didn't stop him when he put his hand under her blouse. There had been too much sadness today. She was all worn out and weary with sadness. This wasn't sad.

His big hands started working at her blouse buttons and it took him ages, then ages more to undo her bra, and it was like he'd just opened up some precious gift that he was hardly brave enough to touch.

She knew what was going to happen unless she said no. But it was too late now to tell him no, and everyone of eighteen had had sex anyway. Better that it was Ross than one of the Sleiman grandsons, who slept with anything in skirts. Ross had never had a girlfriend in his life.

So she let it happen, and it was seriously uncomfortable but she didn't feel bad about it. She'd comforted him and given him a gift – and little enough, too, after all he and Mrs Bertram had given to her.

'Will you marry me?' he said.

'Jesus, Ross!'

Shouldn't have said that. Shouldn't have. Not today. But she wasn't going to marry him. 'You don't have to marry me just because of . . . of that.'

'What if you get pregnant?' he said.

'I'd have an abortion.'

'You wouldn't?'

'I would so. I'm not marrying you. You're my –' Couldn't say big brother. Wrong thing to say now. Her big brother had become her lover, sort of by default.

She didn't pack her bags and run away. Mummy was in hospital, getting her share of attention and it would have been a good time to run. And she should have, before Ross got up the nerve to try it again. But he did, and they did it again, and it sort of got to be a habit in the month Mummy was in hospital.

Everything was okay for a while. She went to football functions in Melbourne, and sex was okay. Practice makes perfect, and Ross liked to practise. Maybe one day they'd get it right. She'd gone to worm-fingered, sleazy Sleiman to get the pill.

The winters were good; Ross spent his time driving backwards and forwards to football matches or training. The summers were not so good. They didn't like the same things. She bought a tape of 'Runaway Girl' and every time she played it, he turned it down. She loved fiery hot pizza but he always ordered a ham and pineapple. They broke up once over pizza, and once over 'Runaway Girl', but she went back to him. He had no family, apart from a few cousins in Tasmania.

Then he did his knee at the beginning of the '93 football season and he had to have an operation. She met another side of Ross. He was almost twenty-eight and his footy years were over. Sally was twenty-three.

'Well, when are you going to be ready to get married? That's what I want to know.'

'I'm here, aren't I? I'm cooking your dinner. I moved the sheep, didn't I? What's the difference, Ross?'

'There's a lot of difference. I want to have kids.'

'Well, I don't. I've got two big kids to look after already, and I sure as hell don't want any more,' she yelled at him that night, and she turned on 'Runaway Girl' and played it loud, made the old farmhouse walls vibrate with it. He hobbled out to the mains on the front verandah and pulled out the fuse. They'd argued on in the dark.

'I want you here with me, Sally. It's crazy. We've been together for six years and you're still running home to her at night. Tell her that it's your life.'

'Is it? Is it my life, Ross? Why don't the pair of you do a King Solomon on me? Cut me in half. You can have the legs and sex bits and Mummy can have the hands and the ears,' she said.

And what is left for me? What is left for Sally De Rooze?

Nothing. A big fat nothing.

Most of their friends were getting married, a few had started their families. A year passed before he wore her down and they set the date, booked the church, booked a honeymoon in Bali. Just for seven days. They were going to pay Mrs Jenner to stay at the flat with Mummy until they got back. They'd fixed up a room at the farm so she could move in with them.

Then she did it again.

Sally was taking up the hem of a skirt when out of the blue Mummy picked up the scissors and stabbed herself in the breast. The blades were not long enough to do much damage, but the Sleaze found the lump while he was putting in a stitch.

So the wedding was off – which was a bit of a relief. Sally used her annual holidays that year travelling backwards and forwards to the city hospital. No more head-sick now for Mummy. This was full-on sick, with the Melbourne doctors finishing off the job she'd started. They cut her breast off.

Life in that housing ministry flat altered that year. For the first time since the car accident there was something resembling sanity at home. The mother Sally had known as an eight year old had come back. She cooked meals, swept floors, had food in the fridge.

And Sally knew why.

Mummy had got her bookings back.

All the dates were written down in her diary. All the phone numbers. Specialists bookings. Hospital bookings. Therapy bookings. She had long phone conversations with Mrs Smith and

Mrs Hudson, who also had their bookings, the three women travelling to Melbourne together.

No more talk of Daddy and the boys now. Mummy talked cancer, spoke of the amount of people who lived on this side of town who had died of cancer, spoke of the other dead too, of Grandma and Aunty Bernice.

Grandma had booked herself into a Melbourne hotel one weekend then taken a dive off the roof because Papa had been playing around with the slut from his office. Sally had not known how Grandma died, just that she'd done it when Sally was three. And to put some icing on the cake, Mummy spoke of Aunty Bernice. She had died of cancer of the breast.

Little runaway girl
Keep on running till you get to the place where you want to be
Catch a moonbeam, or a star –

Get out the rubbish bin, here comes Sally De Rooze, born 1970 died 19– . Never saw anything, never did anything. Never will either. Born with faulty genes. Toss her on the mulch heap. Any place will do.

Catch a moonbeam, or a star. Hold it high and you'll see far –
It will light your way o'er mountain and the sea.

'I'm going to get a job in Melbourne, Ross.'

'Don't start that again, Sally!'

'Oh, shit. Please listen to me, Ross. I don't want to marry you.'

'And I don't want to listen to that rubbish again, and stop your swearing.'

'Karen Matthews doesn't say "shit". She's spent ten years of her life chasing after you, Ross, and she's the right height.

She's got good genes. Her grandmother is ninety-five not out.'

Ross didn't want Karen Matthews or her grandmother.

Little runaway girl. Keep on running till you get to the – to the – to the –

'I'm jinxed, Ross. My grandma took a dive from a hotel roof when I was three. My aunty died of cancer when I was six. My father and little brothers died in a car crash when I was eight. Your mother died four years after I met her and Mummy is sick again. She thinks it's gone to her liver. Just let me go. Please.'

'They gave her the all-clear two years ago. There's nothing wrong with your mother that a swift kick up the backside wouldn't improve. So when are we getting married, for Christ's sake?'

Little runaway girl. Keep on running –

'Shit!'

Just – just keep on –

'Shit!'

Just

sally de rooze

august 1999

Rain was belting down. Her windscreen wipers squealing for mercy, she almost missed her turn out of Toorak Road. As she swung a too-fast left, the rear of her car slewed, floated a while. She needed new tyres. Needed a lot of things, but didn't need the rain even if Melbourne did.

She swung a left again into Bollinger Street, where the gutters ran deep and naked trees stood like a regiment of dark skeletons with wet feet. Her right blinker on, she gave way to a brown Ford exiting the narrow driveway, then she drove on down to the car park at the rear of the flats.

And his hulking great bike was parked in her bay again!

She paid for that space. She paid twenty-five dollars extra a month to have a roof over her car, not to keep a Harley dry. But its owner was a big black question mark and she was just a small, insignificant dot. She hadn't fought hard for her under-cover park in the early months, preferring to park in one of the front bays. They were well lit by streetlight and closer to the flat entrance anyway, and May and June had been fine. Only since July had she been waging a paper war against that bikie, and tonight her little car wasn't going to sit out in this downpour so his bike could stay dry.

She moved her car level with the window of Number 14, the heel of her hand leaning on her car horn.

Beep-be-be-beep. Bee-eep. A long overdue demand to be heard. Beep-be-be-beep. Beeeee-eeep. She leaned again, prepared to sit there with her hand on the horn until she was heard. Nobody ever listened to her. Ross didn't. She could talk to him until she was blue in the face but none of it got through.

Then the slam of a door. The wet slap-scrunch of boots on concrete and a heavy hand probably added an extra dent to her rusting boot.

'Back up,' the bikie yelled. Maybe he'd read the multiple messages she'd been sticking on his bike's precious paintwork with Blu-Tack.

She wasn't going to back up for him or anyone else; never again. The car inched forward; its bumper nudging the concrete wall. She waited for the Harley to disappear into the rain, then her rust-bucket yellow Datsun 120Y claimed its space in the sardine can, between a white Camry and an old silver Commodore.

So dark once her headlights were off. No outside light, or none that worked. She glanced up at the building, an ugly concrete cube with a flat roof and three levels of long windows where only slim slits of light escaped from behind closed blinds. No welcoming light from her own window, either. Hers was a front flat, her main window looking down on Bollinger Street. She drew a deep breath, locked her car; then, her bag over her shoulder, a large plastic Myer bag in her hand and her umbrella snapped open, she stepped from beneath the meagre shelter into the deluge.

The flat entrance, a black hole in the side of the concrete block, was directly opposite a concrete wall of letterboxes. Tonight, soggy junk mail drooped from each gaping slot. She emptied Number 11's box and, wet paper in hand, ran for the stairs and shelter.

Five bedsitters on each floor; five brown doors with brass numbers opened off a narrow passage. The building may have been new thirty-odd years ago, but now the doors needed a paint job and the brass needed a polish and the concrete stairs needed a scrubbing brush.

Dark as pitch on the second flight, that solid, black, lung-sucking dark, and the fluorescent tube on her landing, a stuttering, ghostly glow. Imagining the big bikie's flick knife cold between her shoulder blades, she scanned behind her, keys held like a weapon in her hand.

Her phone was ringing. It rarely rang. Probably the guy from Blackburn with the office job and he'd hang up before she got in.

'Damn the lock,' she said; the key wriggled, withdrawn and inserted again as a door opened behind her. She spun around to face an attack from the rear but it was only the little girls from 13. She smiled at the dark-eyed duo.

'Hello,' they said before heading for the stairs, bundles of multicoloured tracksuits in their arms. Tiny kids, ten and twelve. They looked less; they looked Asian but spoke with Australian accents, and they had Australian names: Helen and Elizabeth.

How could a family of four survive in a bedsitter? They did; they had a sewing machine in there too. Sally could hear it now, that familiar zip zip zip – like Mrs Bertram's sewing machine. She'd never sighted the person who sewed the tracksuits, but had met the little Asian guy and his girls carrying their bundles up the stairs or down to his white kombi van.

'Bloody key!' It helped sometimes to swear at it. She'd contacted the agent three times about her lock, her dripping tap and faulty lightfitting. He made a lot of promises but did nothing.

Then the key turned, and the phone was still ringing.

She hit the light switch and hallelujah, the globe didn't blow. Her mail and plastic bag tossed on to the kitchen bench, she snatched up the phone. 'Sally De Rooze speaking,' she said, striving to sound tall, infinitely employable.

'G'day, love. I've been trying to get onto you since six.'

'Hi, Ross.' Disappointment. 'I worked late.' She'd wanted the call to be from the guy with the job at Blackburn. 'I gave you my work number.'

'You wouldn't have wanted to hear this at work. Your mum is back in hospital.'

'I don't want to hear it here either.'

'I know. Sorry, love, but she was attacked by an intruder, or so she said.'

'What?' Her hand felt for cigarettes.

'Mrs Jenner called me around five. I drove in and took her to the hospital. Apparently some bloke got in and –'

'Is she hurt?' She sucked on the cigarette. 'Did he mark her?'

'No. She looked fit enough. Just – you know, love.'

'I know.'

Five minutes later she hung up the phone. She stood a moment, staring at her shoulder bag, then she placed it on top of the fridge, slipped her arms from her parka and shook it. It shed its own small rainstorm to the floor, arced its spray of raindrops over her bare beige wall – a spotty rainbow, but no pot of gold waited at the end. She shook the silky pink fabric again, overlaying the larger spots with a finer spray.

'Temporary beautification for a very temporary life,' she said. 'Mummy has decided I'm going home.'

Parka hung behind the door, electric jug set to boil, coffee in her mug, she gave her attention to her mail. No reply from Raelene Mason. It was years since she'd written to her, and she hadn't really expected a reply. Hoped for one, though. No job offer either. She wanted that job. It was in a little one-man office and the money wasn't bad. He'd said he'd contact her.

A brief glance at the cover of a jewellery catalogue from Gemsgalore. Too wet to open, it went straight in the bin. She opened a wet please-pay bill from her dentist. It would dry out by next week; she couldn't give him anything this payday. A postcard of Sydney by night, addressed to Miss C Wong. She'd moved out of Number 11 in May and hadn't bothered to leave a forwarding address, but the United Energy bill wore the right name. Too soggy to read, it fell apart in Sally's hands.

'They'll send me another one.'

The rubbish bin got the lot, except for a plastic-coated cardboard pizza ad, the dentist's bill and the postcard. She had never been to Sydney, and no-one ever sent her postcards, so she claimed this one, fixing it to her refrigerator with a smiling cat magnet.

Her small television was perched against the wall on a red plastic storage box. The power turned on, she stood flicking through the channels with the remote control until she found a nature show on Channel 2. It was fuzzy, buzzy, but experienced fingers twisted the rabbit-ear aerial until the picture became clear enough.

Bread in the toaster, coffee made, she took up the Myer bag and from it removed a long black overcoat.

'I love it, I love it, I love it,' she said, slipping it on as she stood before the television on which a giant redback spider and her anorexic mate performed their lover's ritual. She hadn't known about the redback's bad habit of eating her mate. While the little male redbacks in Ross's outdoor loo offered their sperm, the females were pumping in a food digester, readying lover for supper!

'Cannibals come in many forms, Sall old gal,' she said.

The toast popped and she walked to her cupboard, searching for a can of baked beans. She found peanut butter and a tiny tin of passionfruit pulp bought weeks back. It didn't taste the same out of a can, but it filled an occasional need.

Passionfruit were meant to be eaten fresh off the vine, cut in half, the pulp scooped out with a spoon. Or when they were old, a fingernail hole must be drilled and the contents sucked from the wrinkly sack. That's how her father had eaten them in passionfruit season. But the season was winter and canned pulp on toast didn't tempt her tastebuds. She chose the peanut butter, plastic, salt-free paste, and took her meal to the television; there she sat on the floor, eating toast, sipping coffee, thinking of Geelong and Raelene Mason and the passionfruit vines, a wall of green between the two houses. Strange flowers like purple/pink suns. From the squeak-squawking swing, she and Raelene had watched over the passionfruit that first year, watched the suns turn into hard green moons and grow fat, turning from green to purple.

A shake of her head dismissed Geelong. That was the past and this flat was her future.

Not much of a flat. Tonight the window was wet with condensation. Too much water in too little space and no ventilation. A kitchenette and its drip-dripping tap on one side of her front door and a tiny bathroom with its shower and toilet on the other, a living room/bedroom, a short bench, a long window, and all in an area no larger than a cheap motel room. Maybe that's why she'd taken it – because it looked like a motel room. Book in, book out, and leave no self behind.

The wardrobe backed onto the kitchenette, which created a space on the other side for her fridge. There was a small electric heater beside the wardrobe, an energy guzzler. She rarely used it. Number 11 was just a place to sleep, and Bay 11 a place to park her car – not that black bikie's Harley.

She'd bought her queen-size bed second-hand. A bad buy, it swallowed most of the living area, but it was warm with its quilt and electric blanket. She reached across now, turning the blanket control to number three. Give it fifteen minutes, time for another cup of coffee and a muesli bar, then she'd crawl into bed with Sue's book.

Sue had a house full of books. She was Sally's private lending library.

Thursday tomorrow. Another late night. Nothing better to do, though, and the extra hours turned a subsistence wage into something she could almost survive on while she searched for something better.

The supermarket where she'd worked for years had changed

hands six months ago, the new owner employing his daughter as checkout chick. There was little work to be had in Lakeside. Sally could have got a job cleaning at the hospital but she loathed that place. She'd waitressed at the Royal Hotel for a while but Ross hadn't approved, and he'd been pushing again for a wedding. Then she'd seen the ad in *The Age*, applied for the job and got it.

Her mother wasn't happy, nor was Ross. Sally no longer knew if he was what she wanted or just what she had. Or maybe she'd always known and was too scared to admit it. Poor Ross, she'd wasted so much of his life.

She did love him. Couldn't have handled Mummy's little emergencies without him. Hated the way he had his hair cut. Hated the way he ate. Hated his nagging. But she did love him.

Loved him like she had when she was fourteen. Big brother love.

'Sally Bertram,' she said. 'Sally De Rooze.'

She liked her name. It sounded tall, elegant. When she spoke her name on the phone she felt tall, but when people saw her in the flesh they saw the runt of the litter, held back from the teat of life. She'd reached her full height at thirteen, four foot eleven when stretched – an undergrown twenty-nine year old, suffering from a semi-permanent loss of direction, because every time she found a direction Mummy dropped a concrete block in front of her so she had to veer off and find a way around it.

'Concrete-block time, Sall,' she said.

A glance at the wall phone. Too late. She'd call the hospital tomorrow from work. A cigarette lit, she mind-travelled on until the nature show ended then, the remote pointed, she quick-flicked by cop shows, past hospital shows, until she found the news headlines.

Train crash in India. Gunman in Melbourne. Drug dealers in Bourke Street. Bleeding hearts demanding shooting-up centres, while most Melburnians were more worried about who was going to win the premiership.

What a crazy world. What a cold, fragmented city. A lonely place. Six times a week, and twice on Sunday, Sally decided to go home. She couldn't break into Melbourne, except with Sue, who was a total nutcase but a collector of people. She had collected Sally, having swept her up from the tearoom floor at work one morning. 'Can I bot a fag?' she'd said. 'I've given them up.'

The television was Sally's friend and family. Even as a kid she'd turned on the television as soon as she'd climbed out of bed in the morning, turned it on when she'd come home from school in the afternoon. Rarely looked at it. Just company – someone to talk at her.

She stood then and hit the off switch, and she walked to the window, looking out at the street through the beige bars of her Venetian blind. Ambulance or cops screaming off to some new emergency. Dark, old Melbourne town; like a great black beast it growled outside her window, ready to pounce on its scuttling prey.

A shiver travelled from neck to knees. She rubbed her arms, rubbed her left foot with her right.

Small feet. Small hands too. But her nails were long, strong, painted a salmon pink. She was proud of her nails. Pale blonde hair, she'd had it cut short today at lunchtime. It fell straight to the point of her chin then turned under. Ross wouldn't like it, but her face was small, the short hair suited it.

'An elfin face,' Mrs Bertram had said to her once. 'What a bloomer you're going to be, my Sally De Rooze, with your beautiful smile. You'll have to learn to show that smile more often.'

She had learned to smile, but she'd never opened fully into bloom. Mummy had given her no room, and Mrs Bertram had died before she'd finished sprinkling her growing dust. At twenty-nine Sally De Rooze was still waiting for life to begin. She didn't know what she wanted her life to be. Didn't know where she wanted to be, what she wanted to do, but she'd have to find out soon or her life would be over.

That's why she'd taken the job at Phonepross and a lease on the tiny bedsitter – to find space enough to bloom.

'Should have got a bigger flat, Sall old gal,' she said. 'Or shouldn't have taken such a long lease, you bloody idiot.'

a set of wheels

'Some you win and some you lose,' Walter O'Leary said as he emptied the glove box, picked up his vanilla slices and stuffed the lot into a supermarket bag. The key he left in the ignition, and good luck to any car thief who might get it going, he thought as he stepped into the rain, slamming the sagging door behind him.

He'd hired the car from Rent-a-Bomb, an old Toyota, twenty dollars a day. He'd considered it good value, unlimited miles around the city – not that Walter stayed in the city, but the car had taken him where he had to go and got him back again. Until tonight.

He couldn't see his watch face but he knew it had to be close to ten. He knew he was somewhere on Ballarat Road too, and not far from Flemington Racecourse; there'd be a train station around someplace, maybe a tram. He'd give Rent-a-Bomb a call before he left in the morning, let them pick up their own trouble.

A sporty little red job drove by. Walter lifted his thumb hopefully, but the driver ignored his plight.

Money. Some people had too much of it, and most of them

had too little. Not much use unless you spent it, but it did offer choices, he had to admit that. He'd never had much of it, so he'd had few choices in his life.

Cars whizzing by, spraying water while he footed it. He owned a reliable set of wheels; his '72 Holden still moved him from A to B. He'd looked after that car and it had looked after him, but it wasn't here and he was, and he was getting wet and walking always made him hungry.

He opened his plastic bag, sheltering it with his body while easing a vanilla slice from a damp paper bag. Sticky. Walter had bought half a dozen vanilla slices on the trip south, and he'd buy the other half dozen on the way back. They still knew how to make vanilla slices in Dubbo.

Head down, he bit into the slice, munching now as he walked.

'Fresh enough,' he said, turning the slice before biting again. He'd learned how to eat vanilla slices the year he'd got his first job. There had been a bakery in St Kilda, right on the corner, and every Friday night on his way home, he'd buy two. One for him and one for Mother, and the dog got to lick the icing off the paper bag.

He ate his way around the slice while the rain poured down, his teeth not applying too much pressure. Too much pressure squeezed all the custard from between the pastry slices. You had to circle around vanilla slices, creep in on them until that final bite. Thick custard, a gluey consistency, but it didn't taste like glue. It tasted like yesterday, and his yesterdays were a damn sight better than his todays.

White icing stuck to his hand and the rain melted it, trickling it down his wrist to the cuff of his shirt. He licked, licked again before reaching in for the second slice. No use keeping them. They'd been in the bag for three days already. He'd saved the last two to give to his boy, but they'd had another argument, and that was that. He hadn't seen him since May. Should have got down here before this, but he'd written once a week – and received one reply for his trouble.

'Ah well, two out of three's not bad, Walter.'

Traffic lights up ahead. He walked faster, the rain flattening his hair, straightening his curls and stretching them long to drip their excess beneath his jacket collar.

Melbourne. Drive off in the morning with the sun in your eyes, and walk home in the rain. He'd been born in this city, spent two thirds of his life in this city, but he'd never got used to the weather.

The traffic lights stopped his progress, and stopped a taxi. The last of the vanilla slice stuffed into his mouth, he stepped onto the road, knocking on the taxi window with a sticky hand. The driver eyed him, saw drowned rat, probably thought of his upholstery, but his back seat was empty, and his back door unlocked, and Walter was out of the rain.

'Swan Street, Richmond,' he said, taking a handkerchief from his pocket, wiping his face, mopping his head, spreading icing sugar.

The taxi smelt new, but its newness was being overlayed by the odours gathered from its passengers. Walter sniffed. He was adding a wet animal smell to its scent of mixed humanity. His old suit jacket, seventy-five per cent wool, smelled like a wet dog. It wouldn't dry overnight either, but he wouldn't need it on the bus.

They were in Flinders Street when he saw the fire.

'Something's burning,' he said. Across the Yarra, he could see flames billowing into the night sky.

'It's the casino.' The driver was a surly bugger. First words he'd said.

'Burning? They just finished the place, didn't they?'

'Burning gas. They've got these chimneys that shoot out gas. I read somewhere what it costs them a year to burn it. Forget how much, but it was a bloody fortune, the stupid mongrels.'

'What are they doing it for?'

'To get your attention, I s'pose. It worked too, didn't it?'

'A nice place?'

'A nice place to do your dough. I know a bloke who lost his house and wife to that place. He shot himself,' the driver said, and said no more.

Walter didn't have a lot left to lose. He'd already lost two wives and never owned a house. He scratched at his back as he stared at flames the rain couldn't extinguish, watching them until they disappeared from view. Scratching didn't ease the itch; that old burr in his singlet itch. Only one way to scratch that one.

the mouse pack

The rain had stopped this morning, and Melbourne was colder without it. The old yellow Datsun didn't like the cold, complaining long and hard as Sally leaned on the key, her foot playing the accelerator. Then the motor coughed up Melbourne's noxious gases; it blew blue smoke and caught, running ragged for minutes while she sat there, watching the fog of smoke and condensation belching out, choking neglected grey shrubs.

Sky foggy, windscreen foggy, she turned on the radio and backed out, the wipers flicking, her hand wiping fog from the inside of her windscreen.

Thursday, payday, the only reason she'd got out of her warm bed this morning. She'd have to go home tomorrow night. Didn't want today to turn into tomorrow. Or maybe she did. Didn't want Ross. Or maybe she did.

A red light stopped her at Toorak Road. A dozen cars before her and more behind. She couldn't move two hundred metres from her flat before old dictator Melbourne got into the act. Her fingernails tapped the steering wheel in time to the clicking of her turning signal.

Click-click. Click-click.

'Move it,' she pleaded as a tram trundled by. Crowded tram. 'Ought to tram it. No car-park fees.' She lit a cigarette, the reason why she didn't take the tram – didn't take health hazards seriously. Then she was in the traffic, trapped in the stop-start, stop-start obedience to the traffic light computer. 'You're all brainwashed mice,' she yelled.

The old radio had had its day, it was all static and buzz.

... thirteen-year-old Carla Miller was found this morning. Carla was reported missing at seven when she hadn't arrived at her Glen Waverley home ...

Static won the day as a tram rocked by.

'Poor kid,' she said, fiddling with knobs, picking up a female voice wanting to sell her a mobile phone she'd love to own but couldn't afford. A fast twist of the knob cut her off mid-spiel and the car crawled on.

Her office was on the twelfth floor of a middle-aged building in Collins Street, the top floor. A huge white space of no space, it had two phones per square metre and a mouse-plague of people all dialling to the old queen rat's commands. Of the twelve Sally had been with during that week of training in May, only the great gangly guy with pimples, the big woman with the knotted veins in her legs and miserable old coot Ron had remained with Phonepross. Out of the next group of eight, two had stayed on. Then nine came in for training one Monday morning and one came back the next day. It was around that time Sally had stopped counting and accepted the fact that she was just another mouse, fighting for survival on leftovers, just doing what it took to evade Melbourne's fat cats. Each day was more of the same, the traffic, the phone calls, the same old pitch.

'Mrs Dargan? Good morning. Sally calling. You have been chosen this morning to receive –'

Mrs Dargan did not wish to be among the chosen. 'How do

you keep getting my number?' the faceless voice snarled, and somewhere in Melbourne a phone slammed down.

So many of those she called were onto this game now. Each week it became harder to get the sales, but five days and several nights a week, Sally sold hard.

Bells were ringing this morning, the bell ringers' names scrawled on the whiteboard. The supervisor bawled and pleaded and flattered. Noise. The constant hum of a moving mouse-plague, gnawing its way through the fat Melbourne telephone book.

Body without mind sat on that chair. Just the left wrist where a watch ticked, but slowly. Just a finger picking out numbers. Only the mouth of the fake smile, and the phoney voice of good news. 'Mr Donald. Good morning. Sally calling. This morning we are –'

'No thank you, my dear.'

Twelve weeks of dialling. Twelve weeks of Monday morning pep talks and the supervisor's same old client expectation spruik, the same old call target, and we-are-not-meeting-our-sales-target whip. Sally tuned out at pep talk time, tuned out and scanned the crush for new faces, placing mental bets on how many from this morning's new batch would last out the day, the week.

Morning tea at 10.30. She needed a smoke. Only three left in her packet. One for morning tea, two for lunch – if Sue didn't bot. She'd have to buy a new pack at lunchtime and she couldn't afford it. Ought to give it up.

No sale.

No sale.

Again she glanced at her watch. Time was on a go-slow strike. Maybe she'd get a letter tonight from the guy with the job in Blackburn, or she might hear from the woman at the agency. Maybe she should update her computer skills – or go home to Lakeside. Give up. Give in. Get her mother out of the hospital, marry Ross and breed.

Didn't want to breed, that was the only fly in the ointment.

Didn't want to play Mummy to a tribe of kids. Kids needed stability and long-term commitment, and she knew she didn't have the staying power to commit for twenty years.

But what else was there?

Probably nothing.

It was mid-May when she'd left Lakeside. She'd taken a twelve-month lease on the flat so she'd be forced to stay away. May to May, that's what she'd told Ross.

'Just one year, Ross. Just give me one year.'

One year away from him and her mother, and maybe she'd find out who she was.

Poor, tolerant, safe Ross.

The Bertrams had trapped her too young with their safe and it had been so good after too many years of not safe, but safe wasn't a basis for marriage and babies. There was supposed to be love, passion. Or something.

She had to find out what was missing. She had to find out who lived within her – if there was anyone real left within her, or if she'd become segments of flotsam, bits picked up from the Bertrams and from foster homes all over south-western Victoria until all that was left of the original was a Sally shape wearing an agreeable Sally smile painted with lipstick on a yes-woman mouth.

She never rang Ross, but he called most Sundays. He had the stock and the dogs and only sixty-year-old Charlie Glen to help him; he rarely got away from the farm. He and Charlie had driven down in the truck to move her to the flat in May. They'd picked up her second-hand bed from Glen Waverley, her bruised third-hand fridge from Ashburton, and her miniature kitchen setting from Blackburn. She'd done her shopping through the *Trading Post*, where those in Melbourne advertised their discards when they could afford better. They'd hauled her purchases up the stairs and Ross had seen the unit for the first time.

'It's small, love,' he'd said.

'I like it small.'

'You'll need some drawers and a comfortable chair.'

'I like it bare.'

Paring her life down to basics had been part of the deal, stripping herself of all she had been, weeding out all props so there was nothing to hold her to the past, or to hold her from a future.

The rent was steep for a cold concrete cavity with as much personality as the inside of a cardboard carton, and the bills were piling up. In May she'd had over fifteen hundred dollars in her bank account. Now she was gainfully employed, her balance was down to five hundred and twenty. She'd been going out with Sue, seeing a few shows, doing what people did in Melbourne. Then yesterday she'd put her two hundred and eighty dollar overcoat on Visa. Shouldn't have. Should have put it on lay-by, but she'd wanted it now. And she loved it, loved her new hairstyle too, and her platform shoes.

At ten she made a quick call to the hospital. Private calls were verboten in this place; she made it while the supervisor was in the loo. The sister gave her the usual jargon, which meant her mother was okay.

Hair pushed behind her ear, her mind cleared of Mummy, she dialled. This one would be a sale. 'Good morning, Mrs Dunn. This is Sally, calling on behalf of –'

'Who?'

'Sally. I'm calling on behalf of –'

Disconnected.

From the workstation opposite, the pimply guy stared. He spent all day staring at her with his big baby-blue eyes, one finger engaged in picking at his pimples. He looked like the brother of Frankenstein's monster but sounded like everybody's wimpy halfwit son.

Sally flashed him a smile, just to make him blush and flush his pimples. God only knew how old he was. He could have been eighteen or a retarded thirty.

A chook cackle erupted to her left. Heads turned, faces eager for anything that might break the boredom. Pimples thought the cackle was aimed at his blush and his peach pink became a diseased strawberry red.

Giggles and sighs, coughs and cackles became badges of identification on the twelfth floor. Sally would have recognised that chook cackle if she'd heard it in the middle of Bourke Street during a blackout, but if she collided with the cackler in the toilets, she wouldn't know the face. And there was a guy to the right, prone to great brays of laughter. She'd heard that laugh when she went to a singles bar with Sue. Swore it was him, but although she'd searched the faces, she hadn't recognised a workmate.

Pimples never laughed. He had a nervous cough, a clearing of his throat, which he did before every call, and ten times per call. But he stuck to his spiel, got enough sales.

On his left, old coot Ron leaned, his dentures clicking, his worn-out old rat teeth eager to escape, to snarl, to bite. Rabid old sod. 'G'day,' he'd say. Clackety-click. 'Voice of good news calling.' Clackety-click. 'I got an offer too good to refuse today.' Clackety-click. Old creep, in his stale sweaters and vinyl shoes that smelled of rotting feet.

A crazy, nameless place. So many came for a day or two. So many left. No gain in remembering names – like in the foster homes where Sally had served time; she'd get to know a few names then be moved on, or moved home. It had been easier to leave the nameless behind. Names had a way of gluing themselves to you. Like at home. She knew everyone in Lakeside.

'Carla Miller,' she said as she glanced at the window and thought of the murdered child. 'Carla Miller. Glen Waverley.' Somewhere outside of that window, somewhere out there, a mother was crying.

She sighed. The sky still looked grey. More rain coming. Sally wanted sunshine and escape to a dry roof. She wanted a smoke.

Society's outcasts, smokers, they'd been banished to back alleys and rooftops all over Melbourne. They didn't argue about it, didn't fight back. An accepting pack, price hikes and anti-smoking campaigns didn't have them protest marching in the streets. At lunchtime some of them went down to a coffee shop which still allowed smoking but made you pay for the privilege. Coffee was free in the tearoom and the roof only a staircase and a heavy door away.

It was an alien place, a grey-black concrete and metal landscape, high above the world and silent. No phones on the roof. Age and sex didn't count on the roof. Up there nothing counted except the right to stand in the biting wind sucking smoke to fill that inner emptiness, blowing it out, watching it hit the cold air and make clouds, watching it go up, watching it go down, hands at peace, head at peace.

A second group escaped to the roof on fine days. They were non-smokers Sally named the green bunch. They spoke conscientiously of conservation while eyeing the smokers and wondering if they could sue for smoke abuse when the wind changed direction.

There was a third tight group at Phonepross, the tearoom group. Old coot Ron, Pimples always at his elbow, Mrs Varicose and her knotted veins, Sue, toy boy Norm, married Red, and a few Sally had not yet named. They had stamped their claim on the tearoom, where they munched on packed lunches and the world's ills, then spat out their simple solutions.

Tea break came slowly today, lunchtime even more slowly, but it came. By 1.30 the clouds were firing rain bullets at the roof, so the tearoom, a partitioned cubicle at the rear of the spaceless space, was crowded. Old coot Ron sat at the head of the table, Sue beside him, already scoffing a bag of potato crisps, dipping them into a tub of apricot yoghurt. At the opposite end, as far away from Ron as possible, Varicose nibbled on diet crackers spread thick with peanut butter, the crumbs spilling onto her massive breasts like dandruff. Pimples, on Ron's right, stared at the breasts while he ate meat and tomato sauce on brown bread. He left his crusts on his paper bag, then picked up his apple, looked at it, like he always looked at it.

Sally smiled, wondering if today he'd bite it, put the apple out of its misery. It almost made it to his mouth. No. He placed it back on the table, turning it in circles with one long finger while his other hand picked pimples.

Old coot Ron ate rough male-made sandwiches. Sally could visualise him standing at his Bayswater bench, tossing everything in sight over his shoulder onto the bread. Meat, tomato, hunks of onion, beetroot; his sandwiches looked like him. Stale. A bit thick.

'I've been in work since I was bloody thirteen years old.' A slice of beetroot fell onto the table. Ron clawed it up, pushed it into his mouth without missing a beat. 'Anyone can get work if he wants it,' he said, spraying beetroot as he elbowed Pimples' pimple-picking elbow. Pimples squirmed, looked at his apple and blushed a beetroot red.

'You put me in the Lodge for a week, and I'd fix this country. Bring back national service. Put all the bloody kids in for six months.' Another elbow jab at Pimples. 'Turn them into men,' old Ron recited for the umpteenth time. Horrible old man in his pilled hand-knitted sweaters, his stained trousers, fly always gaping. God help his grandkids.

Varicose, grossly overweight, changed the subject. 'Did anyone hear the news this morning? Little Carla Miller.' Varicose had twelve-year-old twins, Tania and Paul. 'I can't help thinking of that poor mother,' Varicose said.

'Why wasn't she at home, keeping her kid off the street? What was she doing letting her wander around in the middle of the bloody night?'

'She was picked up at 6.30, you miserable old sod,' Sue said. 'And what were you doing at 6.30 last night?'

Old was the insult. Ron's hackles rose and his voice rose with them. 'If you'd lived half as long as me and seen half the things I seen, then you wouldn't be so bloody tolerant.'

'I'm not fucking tolerant, am I? And when I've lived half as long as you, I'll have enough sense to keep my mouth shut when I don't know what I'm talking about.' Sue came from a large disapproving family; she had learnt to speak fast and loud.

'And when I was as young as you, bloody women spoke like bloody women and they knew their bloody place, bejesus.' Ron's snarl sprayed onion breath. Two silent eaters stood. Got away.

'What is their place, Ron?'

'They didn't wander around the streets at night with their bloody nose rings and dresses up to their arses. They're out there asking for it, I tell you.'

He made Varicose wish the table was longer, wish she was at home looking after her twins. He made Pimples pick up his crusts and stuff them one after the other into his mouth, seal his mouth. He made Sue stop licking yoghurt from the container and turning the air blue. She had an interesting turn of phrase. She could wedge two four-letter words in a three-word sentence when pushed.

Ron snarled a few final words over his shoulder as he left for the loo, his fly gaping at the ready.

'Do up your fly, you flashing old fuck,' Sue yelled. She always got the last word.

The tearoom settled down. Slowly, new conversations began.

A bunch of rejects from the factory of life, Sally thought as she tuned in, or tuned out, catching snippets here, there, everywhere. Sue spoke across her to toy-boy Norm, a chinless wonder with a ratty ginger moustache who would have been better off growing a beard. He'd been at Phonepross almost as long as Sally.

'They found her on the South Eastern Freeway. Tossed out of a car.'

'Cindy knew her, you know? She's from Glen Waverley.'

'Cindy?' Sally said.

'Yeah. She said that Carla lived two streets away, said she was in the same class as her sister. Not the type to get into a car with a stranger.'

'Was she raped?' a no-name asked.

'No –' The speaker was married Red, a quiet one who rarely opened her mouth. Many eyes urged her on today. Red had an aunt, married to a cop in Homicide. The tearoom group gained a lot of inside information from Red, who now bit into a neat triangle, ham and cheese. 'I'm not supposed to say anything about it, but because he didn't . . . rape her, they think he might be old, or . . . or something.'

'He stripped her?' Sue wanted the details.

'And strangled her, and he tied a pink ribbon around her waist in a huge bow.'

'Some sort of a sicko,' toy-boy Norm said.

Red turned to him, flashed him a smile. 'Yes.'

'The world's full of them,' Sue said. She was twenty-nine, Sally's age, married at twenty, now getting a divorce. She had a nose ring, a tattoo on her calf and she changed her hair colour every other week. It was purple today, with a deep blue fringe. Sally turned from her to Norm, then back again. Purple one side, ratty ginger on the other. Red across the way in her prim white collar and black cardigan and her neat triangular sandwiches, her husband down at the bank, her five-year-old daughter at school.

'Cindy was saying the mother is devastated,' the no-name said.

'It's terrible. It's just . . . just terrible. I have to leave the twins in the house when I leave for work since Mum went up to live with my brother,' Varicose said.

'Which one is Cindy?' Sally asked.

'The one with the long red hair. Always with young Rosy,' Norm replied, and his eyes stayed on to stare a while, his ratty moustache twitching in a hopeful smile.

He was in his early thirties; his wife was forty-nine and the breadwinner, an orthodontist. They had two girls. Poor Norm, bought and paid for seven years ago. He'd looked after the kids until they went to school, now he paid for their after-school care with what he earned at Phonepross. He loved the place, loved the company, always hung around the women.

I don't belong here, Sally thought. This is a transitional period. I won't belong here. She glanced over her shoulder at the standers who also knew they didn't belong. Some would pick up their pay today and never come back. The supervisor would tell a few not to come back. A couple might hang around for a week or two, then grow tired of listening to old coot Ron, and of watching his dentures' daily battle with the beetroot.

She smiled as she turned to Pimples and caught him staring at Varicose's jutting breasts. Her eyes slid down to his apple. Was it the one he had brought in yesterday, and the day before that? She looked at her watch, fifteen minutes left; without a word she stood, walked to the passage and up to join the crush of smokers fighting for space on the concrete stairs, where they blew their smoke out the door while the sniper rain's bullets picked them off, one by one.

No-one mentioned Carla Miller up here. Crushed together like smokes in a packet, they coughed and wheezed, and left their lungs and the problems of the world to fate.

and friday

Time stood still in this place. The wall clock was controlled by the supervisor. No doubt it ticked as other clocks did, but the hands didn't move until she gave the order

Case packed, waiting in her car boot. Petrol tank full enough. Money in her purse. Smokes in her pocket. Finish work at 4.45. Be in Lakeside before eight.

Tick-tick-tick-tick-tick-tick.

One hour gone. Another hour waiting in the queue. Long, aching hours of repetition while the voices on the other end of the phone merged into one.

Until old Mr Fisher. 'You sound like a happy little soul,' he said. 'Go on, tell me what you're selling today and I'll see if I want to buy it. My little granddaughter works in one of those places.'

'How many grandchildren have you got, Mr Fisher?'

'I'm a Pop eighteen times over. Eighteen grandchildren, seven great-grandchildren and two more on the way.'

'There should be a law against men like you.'

Mr Fisher laughed and Sally laughed with him. Poor old guy,

eager to chat to a young bird. 'How many children did you have, Mr Fisher?'

And the line was cut, the sweet old guy with his eighteen grandchildren lost somewhere in Melbourne. Sally swung around. The grey-blonde supervisor towered behind her; she'd been plugged into the call, doing her spot checks. She liked to listen in, catch her workers making private calls.

'I do not give the ratsus how many children Mr Fisher is having. You do not give the ratsus. This is not what you are pay for. For talking how many children. You understand?' A broad expanse of solid buttock. Sagging mammoth breasts too weighty for the thick jaw, they dragged it down, dragged her fat lips down, her lower eyelids down. Bloody hard, old, no-neck monster. She liked saying 'ratsus'. Sue had been at Phonepross when the big boss, an American, imported that expression, but the supervisor had claimed his 'rat's ass', making it her own. 'Is not you place for asking how many children. Is what you learning in the training? No? How many sale you making?'

'I've made five.'

'I am not hearing you bell ring. That is why you having the bell. Yes? You ringing bell. Or right. You name going on whiteboard. Or right?' She reached over, hit the bell, tried to drive it through the fake wood. Then she bawled: 'This one is making five sale. Everybody give clapping, please. Clap. I want to hear the clapping.'

Sally's gaze dropped down to the tree-stump legs, to the flattened shoes as many hands left off their dialling to clap. Trained mice. Ring the bell and get to eat. Ring the bell and get to mate.

'You working tonight?'

'Sorry, I have to go home.'

'You no good for me. I think you better staying home, eh?'

She walked away and Sally turned again to the phone, her eyebrows raised. Had she been sacked? Workers fell like ninepins in this place.

On the dot of 4.45 she left the office and drove across the

city, still not confident on Melbourne's roads. Her eyes scanned left, scanned right, scanned ahead, her brake foot at the ready. She crawled with the traffic to Ballarat Road. Could have taken the Tullamarine Freeway, but it was going to cost her soon to use it, if they ever got all of the nuts and bolts in the right places; anyway, this was the road she'd driven with Mrs Bertram, so this was the known, the preferred, way home.

The sun in her eyes gave way to the semi-dark of winter twilight before she turned off the highway at Bacchus Marsh. She'd had a picnic there with Ross and his mother one day when Bacchus Marsh had still been a pretty country town. Too close to Melbourne, the city had swallowed it up in the great suburban sprawl. New estates everywhere, traffic thick on roads never meant to carry the load. Poor little country town, its personality lost.

The night grew dark and the road she travelled narrowed, for the last ten kilometres winding up and around misty mountains. She sat forward, watching the trees and the scrub on the sides of the road for glowing feral eyes. Wouldn't want to brake on this road, rock wall one side, long drop on the other. An eerie section, her headlights hitting the trees made them glow green. She hated this part of the journey, almost home but lost in another world. Not much traffic, thank God.

Then that last long, slow curve down, and she breathed a sigh of relief as she saw the lights of Lakeside, the lonely glow of scattered farmhouses.

No mist here, but frosty cold. She drove directly to the hospital car park and found a space, familiar space. How many times had she parked in this same bay?

Countless times.

She loathed the hospital. Didn't want to face the sisters again, smell the place again. Didn't want to be here. Didn't Mummy owe her one lousy year?

'Don't expect *her* to pay her bills,' she whispered as she walked the corridor, her heartbeat fast. At the door she stilled her thoughts, took a deep breath and fixed on a smile.

'Hi, Mummy,' she said.

Like two peas in a pod, both miniature blondes, but her mother's eyes were a lighter blue and her hair had been permed into a dry Harpo Marx frizz.

'You know my precious daughter,' Glenda De Rooze said to her ward mate, her pursed lips attempting a smile.

'I certainly do. My goodness, you're like two peas in a pod,' the woman replied.

Then Ross walked in and suddenly the ward was too small. No coat for Ross, just short-sleeved shirt and jeans. Too big, too healthy to be in this place, he looked uncomfortable, shy with these women in their nightgowns. His hand on Sally's shoulder slowed her heartbeat, and she leant against him, safe, stepping back with him, making room when the sister entered, making room together.

They stayed for an hour, stayed until the Harpo Marx frizz was spread on the pillow, and her mother content with her nurses and her pills and television show.

'See you tomorrow, Mummy.'

'Thank you for coming all this way, my precious girl.'

Outside in the dark, Sally's smile sagged at the corners and her shoulders slumped.

'You look tired, love. Want to go someplace for dinner, or will we shove a pie in the oven?'

She lit a cigarette. 'I thought I'd go home. Clean up the flat for her.'

'Do it tomorrow.'

Do it tomorrow. Why not?

She followed his ute home to the farm and drank a beer while the pies heated. They ate late, then went to bed. No passion, but a comfortable and familiar bed, a comfortable and familiar partner. Warmth. Safety. What else was there? She slept well.

The Bertram family had owned the farm for sixty years; remnants of three generations lay rusting in shed and paddock. The old weatherboard house, built by a prior owner, looked rusty too. Old and tired of hanging on, it clung to the side of a hill with its rotting stumps, determined not to slide down.

But in the kitchen a modern wood stove never went out, and the open fire in the lounge room had a log burning there all winter. Warmth hid the stained wallpaper and flaking paint, warmth disguised the worn-out furniture. Although she'd been dead for years now, this house was still Mrs Bertram's house. No chair had been moved from its space, no embroidered cushion discarded, no inefficient '60s lamp replaced by today's.

Photographs of Ross hung on the long wall. Ross as a baby, a toddler, a schoolboy. At his side a young soldier in his vintage '40s army uniform looked down on today with Ross's eyes. Mrs Bertram, the child, was there beside an old frame holding a so-serious study of an Edwardian bride. So many photographs, and such a continuity of features. Was it any wonder Ross wanted to continue the line? She smiled at the toddler Ross. Her babies would look like him – snowy-headed, snub-nosed.

He wanted six kids. Grow our own farm labourers, he joked. God help her waistline. God help her pelvis too. He ran a mixed farm, fat lambs and prime beef, but it wasn't labour intensive, and his house wouldn't hold six kids anyway.

It was a typical farmhouse – dark passages, three bedrooms and the sleep-out, verandahs front and back. Mrs Bertram's front room would make a good nursery, close to the kitchen and Ross's room. They'd have to paint it, get new curtains and floor coverings, and they'd need to put up a decent fence around the house. There were two big dams.

So, do it, she thought. Just do it and be done with it. What else was there other than a safe marriage and babies?

Mummy installed in the sleep-out, that's what else.

There had been a heavy frost last night, and this morning each blade of grass was a small ice sword, but the sun was out and prowling Lakeside. It would be a nice day. Sun on her back, the open fire's warmth on her face, she looked at a photograph of Mrs Bertram and wished her alive, sitting, chatting in the lounge room – a strong foundation on which a new generation might be built.

Ross came from the kitchen to stand with her before the photograph of his mother. 'She would have been fifty-three tomorrow.'

She reached up and ran her hand across his scalp. 'Why do you get it shorn so short, Ross?'

'Saves combing it. And why did you get yours cut?'

He led her to the kitchen. Porridge bubbling, fry-pan waiting to cook eggs. Toast ready. She'd loved these breakfasts when she was fourteen, loved this dark little kitchen.

'No porridge for me, thanks.'

He served her a heaped bowl anyway. 'Eat,' he said. 'You've lost more weight.'

She ate her porridge, ate a greasy egg on toast too, then they lit cigarettes, sipping coffee and smoking companionably over empty plates.

A sunny day, she spent it in the paddocks with Ross and his laughing dogs, and she bottle-fed three stupid little lambs who thought Ross was their mother. All baby things were beautiful, lovable. She'd love Ross's babies.

'Jesus, I miss you like you wouldn't believe,' he said that night in bed.

'Miss me, or sex?'

He might have been a sex maniac, but he wasn't into talking about it. Solid, reliable, unimaginative Ross. Everyone loved him, trusted him. Why couldn't she stop seeing his faults?

'Let's do it. Get married and get her out of that hospital.'

And confront her misery every morning and her tears every night? Can't. Won't. Don't want to. The supervisor's tirades were preferable. Old Ron's recitations and beetroot sandwiches were preferable. The bikie in Number 14 was preferable to living with her mother again.

'I've got the lease, and I can't just up and leave my job, Ross. I'd have to give notice.'

Liar. She probably didn't have a job. He didn't question her words. He didn't question anything. Why didn't he? Why didn't he say, Look, I'm tired of running around after your mother, tired of you stuffing my life around? Make up your bloody mind what you want to do.

He couldn't, that's why. It wasn't his way, that's why. Like Rusty, his gentle Labrador, Ross's love, once given, was unconditional.

face down

By 10.30 Sunday morning Sally was at the housing ministry flat. A tornado had been through and left its destruction behind. Dust, a chaos of cups and plates, saucepans, an empty port bottle or two. She tossed leftover food into the bin, piled the dirty dishes in the sink and left them soaking.

Where to start with the rest? She rescued the china goose girl from behind a bottle and she washed the pretty china face with the dishcloth.

There were twelve ornaments in all, perched on shelves and tables, on cabinet and mantelpiece. Her grandmother had collected them fifty odd years ago. A round dozen.

She turned in a circle, thinking numbers while staring unseeingly at cheap curtains and purple carpet. Someone had actually paid for that carpet when purple had been having its brief day of fashion. Thankfully most of it lay hidden beneath cheap furniture, leaving only narrow paths of purple in between. She loathed it, loathed its constant reminder that the flat had belonged to another before she and her mother had claimed it.

Her glance swept over her grandmother's heavy dining room

suite, jammed in against the lounge room window. She turned to the cabinet, then, without looking, her hand reached for a photograph. She placed it face down, felt for the second in its matching wooden frame. It went face down too. For the last eighteen years she and her mother had waged their photograph war, Sally turning them down, her mother turning them up again, and not one word said.

Guilt? Unresolved condemnation? Probably. She shrugged and walked to the larger bedroom, where she took a lightweight dressing gown from behind the bedroom door. It was clean enough. Three nightgowns taken from the dressing table drawer followed the dressing gown into a plastic bag. She added a handful of undies, then sorted through the pile of dusty make-up, packing her selection to take with her to the hospital.

'They had a bad night with her, Sall,' Deb Davis said. 'I'd let her sleep.'

'When are they planning to send her home, Deb?'

Deb, the smart one, had remained at school, gained a profession. Twice now Sally had asked her to be bridesmaid. Greg, her partner, was Ross's mate, and would be his best man. They didn't understand why she'd moved to Melbourne. No-one understood.

Deb spoke quietly as she straightened the bed-cover. 'She's supposed to go tomorrow, but last night she was screaming with pain. Why don't you have a word to Dr Sleiman? He does his rounds at five.'

Sally shook her head. She stayed well clear of Sleiman the sleaze.

On Monday morning she was up at dawn and on the road before six, but traffic came to a halt twenty kilometres out. Late for work, the Monday morning pep talk over, the workers were wandering to their desks as she sidled in, sidled up to her phone, hoping she was still among the employed.

'You coming back, eh?' The supervisor bore down on her.

'My mother is sick ... in Lakeside. The traffic was chaos. I'm very sorry.'

‘Sorry’ was a word the supervisor didn’t understand. Late she did not want to know about. Traffic. What was traffic but machinery obedient to her will? She spoke with a strong European accent, and bias. A hard old dame, a cock-eyed racist, as politically incorrect as old coot Ron at times; they just fought on opposite sides of the racism fence.

‘Is number one Australian excuse. My mother is sick. I am hearing it many time. Ah, so sorry, my poor mother is very sick.’ The supervisor’s fat lips sucked and her neck expanded, blown up with quick gulps of air. Introduced cane toad, spitting poison, its tongue whipping the native fauna into shape. ‘I am not pay to give the ratsus for you sick mother. You want to work, or you not wanting work. Is not material for me.’

Her name was Ras-something . . . Rasputin perhaps, but with a few extra syllables, unpronounceable to the average tongue so they called her Queen Ratsus. She had three minions who scuttled around her, ringing bells, patting backs and preening when the big queen praised. Sue was a minion, she scuttled and preened, but in the toilets she let the truth rip. ‘Fucking old whore. She needs putting down.’

Life was a telephone. By day Sally palavered to strangers, buttering them up to buy; by night she indulged her mother, bribing her with promises. Too many hours spent on the phone, her neck ached, her head ached, her heart ached. Payday on Thursday; pay gone by Friday.

Bloody Friday. She’d made four lousy sales – and felt guilty about the ones who’d bought. The job was getting to her. Too many sad old people eager to talk to someone, even if the chat cost them; she felt like a thief, stealing their pension cheques. Hated the job. Hated feeling guilty half the time and a failure the rest of the time. Hated the lies she told, and the insults she received. Hated the ones who wanted to talk but not to buy. Bloody Friday.

Then Ross called.

Ratsus was probably listening in, but it took only a moment for him to say five little words.

'Sorry, love. She's back in.'

It took only a moment for Sally's response, almost a cry. 'I called her last night, Ross! She was fine. What's she playing at?'

Only moments. But the old Queen Rat bore down on her. 'You spending too much time with personal phone call.'

'As you probably heard, my mother was just rushed to hospital.' Hardly rushed. 'She has cancer.' Had cancer six years ago. One of the lucky ones, Mummy.

'How many sale you making?'

'Four.' Hospital, the big C, cut no ice with Ratsus. Only sales were important.

'Four is all?'

'Yes. Four is all. It's impossible to make the sales. How do you sell books of raffle tickets for forty dollars? It's hard enough to sell a twenty cent ticket at the local pub in Lakeside on a Friday night, let alone a whole book of tickets for forty dollars. All I have to say is raffle and they hang up on me. What am I supposed to do? Call them back?'

The supervisor was momentarily taken aback. 'Impossible?' She'd misunderstood the meaning of this word when she began keying English into her mental hard drive. Impossible was what she expected from her workers, what she would have. 'You will do impossible or you go now. Is not material for me.'

The rent had been paid but the Datsun still needed new tyres. Every time she hit the brake she went for a skid. This was supposed to be her year, now it was spinning in circles. Couldn't stop the wheel and jump off because in Melbourne Queen Ratsus sat in the driver's seat, cranking it up, and in Lakeside her mother sat tightening the bloody screws.

It was 5.25 when she left the twelfth floor office that night. The roads would be full. Better to wait now until seven, wait until the cars got to wherever they were going.

In number three lift, one hand in her pocket fondling her cigarettes, she decided to give up the battle. She'd pack up her junk, get Ross and Charlie to drive down on Sunday and pick it up. Let the agent try to squeeze blood out of a stone. Anyway her mother was sick. That was number one Australian excuse and good enough to break a lease. She was going home to babysit her mother until they both died of old age.

The lift had gone crazy. It was stopping between floors. It hiccupped at six, but it stopped. A woman stepped in. It had a brainstorm at five. They picked up two young guys who grinned at her when the doors refused to close. Ratsus had keyed one of her pet viruses into the lift's computer.

Then it stopped at the fourth floor, and as the door opened she saw him against the light. And he ... God! He was something else. But the doors closed on him and he was gone.

Tall. Tall and fine. Elegant.

The lift jerked. The doors opened again and he was still there. He smiled. At her or the indecisive door.

It gave up. It let him in. What door could deny a god?

There was plenty of room in the lift, but he stood beside her and her heart skipped into top gear as she glanced up at his face, then quickly down. She swallowed. The lift stopped at three. Two more workers crowded in. She didn't see them. She was riding a time machine and he was riding beside her. He was a Roman god and she his slave girl. She had peeled grapes for him in another lifetime and fed them to him one by one.

God, but he was gorgeous.

A fast glance at the hand holding the briefcase. A long, fine hand. Well-shaped fingernails. Ross's were grimy stubs. Her eyes studied the slim briefcase, the black umbrella in its sheath, not brave enough to look higher because she could feel him looking at her.

She looked at his black overcoat, a perfect match for her long black overcoat, wool from the same sheep's back. The lift stopped at two and a herd stampeded in, forcing the twin black overcoats together in the centre of the crush. Wool fibres recognised their own. They cleaved.

Then it was over. They were at the ground floor and he stood back, signalling with an open palm for her to precede him. She sighed out a breath, held too long, as she walked away from him and into misty rain.

But she stilled her feet. Her back pressed against a grey Melbourne wall she was unaware of the rain as she watched the black overcoat walk away, black umbrella unfurled and held high. Strangely silent city. The trams were trundling by, people hurrying, but she was not a part of this movement. She'd been swept into a time warp, carried back to another century, another world.

The rain moved her feet. Rain on her not-yet-paid-for two hundred and eighty dollar coat.

Idiot, she thought. I just decided that I was going home to babysit Mummy and marry Ross, talk cows and bulls until hell freezes over. Have six kids who'll talk cows and bulls too. There are worse things than cows and bulls. Look on the bright side. No more fighting the bikie for my car space. No more miserable flat. No more dripping taps. No more phones. No more sad old men. No more Ratsus. The year of Sally De Rooze has been cut short. She's getting married.

But her back remained pressed to the grey Melbourne wall, and though the black overcoat and umbrella were long gone, still her eyes looked off into the distance.

Go then. Start driving.

'No. I'm going to see him again. I'm going to know that guy.'

the black swan

All weekend Sally thought of the guy in the black overcoat. She thought of him while sitting beside the hospital bed in Lakeside, and also when she was in Ross's bed. She thought of him on the long drive back to the city. Thought of him. Thought of him.

Her mother was going home tomorrow, cured again by attention. If you could only bottle attention, develop a robot with half a dozen ears and matching sets of hands, Mummy would have been fine. The hospital was organising Home Help and Meals on Wheels; two pairs of ears and hands might do the trick – for a while.

Warmth was in the city air that Monday, the magnolias in bloom, the lawns fresh-cut smelt green. Summer would come and get the year of Sally De Rooze on track. It had suffered a minor hiccup, that's all.

At work they had a new client. No pushing people to part with hard-earned cash; Phonepross workers were supplying a service; they were passing on information. Pimples looked relieved. He'd lost his nervous cough. At lunchtime he and

Varicose joined the crowd on the rooftop and Pimples took out his own packet of cigarettes. Sally actually heard him laugh. Sunshine bred laughter, and laughter was medicine.

That evening, convinced the god in the black coat would be in the lift, she left work early and rode down in number three. The lift didn't stop at four.

She rode back to twelve in number two lift. 'Lost my smokes,' she lied. They were in her coat pocket. The lift stopped at four, but he was not waiting.

It was 5.15 when she caught number one lift and rode up with three girls to nine, then rode down again with three more.

He didn't work in this building. Of course he wouldn't. He was a businessman on his way down from an appointment, that's all. He'd probably flown in from London for the day and she'd never see him again.

She walked out to Collins Street and looked at the people.

Nothing to do on Monday nights in Melbourne. If she had a video player, she could have hired a good movie, but she didn't own a video player, and what use was a television without a video player? Old coot Ron swore that the commercial channel bosses had shares in pay TV, that it was a conspiracy – feed the viewers drivel and force them to pay for their viewing.

Hands deep in her pockets she looked above the tall buildings, wanting to see the sky. Grey sky. Clouds were moving in. If she had a cat she'd have a reason to head for South Yarra, but she couldn't have a cat. No pets allowed in her block of flats. Beige walls and ceilings, cheap brown-beige carpet on the floor, a stone-cold beige squat with the Chinese water torture tap and hours to fill before she could go to bed. Lonely.

She walked back. It was warmer out than in. She rode number three lift to the eighth floor and the place looked deserted. Only a few boxes and a mop in the corridor. She picked up passengers on seven and returned with them to the ground. No-one was watching, so she pressed six and rode up again. Six was occupied. Two men rode down with her. Not the right men.

A strange world. How many people spent their weekdays in this block of offices? Row after row of identical windows. People stacked on top of each other like a huge sandwich of humanity. She thought of the Turkey earthquake, imagining these concrete floors settling. How many would die?

She was on her way back to the street when number three lift disgorged its passengers and waited, its doors wide. Almost 5.25. Almost time-warp time. Just one more try. She entered and the lift moved, taking her where it would.

To four. And he was there, standing apart from two other businessmen, head and shoulders above them, but only a few centimetres taller. Not as tall as Ross, but slimmer, so he looked as tall. Tonight he wore a dark suit and it screamed expensive, but he'd make baggy Kmart shorts look expensive. The other suits faced the lift doors as it started its descent. He turned to her and smiled.

'We've met before?' he said.

'I work on twelve. Phonepross. Telemarket.' She always added the 'telemarket'. Phonepross sounded like phone-a-pro. Crazy name. Queen Ratsus had probably thought that one up. She breathed deeply, lowered her chin. He didn't know she had been riding the lifts for half an hour, waiting for him. He'd think she was just another worker eager to get home. She looked at her watch, shook her head, her foot tapping.

He studied her from his greater height. He saw the bobbed pale gold hair falling forward, the points meeting, framing an original face. A nice mouth; small, straight nose. He saw the long black coat, its collar turned high and he wondered who was hiding beneath it.

She glanced up and he smiled, studied her navy-blue eyes and dark lashes, the fine dark brows. No pencil, no mascara required, unusual in one so fair – or had her hair colour come from a beauty salon? Then her chin tilted down, her navy-blue eyes were cast down. He watched her right hand pick at pearl-pink nail polish. Hands bare of rings. It pleased him. Then the hands left off their varnish picking, as if aware they were under scrutiny, both diving deep into her coat pockets.

He looked down, past the pockets, beyond the hem of the overcoat and he saw an inch of black stocking, of slim ankle. He saw the small feet in platform shoes that made her four-eleven into five foot two. And he liked what he saw.

The lift filled on the second floor. Maximum load twelve, the sign said; second-floor workers didn't work with figures; they kept herding in, giving him reason to move closer. Fifteen filed out at the ground floor like sheep exiting a pen.

'You might be able to answer a question for me,' he said, still at her side. Her eyes opened wide, surprised, pleased he had spoken. Her chin lifted and her hair flipped back. Clean. Fluid. Clear pale skin. A natural blonde, he decided.

Then they were in the cold, the fine day having given way to the chill of night.

'I always wanted to know how telemarket girls know the exact second to call, just as I sit down for dinner,' he said.

'Ve have our means.'

He laughed, and she smiled. 'Hey, what's the difference between a financial adviser and a supermarket trolley?' She shook her head, shaking raindrops from her hair. But she was looking at him, and he wanted her to keep looking at him. 'The financial adviser can hold more booze but the trolley has a mind of its own. One of my clients told me that one today.'

'I'll have to remember it,' she said.

He'd hoped she'd pick up on the line, maybe suggest a drink. No? Not tonight anyway. 'No gain in standing in the rain, I suppose,' he said. But he didn't want to leave. Not yet. And she was in no hurry.

'I thought the rain had gone up to Sydney. The sun was out when I drove down this morning.'

'Where did you drive down from, Telemarket?'

'Lakeside.'

He unsheathed and flipped open his umbrella, and for a

moment it sheltered her. 'Are you going my way?' His open palm signalled right.

'I'm parked to the left,' she said.

'It's been nice talking. See you in the lift some time.'

He worked in her building! Hewitt and Rodes, Financial Advisers, were on four. Old coot Ron had a friend who had a friend who had consulted them. Old Ron said they were squatting down there like a flock of vultures waiting to fight over the savings of poor bloody old fools and they weren't going to get his.

Not Sally's financial adviser. He was a serene black swan. She watched him now as he flew away into the night.

Don't feel like this, her head warned. He's class. Slow your heartbeat. Still that ache for a stranger's touch. 'As if he'd ever look at me.'

But he had looked at her. He'd ignored the guys who got into the lift with him and he'd stood beside her, walked out with her, really looked at her.

Swans live long. They mate for life.

What am I thinking?

I'm thinking that I want to flap my crippled wings and learn how to fly at the side of a swan. That's what I'm thinking.

Her car was cold tonight. Poor little car, waiting in the car park all day. Bought new by Mrs Bertram in the late '70s, Ross had given it to Sally when his mother died. It cost a lot to park it in the car park, but she felt safe in it when she worked late.

Tonight the car knew its driver had been disloyal to Mr Fixit Ross. Its starting motor growled and complained for a long minute. But the motor coughed, it caught and the little car carried her out onto the roads where its windscreen wipers swiped at fine rain and its heater worked overtime to warm the fickle feet of its driver. Its lights scanned the road ahead, brakes at the ready, aware that the driver's mind was not on the job tonight, but away, planning treachery.

In Lakeside, Sally had worked hard at doing the right thing, even if she hadn't wanted to do it. She'd become the original mush-mouth. What a wonderful, caring daughter, people said. What a lovely quiet girl, they said. Always so eager to please, they said. She'll make Ross Bertram a good wife.

Only Sally knew that she wouldn't make him a good wife, because only she knew that she wasn't really Sally mush-mouth. Not underneath. Not down deep. The thirteen-year-old was still in there somewhere.

She used to know how to fight for what she wanted. Even before Daddy had died. She used to fight with Shane. He was Mummy's boy and younger, but as big as her. She'd elbow him at the dinner table. He'd punched her one day and she'd hit back with her gold bangle, made his nose bleed. She'd pushed him off his trike and made him skin his knee. Hid his football under the house. Nicked his bag of jelly babies and ran with them to Raelene's house and they'd eaten the lot. And Carol Rigg. She'd hosed Carol Rigg that day. At eleven she'd known who she was. Then Mrs Bertram had come into her life and bad Sally had been forced underground.

Well, she'd just crawled out of her hole, stunted but still alive. She was stretching, she was reaching high. She wanted to sleep with that elegant black swan. She did. And it was that warm earthy want she read about in Sue's books, that weak-kneed, heat-in-her-belly want she'd never felt for Ross.

Sue was a manhunter, always on the prowl. She said that the only reason she hadn't kicked her husband out six years ago was because he'd been good in bed. Even in the early days, sex with Ross had not been some grand passion – more a payback for what he and his mother had given her. She'd stayed with him because she owed him.

'Like a prostitute,' she said. 'Paying my bills on my back.' Her cigarette butted in the overfull ashtray, she lit another then glanced at the fuel gauge, hit it with her knuckles. Sometimes it stuck. It wasn't stuck. It was empty again.

Her blinker on, she edged across the traffic to the left lane and swung a sharp left into a service station. While fuel was metered in she looked at the cars whizzing by. How could the earth hold enough petrol to keep filling them up?

Leave that one to the Arabs, Sall old gal. That's why they have earthquakes over there. Sucked all the filling out to sell to the cars of the world. Probably. That's why I'm having an earthquake. All of me got sucked out to keep Mummy going.

A sleek black car pulled in to the next pump. She couldn't see the driver. Maybe it was her black swan's car. He'd looked interested. If she had been Sue, she would have asked him to go for a drink, and he probably would have accepted. That's what people did in Melbourne.

The petrol cap replaced, she walked by the black Mercedes. A woman was filling it, not the black swan, but Sally knew where to find him, and she was going to see him again. She was going to pursue him until she caught him. Maybe she wouldn't know what to do with him if she did catch him, but she'd worry about that later.

That week she bought a packet of condoms at the supermarket, placing them safe in the zip compartment of her bag. Just in case. How she was going to ask her elegant swan to use a condom, she didn't know. She bought a cask of wine and two wineglasses, then decided that he looked like a Jim Beam man, so she bought a small bottle and a whisky glass. Vegemite glasses might be good enough for her. Not for him.

'Would you like to come around for a drink, Brent?' she practised. Or John. Or Rick, maybe. 'Would you like to come around for a drink one night, Rick?'

It was just a game she was playing, but all week she played the game, creating for him a background, a past, and a future where she would be. Sally and her black swan living, loving, dining at classy restaurants with his family, Sally watching her p's and q's.

I bet he's got brothers. I bet he's got grandparents somewhere, still snapping their bills at each other in some well-feathered nest. And we'll live at his flat – no, his penthouse, high above the city. Palatial, sparsely furnished. Expensive pictures on the walls. Dark landscapes. No. Moonscapes. And we'll make love on a water bed between black silk sheets.

A slow week, that one. She looked for her black swan in the mornings and when she went down at lunchtime. She rode the lifts at 4.50 and 5.15. No sign of him. Then on Friday, she remained late at her workstation when others ran.

Ratsus was pleased. 'You scratching my back. I scratching yours. Or right?' she said. She didn't know about the 5.25 time warp.

And he was there again, in number three lift at 5.25. A creature of habit. Tonight he walked out to the street with her.

'Lovely weather for ducks,' he said.

'And for swans.'

'You barrack for the Swans, Telemarket?'

She laughed, amused by her own words. 'No. No. Not really. I used to be a Footscray supporter.'

'Why Footscray?'

'A friend used to play for them.' Ross, too easily relegated to friend, but he had been a friend before he became her lover, so it was no lie. She continued walking at the side of the black overcoat, away from her car park. Companionable, they unfurled black umbrellas, the petite blonde stepping quickly in her high-heeled shoes at the side of elegance.

'What are you doing tonight, Telemarket?'

'Going to the casino with my girlfriend, Mr Midas.'

He laughed at her quick reply. 'The name is Matt,' he said. 'Matt Marsden.' He offered his hand, and she took it and her heart leapt high.

'I'm Sally. Sally Telemarket De Rooze.'

'Nice talking, Sall. See you soon.' Slowly he released her hand and he took out his keys, pointing with them into the dark cavern of a small car park. Close by, a blue station wagon beep-beeped and its rear lights blinked.

What a clever car. It wasn't the black Mercedes, but it looked new and it called its owner to its side, claimed him. And why not? He was worthy of claiming. Soon Sally would claim him too. She'd beep and he'd come to her side, but tonight she had a longer walk to her little Datsun that didn't blink or beep.

'Matt. Matt Marsden.' She said his name as she looked at the hand he had held so long. 'Matt Marsden.' He had bestowed on her the precious gem of his name. And she loved it. 'Matt and Sally Marsden.' It rolled from her tongue.

As the crow flew, South Yarra was no distance at all from the heart of Melbourne. In Lakeside Sally could have driven the few kilometres in minutes, but Melbourne was an impenetrable mass at 5.30, a pile of slow-moving metal intent on blocking her way, lights stopping her, the city beast fighting her at every turn. She made it to the flats and the bike was in her space again, so she backed up and parked out front, not wanting to fight him tonight. She wanted to think beautiful thoughts of Matt.

'Would you have time for a drink tonight, Matt?' Sally practised. 'Can I offer you some cheese, a biscuit?' What did people eat with Jim Beam – or did they eat with it? She was stepping from the shower when the phone rang. It would be Sue still wanting to go to a pick-up bar instead of to the casino.

'No, and make it fast. I'm naked,' Sally said.

'Wish I was there, love.'

'Oh, shit. Don't tell me, Ross. Please don't tell me. I don't want to know.'

'She's really into it this time. Collapsed in the main street. Sleiman wants to talk.'

One way or another, Glenda De Rooze was going to drag her daughter home.

'I'm going out tonight, Ross.'

'Who with?'

'Sue. Oh, shit, Ross. What's she trying to pull?'

'Stop your swearing. That's not going to fix anything.'

'What am I going to do with her?'

'I'd get up here if I were you. Have a talk to him. I think

he's planning to send her back to the ... down to Melbourne again.'

She sighed. 'I'll call Sue. If I can't get her, then I'll be up there tomorrow.'

Sue was still at work. She took the call but she wasn't happy. Sally wasn't happy either. She packed a case fast and was halfway down the stairs, cigarette in hand, when the bikie overtook her, or tried to.

'Smoke in your own space,' he said.

Without his helmet he looked less African and more Maori, maybe an Islander. All men she measured by Ross, and this one was as tall, or he appeared so on the narrow stairs. Long-limbed, broad across the shoulders, not to be tangled with, she decided as she stepped to one side, an apology on her tongue. But the apology tripped over on its way out. She'd spent her life apologising for being alive and he'd picked the wrong night to take her on.

'You park in your own space and I'll smoke in mine,' she said, stopping there, the cigarette like a weapon before her. The world was full of it, everybody telling you what you couldn't do and where you couldn't do it.

'You'll be a wrinkled-up old hag before you're thirty,' he said, slapping the cigarette from her hand, grinding it beneath his bikie boot.

'And you'll be in jail for assault.' Her voice high with surprise, she shoved him in his black-clad knee with her case, then, using it as a barrier, continued on slow, right down the middle of the narrow staircase to the front door, expecting a push, or a knife in the back, but ready to give him a run for his money if he tried it.

'Power to the bantams of the world,' he said at the door.

'We're just another minority group. Get used to it.' She ran out to her car, parked in the street; he walked down to her parking bay.

'Smartarse moron,' she said, tossing her case in the boot. 'But

I'm a maniac. I shouldn't have done that. What's got into me?'

Frustration had got into her. Anger at the two-hour drive before her and Mummy manipulator supreme at the end of it. Mummy, who wasn't going to give up until she got her way. She always got what she wanted, first from Daddy, then from Sally. Always had. Always would. Some things are concrete cast.

games

It was close to nine o'clock before Sally reached the hospital and found the car park full. She pulled in to the kerb beside a no-parking sign. The narrow-gutted little road prickled with no-parking signs; residents in this street had gone on the warpath two years ago, angered by cars always blocking their drives.

And she didn't need a parking ticket. She drove around the block, looking for a space, aware that her mother would be waiting, eager to relay her fake collapse in all of its glory. No space. No space anywhere for Sally.

'And I've had enough of her games, and it's too late anyway. Visiting hours are almost over.' She pulled the wheel around, turning onto the road that led to Ross. Two kilometres out, she aborted that visit. Didn't want to see Ross. Let him think she'd gone out with Sue.

'Matt Marsden,' she said, and she drove to her mother's flat.

The front door opened readily to her key, and there was no dripping tap to greet her, only the musty smell, the dusty smell of home. She turned on the exhaust fan and the gas heater before walking to her room. There she changed her sheets, wiped some of the dust away with a pillowcase, then tossed it with the sheets into the washing machine. A mess of towels was stuffed in the laundry hamper. She tossed them into the machine. Angry now, cleaning, putting junk away, slamming drawers and doors, shoving empty packets into the rubbish bin, kicking the bin.

What had happened to the Home Help lady, or had she taken one look and retired defeated?

Out of laundry detergent. That was normal. There was a dribble left in a bottle of woolwash; she emptied it over the towels, then added the last of a packet of bleach. Solidified. It would dissolve.

The kitchen bench tidied, washed down, she turned to the cluttered table, tossing more junk into the bin. Filthy tea towels were added to the load in the washing machine. She reset it, gave it a second cycle with an added dash of dishwashing detergent, then used more of the detergent to wash the floors and the bath, the toilet. Her mother didn't use much dishwashing detergent. Always plenty of that left.

It was late when she filled the bath and sank gratefully into deep water. Comfortable and well-known, this bath; for an hour she lazed there topping up the hot from time to time, using her toes as fingers on the tap.

She slept well that night and by eight she was out, jogging safe streets to the corner shop where the old guy knew her and her brand of smokes. He tossed a packet at her as she walked in the door. 'G'day there,' he said. 'Long time, no see, dear.'

She didn't need the cigarettes, not today, but she'd need them tomorrow so she bought them, and a tub of yoghurt. She spoke a while of Melbourne and her flat and her job, and he spoke of Lakeside and his grandkids. Then he said, 'Did you hear the news? Three kids and their mother murdered last night.'

'In Melbourne?'

'Yeah. They're looking for the father.' He offered the *Herald Sun*. 'It's on page two. A taxi driver reckons he saw the tail lights of the bastard who did it. Poor little buggers, never had a chance. Killed in their beds.'

Sally added the newspaper to her purchases, handing over ten dollars and receiving fifty cents change. Then she remembered laundry detergent and bought a packet. Spent money like water every time she came home.

By midday the musty smell was leaving the flat as the more familiar smells of smoke, coffee and lemon-scented dishwashing detergent ousted it. This place was home. She knew every cupboard, every corner, every rip in every chair. All morning she remained there, washing machine chugging, dryer turning, laundry ironed as it dried to be hung or placed in the linen cupboard.

At two o'clock she locked up and left for the hospital.

'She's in the old building. Oh, and Dr Sleiman left a note. He wants you to give him a call, Sall,' Deb said.

'Are they sending her down to Melbourne again?'

'I think that's an option.'

Sally walked on, plastic bags slapping at her legs as she hurried down the enclosed walkway that led from the new building to the old. It was narrow, ceramic tiled, glass domed. Her footsteps echoed strangely there. Matt Marsden, they sang. Matt Marsden. Magic words, they lifted her chin, helped her pin on a smile for Mummy.

Nothing in this ward to smile about. Four beds, and the three heads on the other pillows were grey, toothless ones. One of them was Karen Matthews's grandmother, ninety-nine not out. Her mother, propped high on pillows, was glancing through a magazine. Her hair hung limp and too long; she wore a sexless blue hospital gown that gaped at the armpits, flaunting her broomstick arms and her scars.

'Hello, beautiful,' Sally said. 'Just love your gear. Where did you get it?'

'It's easier for the sisters.' The reply was defensive, petulant.

Sally took a gown from one of the plastic bags, the salmon

pink. 'Sit up and I'll help get you out of that shroud.'

'Leave me alone.' No precious girl today. The three sleeping grey heads couldn't hear her.

'If you look good, you feel good, and believe me you do not look good. Up you get and no arguments, Mummy.' With little help from her mother, she dressed her in salmon pink, quickly buttoning the bodice, hiding the stick-like arms. 'Now, sit up while I fix your hair and we'll go down to the lounge for a while.'

'I'm not well enough.'

All afternoon the woman refused to move from the bed and Sally remained with her. She trimmed her mother's too-long nails, painting them salmon pink to match the gown. She fussed and brushed the lank hair.

Still no Ross, but each footfall in the corridor turned her head. How was she going to tell him she'd been here all night? She should have called him.

Teatime came early at the hospital and he still hadn't arrived. Karen Matthews had been chasing him for years – maybe he'd started jumping his fence like his bull.

Her mother wasn't eating her meal. Determinedly Sally fed her the vegetable broth, loading the spoon, offering it, offering the buttered bread, pushing her mother to eat as she pushed the voices on the phone to buy. Eventually the mouth opened.

She'd lost so much weight. Probably starving herself, thinking she was punishing her daughter for leaving Lakeside. The sisters gave efficient professional care but they didn't play feeding games, didn't watch her every move. And down this end with the old ladies, God only knew what she'd get up to. Mummy was a sly one, and the sooner they got her out of this ward, the better.

'Why did they put you down here, Mummy?'

It was the opening her mother needed. 'You know why. I'm dying.'

'Yeah, yeah, yeah.' Sally stood and drew the curtain screens, creating a false barrier as other visitors wandered in to sit beside other beds. She could still hear them. Wills and pills and priests. This ward was bad for Mummy.

Sally overrode the voices with her own. She told wild tales of work, mimicking Ratsus's accent; she spoke about Sue.

'She's nice, really nice, and kind-hearted, but she hides it beneath a hard exterior. She dresses like a dork, but she's smart. Did two years of university, but she dropped out and got a job when she married her ex. Her parents have got a mansion out past Doncaster. I drove her out there one day for her mother's birthday. She didn't take a present, said her presence was present enough. She had an interview for a job at Myer on Friday. I hope she gets it.'

'I was sent to work there when I was barely fifteen years old,' her mother said.

'I wouldn't mind working there – they get a staff discount. I've always loved that place, Mummy, ever since that Christmas when you and Daddy took us to see the window. I thought it was magic.'

'Don't!' A hand was raised. 'Don't.'

'Sorry. Anyway . . . anyway, I saw the most gorgeous blouse there last week. It was white satin, and it had embroidery all over the front and collar, and even up the sleeves, but the price was out of this world.'

An unfamiliar sister entered and Mummy patted Sally's cheek. 'This is my precious girl. This is the one I wait for all week,' she said. 'Such a happy girl. Such a joy to me.' Her timing was still good.

Sally offered her mother a spoonful of apple mush.

'I can't eat, darling. Sister understands.' Then sister was gone, taking Mummy's smile with her. 'There's a letter for you in the top drawer. Mrs Jenner brought it in.'

'Who is it from?'

'An invitation to something.'

It had been opened. Sally's mail had always been opened

before she got to it. A pity Mummy didn't show the same interest in her own bills. She glanced at it – an invitation to Gina and Rob's baby's christening on Sunday week. Another present to buy. The card dropped into her bag. 'I wrote to Raelene a while ago. Haven't heard from her. I think they must have moved.'

'Who?'

'Raelene Mason.'

'I don't know the name.'

'Of course you do. Our old neighbours. When we lived in Geelong. I wrote to her for years when I was a kid.' Her mother's head was shaking. 'They lived next door to us in Geelong. Raelene Mason. She had a little brother, Jamey, and a little yappy dog that used to drive you . . . everyone up the wall with his barking.'

Glenda shrugged her bony shoulders. She looked tired, or bored. Sally picked up a magazine, flipping pages while thinking of Raelene and Carol Rigg, seeing them in her mind's eye as they had been back then. Carol, pudding-faced with glasses. Raelene, thin with long black hair. Probably married now, with kids.

Fatso Carol Rigg, swinging that last day. Singing.

Stare, stare, monkey bear.
Everybody knows you swear.

Her forced smile slowly disappeared as she looked away, looking through the magazine and back, way back. Sad, that old swing noise. Squeak-squawk. Squeak-squawk. Memory stung, and she allowed her mind to wander in search of better days.

Daddy. He'd bought the swing-set. Its squeak-squawk had been a happy sound back then, as if it had been laughing along with her and Shane and Raelene.

The next-door garage had been built on the fence line, an easy climb up to its roof from the trellis, but a long jump down. She and Raelene hadn't been allowed to climb up there. But Sally had climbed. After Daddy had died, Sally had climbed often.

'I see you for a few hours a week and you sit there reading magazines.'

'I come here to visit you and all you want to do is lie in that bed. I've run out of conversation.' She turned another page. 'He's a hunk, isn't he?' She offered the magazine. 'He looks a bit like a guy I met in Melbourne,' she said. Her mother turned her eyes away.

'Melbourne. It's all Melbourne. What about me?'

'Okay. What about you? Want to get dressed and go down to the pub for dinner? Have a couple of glasses of wine and get happy.'

'Stop tormenting me.'

Old memories raised old anger, a creeping anger. It wasn't good. Anger got her mouth going, led to a black hole that could swallow her up. She could wallow in that hole for days, reliving the accident, going mad with trying to alter in her mind what had happened that night. If she'd kept her seatbelt on and helped Daddy watch the road like Mummy used to . . .

Watch it, Bren, Mummy would say. That car is turning, Bren. Slow down. Check that the back window is locked, Bren.

If she hadn't climbed over the back. If she'd reminded Daddy to check the back window. That's what she should have done. Should have left Teddy in the back –

She stood abruptly and poured a glass of water, tossed it down and forced a smile, searching her mind for a place to go, a lifeline to hold on to. Only Ross. Only the farm. She should have gone out there last night. Should have.

Guilt and anger now. A bad, bad mixture. She played with her cigarettes, sat again, foot tapping as she glanced at the magazine.

Matt. Matt Marsden.

'He's a financial adviser, works on the fourth floor of my office block. If you could take the best of a young Sean Connery and add a dash of a young Richard Gere, then you might end up with something like Matt. He's dark, and tall – not too tall, and he dresses like he stepped straight from the pages of a fashion magazine.'

Her mother's hand waved the words by as she looked at the curtain screen that hid the door. She was waiting for Ross. She liked him well enough. Not a great talker but he knew how to listen. There were things she wanted to discuss with him today.

'I changed your sheets, did the kitchen and bathroom floors. I'll finish it off tonight, so you'll have a nice clean place to go home to this time. You might feel like staying there for a while.' Sarcasm wasn't good. Watch it, she warned herself and she rattled her cigarettes, wanting out. Out in the air. Space.

'I won't be going home.'

'Has Sleiman said anything to you about going to Melbourne?'

'He knows that I'm dying.' Her mother nodded towards the right. 'Her kidneys have shut down. She's only got days. And old Mrs Thomson. Mrs Matthews. This is where they put you to die. Everyone knows it.'

'People don't die of starvation overnight. It takes years. Give it up, Mummy.'

'Shock can bring the cancer on again. It's come back on me.'

'Cut the crap.'

'I'm in constant pain. It's gone to my liver.'

'It was in your liver two years ago, wasn't it? You're still here.'

'This time it's different. I can feel it.'

'Right.' She reached for her cigarette packet, caressed it with her thumb.

'There's some of Bren's insurance left in the National Bank, and my pension is paid into the Commonwealth. It will be barely enough to bury me.'

Sally tapped her foot, keeping time with her tapping fingers on the packet. This time it was different. Next time it would be different again. But it had never been any bloody different.

'Don't worry about it. I'll put you out for recycling and spend the money on a trip to the zoo. Come on. Out of that bed, Mummy.'

'I haven't made a will. It might be better to close the insurance account while I'm still alive.'

'Oh Jesus, Mummy.'

She'd heard it all too many times before and she didn't want to hear it any more. Bloody insurance money. Daddy and the boys' blood money. She'd hated it then and she hated it now. It had given her mother the means to keep moving, not moving on, just moving the same hell and Grandma's dining room suite and china to an even greater hell.

Her stomach growled. Anger or hunger. She forced it down with cold water. Down. Down. She needed a smoke. Had to get outside, have a smoke. A cigarette made the intolerable almost tolerable.

'I want to make a will.'

Sing a song of sixpence, a pocket full of rye.
Four and twenty black birds baked in a pie.
And when the pie was open –

'There is no will!'

'My goodness. And you with all of your millions. Tut tut, Mummy. You have been remiss. We must get onto that.'

'I want to see a solicitor. I want to put my last wishes in writing. You won't waste any time on me when I'm dead.'

'Then get out of that bloody bed and go and see a solicitor. I'm not stopping you. I'll make an appointment for you. You can write it in your diary.'

That got her mother up on her elbow. It raised her voice above the petulant whine. 'You're cruel. You've got your grandfather's cruel, selfish streak in you.'

'That's why I'm up here. Change the subject, please, or I'm gone.'

'I knew it the day you were born. You're him all over. You run away when the going gets too hard, don't you?'

'Yeah, and this is too hard.' She walked to the door and her mother's eyes narrowed.

'Don't you bury me in this cemetery. I want to be with Bren and my boys.'

'Can't you see that this bullshit has got no impact, that it no longer gets past the outer ears, Mummy? Don't you know that we can all see right through your games? Get out of that bed and let me take you home.'

'You want me murdered in my bed? It's not bad enough that I'm dying.'

'There was no intruder. He's in your mind. He's always been in your mind, Mummy. We spent half our lives hiding under a bloody bed from your imagination.' Sally was at the door and the old ladies' visitors were looking at her. Mrs Matthews stared, and old Donald Thomson. She ran her fingers through her hair, scanning the corridors for Ross. Where was he? She couldn't stand being here much longer. She was going to blow.

'It will be over soon, and no trouble to you. All you'll have to do is fill in the date.'

'Hey, did you hear the joke about the hypochondriac who finally died at the ripe old age of a hundred and fourteen? She'd preordered her tombstone too, had it engraved. *And you refused to believe me when I told you I was dying*.'

She was back at the bed, an unlit cigarette in her mouth, willing Ross to come, to save her from her tongue, but he wasn't coming.

'Two of a kind. Selfish. You always were and ever will be. You never thought of anybody else but yourselves.'

'Two of a kind, all right. You and me, Mummy. Two crazy bloody peas locked into a dried-out pod. Shrivel up and die in here if you want to, but I'm not dying with you.' Her mother's tears began their trickle. 'Stop that. I'm sick of your tears and your act. I'm sick of feeling guilty every day of my bloody life.

I am not coming home. I – am – not – coming – home, Mummy.'

Then they were both weeping. Her mother could always squeeze a few more tears out of Sally. For twenty years, tears had been their mother and daughter togetherness.

Ross walked in and found them howling. He stood back until Sally wiped her eyes and walked away to stand before the window, then he sat on the chair close to the bed.

'How's it going then, Mrs De Rooze?'

She took a tissue and dabbed at her eyes. 'I'm dying, Ross. Why is everyone trying to keep it from me? Dr Sleiman has said something to you.'

'He said you're dying of starvation, that's about all. Wrap yourself around a pie and chips and you'll be a new woman.' He looked at Sally. But Glenda De Rooze had a listener, and she demanded her listener's undivided attention. Her sharp little salmon-pink nails gripped his arm. He turned his eyes to her.

Tears trickling, she told him to take the withdrawal forms from the second drawer of her locker, and she told him to close the National Bank account and to withdraw her pension each fortnight to put it in his account for her funeral.

'And sell the furniture, Ross. The dining room suite is worth thousands, and the ornaments. I won't see the end of this year.'

He offered a dry tissue, then moved his chair back, creating distance as he searched for and found the bankbooks, the withdrawal forms. 'It'll be worth seeing. I was reading the other day that they reckon this millennium bug could close the banks, send our accounts into cyberspace, ground all air traffic.'

'What have I got to live for? My own daughter can't stand to be near me.'

'You know that's not true. Sally's up here every weekend, running herself ragged. She's getting damn near as scrawny as you.'

'I've become a burden to her and to you,' she said.

Ross couldn't bring himself to deny that one, so he scratched his chin and looked at his shoes.

The clouds were trying to rain. Sally pressed her face to the glass. Cool glass. She watched a rain tear hit the window, and she reached out a finger to it, her other hand wiping at her own as she listened to the same old thumbscrewing crap she'd been listening to since she was eight years old.

'So, what's your doctor saying about this last effort?'

'Will you listen to what I'm saying?'

Ross stood and rubbed at his jaw, then he took his mobile phone from his pocket. 'I'll go and give Sleiman a call, love,' he said. 'Excuse me a tick, Mrs De Rooze.'

Sally walked to the bed and whipped the yellow screens back against the walls. Ross was in the doorway, his ear to the phone. He raised a hand. 'Doctor.'

'Out of that bed, or I'll drag you out. And you know I can.'

Her mother's hand found the buzzer and she buzzed it. Buzzed it long as her feet moved, burying themselves beneath the bedcover, trying to run faster to her tombstone in Geelong.

Ross covered the mouthpiece. 'Leave her be,' he said. 'Leave her. They're trying to raise Sleiman. He's on his way here, they think.'

addressing the situation

Sally was in the long walkway when Sleiman came poncing towards her. He'd looked like a thirty-year-old parrot eleven years ago, and she hadn't looked at him since. He'd had a wife then, but she'd flown the coop with his little fledglings.

Sally walked by him, her face turned to the wall. He preferred to speak to Ross anyway. Ross Bertram had a bit of money and to a Sleiman, money spelt class. Sally and her mother were bulk-bill nobodies. The two men followed her to the new building, the doctor speaking gravely to Ross, his parrot beak managing a private school accent.

At the main entrance Ross took her arm, drew her feet to a stop. 'I think you ought to listen, Sally,' he said.

'She is refusing to admit herself voluntarily for further psychotherapy, Miss De Rooze.'

He always managed to take the tall from her name. They were all the same, he and his brothers; they thought they owned this town and everyone in it. Doctor, lawyer, banker, there was a Sleiman finger stirring every pie.

Her open palm waving his words away, she glanced at his shoes.

Maroon. They matched his trousers. Her eyes continued to scan up. Pea-green jacket. Yellow shirt. Beaky nose, an overly long top lip. Her eyes roved up to the face, the sparse hair. His feathers had fallen; now the reptile within was attempting to get out through his scalp. Dry, freckled, scaly scalp. She looked at his eyes, reptilian, droopy lids, then she turned away from him to the rain, a heavy shower beating itself to death again on grey concrete.

'She needs to be at home, Miss De Rooze.' He oozed concern, crawly concern. 'It is a difficult situation for you, I can understand this,' he said, his hands interlocking, his fingers squirming. But he held them back, controlled them. 'She asked me to speak to you today.'

She shrugged, glanced at the moving mouth. Beaky little mouth sucking on seed. His jaw stretched forward, stretching his neck as his long top lip attempted to hide his buck teeth. They all had buck teeth, inner beaks. They needed a dentist in the family.

'There is ... is no simple answer in these cases, and at this stage I am not certain that further psychiatric treatment is warranted.' He wrung his hands and one reached out to touch her. She stepped back quickly, well out of reach, and turned, her shoe squealing on the tiled floor as she opened the door and walked outside. They followed her.

'Are there any other relatives who can assist with her care?'

'No.' Ross replied.

Wind whipped the rain now, driving it beneath the small shelter. Wetting, weeping rain. But clean. Free. Sally turned her face to Melbourne, wanting its freedom.

'She's pulling the old emotional blackmail bit again. You know that as well as we do,' Ross said.

'Since the intruder, she is afraid to live alone. She needs to be with family.' Sleiman stretched his lips in what served as a smile.

Sally lit a cigarette. She couldn't have freedom so she'd have smoke.

'There is an excellent network of support in Melbourne. The situation ... will need to be addressed.'

Good old '90s jargon. He was full of it. The world was full of it. She sucked smoke, blew it at the rain. She'd been addressing this situation for twenty years. She'd been looking at the big picture too. She sucked more smoke, sucked it deep.

Ross was talking. Let them work it out between them. Two men, speaking importantly, tossing a glance at bulk-bill Sally then dismissing her. People were walking in, walking out, gawking at her.

They'd always gawked at her when one of the welfare flock had come knocking on Mummy's door, mouths parroting jargon. Carers who didn't care. They had their own to care for; their own at home in their safe little houses.

Out of sight, out of mind, little Sally. Starve her. Drag her out of school, drag her out of bed. Pack her up in newspaper. Pack her off to someplace.

She felt the sting of self-pitying tears but she sucked smoke and stared at the sleaze. Saw his hands when she had been an embarrassed eighteen and she'd gone to his surgery to ask for the contraceptive pill. He'd got her on his examination table and assaulted her with those white hands.

Always someone forcing her to do what she didn't want to do.

Not any more. Not any more.

'Do you have any suggestions, Miss De Rooze?'

'Yeah. I suggest you ... you look at the big picture,' she said. 'I've been looking at it for years and I just decided that I'm not buying it.' Ross flinched, frowned, but her tongue had come loose and she let it flap a while. 'And ... and I also suggest that as you're her doctor, paid by Medicare to address this particular situation, that you address it, but not to me, because I get enough bloody junk mail already.'

'Sally!'

She walked away then, walked through the rain away from

Bertram disapproval, her hands shaking, her head shaking, her stomach and her legs shaking.

Shouldn't have said that.

Christ! Who had said that?

Sally De Rooze, that's who. Sally De Rooze, almost thirty, and angry, and to hell with Bertram disapproval too.

No keys in her bag, she couldn't get out of the rain and she began hitting her forehead against the cold, wet metal of her car, hitting it hard, hurting it. Then Ross was beside her. He drew her from the car, tried to hold her but she pulled away, found her car keys in her coat pocket and opened the car door, got in. He folded his oversized frame into an undersized seat as the rain grew heavier.

Black sky tonight, black hills in the distance. She'd liked those hills once. They'd locked her mother in. Now they were trying to lock her in.

He lit two cigarettes. 'Want to go to the pub and grab a drink?'

'What does it matter what I want? I'm just a commodity. I'm just an article of trade.'

He smoked in silence, waiting. That was the way to handle her moods. Just count to ten and try again. 'We ought to go to the flat and start packing it. Call her bluff.'

'Don't try to beat her at chess, Ross. She's made her move. I made mine, but she always wins in the end.'

'We're going to have to move her in with us when we get married. We've always known that.'

I don't want to marry you, she thought. But what did it matter what an article of trade might want? Marriage was the only long-term solution. Years ago, when they'd planned that wedding, they'd painted the sleep-out, made it fit for her mother.

The key in the ignition, the starter motor groaned and the motor fired. She opened the window to clear the fog, set the windscreen wipers wiping and drove Ross to his ute, then turned her little car towards the only home she clearly remembered.

She'd stopped putting them in her memory bank, allowing them all to merge, the flats, the motels, the towns, the streets, the faces of the part-time families who had fed and housed her until her mother came home from hospital to starve her again.

The old fridge had been with them forever, and the grey laminex kitchen table with its four tubular metal and vinyl chairs, probably bought second-hand thirty years ago. Daddy hadn't made enough money to buy what Mummy wanted. New furniture had been put in the 'next year' basket.

Her hand traced the old table. They'd made furniture too strong in the old days. The laminex was lifting at the edges, and the vinyl chairs were ripped, but the steel legs were strong. She kicked a chair from her pathway as she walked into the lounge room, where she wiped at the dark wood of Grandma's dining room table.

It was an old suite, but not antique. The chairs had always been too good to be used, except by determined dust. It had followed their every move, followed them from their house in Geelong. Wipe it away one day in Ballarat, and a week later it had tracked them to the next place. Sixteen years ago dust had followed them to Lakeside and, like Sally and her mother, it had settled there.

The ornaments were dulled by dust. Poor worthless dust collectors, they'd be safer in a box. Sally picked up the goose girl, a pretty thing, all pink and white and gold. It looked like fine china, from a distance. When she'd wrapped it that first time, twenty years ago, it had been over three handspans tall, now it was a bare two. She stood there fondling it, dripping tears or rain onto it and onto the paper she'd spread on the dining room table. A heavy drop fell on a supermarket ad, making a paper apple look fresh and dew-wet. Carefully she placed the goose girl base down. She'd always wrapped that one first.

How many times?

She didn't know. But she knew the goose girl's shape with her eyes closed. She knew the point of the goose's bill, the goose girl's wide-brimmed hat. She knew where the pink china arm curved down to the golden basket with its dozen eggs. She knew it and loved its worthlessness, so she wrapped it well and safe for the next move.

So many towns. She started charting the shops, the streets, trying to recall differences. There was the school with the bike sheds down the side and there was the little brick school just over the road. There was the school with that little redheaded male teacher and the school with the old bell.

Funny. She could remember the schools, but not the rooms she'd slept in, except in that first house at 29 Carter Street. Eight when she left it, almost eleven when she'd seen it that last time and pelted Carol Rigg with green passionfruit. She'd had a good aim. Always had a good aim.

The newspaper parcel in her hand, she stared at it. Poor little goose girl, wrapped up again, an anonymous parcel of old bad news. She hated newspaper, hated it. Hated wrapping up her life in it and carrying it away to unwrap in a strange place.

The ornament placed on the table, she picked up the china lady with the blue parasol and the dirty neck. She had come out of a finer mould. A fragile lady, not tough enough for this world, she'd lost her head years ago between someplace and the next. Now she was stuck together with old glue, no longer perfect. The china man might have been perfect. She didn't look, but wrapped him quickly, then the voluptuous lady with the cat, a chip off the cat's nose. It had taken a tumble one night, landed on the hearth.

She wrapped the eagle, his wings spread in flight, then the farm boy, a worried lad that one, seated on a grassy knoll with his red apple. He'd lost his elbow when he'd moved to Lakeside, and Sally hadn't been able to glue his bits together. She'd given up, tossed them in the bin with the new mouse dirt. Now he had a hiatus elbow. The rust-clad shoulder curved down into space. The hand and his apple were grafted to his chest. He couldn't lift the apple to his mouth any more because he had no elbow to bend.

There had been too much glue in her life. Too much makeshift. Only the Bertrams hadn't been makeshift. Worthless bitch, she thought. I'll marry him because it's the only way out of a fix and I'll hate him in a year, but I'll stay with him and I'll chip away at him until he becomes worthless too.

She turned from the newspaper-wrapped pile to Ross. 'Sorry.' He looked at her, quizzically. 'Sleiman. Sorry if I embarrassed you.'

'Don't worry about it. He knows you were upset.'

She wrapped the china wolf, his heavy foot holding down a wide-eyed fawn. Poor little fawn, he'd lost an ear. He'd had it in Geelong. She reached high for the elephant and his red-turbaned Indian rider, lifting them carefully to the table. A weighty one, it had a chip off the old turban. She had smoothed that chip with a nailfile then dabbed on a spot of nail polish. Not quite the right red but close enough given the fact that it had been chosen on the hop from Davis's pharmacy. The shepherd and his Lassie dog with a glued-on tail, a little white-haired professor reading from his chipped book, the white doves, the dancing lady – they looked good from a distance but, like the dining room setting, they were never destined to become antique. Just junk. Pretty junk.

When she started wrapping the photographs, she turned her head away, closing her eyes while placing the frames face down on newspaper. Her father's first, a ten by eight. He was wrapped up fast and well, then the three boys in a matching frame. The photographs had always been wrapped after the ornaments.

A large, heavy framed photograph was lifted from its place over the mantelpiece. Her grandmother had sat for that one only a week before she died, so Mummy said. No smile on her face, but she'd had nothing much to smile about with her philandering husband. Probably planning her long jump when the camera clicked. If she'd done it to make her husband feel guilty, it hadn't worked. He'd still taken off with his girlfriend a week after her funeral.

The smiling Glenda, a bride in an oval frame, Sally eased carefully from the hook above the crystal cabinet. She looked at that one but couldn't remember that happy face, so much like her own. Different eyes, though, a paler blue and close set. Similar smiles. Same teeth. The same, only different.

'Tell me that I love her, Ross. Convince me that I care about her. I must, or I'd just run and keep running, wouldn't I?'

'She loves you too, in her own way.'

'Like she loves the microwave – fast and efficient. She prefers the microwave.'

He shrugged, walked out to the back porch for a breath of air, stepping high over boxes of junk and empty bottles. He braved the drizzling rain to empty a large carton into the green bin, then returned to the kitchen, placing the carton on the table where he began filling it with the wrapped ornaments.

Sally watched him. Wrapping them in newspaper was one thing, sealing them in a box was another, but while her head denied it, she picked up a green texta and wrote on the cardboard. GOOSE GIRL. That's what she'd done whenever they'd packed up for a move – easy to find the important items when they got to the next place. Raelene's mother had taught her that trick; she'd helped pack up the Geelong house.

A cigarette taken from her packet, she lit it while watching Ross's hands. He was an inexperienced packer; the Bertrams had never moved.

Sally Bertram would never move again.

Sally Marsden might fly north for the winters.

He'd used the last of the paper and was looking around for more. There'd be another pile of it stored in some corner; she and her mother wouldn't have survived without it. It cleaned windows, lined shelves, lit old stoves, heated water in an ancient chip heater at one of the flats. Somewhere. It polished the school shoes, and made inner soles when school shoes had holes. And it wrapped china. Cheap, disposable, like their lives.

She walked to the laundry, checking the cupboard there; its

lower shelf was stuffed with old papers. She removed a bundle, dumping it on the floor at Ross's feet.

'She's been starving herself since I left. There's nothing in her cupboards. Nothing in the fridge. She probably sat here at night, planning this.'

'I'm sick of talking about her. I've told you what we have to do.' He left her defrosting the fridge and drove to the Chinese takeaway. He liked his food, and he'd put on weight since she'd left. He'd be a fat old man if he lived long enough to grow old. Near nine he returned, bringing with him a pile of supermarket cartons. They sat in the midst of them eating Chinese and discussing bills, and when Sally pushed her half-eaten meal away, Ross cleaned up her leftovers.

At ten they found the old guitar case beneath more newspapers and a cloud of dust. It had been there, on the top of her mother's wardrobe, undisturbed for sixteen years. Inside the guitar case was a packet of photographs and a bundle of sheet music; the rubber band that once held them together had perished. Sally took the case back to the kitchen where she wiped it clean with a sponge, squashing escaping silverfish with the same sponge. She mashed a cockroach beneath her foot, then sat looking through the handwritten music while Ross dragged the vacuum cleaner from the cupboard.

She began humming along with the cleaner and, slowly, words she hadn't thought of in years started playing in her mind. A time warp that guitar case, a part of some life she'd lived. She began singing the lost words, found written on silverfish-nibbled paper.

Then the vacuum was off and her singing stopped mid-sentence.

'Is that one of your mum's songs?'

'Daddy used to love that one,' she said. The sheet music placed in a plastic bag, she sealed it, safe from silverfish. A brief glance at the photographs was enough. Shane and Grandma. Sally and Shane, the little girl face scribbled over with red biro.

There was one of her father in short shorts, digging in the garden, Sally almost out of frame – not a lot of red biro required to wipe her out of that one. Just the past. Just sad. She sealed them into another plastic bag.

That night she slept in her own narrow bed, her childhood bed, transplanted to many towns before it settled down to grow old and rickety in Lakeside.

'You go home, Ross.' She kissed him goodnight, but made no space for him beside her in the bed.

'Might as well,' he said.

empty rooms

Ross didn't go home. He found a musty blanket instead, and he lay on the green vinyl couch. It was too hard but, unlike Goldilocks, he had no choice. It was too slippery as well, and the cushions beneath his head were lumpy. He catnapped, and woke, altered his position. Around two he thought of Sally's mother's bed and took his blanket in there but the room smelt of her. Stale and bitter. He returned to the couch, where he dozed until dawn.

His back was stiff when he crept in to check on Sally, still sleeping like a baby, soft, soundless sleep, as if in dreams she had no energy to waste on breathing.

He knew her father and brothers had died in a car crash, but little else about her early childhood. What he had learnt of that time had come from his mother. A closed book, Sally; its covers sealed. Rarely did he get to see beneath the seal. She'd planted a passionfruit vine at the farm and told him of the ones she'd left behind in Geelong. She'd spoken of Ballarat when they'd driven there one day to go to a wedding. She'd shown him an old brick house and a school.

'I liked that school,' she'd said.

He'd got to know the brat of fourteen, and over the years she'd grown into his life. Watching her small hands at work – using his mother's knives, her bowls, crocheting baby things for newborns – was like watching his mother's hands at work.

And the biscuits she baked, and the roast dinners. He knew her well in his house, knew her body in his bedroom, but he hadn't recognised the one at the hospital. At fourteen she'd had a barbed tongue; these days she rarely let anyone feel its edge. Sleiman had felt its edge.

At five Ross drove home to the farm to feed the dogs.

Her hair dripping, looking like a half-drowned waif, Sally walked from the bathroom when she heard him return. 'You're early,' she said, staring at the walls bare of photographs, at the cabinets and windowsills bare of ornaments, the old fridge looking white, stripped of its many magnets and useless information. Her phone number and address had clung to its side since May, but her mother had never called that number.

She turned to the table, saw the breakfast cereal and the bread, the jar of homemade apricot jam. 'The Bertrams and their food.'

'You've got to eat to live, love.' He kissed her, but she drew away. 'I was hoping you wouldn't be up. I was going to crawl into bed with you for a while.'

'I'm all wet.'

He was already eating when she made her slice of toast, and still at it when she started moving the furniture, sweeping up. He moved her mother's bed, stood it upright against the wall, exposing balls of fluffy dust and a lost shoe, another pile of newspaper.

All morning they moved furniture and cleaned, then at two they drove to the hospital. Tongue in cheek, Ross told Glenda De Rooze that they'd made a start on packing up the flat. 'Thought we'd just check with you, make sure it's what you want before we take your stuff around to the auction rooms.'

'Go ahead and sell it, Ross. I knew I could rely on you.' She didn't look at Sally.

'And when you change your mind tomorrow, Mummy?'

'You still don't understand, do you?'

'No,' Sally said. 'No, but then I never did understand you. You could probably say that you were one of the truly misunderstood.'

The woman's eyes swept over her daughter, dismissing her as she turned again to Ross. 'Call the housing ministry on Monday. Explain that I have been unwell for some years, that I am no longer able to live alone, that I have been forced . . . forced by my own daughter to give up my home of sixteen years.'

'You'll have to tell them that yourself, Mrs De Rooze.'

'Think five minutes ahead for once in your life, Mummy. I've got a bedsitter and one bed. You'll have nowhere to live when Sleiman kicks you out.'

The woman's small teeth bit, and her mouth grew ugly. 'Live? Live? You made sure I had nothing left to live for, didn't you?'

Sally walked away fast. Ross followed her to the car.

'What did she mean by that, love?'

'Who knows? So. So, what's your next move? This is your chess game.'

'We'll see what Sleiman decides to do with her, and play it by ear. If she rings the housing ministry, then I suppose we move her junk out to my shed.' He grinned, pleased with his day's work. Six for Glenda De Rooze and half a dozen for him.

A spring wedding now on the agenda, Ross was a satisfied man when he tossed the old green couch onto his truck early the following Sunday morning. Glenda was nobody's fool. She'd made her calls; hadn't paid her back rent, though.

He tossed the green vinyl chairs onto the truck's tray, rips and all. 'Ten bucks the lot . . . or straight to the tip. What do you reckon?' he asked three freckle-faced girls, Mrs Jenner's grandchildren, who shook matching red heads. 'The tip, I reckon.'

They nodded emphatically, then one by one he lifted the girls to the tray, catching them as they jumped, swinging them high.

'Anovver one,' the smallest said, so they all had another turn.

Sally smiled, watched him as she carried out the dining chairs. So good with kids – he should have had his own.

The heavy timber table was loaded carefully, Sally on the truck's tray guiding it, Ross doing the hard work. They tied it down well. The grey laminated kitchen table and grey chairs were dump material, but they were tossed on, just in case.

Ross took extra care with the washing machine. 'That should make a couple of hundred,' he said. He wheeled the old fridge outside on his trolley. A happy man today, he didn't know his own limitations. Six-foot-four of muscle, his waist was not as slim as it ought to be, but his shoulders were broad. Footballer's legs flexed, hands that had once made a football look like a toy reached low, heaved, and the fridge was up.

He leaned a while then, gazing out at the street, catching his breath. People were moving about their Sunday afternoon business, taking advantage of the windy sunshine. Lawn mowers roared, an elderly Ford drove slowly by.

'Who's that?' he asked, watching it pull into the drive next door.

'Sally doesn't live here any more,' she said. They watched the car do a three-point turn then drive back, the driver hidden behind darkened windows. 'It looks like a retired Mafia mob car. Karen Matthews could have hired a cheap hit-man to get me out of the picture.'

Ross grinned and turned back to his load. 'She's been calling in a couple of times a week since you left. Bought me over a lemon meringue pie last week. You'd better keep an eye on her.'

'The way to Ross Bertram's heart is through his stomach. That's one of the courses down at the high school. She majored in it.'

The carton of ornaments went into the truck's cabin. They put the television on the back seat of Sally's car. Then the vacuum roared again and dust flew. Little talk now. All words, all sounds bounced against the empty walls, came back hard and hollow, like the Geelong house when the furniture was gone, and the Ballarat house, and that first flat in Carlisle Street. It was cold too; the heater had been turned off, the pilot light extinguished. Cold and dead. Just another place, just another life, another part of Sally being left behind. How was she expected to find herself? Bits here, bits there, bits and pieces everywhere.

One corner of Ross's big tin garage took the furniture. Supermarket cartons were stacked on the fridge and on the kitchen table, but the dining room setting he squeezed in beside the lounge room window. It looked cluttered. It looked wrong in Mrs Bertram's lounge room.

'Put it in the shed, Ross. It's just mass-produced junk.'

'It hasn't got a scratch on it. We'll leave it in here, see how we go. I might build a bit of an extension onto the kitchen side.'

A good man. Good and honest and down to earth. They'd have a good life together. And Mummy would be better out here than in town. Dogs to bite the imagined intruders, too far for her to walk to the bottle shop, and she was never as bad when Ross was around.

Sally looked at the dark wood of the table. Didn't like it. Never had. Didn't want it to haunt her future as it had haunted her past. Didn't want to live with her mother, clean up her mess again, find her pills again, cook her meals she refused to eat. Didn't want to wake up every morning to her demands or her tears. Live with her, rot with her. Didn't want to any more.

The linen was washed and Ross's dryer worked overtime, but it was a big one. It took the sheets, the towels. Everything was washed. Clean. Everything had to be cleaned, sealed in plastic bags, then taped into cartons.

Night came down as she sorted through old clothing. Her mother's few good frocks were hung in the sleep-out wardrobe, two pair of shoes placed on the wardrobe floor; the rest she stuffed into a plastic bag, sealed it, then sealed the bag in a carton. Sealed the carton too. Sealed it tight. MUMMY, she wrote on it. MUMMY in black biro.

She found her pink parka. Old but warm. Ross had bought it for her when they went up to the snow one weekend. She shrugged and hung it in his wardrobe. It would be good for the farm. A few items she placed inside the guitar case, which would be returning to Melbourne with her.

An expensive case, as the guitar it had once held had been expensive. Daddy and Sally had bought it one Christmas. They'd hidden it at Raelene's house until Christmas Day.

'What happened to the guitar?' Ross stood amid the chaos of his lounge room, watching her work.

'God knows,' she said. And no doubt He did, but Ross didn't need to know.

At 11.15 he started yawning and looking at the bedroom. 'Are you going to be much longer at that?'

'I'm going back.'

'To Melbourne? Tonight? Why?'

'Because the traffic is too heavy on Monday mornings, that's why.'

'Then don't go back. Give your boss a call and explain the situation.'

'I can't.'

'Do what you like then. Don't worry about me. I'll have a cold shower.' He walked to the bathroom and yelled, 'Make sure you phone me when you get there.'

'You'll be asleep.'

'Phone me anyway. And drive carefully through those bloody hills.'

She drove carefully through the hills, the car crawling around the hairpin bends, and all the way she sat forward, watching the sides of the road.

'Bloody kangaroo,' she said. 'Bloody useless kangaroo.'

trams and plans

september 1999

'Sydney office is ahead. Is well ahead of target. What can I do? So I losing my job.' An actress who had missed her calling, Queen Ratsus played to her captive audience. She was an old and broken woman, worn down by life. 'And you caring? Eh? Do you caring that I lose my job?'

Sally leaned there, not caring, while the voice built to a crescendo. 'No. You do not caring because you are all lazy. You come to here for the bludge, because in Australia you having it too good.' The old woman blew herself up until she filled the room. Fluorescent lights flickered, dimmed, then glowed brighter, glowed on her, and she was young again, shedding the years with her insults.

'Heil Hitler.' It came from a new face in the front row. Not a young face. Not a big man, but his heels clicked smartly and one of Ratsus's audience goose stepped away.

They watched him go, heads bowed low to hide the smiles. But the old queen wasn't about to let him get away. Her eyes fired electric darts that stabbed him in the back, and for a moment his sweater glowed blue and he turned, looked back.

And she had him, now she'd reel him in, shackle him to a phone, whip one more lazy Australian into shape.

He made it to the wall of lifts; then, his middle finger raised, he saluted her, and the lift doors closed behind him. One mouse had scrambled out of the rat-trap to run free.

Ratsus turned on the desperate who remained. Smiles had been sucked away. Sue wore her serious face beneath chewed black hair. Striped with red today, it matched her gipsy-style red skirt and black layer-upon-layer shirts, her shoulder-length earrings. 'Teamwork,' she hissed, elbowing Sally in the ribs.

'Teamwork. We are team. Yes? If we do not pulling our share, we letting our working colleague down. We all must pulling our share. Sell now. Go. Sell. Sell. Sell. We showing them. Tonight we will be ahead of ratsus Sydney. Sell. Sell. Sell.'

Sally clicked her own heels, saluted, but allowed the salute to end in a brushing back of her hair as she wheeled around, quick-marched to her phone.

No sale.

What did it matter? She was going to hand in her notice today.

No sale. No sale.

A displaced person, that's what she was. Just Sally threads blowing on the wind. Never settled long enough anywhere to get herself attached to the great seething carpet of humanity. Didn't match, anyway. Never had. Just kept getting in the way of the carpet weaver.

Needed snipping off.

No sale. No sale. No sale.

While her mother had paid the rent on that flat, Sally had had a home, or a place to point her thumb at. Now someone else would call the flat home, like Carol Rigg had claimed the house in Geelong.

A beautiful variegated camellia, bought five years ago for her mother's birthday, had been planted in the earth near the front door of the housing ministry flat. Sally couldn't move it. She'd wanted to, but Ross said it was too big and the wrong time. They'd left it behind, like the passionfruit vine had been left behind, while displaced Sally moved on, or didn't move on.

Shouldn't have planted that camellia. Shouldn't have freed it to the earth. Should have bought a big pot, trapped its roots in the pot. It was crazy to keep on planting gardens for someone else to watch bloom.

Distanced from the selling game today, her nerves were split ends. She wanted to talk, needed to talk. She wanted to open her mouth and let it all pour out. And she tried it on the roof at lunchtime. She offered Sue a cigarette and they lit up, puffing a while in silence.

Unreal up here on the roof. Great scene for a science fiction movie. Above the world, above the wires and trams. All the little people, colourful beetles bustling below.

Ladybird, Ladybird, fly away home.
Your house is on fire and your children alone.

'I'm giving notice today. I've got to get married,' a beetle said as it hung far over the concrete wall, wanting to flap its wings and fly away.

'What for?' Sue said.

'Good question.' Sally sighed, brushing windblown hair from her mouth.

'Have they heard of abortions in Lakeside? You're fucking mad.'

'It's genetic.' She sucked smoke, blew smoke over the wall. How to explain the unexplainable? Why bother? Just lean a little further and fly. She sighed, straightened.

'I'm not pregnant. Just coming apart at the seams. I'm up there, I'm down here, I'm up there. I'm in that car half of my life, spending money I haven't got.'

'Tell me about it.'

'It's all come unravelled. I'm coming unravelled.'

'Who wants to be ravelled? It's just another word for screwed-up. Who are you marrying? Not the farmer?'

'Yeah.'

'You? Slopping out the pig yard?'

'He hasn't got pigs. I herd sheep and talk bulls. He's probably one in a million.'

'The bull?'

'Ross. How many guys do you know, Sue, who'd take in their mother-in-law?'

'What's in it for him? Has she got any money?'

'No.'

'Bugger. I was going to offer to marry you myself. Give us your lighter again, will you? This fucking thing has gone out.'

That night Sally drank two glasses of wine with a peanut butter sandwich and she called it dinner, then she went to bed early to save on heating bills. The old dream came for her. Out of the dawn, it came. And it came hard.

Flames. Smoke in the sky. Moon like a yellow balloon, dipping, diving, running away from the smoke. Smell of grass. Smell of burning.

'Sally! Sally!'

Daddy's face at the back window. Telling Sally to open the door. Mummy, sitting on the grass, singing in her cowgirl hat, singing her you killed 'em song.

'I'm sorry, Mummy. I'm sorry.'

She was on the bed, on her knees, sobbing, her hands against the cold, blank beige wall, her eyes staring without recognition at the makeshift bedside table, stack of yellow and white telephone books, digital clock glowing red. Red embers. Like the burning.

Just the clock and that same old dream. At eight she'd named it the fire-dream; the name had been good enough now for twenty-odd years. She closed her eyes on tears. Closed them tight. And she counted while she rocked there on her knees. She counted slow; counting, counting until the tears stopped trickling and her eyes could confront the red figures of the clock.

Six-fifteen. Six, colon, one five. That's all. Just the clock.

A long, shuddering sigh.

Thursday, payday, with Friday leaning over her like the grim reaper. She'd have to hand in her notice. Go home.

Delete home. Have to go to Lakeside. Go up there and watch a bitter mouth spit out insults for the next fifty years.

Wet sky dripping. Tap drip-dripping. Sally drip-dripping again.

'Put it in the too-hard basket. Be a fibre and float,' she whispered, swiping at her eyes with her palms. Her hands were still shaking as she reached out to her stacked bedside table for cigarettes.

Only the leftovers of the dream. She'd be okay in a minute. She walked to the window to look out at Melbourne.

Matt was out there somewhere. He was beneath one of those roofs, showering, shaving. Somewhere in the distance there was a penthouse and he was inside, drinking coffee, selecting his suit for the day.

She showered at seven and drank her coffee slowly, dressed slowly, holding the unravelling threads of Sally together with pantihose and make-up, a short black skirt and a new blue sweater, her black overcoat. She looked okay. She looked together. No-one could see the fraying mess beneath that coat, but no-one ever had. Artist of camouflage, Sally De Rooze. Composer of silence.

Her umbrella in hand, her bag over her shoulder, she picked up her car keys and for a moment stood looking at them, then she tossed them onto the bench, tucked her umbrella beneath her arm and slammed the door. The bikie wasn't going to get a free park today.

A weird little guy with a suitcase followed her along Bollinger Street and across the road to the tram stop, and he stood beside her, watched her light a cigarette. Too many cigarettes this morning. She'd been chain-smoking since she'd crawled from her bed.

'Bad for the lungs,' the little guy said. 'And don't I know it.'

'So is breathing exhaust fumes, so go and lecture a truck,' she replied, and she turned away to look for the tram. One in the distance, whether it was coming or going, she couldn't tell.

Feeling his eyes burning through her coat, she spun around fast and caught him staring, head to one side. She'd seen him somewhere before. Not at the flats, though. He'd come from further down the road.

'You catch this tram every morning?' he said.

People didn't strike up conversations at tram stops, and he was too old to be trying to pick her up. He was wearing a navy suit and a tie, looked as if he was going to work, apart from the small brown case at his feet.

'Is that a big briefcase, or are you leaving home?' she said.

'Going home.' His eyes refused to leave her, but other travellers were grouping and the tram was close. She dropped her cigarette, ground it into the pavement and stepped on board.

A bad day for public transport, and peak hour the wrong time to try it, the seats all taken and the ticket machine way up the other end.

'If they want me to buy a ticket, then I say let them sell me one.' He was still behind her, and his silly little voice made the hair on the back of her neck stand up.

She fought her way to the machine and bought a ticket. He didn't; he was still staring at her as the tram trundled on, trying to toss her to the floor at every stop and acceleration, but it was a fast and efficient way to move people around. Just learning to sway with the crush of humanity, to get the rhythm and she was in the city. She stepped from the tram and walked quickly away.

Walter O'Leary and his case were not far behind her. He followed her down to Collins Street. She turned once, perhaps she saw him, so he placed his case down and scratched his back. When she'd gained some distance he followed again, saw her enter her office building, then he hopped a tram to Spencer Street Station.

His hire car due back last night, he'd been late getting into town, very late, so he'd taken it in early this morning, parked it out the front of the yard, the keys in the glove box.

His old watch told him he had almost four more hours to kill before his bus left, and his case, though small, was growing heavy. He took a luggage locker and stood admiring a young woman in a black overcoat. Walter was watching her instead of watching where he was walking when a big woman, pushing a case on wheels, ran over him.

'I'm sorry,' he said.

She wasn't. She reminded him of Elaine, his first wife.

Black coats and suits everywhere this morning, Melbourne's winter uniform, her army assembling, then marching off to do battle with their computers.

Elaine had stepped into that uniform early and never got out of it.

'Black is for mourning,' she used to say. She'd spent most of her married years mourning the years she'd spent with him. Not that he blamed her.

going, going, gone

All day the clock in the Collins Street office had ticked slowly. All day Sally made the calls, her eye on that clock, and as the hour grew later, her plans grew more inventive.

I had to have the brakes done, Matt. They're down to the metal.

'Good afternoon. Today we are offering you –'

I took the tram to work this morning. Had to put the car in for a service, Matt.

Liar, liar, your pants are on fire.

'Mrs Matthews, this is Sally calling –'

I put the car in for a service, Matt. The motor keeps stalling. It's this cold weather. Have to buy a new car, I think.

What with, you liar?

Why shouldn't she lie? They lied to her at interviews. Like the one she'd given up lunch to go to last week. 'We will be putting your name forward, Sally.' The woman at the agency had sounded so genuine.

They hadn't called, or not when she was home. She needed an answering machine. Dozens of interviews she'd gone to since

May, but employers wanted references and qualifications. She had none. And she knew she applied for the wrong jobs – which paid better than the right ones.

There was plenty of work for waitresses and sandwich hands, checkout chicks and child-carers, and they paid a pittance. After the taxman took his cut, it was impossible to live on what they offered. At least at Phonepross she could do the extra hours, make ends meet. She'd have to do a computer course at night school, get some qualifications.

But Sue had an education, and an answering machine – with a Sue-type message. *Five-foot-eight, overweight, don't stand there and salivate*. Though her guys thought it was a lark, it hadn't got her a highly paid job.

And so the clock ticked on, but slowly.

While Walter O'Leary repositioned his limbs for the umpteenth time and tried to ignore his seat companion's thigh, which was hard to ignore, Sally was placing her phone down.

The time was five minutes past five.

She walked to the toilets. There were six cubicles, all new and white. White tiles. But the basins were grimy by this time of day, their matching wall of mirrors smeared, splashed by Queen Ratsus's mouse plague.

Forget Matt Marsden and hand in your notice. Go back in there and do it. Now.

Her reflection didn't like the idea, it grimaced.

'I had to put the car in to have the brakes done, Matt,' her reflection mouthed, and smiled. The mirrored face appeared happy with that lie.

But she couldn't, wouldn't do it.

Minutes used up in combing her hair, touching up her make-up, gluing the external Sally threads together for their tram ride home. There was little to do about the inner Sally, who was coming unstuck fast.

'I couldn't start the car this morning, Matt,' she mouthed and a trio walked in, glanced at her. She didn't know them. They walked into separate cubicles, not allowing closed doors to interrupt their conversation. Now Sally recognised them. They were the trio with the chook cackler. Young. Probably students. Motionless, she eavesdropped on the conversation; not a part of it, but clinging to the lives of others. A bit of fluff on someone's jacket, easily brushed away.

'Pass me under some paper, will you, Cindy?'

Number five cubicle got her paper and number four cackled.

Sally listened and thought of Ross's hen yard, thought of gathering the eggs, frying them in an inch of fat for the rest of her life. Thought of Ross in twenty years' time, his stomach hanging over his belt, her own stomach sagging down to her knees after producing six Ross-sized babies with heads like watermelons.

'Hey, you know those shoes I was looking at in Myer's, well Mum got them for thirty-nine dollars with her staff discount.'

So the cackler had a healthy mother working at Myer. Sally combed her hair, and in the mirror watched Cindy vacate the cubicle. A gorgeous, tall redhead. No loose threads on Cindy, all together, her ends knotted, snipped off clean. Free Cindy, young and free to go out with her friends on Saturday night, to play and fall in love.

And Sally wanted what Cindy had. She wanted to be in love, wanted the real thing, and she was going to have it. Her borrowed books beneath her arm, she turned on her heel, leaving the trio cackling there.

At the lifts too early, she stood at the noticeboard, conveniently placed beside the lifts.

'Lost, gold purse. Reward. Patricia.' Scrawled hurriedly by a shaking hand.

'To rent. Bungalow in Burwood E. Close to tram. $50 per week. See Joyce Rogers.' Large neat handwriting. Which one was Joyce Rogers?

'Left in ladies loo, black woollen jacket. Pam.' Computer print-out.

She checked her watch. Almost 5.25. Time-warp time. Now

she pressed the down button and watched the lift doors. It would be number three. It would be three. If it wasn't three, then she'd walk back and give notice. That was fate.

Then number three opened and she stepped inside, pressed 'Close', pressed 'Ground' and the lift stopped at four.

He was there.

So. So this was her plan, planned for weeks, planned all day, planned since the fire-dream this morning. Planned at the tram stop, the weird little guy at her side. She was here and Matt was here, and right or wrong she was going to go through with it.

As he entered the lift he smiled, glanced at the books she was juggling and at the large shoulder bag, the umbrella beneath her arm.

'You're loaded up tonight,' he said.

'Hope I get a seat on the tram. I had to put my car in ... to ... have the brakes done.' Practised too long, the lie came out flat. 'I went for a skid last night.' She turned to the door, watched the numbers. Stupid idiot. You didn't go for skids when your brakes didn't work; you went for skids when they did. Stupid idiot. She felt the blood rise to her cheeks.

'Can I give you a lift?'

'No, I'll be fine, thanks.' Too abrupt.

Last chance. Going. Going.

Don't kill chance before it's born. You're almost thirty, Sall old gal.

Going. Going.

And too quickly she added, 'The tram stop is only two hundred metres from my door. It's very convenient.'

'Why stand on a tram when you can sit?'

'If you're sure.'

He was sure. He lightened her load by three paperbacks and they walked from the lift to the street where rain pelted down.

No more thinking now. Couldn't allow herself to think. 'My flat is in South Yarra, Matt.' She loved saying his name. Such a perfect name. I want him, want him. Never felt like this before.

Never felt this throbbing ache, this aching need.

'Which way do you go?' she said, stepping quickly, lightly at his side, where she belonged.

'Your way tonight, Sall.'

Then they were in his car park and his car beeped for her, called her to it, and she was in his car, and his doors were locked and her seatbelt fastened, then together they drove towards Spring Street.

He's just giving me a lift home. Just a friendly lift home.

Maybe he was, and maybe he wasn't, but for this moment she was locked with him inside the warmth of the big station wagon, the Melbourne rain weaving a silver curtain between them and the world. He was beside her, and she was where she wanted to be. She was flying beside her black swan and for once she wasn't thinking of Mummy or Ross.

The car smelt of him, and the smell was intoxicating; every nerve in her body opened, feeding on the scent of him. And it was gluing her unravelling threads together. She had breasts again and her breasts wanted his touch. They pushed against her coat. She had legs again and they wanted to wrap around him, hold him.

She swallowed, crossed her legs, trying to still that want. She'd only known Ross's brand of love. What if . . . what if he wanted to come in and . . . what if he didn't want to come in?

He spoke little, concentrating on the traffic, but he drove easily, confident behind the wheel. She glanced at his profile against the wet window, and she thought of another station wagon and didn't know why.

White, that one had been. Older. Three boys in the back. Sally got to ride in the front with Daddy when Mummy wasn't there and Shane was always jealous.

Shane threw my Teddy over the back, Daddy. Teddy's lonely.

She turned quickly to the rear of the modern vehicle, looking at the neat space, looking for the three boys, looking for Teddy. Nothing there.

Stupid idiot. Stop it. Her heart racing, she turned again to

Matt. His hands were sure on the wheel, and she loved them. Not large hands, but long, slim. His face in profile was well known to her. He had a perfect nose, a perfect brow where his thick black hair now fell. She'd known it would fall over his brow. Just that little bit. Her hand lifted, wanting to touch it, to brush it back, knowing exactly how it would feel. Soft, heavy. Quickly the hand was drawn back to her lap.

Mad. She was stark raving mad. What was she thinking of? He was just a guy who worked in her building, a friendly guy who had offered her a lift home. I'm reading too much into a friendly lift home, so I won't make a fool of myself. I'll say, drop me on Toorak Road, and he'll stop the car and I'll get out and that will be that.

'Turn left at the next lights,' she said. 'And a left here.' The car drew to a halt in front of her concrete block of bedsitters, and she wished she lived in a mansion fit for him to see.

'Thanks very much, Matt.' She reached for her books. Sue was educating her, lending her books she never would have thought to buy. She tucked them beneath her arm as the rain thundered down. Rain, rain, rain, she prayed, not wanting hope to die yet. And God was listening to her for once. He pelted the rain down and it danced on the bitumen like fish dancing beneath the moonlight over a dark lake.

The motor stilled. 'Wait for it to ease off a bit, Sall.'

He didn't want her to leave. She could feel it, feel the air between them. Pure electricity, any movement now and the car would explode, fling them into orbit.

They spoke a while, spoke of the rain, spoke of the concrete block of flats, and when the downpour steadied to a fine mist, Sally sought the door handle.

He reached across her, opening the passenger-side door. His arm brushed against her breast, and her breast leaned into it and his arm moved imperceptibly against it. She was wearing a bra and the blue sweater beneath her black coat, but her breast was bare and his touch burned. Then the door was open and she was sliding from the car, knowing now that it was over. He'd drive away. And she'd wave and ... and tomorrow, and all of her tomorrows loomed before her like a concrete wall.

Raindrops on her hair and on her lashes. Umbrella snapped open, she stepped away. Shook her hair. Shook her head. How could he drive away and leave her? She couldn't let him. He didn't want to drive away and she knew it. She had to ... had to ... had to at least ask the question.

'I don't suppose you've got time for a drink, Matt?'

These words had been practised too, practised when she'd bought the wine, when she'd bought the Jim Beam weeks ago. Just a game back then. Now the game was in play and she'd made her move. She knew her voice sounded too high. Silly. Practised. It sounded like her supermarket persona, mouthing, 'Have a good day.' She knew he would reply, 'I'll take a rain check, Sall.' She was ready for it.

Better if he did. Better for her mother. Better for Ross.

But the rain was falling now, and no rain check was requested.

'I'd like that very much,' he replied.

The door closed behind them, the small heater was turned on. Black umbrellas, placed side by side, dripped in harmony with the sink tap as she slipped her arms from her coat, shook it and hung it behind the door, not brave enough to look at him. Then she did, and her hand went to her mouth, and he smiled, dropped his coat to the floor and his arms took her, rocked her, while his mouth found her own, and his dark eyes burned the last loose threads away.

'It's been too long. Why did we wait so long?' he said.

She clung to him, wanting, wanton, and when he kissed her again, his hand moved up beneath her skirt. He wasn't into waiting, and she didn't want him to wait; he was pulling her pantihose down and she wasn't stopping him, and she wasn't thinking of Lakeside or bulls and cows. She wasn't thinking. She was helping him and they barely made it to the bed before she opened to him.

'God!'

She was a throbbing nerve and he was inside the nerve and he was stripping off her sweater, ripping it off and hating it because it covered her breasts. Then her breasts were bare and his mouth covered them. But he was still wearing his shirt, his tie, and her hands wanted them off.

'God.'

He was driving into her and she was alive and for once she had taken charge of her own life. His tie was off and her hands were beneath his shirt and he was taking her to places she had never been, showing her sights she had never seen.

No more thinking. Only sensation now. She was the given, not the giver. She was the taker, taking what she wanted and screaming for God. Sally De Rooze, twenty-nine years and seven months old was flying, flying high at the side of her black swan and he didn't find her fledgling wings wanting.

'My, oh my, Sall,' he said when they collapsed exhausted on the bed.

'You are beautiful,' she whispered.

Gone now was the growl of the great Melbourne beast. It was only a kitten purring outside her window. Gone too was Lakeside, and the accusing face on the white pillow. All gone. She kissed Matt's hands in gratitude, kissed each fine finger, each perfect nail. For her, life had slipped into focus. This was the Sally hidden too long beneath responsibility and others' expectations. This Sally had been born to love, to love wildly. This Sally was loved, loved gladly.

Matt drank Jim Beam and she drank wine. Fast. They ate crusty bread and cheese, fast, aware they had to get it down. They made love with their eyes, smiled a lot but spoke little. Lips were better used for kissing and for exploring naked flesh still warm with first love. Then they loved again, wild for each other.

'Yes,' she said. 'Yes.' So it was mad, bad, but finally right, and he knew it was right too, then at 10.30 he looked at his watch.

She was on her back, naked, her mind, her limbs at peace. She was thinking of breakfast. Pancakes for two. No cereal in her cupboard. Eggs. Yes. But no bacon. She frowned, leaned on an elbow and watched him dress, clothing new, strange love in a dark stranger's suit, combing wild, sweet love from his hair.

Her hand reached out. 'Don't go, Matt.'

He took her hand, kissing the palm, closing her fingers over the kiss; he walked to the door, opened it. 'Sleep tight.' And he stepped through the door, dragging it shut behind him.

And she was alone and the kitten's purr was becoming a rumbling growl, low in the throat of the city beast. She sprang from the bed, trailing her floral bed sheet. She hadn't given him her phone number. She hadn't asked for his. The first thing Sue did was to get their phone number.

'Matt.' She tugged at the door, dragging it wide. He stopped halfway down the concrete stairs, laughing at her sheet that covered too little, and he returned to her, his lips finding her own while his cheeky hands stripped the sheet from her, tossing it onto the floor as he lifted her, crushed her to him, in the open doorway.

'Stay the night. Stay the week. Stay forever, Matt.'

'Try keeping me away, Sall,' he said. Then he placed her feet back on the floor and he slapped her bare buttock, and he laughed as he flew away.

love and hot pizza

She didn't go to Lakeside on Friday night. She looked for Matt in the lifts, but didn't find him, so she drove to the flat and waited for him. He didn't come. She didn't go home on Saturday either. All weekend she waited and Matt didn't come, but Ross called on Sunday night.

'What happened to you?' Accusation in his voice.

'It's been crazy this week. They needed me to work. How is she?'

'They can't get her out of bed. She reckons it's gone to her back now. The doctor is going to do some more x-rays.'

X-rays. Blood tests. Brain transplant. Just give me one more week. Please, God, just let me see Matt one more time and I'll live on it forever. Just one more night.

'Have you given notice yet?'

Don't answer that one. 'I'll be up next Friday. We'll talk about it on Friday.'

Monday was a blur, but that evening Matt was waiting for her in the foyer. Wide smiles, a brief touch of impatient hands but no kisses and few words, then a fast drive in separate cars to her flat. And love. God, what love they made.

At twelve he dressed, picked up his briefcase.

'Stay with me tonight.'

'No clean shirt for tomorrow,' he said.

'I'll wash it. It will dry in front of the heater.'

'I'll see you Wednesday, Sall.' He kissed her hand.

Wednesday. So many hours between Monday and Wednesday. Ratsus wanted her to work late, but she left the office at 4.50 and was cooking dinner for two when Matt arrived at six. She was skilful in the kitchen. Tonight they'd be eating a stir-fry. The table was set with new placemats and a candle. She'd bought salt and pepper shakers, glass with silver – or chromed plastic – lids. They looked expensive.

The chicken was ready, the vegetables sizzling when he knocked on her door. But he couldn't wait the five minutes until the chicken heated through. He turned off the gas and he picked her up and carried her to the bed, undressing her slowly, making love to her slowly.

They rang for pizza later and he fed her slices, hot, in bed. And they laughed because they both liked their pizza fiery hot. They kissed, and she drank wine and he drank Jim Beam. Then he turned on the shower and he carried her, protesting, in there.

She'd seen it at the movies, and hadn't known how they'd managed, certain that they'd slip over, break their stupid necks. Now she knew, and it wasn't so stupid. Soapy, slippery sex and no broken necks, just wet bodies and water and God in a rainstorm. She was an instrument he played with his fine musician fingers. She was an orchestra he conducted, making sweet new music on her soul.

But when the music ended and the soap was all washed away, he left her.

'See you Monday, Sall.'

Alone, and only 10.30, all showered and ready for bed. She scraped the stir-fry vegetables and chicken into plastic bowls, and as she placed them in the freezer she thought of her mother, of the meals she'd prepared in advance for her mother.

No more, she thought. No more. Let Sleiman find a nursing home prepared to take her. This is my life. This is how the other half live life, and now I'm living it. Then she thought of Ross and she felt the pain of his disbelief. Didn't want the weekend. Didn't want it.

Thursday. Friday. Two more days and she'd have to go. Face it. Face Ross and tell him. Couldn't face him. Couldn't hurt him. Maybe she'd go on Saturday, early, and drive back. No flat now, no narrow childhood bed, and the Lakeside motels charged like wounded bulls. She couldn't stay with Ross. What was she going to say to him? How was she going to tell him? What was she going to do with her mother?

More junk for the too-hard basket. So let it overflow.

She didn't go to Lakeside on Friday night. Didn't call Ross either. She went out with Sue to a singles bar. Sue's hair was blonde and almost tame; even the nose ring was missing.

'Haven't had any for two months and my neighbour's ten-year-old son is in moral danger,' Sue said. All night she talked sex, or her ex, which was the next best thing to talking sex. She said her father had given her the house deposit as a wedding present, that she'd made all the payments on the mortgage but now the judge had ruled that she had to give her ex forty per cent.

'The old fuck always called him a loser. Didn't want me to marry him. Christ, I hate to admit he was right, but he was. And the bloody judge,' Sue said. 'He wouldn't listen. I told him I'd paid all the bills, kept a lazy dickhead for seven years, then found out he'd been having it off with a sixteen year old up the road – and while I was out working. But did he care? I mean, how could any judge in his right mind . . . Jesus, I'd like to go back to uni and do law, give some of the stupid old fucks hell.'

Sally listened with one ear, she nodded, but her mind was on a seesaw. High. Low. High. Low. Guilt and love. Ross and Matt.

'The manipulating old shit said he'd pay out my loan, if I go back.' Sue was wound up tonight. Sally leaned, mind travelling, only listening with half an ear.

Her little flat was not so bare now. It smelled of Matt, and his coat sometimes hung with hers behind her door and for a while his shoes were on her floor. She found signs of him in her bathroom too. A black hair on a towel, or in her comb.

God, she loved him. Couldn't think of him without wanting him. She wanted him now. Ached for him. Come in that door, Matt; take me away from this place. Tell me I don't have to go to Lakeside and face her, face Ross. Make love to me until my brain turns to mush.

Sue finally ran down, started looking around. She had her eye on a blond, and he and his mate brought their drinks to her table. Steve, and leftover Jim. Sally wasn't into leftovers. She had the pick of the crop.

'Hey! Are you with us?' Sue nudged her.

'In the physical sense. Do you want another drink?'

Three replies to the affirmative. Sally walked to the bar and returned with two glasses of wine. A week ago she would have bought four drinks, wouldn't have had the nerve to refuse, scared they wouldn't like her. Not anymore.

The guys looked at the two glasses as one was placed before Sue, the other not leaving Sally's hand. They stared at her hand, and at the wine, and at their empty glasses, then Jim gave up. He wanted to get going, and he was the one with the car. Steve was dithering, weighing up the pros and cons of Sue's distant bed.

'Can you give us a lift home, Sall?'

'No trouble.' But she ran into big trouble after she dropped the couple off at Sue's. She turned down a wrong street and couldn't find her way back. Lost in Dandenong on a one-way street, and if that wasn't bad enough, she had a run-in with a Falcon that happened to be backing out with his lights off.

The driver bellowed from his window, couldn't get out his driver-side door because her bumper bar was in it, so he crawled across the gear stick.

Late. The street was deserted. She wished a cop car would turn up and book her for going the wrong way. No cop car to save her. Only Sally. She shoved the Datsun into reverse and hit the accelerator, heard the rending of metal as the cars wrenched apart. He had the passenger-side door open, then he was out, grabbing at her door handle as she slapped the stick into first and rattled away. Probably ripped his fingers off. He was standing there bellowing abuse to the night; and he could have taught Sue a thing or two about brief yet descriptive sentence construction.

Her driver's-side front wheel scraped around Dandenong until she found the freeway, then it scraped all the way home. A slow, slow trip, but the wheels kept turning and the little car carried her back to South Yarra and to her bed that smelt of Matt. She slept soundly, wrapped in the scent of his love, slept through the alarm, slept until noon, dreaming heavy dreams of love.

It was around two when she walked down to her car, which looked worse than it had sounded last night. She dragged at her front bumper. Couldn't budge it.

The bikie, tinkering with his bike, placed his spanner down and stared as she wiped her hands on her jeans. Ross would straighten it, if it got her to Lakeside. The boot unlocked, her case tossed in, and she slid behind the wheel. Metal scraped as her wheels turned.

'Turn her off.' He was at her window.

'I'm not going far.'

'You're not going anywhere in that. Turn her off,' he repeated, squatting beside her mashed metal.

She stilled the motor and climbed from the car, watching yellow paint peel away as the rusting metal ripped like paper. With his hands and one foot, he levelled the bumper bar, then slid beneath the Datsun on his back.

'She might get you where you're going.'

'Thanks,' she said. 'Feel free to use my parking space. As usual.'

'Planning to, De Rooster.' Long black hair hung to his waist, and his white T-shirt wasn't white.

'It's De Rooze. Sally De Rooze.'

'I got your notes. All of them. You buggered my paintwork with your glue.'

'It wasn't glue. It was Blu-Tack. It comes off. Anyway, thanks for the repair.'

'Yeah.'

The little car, impatient to vacate its space between Camry and Commodore, almost collected the white kombi van, driven by the Asian guy from Number 13.

'Have you got a death wish, De Rooster?'

'No. Just a slow death sentence. And it's De Rooze. D, E, space, R, O, O, Z, E.'

the marathon man

Ross was pacing the hospital car park when Sally drove in around five. 'You've lost more weight,' he said. 'Do you eat anything down there?'

Living on love. Gormandising on it, she thought, but made no reply. He spoke as he walked with her to her mother's ward, preparing her. 'She had some sort of a fit.'

'A fit. Screaming.'

'A fit. Grand mal, or something, Sleiman said. No mention of sending her to Melbourne, though.'

She slowed her steps. 'Why didn't you call me?'

'By the time I heard, she was okay.' Then they were in the room.

Not the hint of a smile from her mother today, only the petulant, drawn face and a sketchy outline of bones beneath a gaping hospital gown. Cruel, faded gown.

But it was irrelevant. Sally didn't fight the gown or her mother. She told herself it was because Ross was there and she couldn't send him from the room while she stripped the outline and clothed it in lemon. But that was not the reason. She was seeing differently today, seeing as if from a distance.

She watched the nurse's face, saw her professional attention, saw her mother respond to attention. She saw Ross's jeans. Too tight. She saw Karen Matthews and her mother enter and sit beside the old lady in the opposite bed. She saw the way Karen looked at Ross. Hungry eyes, as her own eyes looked at Matt. She saw the way Ross walked eagerly to their side, how he spoke to them. Spoke of bulls and paddocks and Lakeside, because they were Lakeside. Sally and her mother were not.

'We may as well go too, love,' he said when the Matthews women left.

Go where? She couldn't go home with him. Of course she couldn't. 'I'm going back, Ross.' Next weekend she'd bring Matt up here. She'd have to tell Ross, but outside, in the dark.

'You haven't handed in your notice yet?'

'I thought I'd wait.'

His huge hand rested on her shoulder. Heavy. Possessive. Matt's hand was light.

'She's sound asleep. Let's get out of here.'

'She's drugged. Her eyes looked glazed tonight.'

'Sleiman said he's got her on some new antidepressant. It takes a while for them to kick in.' His voice was low. 'Let's go to the pub for a while.'

She shook her head and turned to the other beds, wondering why some people clung to life and others gave up on it. Her family had given up young. Her mother's older sister, Bernice, had died in her early thirties. Her grandmother had been fifty-eight. Sally could barely remember her. Maybe the shape of her in the car, maybe the *pretty* on her dress.

Ross's stomach broke the silence. It grumbled, growled. 'The pub has changed hands. They do a good steak.'

At the hotel there would be noise, friendly faces, hot food. She'd have to eat somewhere. Maybe a glass of wine would lend her the necessary courage to tell him she'd been seeing someone else.

There were three hotels in Lakeside, but the Royal was their hang-out. Always had been. It wasn't the biggest hotel, but it was the oldest. It had character, and an open fire.

Ross ordered a beer and a glass of chardonnay. Sally emptied the glass before he started on his beer. She walked to the bar and bought a refill.

They'd managed to have a life in Lakeside. Mrs Jenner, a single pensioner, had lived for years in the flat behind her mother's. She was one of those sweet old ladies who make excuses for all. She did a lot of babysitting and had been pleased to earn a few dollars Mummy-sitting.

Sally looked at Ross, the words ready on her tongue. I've met another guy, she'd say, but she couldn't do it. She was no good for him, but he thought she was. How could she hurt him? A tear rolled free, tickling as it trickled down the side of her nose.

I love him, she thought. I do. But I'm not *in love* with him and I never was. I am *in love* with Matt. She wiped at the tear and caught another on its way out.

'Crying is not going to help much.'

'I'm not crying.'

'She'll be okay. Try to get her off your mind for a while.'

Let him think her tears were for her mother; she couldn't tell him they were for him, for his trust and his unconditional love that she no longer deserved, and because he was not Matt, and she couldn't tell him about Matt. Not here. This had been their place for years. This had been their corner table forever. It probably still had her chewing gum stuck to its underside.

'G'day Bertram.' Familiar faces stopped to talk a while. 'Hi, Sall. How's the big smoke?'

'It gets in your eyes and up your nose,' she replied.

Then Deb and Greg walked in, saw them and brought their drinks to the table. Deb noticed her red eyes.

'Allergy,' Sally explained.

'Guess who's getting married?' Deb said.

'Not you?'

'We're finally pregnant.'

'Wow!' Sally had a reason to fill her glass again, and she did it gladly.

'We waited until the danger period was over before telling the oldies. Mum's disgusted with us. You could have waited until you were married,' she mimicked in the carping tones of her mother. 'So we're doing it. Doing the whole big white wedding bit, just for her, and she wants it in a hurry. Want to hire a bridesmaid's dress?' Deb said.

'Of course. When?' How many times had she played bridesmaid? Becky, Gina.

'The last Sunday in October. Steve and Toni are getting married on the Saturday and we didn't want to be upstaged.'

'Three times a bridesmaid, never a bride,' Greg said. 'Watch it, Ross. She'll get away yet.'

'Not much chance of that, I've got her furniture locked in my shed.'

She couldn't eat her dinner when the waitress brought it to the table. She ate a chip and it stuck in her throat. She thought of hot pizza. Couldn't have hot pizza. Couldn't desert Ross now he had her furniture in his shed. She ordered a carafe of wine, eating little, drinking fast. The wine was good. It raised laughter. Laughter and friends. What else was there?

They left at ten, the world spinning, but Ross's arm supported her. She giggled and walked on air to the ute, where she had to step up before she stepped in. Her jeans were too tight, or she was too drunk. She giggled as Ross lifted her to the seat, did up her seatbelt, climbed in beside her and kissed her, kissed her long.

'Drop me off at the hospital. I'm going back to Melbourne.'

'Yeah, love. Right. You get behind a wheel tonight and the new cop will shout you bed and breakfast.'

She didn't argue. Her words had been a last-ditch attempt to remain honourable, to Ross, or to Matt. Which one? What did it matter? She was not honourable. She was dishonourable trash, and Matt would probably dump her next week anyway. Ross wouldn't dump her. He had her goose girl in his shed. And he had to fix her car.

'I had a bingle. On Friday. Mashed my bumper and front mudguard.'

'We'll pick it up in the morning, check it over.'

'My nightie is in the boot,' she said as he led her to the bedroom.

'Sounds like a good place for it, love.'

She stepped out of her jeans, left them where they fell, she tossed her sweater onto the dressing table and slipped between freezing sheets, then he was in beside her and so warm. She let him kiss her. It didn't matter. He loved her, and she loved him in an incestuous way, and it was three weeks since they'd made love. He didn't cheat. She was the cheat. Poor sex-starved Ross.

'Just one more dance with me. Just one more song,' she sang, and she felt his smile against her face.

'You're tipsy.'

'Tipsy gipsy, that's me. A homeless nomad. These days I have to find my beds where I may. And I pay with sexual favours, sir. What is your pleasure?'

'No payment necessary.'

'Oh, I always pay my bills. Eventually. Just ask my dentist. Ask my agent.'

How many payments had she made to Ross? How much more did she owe him? How many times had they made love in the past eleven years?

She started multiplying while his arms held her captive. Too much of him, and not enough Sally. But her head so full of wine, if someone didn't hold her down tonight she'd float away. Or had she floated away already? Was she on the ceiling looking down, or on the bed looking up?

She giggled against his mouth, familiar mouth moving

incessantly against her own. Abrasive tonight. He needed a shave.

Her lips unresponsive, she did some sexual calculations on the ceiling, head disassociated from lips. Over eleven years since Mrs Bertram had died. She'd had a few months off when she was nineteen, a few more at twenty-two, at twenty-five, twenty-seven. She'd tried to tell him. Tried to get away from him back then. Tried not to waste his life.

Tried and failed.

Pretend he is Matt, she thought, and her hand traced his face. Big. Fleshy. She reached for Matt's thick black hair, but found Ross's spikes. Bristly. And she sighed. He deserved better than playing surrogate for another man anyway, so she gave up and returned to her mathematical equation.

Fifty weeks in a year, so say I average sex out at four nights a week. That's 200, and if I say ten years? That's easy. Two thousand?

'It can't be,' she said.

'What?'

'Nothing.'

Nothing. That's what she was feeling. Nothing. Her mind wandered away from the bed, wandered off to the schoolroom.

'Criminal negligence,' one of her teachers had said when she told him she was leaving school to work at the supermarket. She could have gone on at school. She'd been as good as Deb at maths – which wasn't saying much, but she'd always had a thing about numbers. Always could hold figures on her mental white-board, do additions in her head. Should have stayed at school. Should have done a lot of things. Not done a few.

And he was done with her body and she was free to move away from him physically. He didn't know she hadn't been with him mentally.

'It's been a while, eh love,' he said.

'A while.' Dishonest bitch.

'What are you thinking about?' he said, on his back beside

her, her hand held captive on his chest.

'That it must be at least 2010 times.'

'What?'

'Sex. Us.'

'Christ! I'm a marathon man,' he said.

the casino

october 1999

Lights and noise all around him. People everywhere, like a river of humanity, and he was being washed along by the current, just flowing, his eyes searching. And fate was kind, because he sighted her beside a roulette table. Edging in, he watched the short blond bob, waited for her to turn and face him.

And she did. But she was the wrong one. Same hair, different face.

Too big, this place, too easy to lose yourself, and anyone else. He shouldn't have been here, but he'd followed her from her office half an hour ago, kept his eye on her for a while, then he'd turned, just to glance at one of the blackjack tables, and when he'd looked back, she'd gone.

The roulette wheel spun, and he made a mental bet with himself. Thirteen. The ball was going to land on thirteen.

It didn't. And there was a winner up one end who was pleased it didn't. He took his chips and left. Smart man. Walter watched an old Asian bloke place his bets, or damn near scatter them, damn near cover the table with his chips. Too much money, he had to get rid of it fast. That sort of disrespect for the green stuff tightened Walter's lungs.

He drew a breath and coughed, wondering how the bloke running the table knew which chip belonged to who. The wheel blurred, then slowed, and the ball landed on seven. Everybody lost. Not one chip sitting on seven so no-one needed to know who owned what chip. The house got the lot and a loser moved away. Walter took his place against the table, his eyes avid as the chips were tossed around again – even after the wheel started to turn they were adding chips.

Just a little wheel. He'd remembered them as being bigger.

'No more bets,' the young bloke behind the table said, looking at Walter.

'Just browsing,' Walter replied.

Thirteen was going to come up this time and he knew it. Should have put something on it. He hunched his shoulders, trying to ease the itch in the middle of his back; his right hand reached over, couldn't reach low enough. His left hand had a go, under his jacket, and up. Couldn't reach high enough. Scratch it like a cow against a post, that's what he needed to do. No cow posts in this place.

'Black.' Someone was betting on black.

Black and red. Maybe that was the way to play this game. He reached into his pocket for a handkerchief and carefully wiped his hands as again his eyes followed the spin. The young bloke was looking at him now, wanting him to play or stop taking up the space, but it was a free country, supposedly, and thirteen was going to come up this time.

It didn't. Which just went to prove the odds against winning in this place.

He should have been at his hotel packing, doing what he was told like a good boy. He'd been down here for a week this time, and when he'd called home last night his eldest boy had told him to get on the bus and get his arse back home. Only one problem with that; he wasn't ready to face that bus. If they ever found out how he was financing his week in Melbourne, Lord help him.

‘Oh,’ he said. Thirteen had paid up. If he’d put twenty dollars on it, he would have been raking in the chips now – trouble was, he’d been thinking thirteen for a while, so if he’d followed his hunch, he would have lost his money before he won it, so to speak.

He stepped back. The odds were too great. It was like backing a horse in a big field; too many to choose from. But if you bet black or red, surely you’d have the same chance as you had with two-up. Heads or tails. He’d played a bit of two-up in his time. Turned twenty pounds into five hundred one night, just tossing the pennies and letting his money ride. Elaine had given him the rounds of the kitchen when he’d got home, but she hadn’t refused the ring he’d bought her with part of his win. Must have been a good diamond in it too, because he’d sold it last week for six hundred dollars, and hired himself a nice little car for two days. Still had almost a hundred in his wallet. He could afford to play with twenty of it, couldn’t he? Poor Elaine – she’d roll over in her grave.

He licked his lips as the Asian handed over a wad of hundred-dollar notes. They disappeared down a slit in the table, like lettuce going down a waste disposal. The Asian got a pile of chips in exchange and Walter stood on, taking up space as that pile went the same way as the last lot, reclaimed by the house.

Money to burn. Money to waste. If he’d had a bit more of it, life might have turned out different. His eyes on the blur of the wheel, his mind wandered away to the little one he’d followed from her Collins Street office. Stalking, they called it these days – an old habit, a bad habit, one of his many, and it had given him the nose of a bloodhound and the tenacity of a bulldog. He coughed, a chesty grumble, and he drew back from that thought, forcing his mind to vanilla slices in Dubbo. Yes. Get on that bus in the morning and get your arse back home before you get yourself into trouble.

A step back, a step closer to vanilla slices.

Then he saw her. She was still with the big, buxom one in

red. Red and black. Opposing personalities, he thought, staring at the petite figure. Black slacks, tight black top, clean blond hair swinging – a little girl all dressed up in her mother's high heels.

The angels made little girls –

The song whispering in his mind, he watched her wander into the crowd again, disappearing once more, his heart now beating like a tom-tom.

Black and red. Red and black.

Slowly he turned back to the table, in time to see the Asian hand over another bunch of lettuce. One gulp and it went down the sink.

'What's your minimum bet?' Walter asked the young bloke in charge of the waste disposal.

'Five dollars.'

'Highway robbery,' Walter said, grudgingly handing over a twenty. 'Put it on black?'

Some you win and some you lose, and what the hell did it matter when the world wouldn't give you what you wanted and tomorrow you had to sit on a bus for twenty-four hours? What did it matter?

He watched the young bloke place his chips down. All four of them. Gone. Not much you could buy with twenty dollars anyway. He'd go back to Richmond, pack up his room and get his arse back home. He sure as hell wasn't doing anyone any good down here – his youngest boy had refused to see him today. I won't be coming back in a hurry either, he thought.

Little ball twirling, around and around; it was making him dizzy. He sighed in a breath and wheezed it out, his eyes not leaving the wheel. He watched it blur, lose all colour, watched the colours re-emerge, watched the ball dance and land on a number, but the number was . . . no, never mind.

'Black.'

'Lordy, Lordy, Lordy me,' he whispered, his pink tongue licking, his hands dripping, saturating the handkerchief. He took another from his trouser pocket and grasped it tight.

'Leave them on black,' he said. That was the way he used to play two-up. All or nothing. These days he was into all or nothing, and usually got the latter.

'Black.'

'Let them ride,' he said.

His chips rode well for a few spins, until the old Asian bloke decided to play black, and he wasn't having any luck tonight, and bad luck was catching. Walter moved his plastic to red.

He was hot, and in more ways than one. His soul was on fire and his lungs were burning, but his back wasn't itching any more. Old Satan had his hand up his singlet, scratching it with his red-hot fingernails.

'Red.'

'Well I'll be damned,' Walter said.

An hour passed or a day. He couldn't breathe. No air left in the world. All soaked up by the crowd surging around him. He wanted to get out, breathe. Couldn't. Couldn't relax either; had to keep one step ahead of that Asian.

It was mounting up now, but he couldn't look on it as money. It was just a pile of plastic, bought with his twenty dollars. That was the only way to look on your winnings when you gambled. Start trying to count it up, turn it into dollars, and it hurt too much when you lost it.

'Place your bets.'

His hands dripped salt tears onto the table, a neon sign in his head started flashing seventeen, and he didn't know why, except that seventeen had been a very good year. It was the year before his old mother had died, and the year before he'd met Elaine; he wouldn't give twopence for his eighteenth year. But at seventeen – he'd gone to the Melbourne Cup and put two pound on Rimfire's nose. And won.

He pushed a minor mountain onto seventeen and noticed that his hands were shaking. His mind wasn't too steady either. If seventeen won, and he'd held back half of his chips, it would be losing. He'd kick himself for not putting the lot down, wouldn't he? He pushed a few more onto seventeen, and he sweated.

'Seventeen.'

He was the legendary Walter J O'Leary. He was the king and he wasn't getting on that bloody bus in the morning. He was never getting on that bus again. He pushed a pile to black, got them on just as the young bloke said, 'No more bets.'

And the old Asian bloke didn't.

Black.

'Lordy, Lordy, Lordy me,' he said. 'My little girl luck.'

The angels made little girls, from rosebuds and from fairy floss and dreams.

green clay

Matt came to the flat, his tie off, his shirtsleeves rolled up, and Sally loved him anew, loved the shape of his arms, and his shoulders. Loved him. Mondays and Wednesdays were their days, and she lived for them, and each week that passed they grew closer. So much to learn about each other.

She'd made Chinese noodles with oyster sauce. Ross liked it. Matt didn't. He wasn't into eating.

'You don't like my cooking?' she said.

He lifted a long noodle to his lips, sucking it up like a kid. 'Worms,' he said. 'I'd prefer to eat Sally De Rooze.' He pushed the plate away and kneeled before her, his fingers walking her calf, her knee, her thigh. Creeping higher.

'Well, I like noodles, and I want to eat. Sit down and tell me about yourself. How long have you been working on the fourth floor?'

'Floor. Did you say floor, Sall?'

'Talk sense for a minute, Matt. There's more to life than sex.' Or was there?

Her feet captured beneath his arms, his mouth crept. 'Still

want to eat noodles, Sall? Still want to talk?' Beautiful, laughing Matt. Beautiful, laughing eyes.

'Yes.' They were both laughing; he'd won her pantihose and he swung them overhead, aimed them at the sink. 'Have you got an uncle, an aunty? How old is your grandfather?'

But he was pushing the plates back, lifting her to the table, trapping her there. Fast breathing now. Words hard to make now.

'You are my family, Sall. You're my mother, feed me. You're my sister, play with me.' Heat meeting heat, burning. The tiny table, rocking, sighing. 'What am I to you, Sall? Tell me. Tell me, Sall. Talk to me now, Sall.'

Plates falling. Forks rattling to the floor.

'God,' she said. 'God. You are my god and I'm your slave girl.'

She stepped on the scales before she went to bed that night, a mug of coffee in her hand. And the scales lied. Forty-two kilograms? She stepped off, placing her mug on the vanity unit, then she checked her weight again. Forty-two kilograms. Almost.

There was not enough of her to go around. Too many people taking too many bites of an undergrown apple. Too many demands to still. Ratsus demanded, and Mummy waited, and Matt fed. God, how he fed on her.

'I have to eat,' she told her reflection.

On Wednesday she left work early and hit a supermarket, bought butter, cheese, sour cream and potatoes, bought vegemite instead of plastic peanut butter, bought two frozen meals and two pieces of scotch fillet. By six the steak was bleeding onto a plate and the frying pan was waiting, the potatoes, boiled in their jackets, keeping warm in the oven. She set the table, then stood at the window, watching for the blue station wagon.

As it pulled into the kerb, she placed the steaks in the hot pan and opened her door.

'A tough day, kiddo,' he said and he kissed her, his hands beneath her sweater, cool on warm flesh. 'Make love to me.'

'There's seven dollars' worth of steak almost ready. We are going to eat it.'

'Is that so?'

He didn't care about money. He took what he wanted, the way that he wanted it, doing what he would with her forty-two kilos. The table on Monday, on Wednesday the fridge was good enough. Her back against its door, the steaks burning in the pan, the smoke alarm began beeping while he hammered her into the fridge.

She was a throbbing sex machine, he the pounding motor. Her shoulder bag fell on her head, then to the floor, spilling its contents.

'Say you love me, Sall. Say it. Say it.'

And gasping. 'Love you. Love you.' Screaming. 'Love you.'

'All day I thought of you, of this place. Don't ever spoil what we've got, Sall.'

'I live for you.'

Fast. Furious. And finished.

Matt silenced the smoke detector with the broom handle, then he laughed at the burned steaks. They'd been plump, though. She sawed the charred sides away, and they were fine, but he asked for a sharper knife. She told him she had a thing about sharp knives, that when she was fourteen she'd thrown away every sharp knife in the house.

He didn't ask why, but he told her he preferred his steak rare.

'And whose fault is it that they're not rare?'

'Not mine,' he said, and they laughed, and she almost choked on lettuce, laughing at his antics as he played chain saw with the knife on burnt steak.

'Brrroooom,' he said. 'Brrrooo – um – brrrum.'

Too much laughter, her stomach cramped with it, and her back ached with it, or from its contact with the handle of the fridge.

'I'm going to be a bridesmaid on Sunday,' she said later. 'My girlfriend, Deb, is getting married.'

'Lakeside?'

'She's been sleeping with Greg since she was sixteen. Never

used a contraceptive because her mother owns the town pharmacy. They're over the moon about the baby, though. I've never wanted kids. Maybe when I'm old. I can see Deb as a mother but not me.' She did most of the talking. He rarely offered information – not even his phone number, but that was her fault. She'd babbled on one night about hating telephones and the voices on telephones.

'I'll make certain that you never hate me, then, Sall,' he'd said, and he'd refused to give her his number. They'd laughed that night, but the joke had grown stale.

She spread butter on a crusty roll and bit into it. 'I thought I was going to be late tonight. I got stuck in the supermarket and I couldn't contact you. Give me your mobile number, Matt? I promise I won't ever hate your voice.'

His hand reached out, brushed her face, her throat. 'We don't need telephones. We've got mental telepathy.'

'I'm serious, Matt.'

He took her hand, kissed it, and she claimed his hand, opening it, studying his palm, his lifeline. He'd told her his family was into longevity, that he lived in Hallam. She'd built a mental image of his home, his parents, and his ninety-year-old grandfather, his sister Chari, and she wanted to meet them.

'Does your grandfather live with you?'

'He's in a nursing home in Daylesford, Sall.' He reclaimed his hand and chain-sawed off a piece of steak, chewed. 'Voooooom. Brum-brum, Brrrru –'

'That's a long way for your parents to drive. Why Daylesford?'

'They live there too.'

'You said Hallam.'

'Nope,' he said. 'Did not.'

'So where do you live?'

He was slow to reply. 'In Hallam,' he said, then he looked at her uncomprehending face and he shook his head, took her face between his hands and kissed her. 'I've got a wife, Sall.'

Blood roared in her ears. She barely heard his next words. She was staring at his mouth. She watched it making words she could not hear, her own mouth open, her head denying, refusing to believe, but knowing it was true. When he left her at night he drove home to his wife in Hallam.

'Why do you think I leave you at night, leave this at night?' His hands were spread, palms up. 'I should have told you before, but you must have known, kiddo.'

Should have known. Didn't know. But where did she think he was going? Home at 10.30 to his mother, to sleep in a narrow childhood bed?

Sue had known. She'd seen him, said he looked married. Sue knew men.

Her throat too tight for words, Sally drew back, away from him, away from this thing she had done.

'It alters nothing. I love you,' he said.

'Alters nothing?' she whispered. 'You're married.' She picked up her knife, tossed it into the sink, snatched his plate; it followed her knife. Landed hard. Broke. Scattered china splattered the tiles with burned steak grease. 'Get out of here, Matt.'

'You love me. You said you'd never leave me, Sall.'

'You're married.'

He talked then. He wouldn't go. He said he was going to leave his wife, that they were sharing the house in Hallam, but not a bed. Hadn't in years. He said he stayed with his wife because the house was in their joint names, but now he had a reason to leave, and he would. He was standing, and he tried to take her in his arms, but she had the sharp knife in her hand.

'It won't end like this. You're mine. I found you and I'm not letting you go.' He backed off, though, away from the blade. 'I can't function without you in my life, Sall. I won't lose what we've got here.'

'Go.'

'Don't do this to us. I come here and forget the world. You are my world, Sall.'

Talking. Talking. Would he never stop with his talking?

She leaned, gaining support from the kitchen bench, and the bench pressed hard against her bruised back. The knife still gripped in her hand, she backed past the kitchen bench, past the wardrobe to the door, and she tugged it open. 'Go. Please.'

'I'm not going to lose you.'

'You should have told me. You should have told me that first night.'

'And this is why I didn't.' He tried to take the knife, but she held it like a weapon before her, and his hand drew away.

'Don't do this to us, Sall.' He was outside the door, still pleading when she kicked it shut in his face, locked it with the chain. She turned the television on, the volume high, and she howled and couldn't find a place to stop.

Fool. She'd been such a gullible bloody fool. He wouldn't give you his phone number because it was his wife's number too. You gave him the perfect out. Dumb bitch.

She walked to the refrigerator for wine, tripping over her handbag on the floor, landing on one knee beside her briefs.

Shivering-cold shame hit her in the stomach like a block of ice. May to May. The grand planned year of Sally De Rooze, and now October was almost gone. She hadn't found herself, hadn't found the great love of her life, either. She'd found Sally Shame, a cheap slut who'd been getting it off with a married man.

Better if she'd stayed in Lakeside, cleaned up after her mother. Better than this. A home-wrecking slut, that's what she was. Prostitute from Phonepross; half a pizza bought her for four hours. Name your position. Name your game.

She picked herself and her briefs up, and what was left of her pantihose, and she tossed them into her rubbish bin. She kicked her handbag across the floor, then picked it up and threw it hard at the wall. More junk fell free.

'Bloody city. Lying, cheating mongrel city. I want the last month back. I want to live it again.'

Need more than the last month back. Need to be eight again, or ten again. Need to be eighteen again. Need a whole bloody life back again. She took her case from her wardrobe, snatched a handful of clothing, tossing it in, then she tossed her case at the wall, concrete wall, and her case was cheap, cheap like her life. It bent. She sat then, sat on the end of her bed, looking at her scattered clothing.

'I've been sleeping with a married man, Mummy,' she said. 'Well, not actually sleeping with him. He goes home to his wife to get some rest. But I've been doing everything but sleep with him. It's sex with a capital F, Mummy. Your eyes would pop out if you had seen the things I've been doing. I've learnt such a lot.' Rubbing the guilt in. Forcing it through her pores. 'On the floor, behind the door and on the kitchen table, Mummy. I never said no to him. You never allowed me to say no, so I never learnt how to say it. Everyone knows how to say no, but not Sally mush-mouth. Yes, I said. Yes. Yes, Matt. Yes, please. And I loved it, Mummy. And I love him. I love him.'

Sinking now beneath a mountain of guilt, she closed her mouth, and guilt became an internal thing, bludgeoned her from within. She crawled into bed, because she couldn't crawl beneath it, curled into a tight ball, her thumb in her mouth, knees beneath her chin, quilt pulled over her head.

Didn't ask him to use a condom either. Brand-new packet in the zip compartment of her bag. Unopened. Didn't know the rules of the big city game. Didn't follow Sue's first rule. Get their phone number. Give them a call around nine on a Sunday morning. Best way to catch a married guy. That's what Sue said. And no sex without a condom. No sex ever without a condom. Sue was smart. City smart. Man smart.

And I'm a dumb blonde country hick and I never do anything right. Never have done anything right. Not in my whole life. I should have stayed in my seat that night, kept my seatbelt done up. I should have helped Daddy watch the road. I would have seen that kangaroo – or got burnt with them.

Shivering. Shivering cold. Shivering beneath the quilt. Shivering and crying, creeping away. Away.

Close your eyes, Sally, and Mummy can't see you.

Close your mind, Sally, and you won't have to see yourself.

Close up.

Shut down.

Poor simple Sally De Rooze, green clay in a fucking artist's hands.

washed out to sea

The black hole came for her in the night and it got her, it sucked her down, buried her. She was an insect, fallen into a cast-iron pipe that ended at the bottom of a pit of sludge. She wallowed there, her brain feeding on old sludge.

Daddy. He's got my Teddy. Make him give it back.

Daddy's driving, Sally-gal.

Couldn't make the pictures go away. Had to make them go. She turned on the television at dawn but it wouldn't kill the internal pictures.

So she'd do a Grandma. That would kill them. She'd drive out to the Westgate Bridge and jump. Jumping was permanent, Grandma had known that. No bungee-rope doctor to spring her back, pump her stomach, sew up her wrists, put a stitch in her breast.

She walked down to the car park in the late afternoon, but the road traffic was a roar. Too hard to force the car out there, find her way to Westgate. Too much traffic tonight to go for the long jump. She emptied her letterbox instead.

Only bills and a wad of junk mail. She redelivered the lot to the bikie in Number 14, then returned to her flat and crawled into bed, stayed there all day, all night. Must have, because the clock bleated its call at 7.15 a.m., and it wasn't Thursday morning so it had to be Friday.

She thought of work. Payday yesterday. Got to get my pay. Got to. Got to keep on going. Got to find a way to keep on going.

Junk on the floor. Junk everywhere. Steak on the sink. Twisted case, open against the wall. Her good blouse on the floor.

Should hang it up. It cost a fortune.

Why bother? Why bother with anything?

What right has she got to live when she killed my beautiful boys?

Screamed. Loud as anything, so half the world could hear her. So all the world would know whose fault it was that Daddy and the boys had died.

What right has she got to live when she killed my beautiful boys?

Cold blue killer eyes, killing little Sally with guilt.

Why didn't you die instead of my Shane?

'Why didn't I die?'

Around two in the afternoon she found a clean glass and the wine cask, and a packet of stale biscuits, and she sat with them on the floor, close to the television, drinking, nibbling biscuits, watching the noise, seeing nothing.

The phone rang. She ignored it and poured more wine.

It rang and kept on ringing.

'Cut the bloody thing off,' she screamed. 'You keep threatening to, so cut the bloody thing off.'

It rang.

Maybe it was him.

But it wouldn't be him. He'd be at work, selling promises, selling lies. It wouldn't be Ross either. No one else had her number, except the hospital, and Sue. Sally De Rooze wasn't in the Melbourne phone book and she'd never be in it now. As soon as she was drunk enough she was going to pick herself up and drive out to the Westgate Bridge. The newspapers would wrap her up.

PROSTITUTE FROM PHONE A PRO WASHED OUT TO SEA

Mummy would be pleased.

MIRACLE CURE – DYING WOMAN RISES FROM HER BED TO ATTEND DAUGHTER'S FUNERAL

Phone ringing. Ringing. Ringing.

And when she couldn't stand it any more, she reached for it. Snatched it up. Shut it up and it was Jolly Julie wanting to sell Miss Wong some fertiliser for her garden.

'You hab da wong number,' Sally said. She laughed then, black laughter, but Jolly Julie decided to sell her some fertiliser anyhow, so Sally told her that she was in the fertiliser trade herself, and she wanted to get rid of a tonne of it. Where would Julie like it dumped?

Julie was lost for words. Her spiel thrown off course, she floundered, still too new at this intrusion game. Sally was not new at the game. She was an old hand and she let all the black pour out on poor Jolly Julie.

'Oh, but Julie. This is an opportunity you can't afford to miss. It's well-matured swan shit, and everyone knows that birds make the best fertiliser. I've got tonnes of it. We will deliver to your door. Six months interest-free. No payments until the year 2000.'

Jolly Julie hung up and Sally laughed and dropped the hand-piece to the floor, let it beep. She laughed as she poured more wine, and for an instant remembered other laughter, remembered Daddy.

Laugh and the world laughs with you. Cry and you cry alone, Sally-gal.

Beep. Beep. Beep.

She looked at the phone, thought of calling Phonepross, asking Ratsus if she had some raffle books for sale. That would be funny. That's what she had to do, think of something funny.

Do something funny. Like the fertiliser. That had been a good one. Or ... or if she owned a hose she could tape it onto her dripping tap and poke it under the bikie's door. Or ... or she could drive into the city and paint a suicide note on Matt's car with nail polish. She knew where he parked.

Her lips stretched in a smile, she forced a laugh and almost saw a glimmer of light at the top of the black hole. 'Let him explain that to his bloody wife in Hallam.'

All afternoon she made her mad plans, forcing herself to laugh as slowly she crawled towards the light, gaining two centimetres, slipping back one.

Got to go to work, get my pay. I'll go in tonight. Friday night. Ratsus will be pleased to get me. I'll work until eight. Got to go. Sell. Sell. Sell. I'll need money for Mummy's funeral. Grandma's bloody dining room suite won't pay for it.

Too bad. Let the taxpayers dig a bit deeper, and with a bit of luck they might get two for the price of one. I'll climb in with her and we'll rot together, Mummy and me. Haven't we been rotting together for twenty years? I mean, why stop now?

And she was down again, drowning in old sludge.

The beautiful guitar smashed against the wall. Mummy wishing it was Sally's head.

Why didn't you die? Why didn't you die?

And after school. Little sprays of red dye, fanning out from Mummy's wrists to get lost in the pink water. And thinking, how long would it take for all her blood to run away?

'Stop it! Stop it!' Night coming now, she flicked on the light switch, but the globe had blown, so she sat in the dark.

Daddy used to drive Mummy to the bookings and she'd come home on a high.

Daddy in his shirtsleeves.

Daddy with melted chocolate frogs.

'Daddy! I want Daddy! Daaaaddy!' The scream touched base. It hurt her throat, frightening her. Silencing her.

Saturday, lost deep in the black hole.

Sunday.

Silent.

No roar of traffic on the roads. She'd stopped fighting. She was dying unborn in the black womb. Embryo cockroach on its back, its legs in the air. Couldn't roll over and crawl down the birth canal. Didn't want to live.

No wine left, she opened the fridge and found the half-bottle of Jim Beam, and she slammed the door on it and the old fridge rocked. A bag of overripe bananas fell to the floor. She took one in her hand, looked at it.

Phallic.

Ran her finger down the smooth skin, peeled it with her teeth. Sucked it. Held its soft mush in her mouth. Choked on it, but she swallowed it.

'I'm sorry, Mummy. I'm sorry.'

Mummy could always squeeze a few more tears out of her. She wept then, loud and uncontrolled, wept until there was nowhere deeper to go, sobbed and hiccupped until the tears slowed to a trickle. Then she picked up the telephone and dialled the hospital's number.

'Could I speak to Mrs De Rooze, please?' Voice full of tears.

'Sally? It's Kate here. Are you going to be okay for tonight?'

Kate? Deb knew a Kate.

Deb?

She cut the connection and screamed. 'Shiiiiiiiit! Deb! Shiiiiiit!'

News travelled fast in Lakeside. It always had. Three minutes later her phone rang. She covered her ears and let it ring until it rang out, but it started up again so she shut it up.

'Sally? What's going on with you? You were supposed to be up here last night for Deb's hen party.'

She couldn't answer him. Couldn't talk to him. Couldn't ever look him in the eye again, look Deb in the eye again. Not ever. She hung up, and seconds later the phone rang again. She took it off the hook, let it dangle.

'Are you there? Sally! Answer me!' Little voice. Distant voice chatting to the cheap beige carpet. 'We've got the wedding tonight.'

Deb's wedding at six. She was supposed to have picked up her hire dress yesterday. Maroon. Forgot the dress and the wedding and Deb.

Couldn't talk to Ross. Wanted to scream at him. Wanted to blame him too, offload the blame onto someone else. Wanted to yell, Give me back all those years I've spent in your bed, years when I should have been out sampling life. Sampling people. Learning slow. Learning easy. Not like this.

'Sally! Pick up that phone.'

'I'm contaminated,' she said, but she reached for the phone, picked it up, held it to her ear.

'Pick up that bloody phone, Sally!'

'Stop your yelling.'

'You need someone to yell at you. Everyone is up here waiting for you, and you can't even pick up a phone and call. I'm up here running around after your mother and you leave your bloody phone off the hook all day. She's up. I tried to call you yesterday to tell you. She's out of bed and eating.'

'For how long?'

'A couple of days. She's been sitting with old Mrs Matthews, reading to her.'

Sally stilled her mind. He'd just dropped a lousy lifeline into the pit of sludge. She could see it coiled there. Lakeside. Mummy. Its ends were mucky, frayed. She didn't want to reach for it.

'Why didn't you call Deb?' Nothing to say. No defence. 'Are you going to be okay for tonight?' Silence. 'There's a lot of flu going around up here too.'

'I'm fine.' Why bother? Too much effort. Let go this fraying line and slip back in.

'Kate said you sounded full up with it.'

'I was holding my nose.' That's what Sue did when she

wanted to take a sickie. Held her nose and rang Ratsus. Smart bitch, Sue. She'd known Matt would be married. You think something like that gets to that age unmarried? That's what she'd said. Smart city bitch.

Ross was still talking. 'You're not looking after yourself down there. Give it up and come home where you belong.'

'I don't belong anywhere, and I haven't got the flu.'

'Have you been to the doctor?'

'Will you listen to me? Will anybody ever listen to me? I'm fine. Can you hear me? I was holding my bloody nose.' She did it now, yelling the words at him through pinched nostrils, and her eardrums popped. She thought she'd burst them, and she swallowed, once, twice. She shook her head, changed the telephone to her other ear. Deaf in one and couldn't hear with the other. She picked up a tear-wet tissue and blew her nose. Her ears began clicking. She wasn't going to do that again in a hurry.

'I was just getting dressed to come down and see what was going on with you.' She didn't reply. 'I'll be there in two hours.' Silence. 'Did you hear me, Sally?' he yelled.

'I can hear you. So can half of Lakeside.'

'Take a couple of pills and get a few hours' sleep. I'm leaving now.'

'I can't do it, Ross.'

'There are people relying on you. Stop feeling sorry for yourself. Did you get your dress?'

'Stay out of my life.'

'I'll be there around two.'

'I didn't get a bloody dress.'

'Jesus, Sally! What's happened to you lately?' Matt happened. That's what happened. 'What about the one you wore for Gina's wedding?'

'It's in one of the boxes in your garage, and it's blue and probably mouldy anyway. No-one will miss me.'

'We'll pick up something when I get there.'

'Oh Jesus, Ross.' He wouldn't give up. He'd be down here.

He'd break her door in. She moaned, looked at her skirt, at her bare feet, and the mess. She'd been doing a Mummy. She wasn't her mother. She wasn't. 'I'll get something. I'll be there.'

'Are you well enough to drive?'

'I said I'd be there.' Better there than here.

He let her go and she walked to the bathroom, picking up jeans, shoes, junk, tossing them onto the bed. She turned on the hot water and slowly stripped; her clothing stank of sweat and stale Matt. She looked at her face in the foggy mirror. Pale, and more like her mother today, eyes swollen, half-closed by too many tears, her hair a mess.

'I didn't find me, Mummy. Just lost the rest of me.' Through the fogged mirror her hazy reflection stared at her. 'Was I ever meant to be, Mummy?' A ghost in that mirror, hazy. Her ghost. Written down to die at eight and something had gone wrong. Lost ghost.

She stepped beneath the too-hot spray, wanting to feel pain. And she felt it.

'Shit!' she yelled and reached for the cold tap, gave herself a shot of cold-water-in-the-face therapy.

She was rinsing her hair when the phone rang.

Naked she ran to answer it. 'I said I'll be there, Ross. You don't need to check up on me!' There was no reply. 'Hello. Hello?' Only silence, but not true silence. The growl of the city beast. 'Hello. Who's there?'

Matt? It was probably Matt, and she'd spoken Ross's name. And a good thing too. Let him know she wasn't sitting here crying for him. Let him think she wasn't, anyway.

'Go home to your bloody wife and stay out of my life,' she yelled and slammed the phone down. As she did, it rang. The thing had gone crazy. Weeks could pass and no-one called. This time she heard the STD beeps.

'You're still there, Sally.'

'And you wouldn't have known if you hadn't been checking up on me. I had a shower. I had to wash my hair.'

'You had a hair appointment up here.'

'Well I'm not up there, am I? I'm down here and stop your nagging or I won't bloody well be up there.'

She threw away the skirt she'd worn since Wednesday night. Tossed it in the rubbish and carried the bag downstairs. She met the bikie at the garbage bins.

'Been having a party?' he said.

'Get a life,' she snapped and she pushed by him, got rid of her bag and some of her shame. Her letterbox was loaded with junk mail. She emptied it on the way back, emptied it into Number 14 and didn't care if he saw her. Back in her unit only long enough to pick up her handbag, she was away, out of that place.

She hit an automatic teller machine hard, then drove to the Queen Vic market. Noise and the jam of people. Smells of food and musty age and brand-new shine. All in together. Leather bags and arty junk. Clothing and kitchenware. Cheap framed pictures, silk scarves and mouldy shoes. Flowers too. She chose a bunch and some fruit, then she walked to a mess of shoes and bought a pair. She bought a bucket of salty chips and a long maroon frock with a split seam. She bought light globes and an ornament, a dark-haired boy and his dog. It wasn't number thirteen of the old collection, but number one of the new, and it wasn't china either. Looked like it. Didn't feel like it.

Back in her car she unwrapped the ornament, wondering why she'd bought it, but when she looked again she knew. It was a little Shane boy, skinny little neck, cheeky eyes.

Lots of parcels to open, presents to herself. She'd wear the shoes tonight. They were black strappy things. Pure luck that she'd gone to the market, it was never easy finding shoes she liked to wear. She'd seen these and pounced on them, sure they'd be too big. But they weren't too big. Perfect, even if they were seconds. And the dress. It was the exact colour Deb had wanted, and nicer than the one at the hire place. A few stitches and it would be okay for one night.

Black lifting, lifting, lifting. Black going, going, gone.

a tangled thread

Lakeside had hidden for years in its valley, no highway leading there and nowhere to go once you got there, except to turn around and drive back out again. Its distance from greedy Melbourne had saved it from the fate of many small towns. No new housing estates for Lakeside. She glanced at her watch when a herd of cows expected right of way at the intersection of Lake and Centre Roads. Farms rubbed elbows with garages and used-car yards on this side of town. Window down, the scent of milking cows and petrol intermingling, she inhaled the scent of home.

Mrs Bertram and Ross had taught her respect for cows, unlike the hoon who had tailgated her through the hills, blasting his horn. He leaned on it again, and when she didn't move he went around her, scattering cows. She followed him through. Might as well. Her right blinker had been going; a right-hand turn would have led her by a back road to Ross's farm, but she was in no hurry to go there. Plenty of time to pop in and see Mummy, ask her if she'd like to go out for lunch tomorrow.

From this section of the road she could see the lake, deep

blue, and the park beside it edged with roses. Postcard pretty today. Lakeside was a pretty town in spring. An old town, a gold town, it had been solidly built in the 1800s. The churches were tall, the banks had flaunted their old-gold wealth. Not much wealth left these days; they played bingo twice a week in the State Bank building, now community centre.

The supermarket had retained its original grocer's windows and grocer's door, hiding the fact that it had extended out the back where a modern rear entrance led in from the car park. A craft shop, owned by escapees from Melbourne, had been put back the way it was a hundred-odd years ago; the department store beside it had never bothered to modernise – apart from their cash registers.

She swung a left and drove on down Hoppers Street, seeing the town as she had the day she and her mother had arrived here. Small and solid. Neat. Old pubs on three corners. 'Accommodation', the sign over the Royal read. Cheap rates. They'd repaired the top-floor verandah recently and restored the lacework. It looked good.

Small towns were into the tourism dollar, and Lakeside had a worthy past no-one had recognised until the 1980s when a schoolgirl had been found in the lake, in a wheat bag, weighed down with bricks. They'd never found the murderer, but Melbourne day trippers had found Lakeside, and the big wheels in town had found the day trippers eager to spend their money viewing old buildings and gold mines. On long weekends and during holiday seasons the town went mad and the motels and caravan park were full. Locals couldn't get a park in the main street, and speedboats took over the lake the Sleiman family had long looked on as their own.

Ten years ago a new wing had been built onto the side of the old hospital. It smelt new, clean, but a renovation with modern floor tiles and modern furnishings hadn't killed the odour of the original building. Red bricks and narrow windows, high ceilings still trapped the pain of a hundred and fifty years. The elderly, the long-term patients, were housed in the old section, more nursing home now than hospital.

Loaded with flowers and fruit, Sally hurried down the last corridor to her mother's ward. A glance at her watch. Time for a two-minute visit. She'd missed work on Thursday and Friday, hadn't even checked in. Ratsus would probably tell her to go home if she went in tomorrow, so better not to go in. Save face.

Her mother's screens were drawn and Sleiman was there with two sisters. They were connecting tubes.

'Mummy,' she said.

'Wait outside, please,' a sister said.

'What's happened to her?' Open-mouthed, open-eyed, Sally pushed forward, in the way, always in the way.

'We don't know.'

'When did it happen?'

'She's coming out of it,' the sister said, her needle feeding drugs into an intravenous line.

'Can you wait outside, please, Miss De Rooze.' Sleiman the sleaze was playing life-saver.

Sally stepped back, placed the flowers down; they still gloated with life and colour. The strawberries from the market, fat and red, she placed on the locker, the red-gold mango she grasped in her hand. Her mother looked like grey death, cold fluid dripping into a fragile arm.

'Did she take something?' No reply. Sally backed from the room, then quickly walked away. She drove to the farm, no longer seeing the town, only Mummy.

She didn't tell Ross. He was in the kitchen, eating apple pie doused with cream. Homemade pie. Karen Matthews had been over the fence again. He could do worse than Karen Matthews, but not much worse. Lanky dobber dork.

'We're eating at the wedding, Ross.'

'Have some.' He offered a forkful. 'It's proper pie.'

A shake of her head and she walked into the bedroom, where she tried the maroon frock. It was too long, but she ransacked the sewing machine drawer until she found maroon thread, a needle. She stitched the split seam, tacked up a fast two-inch hem, pressed the frock and made it to the bride's parents' home on time.

'You could have called us, Sally,' the mother of the bride, carping old battle-axe in navy blue, said.

'This time yesterday, I thought I was dying.' True enough. 'You look terrific.' Not true enough.

'A miracle recovery, by the looks of it.' Short and skinny, tough as steak cut from a twenty-year-old bull's backside was Mrs Davis. How had she produced Deb?

'You know me, Mrs Davis. I always rise to the occasion.' She'd stolen a few bottles of nail polish from the Davis's chemist shop as a fourteen year old – and been caught once. Caught by Mrs Bertram. Hadn't done it again, but every time she saw this woman she remembered that black nail polish.

One more walk down the aisle. She heard little of the service. Her mind was with her mother. More fake smiles for the camera, then a quick stop-off at the hospital. Mummy was sleeping.

'She's fine,' the sister said. 'It's happened before.'

'She's getting hold of something?'

'She's fine now, love. Let's go,' Ross said.

Let's go.

The reception was at the new motel, and thank God for wine. It got her through until twelve.

She hadn't packed a case, had no nightgown, so she borrowed one of Ross's T-shirts. He came from the shower in his giant pyjamas and stood behind her. 'Bed, eh?' he said.

Bed.

It complained as he climbed in. It was allowed to complain. Why couldn't she? She stood at his window, looking at the hills, a solid black wall against a starry sky, Lakeside's last line of defence against the outside world. All right for Deb. She'd been born here. All right for Ross too. Not all right for Sally De Rooze. She'd come from the other side of that barrier and she wanted to be there now.

'Not a bad night,' he said. 'Old mother Davis wasn't too pleased with you.'

'Them's the breaks.'

'Your dress looked good. Where did you get it?'

'The market. I only paid twenty-five for it. One of its seams was split, and another one split halfway through the night.'

'What do you expect for nothing?'

Too much sometimes.

'Hop into bed, love. You'll freshen up your cold standing out there.'

Sally De Rooze, service provider, slid in beside him and he placed an arm beneath her shoulder, drawing her close, kissing her, smelling of shaving soap and toothpaste.

Sense of smell okay. No sense of feeling. Sight was good. Even in the dark she could see Mummy's face on the ceiling. Skull face with white eyes.

His hand brushed her breast, kept brushing and she couldn't stand it. She pushed it away. 'Did she know I was coming home, Ross?'

'Who?'

'Mummy?'

'Yeah, I rang her to let her know you were okay.' His hand slid beneath the old T-shirt, feeling the silk of her briefs and her jutting hipbone.

They weren't watching her mother at the hospital. She had to be watched. You couldn't trust her as far as you could kick her. Sly like a fox was Mummy, little close-set eyes watching you while she sat on the green vinyl couch, sipping port and planning her next move. Watch her, always watch her. Read her moods. Look behind each word she utters. And check your own words too, censor every one before you let it loose, or she'll catch it and fire it back as ammunition. And never, never disagree with her. Yes, Mummy, yes, yes, yes, Mummy.

'She's got hold of something, Ross. She must have. You said she'd been sitting with the old ladies. She's probably knocked off someone's pills. What sort of pills would cause a fit?'

'Do we have to talk about her all night? I hardly ever see you.' His hand crept up, feeling for rib bones, counting rib bones. 'What do you eat down there?'

'Do we have to talk about food all night?' She took his hand, held it as she lay back on the pillow.

'Just tell me if you're not in the mood.'

'I'm not in the mood.'

He waited for sixty seconds for her mood to alter then his hand returned to her hipbone. 'You're skin and bone. No wonder you're not in the mood.'

'If you'd stop feeling my bones and lecturing me about my weight every bloody five minutes, I might get in the mood. I don't lecture you about your weight. You were popping out of your shirt, and your trousers looked as if they were going to split every time you bent over tonight. You're getting as fat as a pig, Ross, and your hair looks bloody awful. Why don't you let it grow?'

'What's that if not lecturing me?' he said. 'Will we or won't we?'

'Jesus,' she sighed, and she gave up.

He peeled away her T-shirt and her briefs. She didn't help, didn't hinder, but she thought of Matt. He'd ripped her clothes off – the grand master of sex and she his willing student. No matter what he wanted to do, or wanted her to do, she'd never said no.

Never learnt to say no. Never learnt to argue for what she wanted or didn't want. No-one to practise on. Oh, she'd screamed that last night – when it was too late. Too late for everything.

You need to practise arguing for what you want when you are young, she thought. You have to argue with your little brothers, argue with little friends. But her brothers had died, and Sally had moved around too often to have friends to argue with.

Poor Deb. She's been a good friend and I nearly ruined her wedding day. How did I forget?

Matt. That's how.

And she loved him. She did, and she couldn't stand Ross's mouth wearing her own ragged. She ached for Matt's mouth and his smooth strong hands. He made her feel alive, made sex into a game they played together.

Ross's hand moved to her breast.

'Jesus!' she said.

'What now?'

'Stop playing around, will you, and just get on with it if you have to.'

'Yeah?' He rolled onto his back. 'Yeah. Well, I don't think I'm that desperate, thanks all the same for the offer.'

She rolled away, placing distance between naked flesh, and minutes passed. 'I'm sorry, but I can't get Mummy out of my head tonight. She looked like a hydroponic vegetable. Tubes pouring in the fertiliser one end, draining it out the other. Maybe she is sick, Ross. People with brain tumours have fits, don't they? Have they done a brain scan?'

'Pity they couldn't do a brain transplant. Go to sleep.'

Silence again. She waited for five minutes, counting them away, then she rose, found her T-shirt and briefs in the bed and she dressed. 'I'm sorry.'

'For Christ's sake, stop saying you're sorry. I said it was all right.'

'It's not all right, and you know it's not all right. You're too accepting for your own bloody good sometimes. It's over, Ross. What we had is over. Can't you see that?'

'Yeah, yeah, yeah. Just go to sleep.'

'I can say that to you, and all you can say is, go to sleep!'

'All I know is, a man can't do anything right tonight. You've got some bloody bee in your bonnet, and I've got to get up in five hours, and just for the bloody record, I'll accept any bloody thing I want to accept. And I'm big and ugly enough to decide what's good for me too. I don't need you to decide for me, and I don't need you to decide how I have my hair cut either. I'll have it cut like I bloody well want to have it cut. Now go to sleep, for Christ's sake.'

She walked from the bedroom and he called after her. 'What have I done now?'

'Nothing. You're perfect. I've got a virus. I'm losing my voice.'

Lost it a long, long time ago.

'There's Aspros in the top cupboard over the sink. Make yourself a hot lemon drink and put some honey and brandy in it. It's in the lounge room cabinet.'

Barefoot and in his T-shirt she walked out the back door, out into the cool and down the gravelled path to pick a lemon by the light of the moon.

It was bright out tonight. Yellow-balloon bright. The dogs barked. They liked to bark on moonlit nights.

'Lay down,' she growled, and they barked like demented things.

'Lay down!' Ross roared from his bed, pleased to have something to roar about. Silence.

There were always lemons on Ross's tree. He had an apricot tree too, and a peach tree. Apples, figs, grapes. Such a continuity of nature. Year after year they flowered and bore their fruit. Year after year. The trees had been planted by the generations that were no more, but their planting sustained. Fruit for all seasons, had Ross. His trees would continue to bear, his sons would pick the apricots on some New Year's Day and their wives would make jars of apricot jam. Ross's sons; they wouldn't be her sons.

Never cut a tangled thread if a little time and patience can untangle it, Mrs Bertram used to say when they'd sat together crocheting the double bedspread.

She'd tried, tried to untangle this mess for too long. It was time for the scissors.

Moonlight washed the land tonight, glistening on the leaves, painting them silver. She wandered the back yard, each step a careful step, a gentle touchdown before her weight was transferred to the sole of her foot. There were prickles and sticks and broken bricks in this garden. Hens wandered here, leaving their calling cards behind them.

The lemons were white in the moonlight, and she picked one, cupping it in her hand, smelling it. It was a lemon, grown on a tree with a hundred other lemons and it knew it was a lemon. It didn't try to be an orange or a grapefruit.

Who was she? Where did she grow?

I'm a hybrid in a pot, no roots dug deep into the earth, she thought. Born to be moved around. Ross is just trying to dig it out of the pot, offer it his acres and room to spread. He doesn't see it as a stunted thing because he doesn't dig deep enough to see the convoluted root mass beneath the surface.

Who was I born to be? Everyone is born to be someone. What if Daddy had lived? Who would I have been? He would have let me be whoever I was meant to be.

I wasn't meant to be a farmer's wife. Matt's slut maybe, like old Papa with his sluts. He'd driven Grandma to suicide with his sluts, or so Mummy said ... or maybe, maybe Grandma's bitter mouth had driven him to his sluts. Maybe Mummy would have driven Daddy away if he'd lived.

She looked up at the sky, searching for a familiar cluster of stars. Beautiful, beautiful gem-studded velvet sky. Silence. She could almost hear the stars twinkling.

Her flesh cooling, she walked the back garden, looking up at her family of stars in the western sky. Daddy star was shining brightly tonight. He was up there looking after Shane, and Robby and Nicky star, and the tiny intermittent twinkle that was Teddy star. She waved to them, blew them a kiss, four kisses, then she stood still and listened to Ross. His bedroom window was at the rear of the house and she could hear his peaceful snores – peaceful from a distance.

Cool now, the breeze teasing her hair, night things on the prowl, scuttling. She stepped back, looked at the grass.

'Old snake in the grass. Are you one of Matt's friends?' She teased the grass with her foot. No fangs. 'I love this place but I don't want to live here. I love Ross, but I can't make love to him. That's a lemon trying to be an orange. Sour. Bitter. Cheat.'

The warmth of the old house drew her back. On tiptoe she crept to the bathroom, washing her feet in the bathroom basin. Mrs Bertram's bedroom waited empty. Ross's room was diagonally across the passage. Quietly she crept into the empty room and she sat on the bed. Bed springs creaked. Dust rose. She sneezed.

'Is that you?'

She tried to muffle a second sneeze. 'No,' she said. 'Just your neighbourhood burglar with hay fever.'

'Come back to bed. You'll have a relapse.'

To bed. To his bed. But never again her bed. She should tell him now, force him to listen.

Too late. He'd spend the rest of the night drinking coffee and smoking, looking at her with his labrador eyes, and in the morning he'd be tired and she'd feel guilty, and she didn't need any more guilt. Easier to lie tonight.

'Go to sleep,' she said. 'I won't be too long.'

She didn't go to bed that night. At five in the morning she dressed and crept from the house, and she drove across the milky white hills, then down, down to the signpost nearly hidden in a bank of mist.

GEELONG.

And onwards, onwards, the sun now in her eyes.

number 29 carter street

Her house was still there, but it looked so old, small, low. How did it get to be so low? How did the trees get to be so tall? Was that huge spruce the one she and her father had planted the Christmas she was five, then decorated with balloons so they couldn't see the tree for balloons? And the liquidambar, not as tall as Sally when the house was sold. Now it was huge. Beneath it a tall woman stood watering a group of pot plants. Sally glanced at her, then away to Raelene's house, old too.

In her mind this street had remained unchanged. She had allowed no brand-new fence to lean, to fall, and she sat now looking at Raelene's front door, knowing that Raelene had moved on, left this old street behind, left Sally behind. They'd written for years, Raelene's long letters had kept Sally attached to Geelong – until Lakeside and Mrs Bertram.

'My fault. I was the one who let go.'

She chewed on her nail a moment, drew a breath and left the car, walked up the drive, knocked on the door. Same door, just a different colour. A pregnant woman opened it. She was not Raelene. She wore a sari and spoke with an accent.

'Sorry to disturb you.' Then back down the familiar cement drive, cracked now, and stained. She looked for the trellis near the garage. Gone, long ago, like the passionfruit vines. All gone. No more green paint. No more of Daddy's emeralds.

All so long ago. Eleven when she'd come here that time and climbed on the garage roof with the hose.

She was pulling away from the kerb when she heard her name.

'Sally? Sally De Rooze?'

She braked, turned to see the tall woman standing beside her letterbox, waving her hose. The motor died and Sally wound her window down while she stared at the woman's face. Not a pudding face. But the teeth, maybe. And maybe the colour of the hair. She wore glasses. Blue glasses. It couldn't be.

'It is you, Sally. I knew it was. You haven't changed one iota.' The woman lifted the hose, allowing water to splash to the nature strip, then she laughed.

'Carol Rigg?'

'Yeah. Or I used to be. Carol Murphy now. I'm back home with Mum and Pops for a while. How are you? Long time, no see.'

Then they were both at the letterbox and Carol Rigg–Murphy turned off the water. 'I was almost going to let you have it when I saw you walking down next door's drive – just for old times' sake, but I thought, gee, what if it isn't her? They'll lock me up for a madwoman,' she said. 'You didn't grow much, did you? You still look about twelve.'

'You grew.' It wasn't easy. What did you say to an old enemy you'd pelted with passionfruit but never spoken to?

'Yeah. Didn't think I was ever going to stop when I was about fourteen. Went from fatso to beanpole in twelve months. Have you got time to come in for a cuppa?'

'I was on my way through. Thought I'd drive by. See if the street was still here.'

'You were looking for Raelene?'

'Yeah.' So strange making conversation with this stranger

who was not so strange. Glasses on her nose. Same nose. Floral dress. She'd always worn floral dresses. And the chin. She still had a round chin. Weird. Chatting at a front fence to a house thief who now wanted to claim her as an old friend.

Why not claim her, she thought. Why not reach out a hand to someone from back then? Someone who knew you back then. She might remember who you were, help put all your pieces back together.

Stare, stare, monkey bear.
Everybody knows you swear.
You've got dirty underwear.

Carol was speaking, going ten to the dozen, but Sally was away. She shook her head, shook her mind back to the moment. 'She's in England? Raelene?'

'I think she's still over there. She went right through school, you know, then went on and did psychology. Then she got a job in England, so her parents went back too. They were poms, nice enough, but after they lost their son, Raelene was like their whole life to them.'

'Little Jamey. They lost him?'

'Oh, you wouldn't have known. He got leukaemia. They kept him alive until he was thirteen, which was about the time Rae finished uni. Then he died, so they sold up and left. I've got their address somewhere if you want it. I wrote once, sent a few Christmas cards. I never was a letter writer like you and Rae. Come in for a coffee and I'll see if I can find it for you. Mum's home, and old Nan is with us too since old Pa died.'

'I won't . . . not today.'

'How's your mum going these days, anyway?'

'She's . . . she's really good. Really good these days.'

'I never knew her, of course, but Rae's mother told Mum a bit about it. God, I'm that pleased to see you. I've been going nuts here. It's a real madhouse with four generations under the one roof. My girls share with Nan, and Jake is in my room. I've got to get myself a place of my own, but I sort of can't decide where I want to live. We used to live in Croydon when I was married, but if I go back then I won't have Mum to look after the kids after school.'

Sally looked at her watch. She'd turned on a talking machine. 'Where are you living?'

'Melbourne. South Yarra. And I'll have to keep moving, Carol. I'll call you. Your mum would still be in the book?'

'Yeah. They're the original stay-puts. Couldn't move Mum and Pops out of here if I put a bomb under their beds. Me and Leo wanted them to go in with us in a milk bar a couple of years back, but no go. Just as well they didn't, really. No money in them. We went broke, then we broke up six months back. Which is a bit sad, but that's the way life goes, isn't it? I'm going mad here, though. Stir-crazy. I'm thinking of putting an ad in the Melbourne paper, getting some other woman with kids to share a house with me. I could work the night shift and she could do days. Share the kids. Have you got any kids?'

'I'm not married.'

'Not married? You've got to be thirty. Really?' Sally shrugged, looked away. 'God. Looking like you do, I thought you would have had to drive the blokes off with sticks. You always were pretty, though. You know what Raelene's mum used to call you?' Sally shook her head. 'She used to say you looked like poor little Alice, locked outside of Wonderland.'

'And Mum was the Mad Hatter.' Sally replied.

Carol laughed and Sally forced a smile, eager to be gone but aware she would not get away easily.

'Gee, you've made my day. Made my week. I just found out that Leo has got another woman. He went back to his old trade after the milk bar. She works with him.'

'It happens,' Sally said.

'Oh, I know. I'll find someone else too.'

Sally stepped back to the car; Carol followed her, leant on the car. Sally opened her car door. Carol held it open.

'I've got two girls – Emma and Rebecca – and Jake, the boy. They're good kids.'

Sally looked to the left, to the right. She glanced at the house across the road. They had built on a second floor. Twin boys had once lived there. Was the man mowing the lawn another stay-put? Dean. Dean or Donny Cooper. Shane used to play with them.

'Are the Cooper twins still around?'

'No. They left in high school. Anyway, I was telling Emma about you and the hose bit and Emma said, "Why didn't you get your hose and shoot her back, Mum?" I mean, that's just the sort of thing that she'd do, but I was an only child and I didn't have the cheek that you and Raelene had. Gee, I thought you were game, running along the peak of that roof like a tight-rope walker, with Pops and Mr Mason creeping after you on their hands and knees. And that other time, just after we moved in and you came back here. You sat up there for hours singing this song about your father and brothers, and playing a huge guitar. It made me cry.'

Sally could remember that night. Mummy at the funny farm, Sally in emergency care, but she'd nicked off and walked home. And she couldn't go in when she got there because Carol Rigg lived there. She'd crept into Raelene's garage and found Mummy's guitar, climbed with it onto the roof.

Behind the wheel now, she played with her keys. Couldn't close the car door. Carol's head was in the way. 'I'll have to go, Carol.'

'You still live with your mum?'

She glanced at the house thief, who already knew too much about her past. 'Yes,' she said. 'I'll give you a call.'

'You make sure you do. I'd hate to lose you again after finding you. Better still, you give me your phone number.'

Sally gave her her Melbourne number but she reversed the last two digits. Carol repeated it. 'I'll give you a call next week.

Oh, and Rae's address – that's if I can find it. Where do I send it?'

She gave Carol Ross's roadside delivery address, but ten more minutes passed before she got away and pointed her car towards home.

'Home.' She said the word, questioning it. For sixteen years home had been Lakeside. Now the hazy shape of the city skyline had become home, and she drove towards it gladly, wanting it, wanting whatever that growling Melbourne beast had to give.

When had she made the transition? In Geelong? In Carter Street?

She hadn't felt it happen. Yesterday she'd driven home to Lakeside. Now she was driving down the freeway to her home.

the world going by

november 1999

She slept late on Tuesday morning. It was close to ten when she crept up on the office block. Ratsus was waiting, patrolling her phones.

'So you finally showing you face, eh?'

'Sorry. I've had a virus. I had to go to the doctor this morning for some more tablets.' She coughed, giving her lie veracity.

Queen Ratsus's trumpet lips blew air in an exaggerated 'Phuuumph'. She didn't believe in human viruses. A virus was a trick played on computers. 'You can use telephone. Yes? I personally am not so sure of this. This is why I asking you. Yes? You can use telephone? You can dial number? Yes?'

'I was too sick, and I live alone.' Sally coughed again, raising a worthy smoker's cough. 'I'm sorry.'

'And I am tired of sorry excuse. You wanting work, or you not wanting work. Is you decision.'

'I can work late all this week.' Ratsus blew more air, but she walked away, and Sally exhaled her own air with relief. She was still among the employed. As she took her seat, Pimples stared, Ron's dentures clickety-clacked and Cindy cackled.

Nothing had changed but everything had changed.

'Sell. Sell. Sell,' Ratsus bawled. 'Why it is we are here?'

And the chorus came back loud. 'To sell.'

'Why we can sell?'

'Because people love to buy.'

Sally sighed. True enough. She dialled a faceless voice desperate for a dose of retail therapy. And she made a sale. The power of positive thinking.

'Sell. Sell. Sell.'

That's what she had to do. Accentuate the positive. Eliminate the negative. And she was back into the swing of the old selling game. Maybe she'd missed it. On the high that always followed the low, she sold hard.

Seven lonely days may make one lonely week, but seven lonely nights made a bulging pay packet. The bills slimmed it down. Then Monday again. Matt's night again, and no Matt. Let him ring. And he had. Let him plead. And he had. He'd get over it and so would she.

Sue worked late most nights and on Monday she didn't want to go home, so they walked to the casino. Sue sat at the pokies and Sally wandered off to watch the laser show and the water dance, and to walk that *Gone with the Wind* staircase and dream. It was a magical place, as long as you stayed away from the tables and the pokies.

At nine she wandered out to watch the lights on the river; a muddy gutter by day, the Yarra added to the magic of this place by night. And the city behind it looked like a man-made mountain range against the sky. No barrier now, that mountain. Home. Melbourne was home.

She sat alone waiting for the fire show, her self-prescribed dose of fire therapy. The first time she'd heard the roar of gas, seen those belching flames, she'd screamed and cowered. Sue had thought it was a lark. She'd laughed, but that night the fire-dream had come for Sally. She'd woken herself with her screams.

Now she forced herself to watch those flames, forced herself closer each time she came here, and tonight she was too close; when the flames roared, she felt their heat on her face. But she didn't flinch. This place was magic land, and the fires here were made by dragons imprisoned in a cave beneath the Yarra. Every hour on the hour they came out to roar their fury into the night sky. Caged things, like her, they just wanted to fly.

It was close to nine-thirty when she went in search of Sue and found her still feeding the pokies' greed. 'Just another five minutes, Sall. I had a win.'

'Quit while you're ahead.'

'Who says I'm ahead? Just five more. I've got that lucky feeling.'

'Five more. I'll be near that bar.' Sally yawned and found an ashtray, lit a cigarette and watched the world go by. And it did. Including the bikie, barely recognisable, apart from his long hair.

He recognised her too. 'No soliciting allowed here, De Rooster. Get yourself down to St Kilda.'

'Get a job,' she replied and turned away.

Minutes later Sue came at a run, flashing notes. 'I told you so. Stick this in your purse.' Sally took the notes, folded them. 'Don't give them back to me. Even if I beg.'

'We've got to work in the morning.'

'Fifteen minutes. I'm on a winning streak.'

'Fifteen minutes and I leave.' She tucked the rolled notes into her bra.

One of the guys from *Home and Away* walked by; he looked at her too, smiled. If she'd been Sue, she wouldn't have allowed it to end at a smile. Then half an hour later, when she walked to the bar for a drink, she almost had a head-on with Sleiman the sleaze.

'Miss De Rooze,' he said.

She shrugged. Nothing to say.

'A drink?' he said. 'Can I –'

She paid for her own wine and returned with it to her ashtray.

But he followed her, his white fingers feeling up a tall glass as he showed her his beaky front teeth. 'Your mother is on the improve again.'

She nodded. What else could she do? If she moved from here Sue would never find her.

'Good to see you looking well. As usual.' The beaky smile.

Maybe she should ask him about pills and fits and brain scans, and better here on her own turf than in Lakeside. She was priming herself, forming the question, when Sue found her.

'Just a twenty thanks, Sall,' she said.

'I'm leaving.'

'Just a twenty. Come on, you mean fuck.'

The sleaze flinched, stared at the red hair, at the nose ring, then down. He sucked seed and walked. Sally walked in the opposite direction.

'You were sucking up the dregs with him, weren't you? *I* wouldn't even look at him and I haven't had any since – Jesus, I've forgotten.'

'He's my mother's doctor. Do you want a ride home?'

'Give us my money and I'll get a taxi. Come on, Sall. It's ready to pay up big. I can feel it.'

'I'm going, going, gone.'

Sue tailed her, caught up to her on the bridge where Sally leaned, watching the dragons' fire again, but from a distance.

'Wouldn't do a seagull much good if he happened to be flying over,' Sue said. 'So let's go if we're going, you mean fuck.'

Sue offered coffee in Dandenong. They sat on the couch with a cat between them while Sally looked around a house that was a home. Sue might have a cheap love life but she had expensive furniture and light fittings. She might have rat-chewed hair and buy her gear from op shops, but her furnishings were tasteful. She had a video player too, and a video due back. She put it on when she made a second cup of coffee and Sally remembered the notes in her bra. She removed them, tossed them onto the coffee table.

'This place must be worth a fortune. How can you afford to pay out your ex?'

'I can't, can I?' Sue claimed the notes, curled up and warm, flattened them and placed them in her purse. 'Have you got any fags on you?'

'Buy your own.'

A fifty-cent piece hit the cat. He spat and moved an inch. 'Anyway, what happened to the married bloke you used to see on Mondays?'

'Easy come, easy go.' Gone, but not so easy. Not yet.

It was near two in the morning when she left Dandenong, and the freeway was just that, almost deserted. Eerie. The whistle of the wind through a slightly opened window sounded like the wail of the damned. Carla Miller's body had been found beside this freeway, near the Springvale exit. They'd never found her killer. Sally put her foot down, forcing the near-bald tyres to turn faster.

Little traffic about, but a car with one light was tailing her; or was it a bike? It had been behind her since Stud Road. She slowed, hoping it might pass, but it slowed too.

Strange, the sound of a silent freeway. Her foot grew heavy again on the accelerator, eager now to get home. She took the exit to Toorak Road and the bike followed her off. Her doors were locked but she reached over, just to make certain. She checked the rear-vision mirror.

The bike was closer. He was following her. Then she was at her turn. No blinker on, she spun the wheel fast, and, thank God, the rider continued on his way.

Too tired, that was her trouble. Tired of sitting all day and half the night, tired of driving. She ran down the drive and up the stairs, one hand rubbing her spine. Matt's last effort against the refrigerator door had left its mark. But it only hurt if she bumped it, and she wasn't into bumping it.

Tuesday, so slow. Wednesday. Slower. Matt called again. She hung up and left the phone off the hook. Then she washed the bathroom floor and her mop picked up a dark hair. She held it in her hand, loving it, still loving him.

Every day was the same. The alarm that woke her, the drive to work, the phones, the faces. She worked through until 8.30 on Thursday night and went home to her dripping sink tap. She'd have to visit Mummy this weekend. Drive up and back on Sunday, ask Sue along for the ride.

Drip, drip. Drip, drip.

'Shut up, you bloody dripping thing,' she yelled at the tap. Like Ross's dogs, the tap ignored her and dripped on. She sprang from the bed to place the washing-up sponge beneath the drip and it sang a different tune.

Splat-spat. Spat-splatter, splash.

How can I stop wanting what I want, want, want?

Splat. Splatter-splash.

'Sally Trash. Trash. Trash. Why fight it?'

Splatter-splash-splash-splash. Splish-splash.

She began singing to the splat-splat rhythm of the dripping tap, singing crazy songs of junk-collecting policemen, then the spat-splat rhythm altered and her song changed, and old words returned to her tongue, each line leading into the next.

Hush now, Sally, go to sleep.
Into the land of dreams you creep,
Ride up high to the stars tonight,
Safe with Daddy and his gentle light.

Nicky's up yonder looking around
In the clouds he's safe and sound.
Robby and Shane play without a care
For God is watching all up there.

lost, sally de rooze

december 1999

'Wanted, female, 20–25, to make fourth for cruise. Leave name and number.'

It was pinned in a prominent position on the office notice-board, a colourful computer print-out with a picture of the cruise ship, done by someone with more advanced computer skills than Sally, who now stood before it, pen in hand. She took down the phone number while strangers, locked with her all day in this phone-riddled space, bunched, punched the already glowing down button.

A lift arrived. Number one. The smokers, male and female, grasped their cigarettes, jostling for a place in the first lift as a second ding'd to a stop. Number three.

Old Ron approached, Pimples at his elbow, a gangly six-foot-six. He wasn't thin, just uncoordinated, as if all of his parts hadn't quite been connected, or were too far away from his brain to be under its control. He needed an extra brain in his hip. People would take them for a pair of gays, she thought. They were always together. The old guy in Number 6, the flat beneath her own, had had a young boyfriend for a while. Maybe old gay guys liked their boys young. But was Pimples so young? Maybe not.

Ron's fly was gaping, again or still, his sweater halfway up his back, greasy grey hair falling over his glasses. Repulsive old coot. Pimples noticed the zip, touched the older man's arm before disappearing red-faced into the lift.

'Plenty a room,' Ron said, tugging at his zip.

She shook her head. No, thank you very much. Wouldn't like to be trapped in a lift with that pair, and she didn't want to go down in number three anyway. She never used three these days. She'd met Matt in three at 5.25.

So many men. The world was full of them. She watched toy boy Norm enter the lift with married Red. There was something going on between those two. They kept flashing each other hungry looks.

'For sale, small refrigerator. $70.' Handwritten.

'Computer and colour printer. See Dave.' Colourful print-out. Nice computer.

She stood there, watching the strangers leave, taking notes, her mind like an unformatted computer disk. Couldn't follow any file to its logical conclusion. Information fragmented. Abort.

She'd gone to an interview at lunchtime. Receptionist at a medical clinic. Why apply for it? Why go to the interview? She'd had enough of sick people.

Mummy. She'd been a prize misery-guts on Saturday; she didn't like Sue, and she made it plain. Ross had been just as miserable when he'd called in and found Sue there again. Everyone had been miserable except Sally and Sue. They'd had a good day, the journey not so long with Sue in the passenger seat. Three times now she'd travelled with Sally to Lakeside, and one weekend they'd played tourist, sharing a twin room at the old Royal Hotel. They'd had a swim in the lake, eaten takeaway on a park bench.

Matt hadn't called now for eleven days; he'd finally got the message. She barely thought of him, when she was away from Collins Street. Here she thought of him; hadn't sighted him, though. When she walked past the coffee shop she thought of him, but most nights she worked late, and when she didn't, she got away from Collins Street before five.

Not tonight. Ratsus had bailed everyone up for an impromptu pep talk, then weeded out six workers. None Sally knew.

A cackle from behind, she turned, met the cackler's eye. Cindy. One of her crowd had got the shove, but it hadn't killed that cackle. Varicose came limping along behind them, looking preoccupied. All she ever had on her mind were her twins, and getting a seat on the tram out to East Burwood, stopping off at the supermarket to pick up something easy to cook for dinner.

So many no-name people fighting for space in a lift, for space in the world. A green-bunch threesome approached. Varicose stepped back, gave way, always conscious of her size.

'A long day,' she said.

'They're all long,' Sally replied.

'I always thought I'd like to go on a cruise.' Varicose sighed wistfully, looking where Sally was looking. 'Are you thinking of going?'

'Thinking about it.'

Christmas was coming. She'd opened a Christmas Club account with the Bendigo Bank years ago, and she paid twenty dollars into that account each week. There would be enough in it to pay for a cruise.

'I've got a feeling it's young Pam and her cronies. I overheard them talking about a cruise,' Varicose said. A nice lady. At what age did a girl become a lady? Varicose wasn't old. Her face looked about twenty-eight, her body forty and her legs sixty. Did size or age determine whether one was girl or woman, or was it motherhood? Become a mother, and the girl flew out of the bedroom and a woman fell into the kitchen.

Sometimes.

'Which one is Pam?' Sally asked.

'The tall one with the short black bob. She's on the workstation beside Dave.'

Dave? Pam? Varicose knew their names, but what was the use of naming people in this place when Ratsus's hobby was weeding her patch.

'I'm almost thirty. They want a twenty-year-old kid.'

Big brown eyes widened. 'I thought I would have been years older than you. I'm thirty-one.'

Sally didn't feel almost as old as this woman with problem legs. She didn't want to be almost as old. Eighteen. She wanted to be eighteen, and Mrs Bertram still alive, still sprinkling her growing dust.

Number three lift opened its doors again and Varicose stepped in, held the door; Sally couldn't refuse to go down. Couldn't say, I never use three, thanks.

The time was 5.25.

They stopped at nine. Three women stepped in. They stopped at six. Two men. At five an anorexic girl stepped on board and Varicose stared at the broomstick legs. Then the lift stopped at four and he was waiting there, looking for Sally as the doors slid open.

He stepped inside but she pushed by him and out to lush carpet and grey-blue seascapes, and he followed her while the crowd in the lift watched the show, watched her run from him.

'Don't do this, Sall.' He caught her hand as she tried the toilet door. Locked. She ran for the stairs, knew where the stairs were, but unlike Phonepross's fire door, this one refused to open. She turned down strange passages, found a dental surgery, dentist working overtime. Matt caught her, drew her to him and he kissed her against a glass door.

Hewitt and Rodes. Financial Advisers. Opposite the dentist.

It was later, at the flat, that she asked the question. They were eating pizza, drinking wine. 'You have left her, Matt?'

'I thought I'd lost you,' he said.

'Have you left her, Matt?'

'Be patient with me. Give me a month or two to get things worked out at home and we can have it all.'

Home. At home. His home. His wife's home. In Hallam.

'I don't want to be responsible for breaking up your marriage.'

'You are my only family, Sall.' He bit into another slice of pizza. 'What I can offer you at the moment isn't enough. I know it, but for the moment we will make it enough, because it's all I have to give.'

For the moment.

He kissed her, and he tasted of hot pizza. For the moment he was with her and she would make it enough. But moments alter from moment to moment. Christmas and its plastic Kmart doll was coming, coming to get her.

'I'm booked into the motel, Ross.' Seated on that hospital chair, back in that place, she couldn't meet Ross's eye.

'You want to be on your own for a bit, love?'

She nodded, looked at her mother, who was sleeping – or playing possum.

Ross sat back, his eyes uncomprehending. He looked at the window. Looked at the floor. Looked at the vase of flowers. At the vacant bed in the corner.

'Old Mrs Matthews died on Thursday. A pity she didn't make it to the new millennium,' he said. 'The funeral is on Monday. Will you be able to stay for it?'

She shook her head. Then she said it. 'I've met a guy in Melbourne, Ross.'

He flinched. He licked his lips and stared at her. She was his first love, his only love. His hand went to his mouth. Covered it. He swallowed hard, then drew his eyes back to the face on the pillow, remembering that mouth of seven months ago, and the words spat from that mouth: 'She'll come running back with her tail between her legs. You mark my words.'

Or keep on running. Take off with some other bloke. He

swallowed again, rubbed his mouth, his chin. Christ, he wasn't about to give her up to some city bloke. Probably just someone she worked with. It would blow over in a month, like when she was nineteen and Wally Martin had chased her up hill and down dale. She'd gone out with him. And that guy from the bank. It would blow over.

He stood, knowing that it wasn't going to blow over, and he turned to the woman in the bed. He blamed her for Sally's leaving. Blamed her for making them put off the wedding five years ago, blamed her, and her alone, for his babies unborn.

Cold sweat trickling down his spine, he knew he had to get out of this room or he'd kill the crazy bitch, suffocate her with a pillow. Had to get out. Do something. Fix something. Dig a hole. Pull out a motor. He stepped back and looked at Sally's profile against the window. An old-fashioned cameo, head and shoulders. Precious. But too young when they first got together. That's why he'd agreed to this year. That, and to let her try to break away from her mother.

Made a clean break, hadn't she?

His head down, he licked his lips, rubbed a hand across them. Then he turned, walked away.

christmas fever

Santa was threatening from every shop window, from every batch of junk mail. Christmas fever had Melburnians in its grip. Like a virus, it infected the city's collective consciousness, doubly infected this year by the millennium bug. So drive faster, Melbourne, get to the end of this bad old year sooner because there's a brand-new century coming and a party to wash the 90's sins away.

Sally was on her way home from Lakeside on Sunday night when a P-plate driver roared by, lane hopping, his passengers laughing. He cut her off. She braked hard, her tyres skidding on the tramlines, but the cars behind her had good tyres and brakes. No crunch. Not quite. Not this time.

The P-plate driver wasn't so lucky at the intersection of Toorak and Chapel, and Sally was only six cars behind him.

The scream. The thunk. The crash. And two cars melded. The screaming and the steam that looked like smoke and they were going to burn and they were going to die.

Close your eyes, Sally, and you won't see. Close your mind, Sally, and you won't know.

Close up.

Shut down.

Daddy. Daddy. Daddy.

Smell the burning. Smell the oil.

Don't think. Don't think. Please God, don't let me think. One. Two. Three. Four. Five. Five fingers. Six. Seven. Eight. Nine. Ten. And five more. Count the letters in the sign, and the stripes on the blind. Count. Keep counting. 273 + 189 = 462 + 53 = 515.

Waiting and counting. Motor off. Couldn't go forward. Couldn't go back. Waiting, counting numbers until the cops cleared a pathway through, until their hands signalled the drivers forward, giving them leave to aim their weapons again at old Santa.

Santa gave Raelene a talking doll and he gave Sally a plastic thing from Kmart. He didn't like her as much as he liked Raelene. Sally had written him a very nice letter, and she'd said please, Santa, and thank you, and lots of love, and she'd posted it off to the North Pole.

It will be over soon, all gone again soon. Brand-new century. Brand-new life with Matt.

And Mummy.

What was she going to do with Mummy when Matt got his divorce? He wasn't the type to take on a live-in mother-in-law. But she'd been better today. Full of energy. Her pale eyes bright, darting things. She'd walked down the corridor, and talked.

Not a good sign. Good was bad. Miserable was great. Something was going to blow. Sally knew it, Dr Sleaze didn't. He'd seen the bright eyes, heard the laughter, suggested an outing on Christmas Day; Christmas dinner at home with her daughter.

'Wonderful, Dr Sleiman,' Mummy had said. 'It's so good to feel well again.'

Home with her daughter? Where?

Before she'd left Lakeside, Sally had called in to the new motel, booking a room for a week, booking Christmas dinner for two. It would cost her a small fortune, but she had her Christmas account money.

Then what? Didn't know what. No answer to that *what*.

'Do a Scarlett, think about it tomorrow.'

Blank space tomorrow. Big fat gap. Spend your life waiting for tomorrow and when it gets there it never was anyhow. Just another broken promise.

And Matt too. Just another broken promise.

'Selfish mongrel!' she screamed at a truck that wouldn't let her over to make a left-hand turn, or at Matt, or at Father Christmas.

She'd see Matt on Monday this week, but they'd have no Wednesday. Santa stole it for Matt's office party and she wasn't invited. He never took her out.

I'm the other woman. I know the rules of the game. It's like he said, if his wife finds out about me, she'll take him to the cleaners. I have to think of the future. Think Monday. Stretch out Monday and make it a good one.

Monday. Just another lying tomorrow.

Matt arrived at six-thirty, drank her Jim Beam, swallowed her last three Panadols, used her fast, made her feel like a prostitute, then he dressed to leave.

'Wham, bang, thank you, ma'am,' she said.

He tried to smile, but his lips couldn't make the grade. He raised an eyebrow instead. Monday had come and now it was on its way out the door.

'How much longer do I wait for you, Matt?' He glanced at her, didn't understand. 'The divorce,' she said. 'How much longer?' He shook his head. 'You're taking her to your office party, aren't you?'

'Don't start, Sall.'

She watched him turn, pick up his shoes, his face clamped, closed. He refused to argue. She watched his eyes as she rolled to the side, drew the sheet across naked limbs. Stranger Matt tonight. He had the Christmas virus with millennium complications.

'I feel used,' she said. 'Abused.'

'We used each other.' His eyes had already left, gone home to the wife for a rest.

'I don't use you. I love you, and I want to be with you every day of my life. You say you can't live without me, but you're leaving me to go home to her.' He knotted his tie, made no reply. 'Let her have the house. Let her have the money. Who cares about money, Matt? I can keep working. We'll buy our own house.' He stood looking down at her, unmoved, unmoving. 'Talk to me, Matt!'

'It's all been said, Sall. If we're patient we'll both get what we want.'

'Nothing has been said! It never is. I need you now, Matt. I needed you to be with me yesterday. A car crashed right in front of me and I thought it was going to burn.'

'Did it?'

'No.'

'You turn molehills into mountains, just for the climb. I can get whingeing and nagging elsewhere, Sall. It's not why I come here. Now I have to go. Have a safe trip. I'll give you a call when I can.' His hand was on the doorknob, and she rose up on an elbow, lonely, angry, the black coming down to get her.

'Have a good weekend,' she yelled. 'Not a problem. Have a nice day. Those lines were perfected by checkout chicks, and I ought to know. I deserve better from you, Matt. Tell me you'll miss me, or give me the rote, ''Love you, Sall''.'

'Love you. I'll miss you, kiddo.' He opened the door. 'Have a good Christmas.'

'I hate Christmas, and I hate you. What have I got of you, Matt? Nothing. She's got it all, and I hate her.'

'Me too, but we've got this room. We've got each other in our cardboard paradise. What more have we ever wanted?'

'More than a couple of hours a week on this bed. I want to get dressed up and go to parties with you, sit in dark pubs, walk down the street holding your hand.'

He stood at the door, his face ungiving, and she thought of Ross's face, an open book. She couldn't read this one. Expensive book, Matt, deep, too heavy for a reader of popular fiction.

'Go then. Leave your money beside the bed, because that's all I am to you.'

He took a two-dollar coin from his pocket and tossed it at her. She caught it.

'I've got no change on me, smartarse.'

'Credit it to my account.' She tossed it at his head, and got him too, on the shoulder. He picked up the coin, pocketed it. 'At this rate, you'll never make enough to retire on, Sall. I suggest you get yourself a financial adviser.' And he left her, left her to drive home to Hallam, to a Christmas tree with lights, and Christmas dinner with the parents. He left her for that bitch he'd take to his office party. Left her, and she packed her case and counted her money for Lakeside.

a naked chicken

Sue was going home for Christmas dinner, under sufferance; her grandfather would be there. 'Chauvinistic old fuck, he needs an injection of lead,' she said.

'You're lucky to have a family.'

'Meet them and still say that. The old sod is a Collins Street specialist and he thinks I should be sterilised.'

Her tribe of brothers and sisters would be there, all older, all professionals, teachers, one a doctor. They'd have turkey and pea-green hair with red spikes, matching red and green beads on a nose ring.

'Why do you do it?' Sally asked, flicking the nose ring.

Sue smiled her twisted grin. 'To nark the old fucks. I voted Labor too, helped oust poor old Jeff. I need putting down.'

Sue's father wanted to pay out her mortgage; in return, all she had to do was go back to uni. Sue wanted to do law, but she wouldn't give in, let her father win.

The more kids had, the more they rebelled; give them nothing and they strived all their lives to gain parental approval. Sally had spent two hours and sixty-five dollars buying her mother a new dress to wear on Christmas Day. Sue was doing her mother a favour by turning up for Christmas dinner, her only presents dangling from her ears.

'Want to come with me? Eat turkey and be my buffer zone?'

'I wish I could.'

'Say that after two hours of them. Ten minutes of their pompous crap and I'm puking.'

A lifetime search for approval landed Sally in Lakeside, alone in a motel room at noon on Christmas Eve; she was weighing a large frozen chicken in her hand.

Christmas was about relatives. Between them, Sally and Ross couldn't raise many. He had cousins in Tasmania. They sent cards. For the past fifteen years Sally and her mother had eaten Christmas dinner at the farm, and tomorrow would be no different. Ross had called last night.

'Christ. We're family, love. We can still eat Christmas dinner together, can't we?' he'd said, his voice not so certain.

What could she say? I've made a booking for two at the motel? Matt might drive up for a night, or an hour? When she'd booked the motel unit she'd convinced herself that Matt would give her one day out of his Christmas.

'Thanks, Ross,' she'd said. 'I'll supply the chicken. You supply the wine, and plenty of it. Mummy is coming out for the day.' She didn't ask him if it was okay to bring her along.

'I'll get some port,' he'd said.

So there she was in a classy room with no view; but it was big and it had heavy drapes and a well-stocked bar fridge, complete with a pricey list for tourists.

'And a naked chicken,' she said. She'd bought it this morning from the supermarket freezer. A quick wrap in the motel-supplied newspaper, into a plastic bag and she carried it out to the car, where she tossed it into the boot beside a foil-wrapped supermarket Christmas pudding. She'd made her own pudding last year.

A sigh too deep as she picked up a parcel wrapped in red and gold. She'd bought Matt a black silk dressing gown, visualising him wearing it in their future mansion. What future? But that was all she had to hold on to today, so she clung to it. He might drive up for a night. Half of her life had been spent pretending that things might get better. She was still good at it.

A second parcel, smaller but wrapped in the same red and gold paper, she balanced on her palm. A shirt for Ross, bought in a hurry yesterday at Target. Sad, really. It had cost a third of what she'd paid for Matt's dressing gown, but Ross would accept it gladly, wear it proudly.

He was like a big kid with presents. She'd always bought him heaps, just rubbishy things. Last year she'd bought him duelling water pistols and they'd spent the day chasing each other around the farm, guns blazing, dogs barking, spinster chickens looking on, cluck-clucking their disapproval while Mummy had disapproved from the lounge room, pursed lips tut-tutting. A fun day. Only one year ago, but a hundred light-years away.

She reached for the third parcel, her mother's dress, then the car boot slammed. She returned to her room, aware that she would have to buy something else for Ross, something silly. She'd have to make it a good day for him; he'd probably refused half a dozen invitations to Christmas dinner.

Shopping was therapy, a place to go when there was no place to go. The main street a solid wall of cars at midday, she turned down a side street and into the supermarket car park, cruising until she caught the eye of a woman pushing her trolley out of the building. She tracked her to her bay, stopping behind her while the trolley was unloaded, slowly.

Time. So much time in the world for some people. Motor idling, blinker blinking, she waited, frustrating other drivers eager to get by, to get home to their Christmas trees. She didn't have one.

'Merry Christmas,' she said. 'Merry Christmas.' She waved.

Some returned her wave. Many had heard about the wedding, and the hair appointment she hadn't kept, and the beautician who had come to the Davis house to do the make-up. Sally had applied her own lipstick smile that day. She didn't belong in Lakeside, not any more. Only Mummy kept pulling her back.

The supermarket car park was for supermarket shoppers. It said so on the sign, but she wandered through the store and back to the main street where she bought a giant rainbow lollipop. Ross would like that. Out front of the menswear shop she saw a pair of Father Christmas pyjamas, complete with white fur trim. Couldn't buy him pyjamas. He'd think it was all on again.

The shops were busy, shopkeepers rubbing their hands in glee. Christmas loosened the purse strings, buyers became desperate. So many faces wore that anything-will-do-him expression, but anything wouldn't do for Ross. For an hour she wandered and browsed, picking up, putting down, until she found a pregnant-cow jug at the craft shop. It looked like Ross's house cow, a weighty udder, its tail the handle, its snout to pour the cream.

Buying presents had always been the best part of Christmas. It was making her feel a bit Christmassy – being in the crush, queuing with the great human horde.

'Merry Christmas,' the checkout girl muttered. 'Merry Christmas.' Like counting sheep as shoppers pushed through the gate, their tired bleating little lambs at their sides.

'Merry Christmas, Jen.' She'd known Jen Larkin since school. Jen, sex mad.

The woman looked up, recognising her. She grinned. 'Bugger Christmas, Sall. Roll on 5.30. And what are you doing back here? I thought you'd escaped.'

'They caught me at the pass and brought me back in chains.' Sally took a hundred-dollar note from her purse, then put it back and handed over her Visa card.

It was nearly three o'clock when she drove out to the farm to face Ross, to get that over with. She placed her presents beneath his lopsided tree, beside the scattering of presents already there, and she saw her name on one. With a smile, she picked it up, felt it.

Ross snatched it, held it high. 'No peeking, you cheat,' he said.

Cheat hurt. It killed her cheeky mood. Soon after, she left him to return to her unit, the naked chicken forgotten in her boot. It thawed for half an hour in the hospital car park while she sat at her mother's side and spoke of the morrow.

'I'll pick you up at ten. I'm cooking dinner out at the farm.'

'*I* won't be going out to the farm.'

'Why not?' The petulant mouth remained pursed. 'We don't have to stay there all day, Mummy.'

'I thought we were going to the motel for lunch.'

'It will be more Christmassy at the farm and the food will be better.'

'Then I won't spoil your Christmassy day. I'll stay here.'

'You'll spoil my day if you don't come, and you'll spoil Ross's day too. I thought you might spend the night at the motel with me. I've got a spare bed. It would be like old times.' Her mother's expression was pained. 'It will do you good to get out of this place.'

'Do me good? One night with my daughter, then nothing, would do me good?' Her mother lay back on the pillow and closed her eyes.

'Don't lie down. Come for a walk with me in the garden. It looks beautiful.'

'Sleep is beautiful.'

'Not at this time of day.' Sally reached for a box of chocolates someone had left on the locker. 'Who has been visiting you?'

'Mrs Jenner brought them. She knows I can't eat chocolate.'

'I haven't seen her in months. How does she look?' A chocolate in her mouth, she unwrapped a second.

Glenda ignored the question. 'I hope you're happy with your new man,' she said.

Two could play at that game. Sucking chocolate, Sally picked up two pieces of what had been a Christmas card. 'Didn't like the picture, or the message?'

'Throw it in the rubbish.'

Tiny writing. *Glenda*. Ripped at the point. Then *forg* – but her mother slapped at the pieces, her eyes filled with their old loathing. 'How dare he. How dare he.'

Sally knew that tone. 'Your father?' She was on her feet, backing away, two small pieces of card still in her hand.

'Throw that filth in the rubbish.'

'You said you never heard from him.'

'He drove my mother to her death then he left us for that slut. He took everything of value, and left Bernice and me to live or die. He didn't care about us any more than he cared about our mother. How dare he send me a Christmas card? How dare he.'

'But you always said –' Sally stared at the segments of card. Tiny handwriting. *love t* – 'You said you never heard from him, that –'

'I saw my mother driven to suicide by his sluts. You understand nothing!' Glenda was screaming now, building up to a throwing attack, but not a lot of ammunition here. Only a glass and a water jug. The box of chocolates.

Sally moved them out of danger. 'Settle down, Mummy. That's enough!' She dropped the scraps of card into the bin. 'See, it's all gone. Finished. Now settle down.'

Small teeth clenched, the woman panted and lay back on her pillow.

Sally turned to the window, then back to the rubbish bin. *Sa – er la th*. 'They're forecasting a nice day for tomorrow.' Good old weather, always a safe topic – but not today.

'And I'll spend it alone. As I've spent every day alone since my boys died.'

'Don't do this. Not today. Please, Mummy.'

'If you hadn't been climbing around in the car that night then they'd all be here with me today.'

'Oh, yeah. And a very merry Christmas to you too.'

'You killed them.' Cutting little eyes, trying to draw blood. 'You can't stand the truth, can you? The truth still hurts, doesn't it?'

'Hurts like hell, so go tell it to the fucking kangaroo, Mummy.' She ran from the ward and she and her naked chicken returned to the motel car park to drip a while in the last of the heat.

Ross came by at eight. She didn't want to go with him for drinks at Greg and Deb's flat, but he talked her around. She painted on a lipstick smile and left the chicken to drip alone in the motel car park.

There was a mob at the party, a happy, laughing mob Sally was no longer a part of. She'd been culled from the herd. She saw the looks, the words spoken behind hands. The expression on Deb's face when she'd walked into the kitchen and caught her talking to Karen Matthews.

'I don't know how she's game to show her face here,' Karen said.

'She's making a prize fool of Ross. I know that much, ' Deb replied. 'I wish he'd wake up to himself and tell her where to go.'

Sally wanted to crawl into a corner and cry, but she wouldn't let them see her cry. Her lipstick smiled. Big smile. Wide party smile. They'd both blushed. Deb pinkly, Karen puce. She and Pimples might make a good pair, both gangly six-footers and great blushers. The image helped keep her smile fixed for fifteen minutes but by 9.30 the lipstick had worn away and she knew she had to get away, go back to the hospital and get that rubbish bin, or its contents.

'Want the last spring roll, Sall?'

'No thanks, Deb.' Probably laced with poison.

'More wine, Sall?'

'Yes thanks, Greg.' It came out of a cask. Probably safe.

Coming here tonight had been a mistake. Sitting at Ross's side was a mistake. She didn't belong at his side any more and everyone knew it. Every time she lifted her head she caught Karen Matthews staring at her – or Ross.

Noise. Chatter, music and laughter and not enough air in this room. She had to move. Get outside that door, get away from Ross and his arm behind her chair. Get away to free air. Breathe.

'I'll take Mummy's dress around to the hospital. I meant to leave it with her this afternoon,' she said, standing abruptly, spilling her wine onto her jeans, her chair, Deb's carpet. Only white wine.

'She'll be asleep.'

'Then she'll think Santa came while she was sleeping.' She picked up her bag. 'We'll see you around ten.' He stood, wanting to go with her. 'Stay,' she said. 'Stay. It's not far.'

Everyone waved, said their goodbyes, but when her back was to them she felt their accusation hit her between her shoulder blades. She turned at the door, in time to catch the lead bullets shot from Karen Matthews' eyes.

Deb lifted her drink. Greg called, 'Merry Christmas.'

'Merry Christmas all,' she said. 'Watch out for the booze bus.'

And she was away and walking. A strange night. Still. The century was old, barely breathing. You could hear its sigh of relief as a breeze brushed the grass on a vacant lot, sweeping up the last of its memories. The party was almost over. Soon it could go home.

All of the little houses. All of the little homes. All of the little parties. All of the mummies and the daddies and the little girls tucked into their safe beds. They'd grow up in the year 2000. Wouldn't remember the 1900s, but her generation would remain trapped in it, probably call it the good old days.

She stopped at the motel to pick up her mother's gift, then ran off again. Running was good, the sound of her sneakers on cement, leaving the last of Lakeside's Sally De Rooze behind.

Bleak place. Stale, sterile place of white light and shiny floors and Mummy. No tears, though. Her mother was sleeping like a baby.

She glanced at the rubbish bin. Empty. On her knees she searched the floor for just one scrap of that Christmas card. No scraps. Her grandfather was lost again.

Two of a kind, Mummy always said. Selfish. They ran away from her in search of something better. Sally had no memory of her grandfather, unsighted in twenty-four years. Through those years, her mother had named him a womaniser, thief, drunk, deviant. She'd come home from the psychiatric hospital ten years ago claiming he'd sexually abused both her and Bernice. Maybe he had, but Sally could remember her Aunty Bernice. She'd been taller than Mummy, and always laughing. She'd kept in contact with her father. He'd been at her funeral.

Sally could remember that day. She and Shane had spent the funeral afternoon with Raelene and Mrs Mason. Mummy had come home crying, then the next thing she was at the front door screaming at someone.

Through the window Sally had seen a man walk away, seen his hand raised in a half-wave, seen him get into a car. Back then she hadn't known who her mother had screamed at. Now she knew it must have been her grandfather.

'Grandpa?' she whispered, testing the word. 'Grandma and Papa,' she whispered. That word felt right somehow. Memory and imagination mingling, she thought of a car, and a red and white checked cloth on the grass. But she shook her head, shrugging off the fantasy.

Christmas cards were easy enough to buy, words easy to write, but words on paper didn't mean a thing. Facing people was the hard bit, being kicked in the teeth and coming back for more was the hard bit. If he wanted to prove that he cared, then let him come here, face her and let them work it out, and the sooner the better.

She kissed the sleeping woman's brow. Safe to kiss her, safe to smell the strange lost scent of her hair, safe with that venomous tongue locked away. Safe even to whisper. 'I care about you, Mummy. You're all I've got, and I'm all you've got.' She pressed on twin tears with her index fingers, striving to push them back when they threatened, catch them before they escaped.

'Haven't you got a party to go to?' A young sister had crept in on her rubber-soled shoes.

'Haven't you?' Sally was slow to turn.

'I drew the short straw. Go home and get some sleep, and half your luck. By the time I get home my kids will be up riding their bikes around the lounge room.'

Sally knew the face of this one but not the name. 'How many kids?'

'Three – and three bikes.' Quiet voices in this room full up with sleep. 'It's not much use waiting for her to wake. She had her pills not long before you came. She'll sleep until around two.'

'Did she say anything about going out for dinner tomorrow?'

'Not to me. She was full of life tonight, though. We had old Joe Campbell's group come through singing carols. She was singing with them and she's really good.'

'Yeah. She used to sing professionally.'

'I believe it.'

'When I was a little kid.'

'Old Joe and his ladies tour around entertaining in retirement homes. She ought to join them. Oh, well. I'd better keep moving.' So young, so capable, her family waiting for her at home when her shift was over.

Sally watched her move about the other beds, envying her. She stood, stretched, then searched for a pen in the bottomless pit of her handbag. 'Could I borrow your pen for a second?' she said. The sister waited while Sally wrote the motel's number on a giant Christmas card taped to the gift-wrapped frock.

Hope it fits. Give me a call if you wake early. Lots of love, Sally Santa.

'It's a dress for tomorrow. If she wants to get out early, I'm at the motel around the corner,' she said, handing back the pen. Then she left.

Late now. Christmas parties all over town. Noisy now. Alcohol kicking in. Back at the motel she transferred the chicken from boot to fridge, then she read for a while, but tonight the novel couldn't carry her away. Things would be okay in the morning. She'd watch what she said. She'd get the chicken on and they'd open a bottle of champagne. Champagne would help. Ross had something for her mother. She'd seen it under the tree. Probably slippers. It would be okay. Plenty of champagne and port.

Distant drumming of music. Bar fridge rattling every time the motor started up, and it was working overtime tonight. At twelve she decided to relieve it by emptying a small bottle of whisky into a glass and adding half a can of Coke. She drank it down fast with two Panadols. Good medicine. At twelve-thirty she hit the fridge again, opening the rum this time and pouring it into the half-full can of Coke. It was enough. Her book down, she turned off the light.

santa dressed in black

She was dead asleep, flat out on her back, dreaming deep dreams, when Father Christmas made his surprise call to her motel room near dawn.

The ringing entered into a dream; it became the doorbell of the redbrick house in Ballarat. Old Papa had come calling this Christmas morning and his arms were full of presents, but he looked like old coot Ron and his zip was open.

She was on her feet in a room as black as pitch. Didn't know where she was, or how to find the front door to stop the doorbell's ring. And why should she open the door, anyway? She couldn't stand the miserable old coot. Didn't trust him either.

But it wasn't the doorbell. It was the phone. It was the phone, and she couldn't find it in the dark. Couldn't find a light switch. Where the hell was it? Where was she? She found the curtains and followed them to the bench, bruising her toe on the leg of a chair but eventually feeling out the noise, stilling that ring.

'Sally De Rooze speaking,' she said.

Poor Sally De Rooze.

Shivering cold in a room that was warm. Teeth chattering cold, her blood turning to ice before the voice on the end of the line had said all of its words. She sat there, in the black, on the edge of the bed, the phone gripped in her hand. She sat there trying to separate dream from reality.

Then she stood, found the door, found the light and she called Ross, because she didn't know what else to do.

'She's done it, Ross. She's done it this time.' That was all she said. And such a stupid thing to say, but Ross knew her voice and he knew her mother, so he understood, so it hadn't been such a stupid thing to say after all.

'Hold on, love. I'm on my way.'

She'd gone to sleep in her jeans and T-shirt. Now she searched the floor for her sneakers. Couldn't find one. Found it beneath the bed. She pulled on socks and shoes, grabbed for her bag and motel key, and drove alone through a misty grey world as the stars started to fade.

In the hospital room she held the slim hand and said, 'I'm sorry, Mummy.' She brushed back the frizzy hair and she kissed the brow and the hand, but Glenda Jean De Rooze, forty-nine-year-old mother of Sally, had left.

The young nursing sister had an arm around Sally's shoulder. Sleiman and the new doctor were at her side. And she didn't know why, until the hand she held grew cool then cold.

She dropped it, and the legs of her chair squealed as she sprang to her feet.

'I'm sorry, Mummy,' she said. 'I'm sorry, Mummy.'

Ross rushed in, his eyes bleary with sleep half-slept. Just get there. Get to Sally. The sister knew him, nodded to him, stepped away from Sally.

'I'm sorry, Mummy.'

Her mother was wearing the same faded hospital gown. She was in the same bed. The same hair was on the same pillow. The Christmas present was where Sally had left it. The card was there, the chocolates there. Just the same.

'I'm sorry, Mummy.'

Ross's arms were around her. He was leading her away from the bed but she kept looking back, expecting something more. Surely God must smite her dead too. There could not be life after Mummy.

But her legs were walking her away and the toe she'd stubbed on the chair was throbbing.

Go tell that to the fucking kangaroo, Mummy.

She tried to pull back, to walk back. Ross wouldn't let her.

'I'm sorry, Mummy.'

And she was in the walkway and Sleiman was talking. Ross was talking. They were all talking, looking at Sally. She was looking at them too, but not hearing. Just shivering, huge shuddering shivers.

Taken a dip in the lake mid-winter? Been skinny-dipping off the Sleimans' pier?

Did that a few times.

She stared at the beaky mouth, couldn't hear its words, but she knew she wasn't supposed to think about skinny-dipping off his pier. She was supposed to die with Mummy. She'd killed her – or made her do it.

Go tell it to the fucking kangaroo, Mummy. That's what she'd said. She could collapse at least. Or bawl. Or something. Do something.

Ross walked her through to the new building, where she'd walked alone so many times before. Past the desk. She almost waved a hand to a shocked familiar face, but she caught that wave, stopped it just in time.

Then outside. She was still walking away from Mummy. Right away now. Each step was taking her further and further away, out into the air and into that perfect split second when night ended and day began. She looked up at the sky. Birds whistling, warbling, looking for the early worm, her shoes crunching gravel as they walked away from Mummy.

The scent of the garden was strong, and so sweet. No daytime odours to mask it. She breathed in sweet and wondered at the flower. Her footsteps slowed as her eyes searched the dark garden, but Ross drew her forward to his ute.

It looked too clean, shiny white beneath the lights. It was never clean because he never washed it. She turned, looked at her lonely little car parked in a dark corner where the dawn light had not yet reached, and she started towards it, started feeling for her keys. The Christmas pudding was still in the boot. Well-travelled, that one. Matt's black silk dressing gown growing cold there. Ross held her back from it. He opened his passenger-side door, so she climbed in. He fastened her seatbelt while she looked past him to the sky.

Blush of a lilac dawn behind the eastern hills, small rivers of gold. She almost commented on the sunrise, but she caught herself in time. This was the wrong time for chatter. Her teeth didn't know it. They were chattering. Had to stop them or she'd break her front filling again. Have to get that one capped one day when she could afford it. She placed a thumb in her mouth, cushioning her chattering teeth. They bit into her thumb.

No traffic on the road. Old Santa had done his job and gone back to the North Pole with his reindeer.

Giddup, Rudolf. Stretch those legs, Prancer. Run like the wind, Dancer.

Go tell it to the fucking kangaroo, Mummy.

Silent dawn. No more jingle bells. No more parties. Just the whispering road noise of a lonely farm ute driving through the dawn streets of Lakeside. Wheels made a different sound in the city. Never silent in the city. Not true silence.

Past the motel. Past that wide empty bed. She wanted to crawl under a bed and hide; that's what she'd always done when Mummy did the *killed'em* song and dance. Hid. But you couldn't get under modern beds, couldn't get anything under them. Except shoes. Shoes got lost under them. And socks. She used to be able to get under beds. So did Mummy.

It wouldn't be the right thing to do, though, to crawl under a bed and hide. Not after phoning Ross, waking him up. She had to go back to the farm with him. Shouldn't have woken him.

Go tell it to the fucking kangaroo, Mummy.

Not the correct thing to say. Shouldn't have said that. Have to do the correct, the Bertram, thing.

I could have saved seventy-five dollars on that motel bed. I could have saved sixty-five dollars on Mummy's dress. Have to take it back and get a refund.

Not correct Bertram thinking. Mustn't think those things.

Why not? As Mummy had always said, funerals cost money.

She shook her head, shook it hard. I've gone crazy, she thought. Not my fault, though. It's genetic.

And it's not my fault. It isn't. She accused me of killing everyone, and I replied, *Go tell it to the fucking kangaroo, Mummy.* If I delete one word from that sentence then it becomes blameless. I becomc blameless.

Go tell it to the kangaroo, Mummy.

Everyone knows kangaroos are always into it, a joey in the pouch, one in the womb, and one hopping by its mother's side. They breed like rabbits.

They were at the farm and she hadn't seen the road. Ross helped her down from the ute and she walked into his kitchen, her thumb in her mouth, tremors travelling through her. She stood before the stove, watching Ross open the flue, poke in two chunks of wood. The kettle began to sing.

Old black kettle. Mrs Bertram's kettle. Cast iron. Big, heavy, but always boiling. Sally listened to the water's gentle song and stared at the kettle's lid until it huffed, puffed. Ross moved it to the side, then he removed her thumb from between her teeth, held her hand, held her captive against him. She shook. Shook him too, and she didn't want to shake him up any more.

He tried to talk to her but his words weren't going in. Head too busy to listen. He pulled a chair to the fire and he sat her on it, drew a second chair close. Her thumb had returned to her mouth. Again he took the hand, the thumb wet. He found her other hand. She let him hold them. His hands were warm. She looked at him, knowing she was supposed to say something, like, it was too sudden, Ross.

But it wasn't sudden. Not really. Mummy had been practising for the main event for twenty years.

Okay then, she'd say, it's not fair. That was normal. A nice normal thing to say.

But life wasn't a game of cricket with umpires in white calling 'no ball'. It wasn't like that. Never had been.

So what was there to say?

Nothing acceptable. Not one word found in her mind was acceptable, but there was a great heavy load of words there, in her throat too, in her chest. Couldn't let them get out. Cast in iron, those words. She had to breathe carefully under them, breathe silently around them, swallow them down or she'd vomit them up all over the floor and mortally wound Ross with the shrapnel of regurgitated words.

She shook her head, withdrew one hand. Movement. Conscious movement was good. She scratched at her head and there was pleasure in that scratch, then she dragged her chair closer to the stove, seeking distance from him. Space. She needed space.

Perhaps he understood. He walked into his room; when he returned he draped her old pink parka around her shoulders, then lit two cigarettes, offered her one.

Good. At least they were doing something. She watched the smoke from the two cigarettes join and spiral up the chimney with the kettle's steam.

A strange day, and long – the longest day of her life. She had sat smoking by the fire in the morning, sat smoking in the lounge room through the afternoon, sat smoking on the back verandah in the evening. Waiting, waiting for the sun to go down.

It had almost given up its fight. The stars would be gathering, waiting in the wings for their time to shine.

She was smoking in the back yard now, and looking at the white clouds to the west that altered as she stared. White swan's-down clouds became the pink of a flock of galahs, a galah-feather quilt, waiting to put the weary sun to bed. But the sun never went down easily on Ross's land. He owned a hill, thus owned the sun for longer than those in the valley. Like an obstreperous child tonight, it clung to the distant treetops, painting them red with its own blood while it bruised, abused the western sky. Not the red of Mrs Bertram's sunset. Mummy's was deep purple, edged in yellow with streaks of blood. A bruise on the landscape.

Then it was gone.

One by one the shy stars peeped out, twinkling, fading, returning, until it was like those other nights when she'd sat on Raelene's garage roof and watched the million candles glowing up there. From Raelene's roof she'd seen the big star that was Daddy and the three small stars, even the tiny twinkle she had named Teddy's star. She'd sat up there for hours at night, singing sad songs to Daddy star, closer to him on that roof, away from Mummy on that roof.

She had known for certain that he was up there with the boys, lighting up heaven and looking down at her, watching over her. Mummy could make up songs, so Sally had made her own special song for Daddy and the boys.

The angels needed new stars for God's heaven
And they slid down the moonbeams that shine
To take my baby brothers and take Shane from my mother
And steal that precious Daddy of mine.

The sky was so clear tonight, Mummy would find them. She'd find them.

She scanned the sky, her head turning quickly as a tear escaped. One lone tear. It wasn't for Mummy, it wasn't, but it blurred the landscape. She walked forward through the blurred world to the high paddock, where she climbed through the fence. Head back, she searched the west until she found her familiar family cluster. No new star had joined them but in Lakeside it wasn't too hard to find a bright star close by, moving in on the merry group to murder their shine.

'Close your eyes, Daddy, and she won't see you,' she screamed. 'Hide behind the clouds tonight, Daddy, and she won't find you. Stay away from her, Daddy, or she'll kill your light.'

lemons and tears

From the back door Ross listened. She'd been yelling about something, now she was singing. He'd expected tears. He could have handled her tears.

He'd never been much into music, or her sort of music, but it was her voice that was breaking his heart – like a cry coming from some lost place within her.

Tears burned behind his eyes. He lifted his chin, defying them to fall. He loved her. He'd always love her. Wedding ring or not, she was his wife. He could barely remember what life had been like before Sally. Always here, always by his side. Little Sally in the paddock chasing sheep. Little Sally running like the wind across the bull paddock, her blond hair flying, the bull behind, the dogs barking.

He walked deeper into the yard, listening.

Christ forgive him, but he was glad her mother had gone. Sleiman was worried. They'd be doing an autopsy.

'Fool of a woman. Spent her life crying wolf. No-one took any notice of her complaints,' he muttered as a tear rolled free. He picked a lemon and bit hard into the rind, an old trick he'd learned at twelve when his father died and he'd had to become the man of the house in a hurry. All day he'd been thinking about his mother, and his father.

The lemon in his hand, he walked deeper into the yard until he sighted the tiny figure walking across the top paddock. So small, like a little kid wandering in the gloom, trying to climb to the top of the hill and run like hell down the other side.

'Jesus,' he said. 'Don't let her get away from me.'

As if he had some business there, he walked purposely to the tractor shed where he stood in the shadows, listening to her song. He couldn't leave her tonight.

He wished she'd howled it out then gone to sleep. Sleiman had said to give him a call if he was needed. Maybe he ought to ring him. Or maybe he'd just watch her and wait it out. He knew her black moods, and he was afraid of them. That was the truth and there was no getting away from the truth.

Four more days to get through until the funeral. He'd tried to get it done sooner, but autopsies and opening up graves took time. His own parents were buried side by side, and what was wrong with side by side? No good for Sally to have her father's grave disturbed. How was she going to handle it? How was she going to handle seeing her brothers' grave again?

And what a time to die. They'd lost Christmas Day. The presents were like some sort of snide joke. And the tree had been a mistake. Christmas trees were for kids and he didn't have any.

His mother had loved Christmas. They'd always had a tree and she'd spent hours decorating it. She should have lived forever. Life is for the living, she had always said. Worrying about what is going to kill you will wipe you out faster than any little surprise fate has got in store for you. It sure had a surprise written in for her, and tonight was bringing it all home again too.

'Bloody top-heavy tractor,' he said. 'Why didn't she leave that paddock for me? I told her it was too steep, to leave it for me.'

Maybe half the tears leaking down his face tonight were for his mother. The other half were probably for himself. He didn't know what he'd done wrong or what he hadn't done right, but he sure as hell had done or not done something.

Things went on in Sally's head that he'd never understood. It was like she was trying to think too far ahead, like she was trying to see tomorrow before it got to today, so she could recognise the problems in advance and fix them before they happened.

These last months there'd been nothing between them, and a man got used to female company. He'd found himself looking around, and he didn't want to look around. Karen Matthews and her lemon meringue pies were even starting to look okay. Talking to her on the phone today had been a relief. And Deb. She'd wanted to come around, but he'd put her off until tomorrow.

Sally hadn't called anyone. Who was the bloke she was supposed to have in Melbourne? Where was the useless bastard now? Whoever he was, whatever he was – if he was – he wasn't doing her any good.

I wonder if she's got his phone number in her handbag. I'll have a look in her bag and give the bastard a call, get him up here where he ought to be, he thought, and he bit deep into the lemon, his eyes still following the small figure. Just a dark silhouette against the backdrop of his land. Little girl lost.

She belonged here, where he could look after her. She needed looking after. Not that what he felt for her had ever been what you might call protective love, brotherly love. Even when she was fourteen, a wild little bugger with a bugger of a mouth on her, he'd loved her.

I should have married her when she was eighteen. Should have hid her pills and got her pregnant. That's what I should have done, he thought.

She was still singing, still belting out that sobbing rhythm. He couldn't hear the words. His mother had said once that there was something in Sally's voice that raised goosebumps on her soul.

He'd never been much into souls but her song was raising goosebumps on his arms tonight. He bit into his lemon and sniffed.

Near ten she returned to the house. He heard her turn on the television, and he looked through the window, watching her, wanting to hold her and howl. So little of her, she looked like a porcelain doll tossed onto the couch, all played out.

That city bastard and her mother have sucked the life out of her, he thought. This is going to finish her off. Two tears tumbled, and he swiped at his tears with a lemon-juice hand, then rubbed them with his shirt-tail.

Had he possessed the gift of words, he might think, 'ethereal', only on loan to me and Lakeside, but he wasn't much of a hand with words, so he stood at the window loving her, wanting her safe in his bed, but knowing now that he might just as well try to trap the north wind in a Foster's stubby.

In the kitchen, a silent search amid the chaos of her shoulder bag could not unearth a name or phone number.

'Useless bastard,' he muttered as he walked outside to tie up the dogs. They were pleased to go to bed, and he wanted his. He crept to the lounge room door, peeped in, hoping to see her asleep on the couch. She was sitting there, her elbow on the arm of the couch, a cigarette in her hand, her eyes following the flashing of the television screen.

Nothing he could say. Nothing he could do. He went to bed. His door was open. His eyes were open and all night the television played on.

dry eyes

The rain had come in the night, and this morning the sky looked grim. Sally made coffee, emptied the ashtrays into the stove, moving silently, pleased that the house was still her own. It was rare for Ross to sleep past 6.30 and the hands of the clock now pointed to 7.45.

No more hospital. She didn't ever have to go back there. Not today. Not tomorrow. Not ever. Nothing to do – not like when Mrs Bertram had died and left her slippers where she'd last kicked them off, just inside the bedroom door, left her make-up in the bathroom, her book propped open beside her bed.

If Mummy had died back in September, I might have cried, she thought as she eased the firebox open, added wood, then eased it shut. I could have gone to the flat and touched her frocks, picked up her old shoes. Nothing left to do. No more tears to cry.

Only a few frocks hanging in the sleep-out wardrobe; and the shoes.

She took her coffee to the sleep-out and she picked up the shoes, rolled them in the frocks and carried them to the kitchen wastebin, forcing them in. Forcing them down.

Rusty barked, and Fred, the kelpie, joined in. Ross always let the dogs off the chain as soon as he was up and about, and they knew that someone was about. She crept from the back door, listening to the squeal as she eased it open, to the sigh as she closed it silently behind her, then carefully dodging mud and puddles, she walked down to the dogs.

They knew she wasn't their top dog, but they wagged their tails and cut their barking to growling yelps. She unclipped chains, patted heads and they bounded behind her to the back door, tails wagging expectantly.

There was a bag of dog chow in the laundry. She poured a measure into their bowls, which they eyed suspiciously before wolfing.

'Too much?' she said. 'Or too little?' Rusty shook his head, so she topped up their bowls and returned the bag to the laundry. Then across the mud to the tin shed, where she stood looking at the pile of junk in the corner while the dogs checked it out for mouse invasion.

It was all hers now, her own lovely big pile of unlovely junk. All hers to haul around the country on her back.

'Worthless junk.' She kicked the gruesome green lounge suite. The old chest of drawers she smoothed with her palm before sliding a drawer open. Empty. Daddy had bought it second- or third-hand. He'd painted it white to match her bed. She looked at the fridge. Old, but still going strong – or it had been in September. Did fridges die from lack of use? But it had never become accustomed to working overtime. She touched its white enamel. It felt gritty, and she wiped her hand on her jeans. She'd been wearing the same clothes since she left Melbourne. They probably stank. She smelt her armpits. A bit sweaty, but no-one had their head under her arm.

She looked for the box containing Grandma's china. It had no value either – just beautiful junk, but this morning Sally needed to touch beautiful, the only beautiful she'd ever had in her unbeautiful life.

The box had been marked. They'd all been marked. On the side of the top carton it was printed in green. GOOSE GIRL. Up on the old laminex table, she reached across and hauled the china down. Heavy, it almost toppled her, but she got it to the floor intact and she squatted over it, searching out the china goose girl, feeling the shapes beneath the newspaper, yawning and wanting to lie down, put her head on the box and sleep.

Not brave enough to sleep, not yet, she took a deep breath, shaking off drowsy as she continued feeling the newspaper parcels until she identified the shape of the arm and the hat and the beak. She yawned, shrugged her shoulders and unwrapped the newspaper, smiling as she handled the goose girl, touched the goose. She felt out the china lady with the parasol, the line of glue beneath her chin. Poor lady, murdered by the furniture movers. Her hand identified the china man; he and the parasol lady were a matching pair. The two unwrapped, she held them side by side, as they had stood side by side for fifty-odd years. She made them kiss, or butt heads.

'How did you do it, Glenda?' she said.

'That's for me to know and the pathologist to find out, Bren.'

The game stopped abruptly.

They needed a bath, both of them, dust and newsprint stained their faces. Have to give them a bath in dishwashing detergent, a toothbrush to get into the crevices. But not today. She wrapped them up in their newspaper and packed them in the carton, china Mummy on top. They wouldn't get up to any games, not with all of those petticoats, and the newspaper. How had they ever got together to breed their wild goose girl?

She smiled then, thinking of that first time the china was packed into cardboard boxes. Her mother must have been young then. Twenty-eight. She couldn't remember the twenty-eight-year-old face. Just the weeping. She could remember that. And the screaming. She'd never forget that. They had no money to buy tombstones for their dead, Mummy had said, so they had to sell the house. Give it to Carol Rigg.

Dead people didn't need tombstones, but Sally had needed that house and her school and Raelene. She had needed her bedroom and her swing-set and the passionfruit vines. And Mummy could still get bookings. The telephone never stopped ringing for Glenda Jean, because the terrible news had got in all the papers and the newspapers called Mummy a great talent.

Raelene's mother and father had come in one night to calm Mummy down. They knew all about insurance. Raelene's father had worked for AMP, and he said how it would be a pity to lose the house. He said that if Mummy went to the bank and explained her situation, he was sure that they'd wait for their money until the insurance came.

Please, Mummy. I want to stay in our house.

Too many memories, my precious girl.

'Precious girl, bullshit! I was Daddy's girl. Always. I followed him around like a shadow. And you hated it.' She stood in the shed but she wasn't seeing the shed, she was seeing the past, remembering, remembering it all.

Exhaustion had taken the edge off old hurt, allowing her to wander the painful places with dry eyes. A cleansing place to wander in the early morning, rain thundering down on a low tin roof. She stayed in that place too long, stayed there until the dogs barked, lifted their ears, until Rusty nudged her knee, and yelped: We're off. Top dog's up.

Almost nine o'clock. Ross never slept this late – probably would have slept later if the phone hadn't called him from his bed. He was sitting in the lounge room in his pyjamas, speaking on the cordless phone.

He'd made the calls yesterday. Mrs Jenner, Mrs Hudson, Deb and Karen. Gina. Not too many. Sally stood in the passage trying to decipher this morning's one-sided conversation.

Ross knew she was out there. He lowered his voice, trying to guard his words, but he had to repeat them. 'With her husband. Yes. The same grave. In the same grave. Yeah. That's what she said. Yes.'

She fought a fresh packet of cigarettes open, lit one. Smoke sucked in. Smoke blown out. Orange embers and grey ash circling as they crept up the white cylinder. She walked into the kitchen.

She felt so calm this morning, calm in a way she had never felt calm before. She'd been worried about Christmas Day and what she was going to do if her mother had refused to leave the hospital. Always and forever it had been, what am I going to do? How am I going to fix it?

No more fixing.

She shouldn't be feeling like this, thinking like this. She should be howling, letting Ross and Deb comfort her. Should be.

He completed his phone call. The receiver was in the kitchen and she heard the click-click of disconnection, that click-click, like old coot Ron's dentures, then Ross walked in.

'She's already got her name on Daddy's tombstone. Will there be any problems?'

A huge smile of relief lit Ross's face and his voice mirrored the same relief. 'All taken care of, love. All done. You don't need to worry about it.'

She took her handbag from the top of the fridge and opened her purse, placed ten clean green notes on the table. Enough there for a holiday. Probably not enough for a funeral. She had a few hundred dollars in her Commonwealth account, and she dug deep into the bowels of her bag until she found her old bankbook, which she placed on top of the notes.

'Put it back in your purse. Just sit down and take it easy today. Deb is coming over to see you at two.'

'Good,' she lied.

He'd picked up her car yesterday, paid her motel bill, collected her mother's personal effects from the hospital. He'd put her case in his room, placed the chicken in the fridge, the pudding on the bench. All under control. Ross's control.

She turned to the sink, picked up the frying pan. White grease had solidified in the bottom of the non-stick pan she'd bought so he wouldn't need to use grease. She scraped the grease onto paper, wrapped it and placed it in the bin. So she'd lost Christmas Day. So they'd have it a day late. Chicken and roast potatoes, pumpkin and peas. Pudding and brandy sauce, the order now for two. She was hungry this morning.

'I had a call from Sleiman. He said that when the shock wears off, it might hit –'

'It hit and ran, Ross.' She looked at his eyes, knowing he wouldn't understand, but she said it anyway. 'It feels sort of peaceful. She got what she wanted for Christmas, and it's like . . . it's like I suddenly realised it's not my fault.'

'Of course it's not. Did you get any sleep last night?'

She shrugged. 'What did you do with the bag you brought back from the hospital?'

'You don't want to look at that now.'

'I do.'

He walked to his room and returned with a plastic bag; she emptied it onto the table.

An unopened Christmas present, a watch, a wedding ring and small diamond engagement ring. Pretty nighties, a dressing gown, a large handbag half-full of death certificates and photographs, a purse containing ten dollars and two melting pills.

She removed the ten-dollar note, then handed the purse to Ross. 'You'd better give it to Sleiman.' He took it, glanced at the pills and at the colourful stains on the fabric lining. She searched on.

Scraps of paper. A small address book. Old photographs, several of them black and white. There was one of a man holding the hand of a little girl, both faces scribbled over with a red biro.

The yellowed envelope emptied onto the table, she sifted through death certificates. Grandma's was there, and Bernice's. Daddy's, the boys'. Marian's? Red words covered that one. *Slut. Whore. Rot in hell.*

Her mouth open, she stared at the name, remembering the

day, mid-May. She'd paid her bond on the flat. Ross and old Charlie Glen were going to help her move in at the weekend. She'd driven home from Melbourne on a high and found Mummy on an equal high, sitting at the table, laughing over the death notices in the newspaper. *Slut. Whore. Rot in hell* scribbled across that page too, in red biro.

My stepmother. I sent him a congratulations card. Posted it today, care of the funeral home. They'll see that he gets it, the evil old swine. I've ordered a copy of her death certificate too!

Ross was staring at the red words. Quickly Sally folded the paper and walked to the stove, pushing it into the firebox, watching the red biro burn. Her mother had liked red biro. Black had not been strong enough to express her hatred. Her hand shook as she added wood to the flames, then she turned the oven control to 'Hot' and set about releasing the Christmas chicken from its plastic while Ross repacked her mother's bag.

Onions found, peeled, cut. No tears. She made breadcrumbs for the chicken stuffing and she found the mixed herbs in the rear of the deep pantry. She found a slim skewer in the knife drawer. Old skewer, Mrs Bertram's skewer, used on every chicken ever cooked in this kitchen.

'You don't have to put on a brave face for me, love.'

'The chicken is thawed,' she said. 'If we don't cook it, it will go off.'

'It doesn't matter if it does. I prefer to eat homegrown anyway.'

'Poor dead supermarket chook, never pecked on green grass and bugs, stuffed from birth with hormones, fake fattened for Christmas. Look at the poor thing, its legs spread wide, still waiting to be stuffed. It's all a farce,' she said.

'What?'

'This travesty of prime chickendom. Tender and tasteless. And your plastic peanut butter is a farce and her church funeral too, and me going along with her church funeral. And agreeing to opening up Daddy's grave so she can prove in death what a wonderful, loyal widow she was.' She shook her head, shrugged.

'I don't know what you mean, love.'

'I know you don't. We slept together for eleven years, didn't we, and you never knew me.'

'Of course I did. I do. I love you.' He was on his feet.

'You love some fake picture frame with its fake photograph that you picked up at the reject shop one day and hung on your wall because it was fake pretty. It isn't my photograph. There aren't any photographs of me, and I've got to go home, Ross.'

'You're not going anywhere. You're staying here until the funeral.'

'I can't be real here, Ross, and reject or not, I want to be real.'

'You're saying silly things, love. You're not yourself. Take a couple of Aspros and lie down for a while.'

'I am myself, and you don't know me. And if you did, you wouldn't want to, so it's better if I go home.'

'You're not driving in this mood.' He picked up her car keys, put them in his pocket, and she dropped the chicken into the sink, the skewer into the drawer; she washed her hands and walked into his mother's room, closing the door behind her.

tranquillity by proxy

Mrs Bertram's room looked as it had eleven years ago, except for the dust and the insects. Insects crept in through the rusting flywire screens of this room that no-one used and no-one cleaned. There was a smell of dust on the crocheted quilt and half a dozen dead blowflies on the windowsill.

They were the right sort of Christmas decorations, better than fairy lights at the window. Big blowflies with gossamer wings and a huge one to replace the Christmas angel on top of the tree, she thought, that's what we need. Get Christmas into its right perspective.

As she fell across the bed, dust from the quilt rose, making her sneeze. Once. Twice. Ten times she sneezed, and she had to get up and shake the dust and dead insects from the quilt. Still she sneezed – until she found a crumpled handkerchief in the parka's pocket and the stubs of theatre tickets. She blew her nose, then looked at the tickets, remembering the night she'd gone out with Sue, and Sue had told her she looked like a ten year old in her quilted pink parka.

Sue and her pea-green hair, dyed to nark her parents and her grandfather at that mansion near Doncaster. Where was Ratsus today? How would she survive without her phones? And the black bikie from Number 14, what was he doing today? And Matt, where was he? Her eyes followed a gangly spider stalking its web in a dim corner, waiting to suck the juices from trespassing prey – it reminded her of Pimples, uncoordinated and slow.

Tired. All of her juices had been sucked out. Brittle, insect in a web, trapped again, and after she'd flapped so hard to battle her way out. Somehow she'd have to find the right attitude. For Deb too. Deb would forgive her for forgetting the wedding if she said the right things, did the right things. Maybe Ross would return her car keys if she found the right attitude.

He opened the door. 'Use my room if you want to have a sleep. There are no sheets on this bed,' he said.

'I'm fine, thanks, Ross.'

He found a blanket and covered her, then he brought her a late breakfast on a tray. She ate it to please him. She drank a cup of tea. Would have preferred coffee.

So warm in the kitchen but freezing in this room. Rain was battering the tin roof. Boxing Day today. Summer. Cricket at the MCG. What a wash-out.

Mind-travelling she lay there, listening to the wire door slam each time Ross entered, each time he went back out. She travelled back to five, then to eleven. She wandered the year of eighteen, then crept up on that year of eight and Daddy. A laughing man, his features blurred. She mind-slipped away from him to fourteen and Mrs Bertram.

Strange, just to stop dead, to lie on a bed, the only action in her mind.

Ross opened the door again at one. The odour of roast chicken followed him in.

'Boo,' she said as he leaned over the bed.

'Have you been asleep?' He kissed her brow.

'Just thinking.'

'You feel hot.'

'Hot head, cold feet and no car keys.'

'You need something to put you to sleep for a while. You're probably in shock or something.'

'Why?'

'You've just lost your mother, that's why.'

She propped on an elbow and reached for the cigarettes in his shirt pocket. Lit up and blew smoke. 'Lost is the wrong word. Lost means that something precious escaped through a hole in my pocket. What she did was to take something of mine and pitch it over Sleiman's razor-wire fence so I couldn't get it back. But she's been doing it forever, so what's new? My house, my photographs, my childhood, all tossed away.'

It was the wrong thing to say. She could tell by his eyes. It didn't matter. She wanted to say it, so she said it. 'Have a look at the photos in her bag. They are all of her and Shane and Nicky. Two of little Robby, none of me. I thought there might be one of me.'

'I'll look later, love.'

'I didn't exist back then, Ross. Little Sally turned up one day in a high school photograph, at the age of fourteen. And do you know why?' She didn't wait for a reply. 'Because your mother saw me, Ross. She brought me into existence. Do you know that when I was fourteen, I prayed that they wouldn't let Mummy out of the nuthouse. Do you know that when she cut her wrists that time, I wondered how long it would take for the blood to run away?'

'Stop it, Sally. Let your mother rest in peace.'

'I didn't have a mother. I just had Mummy.'

He ran his hands across his scalp. 'I'm going to give Sleiman a call,' he said, and he left her, gave her space.

'Whoops,' she said. 'You've blown your car keys now, Sall old gal.'

She heard old Ron's teeth click-click as Ross picked up the phone, hung up the phone. She heard him setting up a small electric heater and smelt burning dust as a warm breath of air wafted in. Feet in the direct path of the heater, she waited, counting the minutes until she heard the car – a maroon Volvo. He'd always driven a Volvo.

Five more minutes passed before the sleaze entered the bedroom, his long top lip covering his beaky teeth. No smile today, not for the newly bereaved. As he approached the eastern side of the bed, she went west.

'I'll feel better if I know you're okay. Let him check you over, love.'

'I'll feel better if he doesn't, Ross,' she said, and the white fingers knew they didn't have a chance with her, so they delved into the bag, found and offered pills – little answers to life's little problems.

She looked at them. How many pills had she popped from those bubble packs? How many had she searched for in the carpet? Small poisonous mushrooms in a field of purple grass.

Ross handed her a glass of water. She took it, sipped it. Not as good as Melbourne water. He popped two pills, and she looked at the tiny things, innocuous in that large, well-known hand. She didn't need pills. She needed her car keys because she was Sally De Rooze, almost thirty, and she hadn't made the kangaroo suddenly decide to hop across the road. It wasn't her fault that the tailgate of the old station wagon was faulty either. Daddy always knew it was, that's why he'd always locked it, and if Nicky hadn't started howling, it would have been locked the night of the fire.

Poor Ross. He looked so worried, like a lolloping great pup, kicked in the gut and not knowing what it had done to deserve it. His tongue out in a grimace, he scratched behind his ear.

'Take them, Sally. They won't hurt you. You've got to get some sleep.'

She shook her head and it felt good, so she did it again. Once, twice, thrice she denied those pills – like what's-his-name in the garden of Gethsemane, before the rooster crowed ... or ... or before the fake Christmas chicken burned. Then her hand reached out to accept her fate. Maybe they'd make Ross feel better.

She rolled them on her palm. They looked larger than they had on Ross's palm, and not so innocent. With a shrug she tossed them into her mouth and washed them down, wanting to be rid of these men who were stealing the heater's warmth.

She watched Ross's eyes as she handed back the glass, and she saw the twin pills' relief hit him immediately. Potent stuff. They dispensed tranquillity by proxy.

'She'll sleep now,' Sleiman said as the two men walked back to the front door, and warmth returned to play on her face.

Sleep might be nice, but what would she dream? Anyway, because they thought she'd sleep, she wasn't going to, just to nark them. That's what Sue would do. Have to get up, though. Have to get up and walk. In a minute she'd get up. When the sleaze left.

She could hear them discussing her.

'Give her one in the morning and one at night.' She yawned. The voices were fading. '... not strong ... help her get through ... take the edge off grief.'

She yawned, warm now. Good old pink parka. Always warm. Feet warm beneath the blanket. She rolled onto her side, waiting to hear the Volvo motor, hear it drive away. Then she'd get up.

She yawned and her eyes closed. Just for ... just rest them ... just for –

some stranger

Mrs Jenner was there with her batch of granddaughters. She always had them for the school holidays. Karen Matthews, her mother, her brother, and Jen Larkin from the department store were there. Deb and Greg had driven down. They'd forgiven her. Deb sat at Sally's side, while the stranger in white spoke about some stranger's gentle mother, and of seeing through glass darkly.

Sally was seeing through dark glasses darkly. They hid her eyes, dry now for five days and five nights. Dry, and tired with reading romance in Mrs Bertram's bedroom. She'd found a carton of Mills and Boon beneath the bed, exactly what she'd needed.

Six cars followed the hearse to the familiar cemetery. Ross held her hand as she walked by the three cherubs, but she waved to them, blew them a kiss, still wishing Superman had been standing watch over their grave.

It didn't matter. They were not in this graveyard. Not fat little Nicky. Not Robby the serious, or silly sausage Shane. It was just a place mark. Like Daddy's grave. Just a place mark.

The rain had gone but the sky was still grey. She had taken two pills before leaving Lakeside, they'd pickled her brain nicely, given her that stunned, newly bereaved look. She felt dazed, or drunk. Ross supported her, he held her until Mummy was safely in, on top of Daddy, like packing the china man and lady up for the next move.

Rose petals were handed to her. She sprinkled a few and swayed again. The wind caught her rose petals. They fell where they would on the fake grass.

Man, with his desire for immortality, had turned waste disposal into a religious experience. Like weddings, she thought. Big white statements, when love is black. Love hurts. Happily-ever-after love only happens in Mills and Boon. Happens over and over, only the names, place names and dates have been altered.

People touched her arm, her hand, her shoulder, as they walked away. Mrs Jenner's grandchildren had been promised McDonald's if they were good. The funeral over, they wanted the pay-off.

'We've been good, haven't we, Nanny? We've been good.' Happy little voices tinkling. New life amid the dead. They'd be the new century's children.

'My word, you have.' Born to mother, Mrs Jenner now mothered her grandchildren. Lucky kids. And so good, sitting in the pew like little redheaded dolls, all dressed up for the party afterwards.

'Stay in touch, dear.' Mrs Jenner kissed Sally's cheek, then took her brood off for McHappy packs, and Sally wanted some too. Wait for me. Wait for me. Take me with you to buy some laughter. I don't want to be here.

Deb and Greg left. Greg had to go to work, sole breadwinner now.

'Oh, Sally, sweetie.' Another hand touched her. 'I'm sorry I'm so late, but I couldn't get the car started and by the time the RACV man came ...'

Sally looked up, and the sun was in her eyes and so was Carol Rigg, now Murphy. Carol the house thief, in her floral dress and navy blazer. Sally stared at the motormouth.

'I saw it in the newspaper, sweetie. They did a bit of a story about your dad and brothers. I've tried to call you, but I kept getting your grandfather and he didn't know what I was talking about. I'm so sorry.'

Sally didn't reply. Couldn't say, that's okay, no worries, not a problem, so she didn't say anything, but she heard Ross say, 'Grandfather?'

'It sort of sounded like him, and I knew I had the right number. The first four digits are the same as Uncle Joe's then 4579. I remembered it because it was Nan's age. She's seventy-nine.'

'It's 4597,' Ross said.

'I'm such a fool. I must have got it twisted. I've been dialling 4579 and driving some poor senile old man crazy.'

Both now had their arms around Sally. Both so tall.

'They're together again. Try to think of it like that, sweetie.'

Sally knew that. She'd wrapped them up in newspaper and packed them both away, and it said so in the newspaper: *Resting together for all eternity*. What could she say to Carol Rigg? Nothing. It didn't matter. Carol's mouth was still working.

She looked at the moving mouth, looked from it to Ross's mouth, and wished they'd both go away. But in Mrs Bertram's Mills and Boon the newly bereaved were sent off to an old aunt, or a stern uncle. No uncle or aunt here today, a loyal ex-lover would have to do. She'd go home to the farm, be a good heroine. There was supposed to be another man in the story, some dark brooding guy who the heroine would end up with. Where was he hiding?

Maybe Matt had looked in the deaths column. Maybe he'd come.

A glance behind her, then to the left, to the right. No Matt. Maybe one of the gravediggers was dark and brooding. They'd be somewhere, waiting. She couldn't spot them, but she saw a little leprechaun, seated on a toadstool, and while she stared at him he disappeared in a puff of smoke, went off to find the end of his rainbow.

Fairy tales and Mills and Boon confused, Sall. Get it together. Keep it together. She shook her head. Had to stay away from fantasy today. Had to go home with the faithful ex-lover, have afternoon tea at the farm with all the people who'd only be coming because of Ross and a free feed.

She needed a smoke, that's what she needed. The grave-diggers were probably having a smoke somewhere, but she couldn't light up beside her parents' grave. Not the done thing. She swayed forward. Back, against Carol Rigg. Carol's arm supported her.

'You're right, sweetie. Lean on me if you want to. I've got you.'

I'm leaning, she thought. I'm leaning on a motormouth house thief.

'Come home with me for a while. It's not far. We'll have a coffee and talk it out.'

'Want to go to Carol's for a quick coffee, love?'

What would they say in Mills and Boon? She couldn't think, and couldn't make her feet move anyhow. The pills had settled in her feet, tranquillised them so she couldn't force them forward, or back, or had her high heels taken root in the fake grass?

Maybe they'd go away if her heels were stuck, give her a few minutes in private with her mother so she could tell her that she knew why she'd had to do it before the thirty-first. It was on the tombstone: 1950–19– .

'The millennium bug claims its first victim,' she said, and Ross picked her up, he pulled her heel roots out of the grass and he was holding her close and it was raining. But the sun had just peeped out to shine a while.

She understood why. And she knew that he understood too,

and she knew now why he'd hated 'Little Runaway Girl'.

Poor Ross, he was making the rain. He was holding her so close, dripping tears all over her.

And the rain from cloudless sky, are the tears I'll ever cry,
For I have no running shoes to tag along.

So now it was time for the dark, brooding gravedigger to come out of hiding and get on with the story.

Don't look behind you, girl.
Little runaway girl.

the new beginning

january 2000

The answer had been in the purse, plus four old fifty-dollar notes, bound with a perished rubber band and stuffed high into the hidden pocket. It was Mummy's escape money, but she hadn't used it.

For weeks Glenda De Rooze had hoarded her pills, and from an unknown source added a few heart pills to her collection, and migraine pills; then, while Lakeside partied, she'd swallowed her grand cocktail. No-one to stop her game; Sally gone home to her motel bed. Dr Sleaze at his lake. Nurse too busy, thankful that the demanding one was not awake and leaning on her buzzer all night.

Sally escaped back to Melbourne on the Friday morning. Weeks ago, Ross had offered his farm for a wild new century's barbecue. Half of Lakeside was invited; he couldn't cancel. He thought he understood why Sally didn't want to be there.

She'd called Sue five minutes after parking her tired little car in its bay – hadn't told her about the funeral, though. She'd wanted Sue's laughter, not her sympathy. They'd met at nine under the Flinders Street Station clock and partied with

Melbourne, two small cells in the solid block of humanity moving on Southbank.

It was eleven in the morning on the first day of January in the year 2000 when rain hunted them from the streets. They caught the tram to Sally's flat and fell onto her bed, one each end, and they slept twelve hours straight, then ate breakfast twenty minutes before midnight – a feast of cornflakes.

'It feels weird, doesn't it?'

'What? No men?'

'2000. There's still water in the pipes. The electricity is still on. The world was supposed to come to a stop at midnight.'

'Yeah, the fucking cons. I was hoping the bank records would go into cyberspace and take my mortgage with them,' Sue said. They laughed and had a glass of wine, and they had never drunk wine on top of cornflakes. It raised raucous laughter. Number 6 banged on his ceiling, and someone banged on the door. Sue wanted to open the door, invite the knocker in, but Sally told her it was probably the big, black bikie.

'I'm not a racist,' Sue said.

On Sunday morning, the phone roused them too early. Only Ross. He didn't talk long, but for a moment reality threatened. Sally took a don't-care pill and Sue wanted to know what she was swallowing. She pinched the pack and stole a little unreality.

They caught a tram to St Kilda in the late afternoon and they walked the esplanade, walked the pier, watching hopeful fishermen toss their lines into the barren waters of the year 2000. They had coffee on the footpath in Fitzroy Street, listening into clever conversations that had no reality. Then unreality wore off for Sue and she remembered she had a cat; she had to go home, feed it.

The chill of winter had settled over Melbourne six months early. Maybe the big computer in the sky had been hit by the millennium bug and turned the seasons around. Sally's heater rattled that night, guzzling electricity while she sat late before the television.

On the third day of the new century she wandered into a music shop to look at guitars. Plenty of money in her purse. She had her refunds from Mummy's dress and Matt's dressing gown, and Mummy's escape hoard, and Ross had refused her thousand dollars. He was going to sell the furniture when the auction rooms opened. She didn't buy a guitar, too old now to pick up where she'd left off at sixteen.

Wandering in the rain, walking, watching people, watching lovers holding hands, Sally the alien, the only one of her breed left to walk in a strange new century, had no hand to hold.

'Sleep is beautiful,' Mummy had said on that last day.

Sleep, beautiful or not, Sally could not find – not without her don't-care pills. She felt tired enough, but her bones kept wanting to jump up and do something. Catch a tram. Drive out to Sue's. Jog around the block. Drive out to the hills. Do. Do. Do something, anything, just as long as she was out of the flat. Mental exhaustion, reaction to the pills, or common imagination, but she was hearing Mummy's voice in her head when she was alone in the flat.

Ghosts were only supposed to hang around their old haunts; still, Mummy had moved around so much, she wouldn't have had any special old haunt, so she'd probably got herself a special haunt dispensation to come and visit me, Sally decided.

This place stinks of smoke, my precious girl.

The words so clear, so Mummy – apart from the precious girl bit, but God or the other guy was probably listening in.

'Which is a sweeter scent than mouse pee, Mummy. You must admit that.'

They had some interesting conversations. The day she took out the old photographs found in her mother's bag, her resident ghost really wound up. Not much to see, though. Old negatives, ancient individual black things, but they made her remember an old camera. Like a black box. Big. Always aimed at something.

Not Daddy's camera. Not her grandmother's either. Perhaps it had belonged to her grandfather.

The death certificates had filled in a few gaps. She'd been closer to four than three when her grandmother had died. Couldn't remember that funeral. Couldn't really remember her grandmother, except the shape of her, and that day in Geelong when they'd had a party with a red checked tablecloth on the grass, cakes in a white bag.

Only Shane then. Shane and Sally.

There were a few condolence cards she had to reply to. She filled an hour writing thank-you cards. It was a Bertram thing, so she did it well and posted them, then met a new tenant on the way back.

Lyn. Tall, thirty-odd and married. They had coffee, and were enjoying themselves until the husband came home. Sally didn't want to go home to her ghost, so she went jogging the darkening streets. What was there to be scared of in a century only days old?

Scared of running until she dropped. Scared her legs would take off and try to leave her head behind. Scared of a future without Matt.

He'd phoned on Monday night. She'd told him she had visitors. 'I'll meet you in town? We'll go to a pub for a drink,' she'd said.

'How long will they be there?'

'I want to go out. I want to sit in a pub with you, Matt.' He hadn't wanted to sit in a pub so she'd hung up the phone.

She didn't want to sleep with him anyway. Didn't want to have him at the flat, not while Mummy was hanging around. Couldn't let her see the things they did, make her comments while she watched them play their games.

Not where you're going to eat, you little slut.

'I didn't get into the habit of eating regularly. At least I got some use out of the table.'

rosebuds and fairyfloss

Day was breaking outside the casino; he'd been there all night, and he was no longer certain if he had been there, or if he'd dreamed he'd been there. His head light, his lungs labouring for air, he knew he had to be dreaming, because if he wasn't, Satan had come to collect his eternal soul, got him a taxi to speed him on his way, and sent one of his angels to make sure he got in it. They'd damn near called an ambulance, but he'd refused that.

Heat was in his chest, in his head, his lungs were barely sipping on air. Always, when he was awake, he carried an inhaler. He never moved without it. Five years now since he'd swapped his smokes for that inhaler and he always kept one in his pocket, but he didn't have one now. He had money in his pocket instead.

'Richmond. Swan Street.' He got the words out, but when he got there, he couldn't get out of the taxi. Got a green note out, though, and handed it to the driver.

'A moment. Just . . . one moment.'

Asthma and gambling. They went together. That's why he didn't do it any more. Not often. Not as much as he used to.

There was a spare inhaler in the zip compartment of his old case. He could remember packing it in with his pills and the photograph. Had to get into that hotel and up those stairs and get it.

Slow movements now. Concentrated effort now. He got his legs out, his feet on the kerb, then he stood, one hand on the taxi.

'Sure you don't want to go to a hospital, mate?'

'Tablets. In the room.' The driver was offering him change. 'Keep it. Can you ... get me ... inside?'

He sipped on air. Had to hold down panic, control the mind and it would control the lungs. But it had been a mindless ten hours. He'd gone to the casino with forty-odd dollars in his wallet and been assisted out to the taxi with enough green stuff in his pocket to choke a horse.

The taxi driver earned his money. Walter had never had much time for Melbourne taxi drivers but he was changing his mind tonight. The driver, a big bloke, damn near carried him up those stairs. He found the inhaler and Walter snatched it and, like a baby given his bottle at bedtime, put it to his mouth and sucked. The driver found the pills too, fished one out and placed it in the open mouth, fetched a glass of water from the bathroom. He earned his money and closed the door behind him when he left.

The glass of water lifted with a shaking hand, Walter sipped. It made him cough, but he was getting enough air in to cough out; he sucked again on his inhaler, and sat on, shoulders hunched forward, head down, thinking of those last hours, those last weeks.

He hadn't intended coming back until April. He'd had no choice. No choice of a room when he'd arrived either. He'd had to take one of the west rooms on the second floor. Didn't like the stairs, or the bathroom, a long hall away. He liked the ground floor rooms.

Walter turned to the window; not a lot to see out there. A

pigeon perched on a cement wall; a high-flying blowfly trying to find a way through the flyscreen.

'I'm not dead yet,' he told the fly. 'Thought I might have been for a while there.'

His tongue did a search of his lips as his fingers combed his silver curls. He needed a haircut. Meant to get one while he was home. Meant to do a lot of things.

Hadn't meant to go to the casino last night. He'd only gone there to get out of this room. Depression had descended on him weeks ago, and every day the room had grown smaller, so he'd hopped a tram and headed for the roulette wheel – and dropped twenty dollars in two spins. It was when he was trying to find his way to the exit that he'd stopped at the blackjack table, just to have a look.

There was a time when he'd bet his shirt on the fall of the cards. Poker, euchre, five hundred. Loved the games. Learnt them as a tot. Always loved handling the colourful cards when his old Dada had let him play. Crisp, cool cards in his sweating little hand. He stayed away from cards now, but old Satan had got to him, sort of whispering in his ear.

Hasn't a lifetime of playing cards been an apprenticeship for this night, Wally?

That's what he said. Clear as a bell. And there was an empty chair, right in front of him. Twenty dollars a game.

He'd have one hand. All he could afford. Just touch the cards, watch their fall.

The only problem with that was he'd won the first hand. It was over and done before he could say *hit me*. He'd got the ace and a ten dealt to him! So he played a second hand, and he'd got an eight and a nine. Anyone with half a brain would have sat on those cards, but he'd had a feeling in his gut that he'd get a four. The dark-faced lad dealt him an ace, and that was two aces down. His head had started keeping track of the fallen cards, not consciously, he didn't do it consciously, just one of his bad habits.

'Give me a three,' he'd said, and the lad had looked at him as if he was senile.

'Not the way it works here.' He'd dealt the card, and his big brown eyes had damn near popped out of his head. He'd dealt a three.

That's when Walter had forgotten time. That's when his asthma had started getting bad.

He sat immobile on his bed, inhaler in hand, his mind replaying his night of triumph. He could see it in detail, see the faces of the other players, see the dealer's smile, hear the fall of the cards. He'd waited for the itch of enlightenment, for that card marked as his. He'd lost a few hands, but won a lot more.

A yawn. Wide. It lifted his head and he caught his reflection in the mirror, saw his old Dada staring back at him – that silver-grey hair, and too much of it. He smiled at his old Dada, remembering the kitchen table and the deck of cards, the slap-slapping of cards being dealt. And his mother. 'Ah, the women in my life.'

The angels made little girls, from rosebuds and from candy-floss and –

That song. It was driving him mad. It might have been all right if he could have remembered all the words, but he couldn't. Just that line kept coming at him.

He turned towards the window. The pigeon had flown away. The blowfly was still buzzing. A breath sighed in and Walter reached with effort into his pocket, removing a damp and crumpled handkerchief, then another from his trouser pockets. He tossed them onto the bedside table and took two clean handkerchiefs from the case, took out his vinyl toilet bag, then stood, stripped to the waist.

He had a container of towelettes on his dressing table. He rose now with effort and removed a wad, using them to wash his face and underarms. He needed a shower, but he was too damn tired to get himself down to the bathroom. Deodorant used liberally, he struggled into a worn white singlet, then reached into the breast pocket of his old suit jacket, removing his bundle of notes.

It didn't look much all bunched up together like that, but it looked a healthy green. A smile crept from his lips to his eyes as he sat again on the bed, spreading the notes, dealing them into groups of one thousand. He'd served eleven players, licking his thumb from time to time, savouring the flavour of money.

Have to ring up Greyhound and get them to alter the ticket. Hire myself a little car again and go out and see my boy. Should have been out there before this. Oh, well, now I can take him something nice. Might buy myself a new suit too. His fingers continued playing with the green, dealing more thousand-dollar piles.

'You're thinking too small, Walter,' he said, and he glanced at his watch. Almost eight o'clock.

Too much green to count, and he knew how much he had. The notes gathered, he folded and pushed the lot into the zip compartment of his case. Not a good idea to stay on in this place. The taxi driver had seemed a decent bloke, but you never could tell who you were dealing with in Melbourne. People looked innocent enough.

He did a quick pack-up of his room; not a lot to pack. He picked up a framed photograph from the windowsill, allowing himself a moment of exquisite pain and pleasure, then he tried to slip it into the zip compartment where it usually rode. Not today. No room in there. He placed it safe between his pyjamas and underwear and, by nine, the old Richmond Hotel had a vacant room – on the west side, half a mile from the bathroom – and Walter was at a used car yard. He wasn't looking at their bombs either. In his youth he'd dreamed of driving a sporty little job, and from the minute he'd walked into this yard, his eyes had been drawn to a low-slung Honda. He'd tried to fight it, but not too hard.

The salesman thought he was being had. They took it for a test drive and for the fourth time in his life, Walter fell in love.

Back in the yard, Walter and his little brown case led the way to the office, then, the case lifted to a chair, he babied the worn metal zips open and started counting lettuce onto the desk.

There were three salesmen watching him, looking a bit suspicious, but he told them of his win, and he sent one over the road for a bottle of champagne, which they drank in the office, toasting him and their sale. He had a sip.

You've got champagne tastes on a beer wage, Walter O'Leary. That's what Elaine used to say. He couldn't deny it. Nothing wrong with champagne tastes when you could afford them, though he didn't much like the taste. Nothing wrong with the sporty little Honda Prelude either. It was black and it had darkened windows and air conditioning, a sunroof, seats that cushioned your bones and a motor that started first pop, then purred like a kitten. It set him back almost thirty thousand, but he had plenty left over.

phonepross

february 2000

Summer had saved its heat for February. The bedsitter was a sweatbox, heated daily by its flat tin roof and still haunted occasionally. Sally spent little time there, working late when asked, then walking into work late the following morning, yawning, but selling hard.

Matt had called two dozen times through January, and he'd caught her in the lift one night, but Sue had been with her, and Sue had a nice turn of phrase. She got rid of him.

Nine days now since he'd called and life was carefree. She had her don't-care pills to turn off care. Good little pills, a new pack supplied on demand by the clinic around the corner.

In and out of the surgery in two minutes, at thirty-six dollars a visit; that doctor could earn more in half an hour than she could make in a week of phone calls. But she made her phone calls. She paid her bills.

New groups had wandered into the tearoom through January. They'd segmented. The tearoom table gained a few faces, others joined the green bunch while the lost drifted up, up to the roof, security pack in one hand, lighter in the other. No introductions necessary on the roof; lepers recognised lepers.

In mid-February Sue removed her nose ring and dyed her longer hair fire-engine red. She and Sally were discussing dripping taps one day when a long-nosed pipsqueak of a kid somehow managed to filter into the small space between them. He must have cut himself shaving – if he shaved; he had sticking plaster on his jaw.

He knew it all. 'I spent twelve months making cupboards for a kitchen manufacturer that went bust. I worked for a while with a plumber. I sold whitegoods at my last job. I can turn my hand to anything.'

'So what are you bloody doing here?' old coot Ron asked. A man of many talents, Ron was not into kidding himself. He was licking up the dregs in the barrel and he knew it, but he could barely get his words in edgeways. You name it, the pipsqueak knew how to do it. Hang curtains, deliver pizzas, sing in a band. It was worth sitting in the tearoom just to watch the play of the young bantam and the old rooster going at it, feathers flying.

Ron spilled more beetroot than usual. A purple circle hit his blue shirt, bounced to his open fly, balanced a while, considering an infiltration into the dark place, but it changed its mind and hit the floor. Sally laughed and Ron scowled at her, lost a lump of tomato then almost dropped his teeth chasing it.

She giggled as she watched him suck his teeth back. Clackety-clack. Munch. Crunch.

Varicose crunched quietly, crumbs from her diet biscuits falling to her breasts, clothed in black. Cracker dandruff. Pimples watched her breasts transfixed, but Sally caught him watching and his eyes swivelled to Ron, to Pipsqueak, while his jack-hammer finger picked.

'Leave your bloody face alone,' Ron snarled, spat beetroot. 'You put a man off his bloody dinner, you do.'

'Speaking of being put off his bloody dinner . . .' a new face commented. It walked, headed for the roof to bot a smoke. He'd have his own pack tomorrow.

This was better than a television sitcom, Sally and Sue supplying the canned laughter. If some producer set up a hidden camera in this tearoom, he could flog his tape for a fortune, give the world some new millennium reality to laugh about.

Pipsqueak closed his mouth long enough to stare at the disappearing back, then opened it again to take a bite of tuna and onions.

The producer would require smellevision.

'He looks fishy,' Sue hissed, and they collapsed with laughter while Ron eyed them from beneath a thatched verandah brow. But they were old hands and Pipsqueak new, so he turned his ire and his beetroot on the new.

They sparred again. Old Ron might be battle-scarred, but he was cagey. He started digging in his spurs and the pipsqueak backed off, his eyes settling on Sally, who was also backing off. Toward the door, cigarette packet and lighter at the ready. Not a lot of talent in this place. He followed her up to the roof and offered her a smoke.

Nobody, but nobody, offered smokes in this place. They might give them grudgingly when asked, but it was a mistake to offer smokes. She took one, let him light it, then stood smoking at his side, allowing him one smoke's worth of earbash time. When he took a breath, she slotted thirteen words in. Fast.

'Do you know how to put a new washer in a dripping tap?'

'I'll give you a practical demonstration, babe. Nothing to it. Any fool can put a new washer in a tap.'

She invited him and his toolbox around for a drink and he wasn't all mouth either, because the tap actually stopped dripping and Mummy hadn't said one word.

'I don't suppose you know how to fix a light fitting.'

'Nothing to it – but it's illegal to muck around with electricity these days.'

'Is it illegal for you drink?' she asked before pouring him a glass of Jim Beam and Coke.

'I'm twenty-two. Almost. How old are you, babe?'

'Twenty-five. Almost,' she lied.

'You don't look it, but I usually go for older women.' He finished his drink, and looked hopefully at her bed. She started washing dishes, clattering cutlery, splashing water.

'You haven't got much space, babe. I've got a balcony, and a good-sized kitchen.'

'All the more to clean,' she said, and she started washing the floor. She washed around his feet, trying to wash him out. But he lifted his feet. 'Well, thanks again for the washer.' His tools in her hand, she offered them, but from a distance. He'd have to stand to get them and finally she'd got him off her chair and on his feet.

'It's been a good night, babe,' he said. The tools, a donkey's carrot held before his too-long nose, she walked him to the door. Dragged it open. He moved behind her. 'Like to go out some night?' he asked, taking the tools.

'Love to.' It got him through the door.

'There's this Karaoke bar down at St Kilda –'

'We'll talk about it at work.'

Matt phoned again on Wednesday. She hung up again. Didn't need someone else's husband. She had Sue, and Lyn from downstairs. Carol Rigg had called twice. Deb had called. Ross rang on Sundays. She had plenty of friends. Maybe she'd go out with the pipsqueak too. Why not? No more Monday–Wednesday-waiting-for-Matt existence. There was a world out there.

The phone rang again. 'Don't hang up on me, Sall.'

She did, but he called back and she sighed, knowing she'd have to talk to him.

'It's over, Matt.' Maybe a twinge of old pain. She took the phone to the sink, holding it to her with her shoulder as she broke one of her don't-care pills in half, swallowed the half, just to keep her resolve strong. She lit a cigarette and blew smoke in the face of the phone. Blew it right down the holes and along the wires and into his ear, mentally watching him prod at his ear, force smoke from the other ear. Little puffs of it. Smoke signals. The image, or the pill, raised a giggle.

'Stop your games. I'm coming around.'

'Wrong. I don't play games any more. Look on the bright side, Matt. You even get to keep custody of your phone number.'

'Is this over a phone number? Get a pencil and write it down.'

'It's not over a phone number. It's . . . it's over dark pubs and holding hands on the Esplanade. It's . . . it's just over. Stop ringing me.'

'I'll be there in ten minutes.'

'You won't be here in ten minutes. You're not around when I need you, so don't come around.'

'I'm spread thin, Sall.'

'You're not spread at all. You hoard yourself for yourself. I know nothing about you. Matt Marsden, doles out financial advice, wife in Hallam. Well, I took your advice, Matt, and I found myself a new adviser and he hasn't got the wife in Hallam. Goodbye.'

'Sall. I need you.'

'You need my bed. Or table. Fridge. Go and . . . go and buy the wife a new dining room suite or something. My furniture is worn out.' She liked that line, and she giggled, blowing smoke down the wires, seeing the white puffs popping out the other end. Dear little don't-care pills. How did people survive without them?

'Have you got someone with you?'

'Yes.'

'Who?'

'Mummy.'

'How long is she staying?'

'Ask her yourself. Mummy,' she called, 'want to talk to Matt? The married guy.'

'We'll go to a motel.'

'Us? You mean you and Sally from Phone a Pro in a motel room? My God, he's getting desperate, Mummy. He'll be offering to take me home to meet his family soon.' Silence then at the other end of the phone. 'A motel tonight, Matt, and dinner with the parents on Sunday?' Silence. 'Should I buy a new dress for Sunday, or will jeans do?'

'Don't do this, Sall. Don't spoil what we've got.'

'What we've got? You can't spoil *nothing*. Give me a call when you get your divorce and I'll see if I'm free.'

She hung up, and hoped he wouldn't drive around, but she watched at the window anyway, listened for that knock on her door.

A married man. You're like your grandfather, you little slut.

Sally bowed to her resident ghost. 'Go home and haunt Carol Rigg,' she replied. 'She's the one who lives in my house.'

It was after seven when she heard him. Just a little knock. A not-so-confident Matt tonight.

She hadn't eaten, so she would let him take her out for dinner. She wouldn't sleep with him, couldn't sleep with him, even if she wanted to, which she didn't. She'd swapped her contraceptives for don't-care pills, and they worked well too, turning off both care and desire, turning off guilt and fear, turning off everything.

No hurry to open the door. She combed her hair, added lipstick, selected her shoes, but didn't put them on. She'd creep to the door barefoot, finger to her lips. Shush, she'd say. Mummy doesn't approve of you, and she's in the bathroom. Just give me a minute to grab my shoes.

But it wasn't Matt standing in the passage. She frowned. Pills could cause hallucinations. She'd seen that on television once. Head to the side, she squinted her eyes at the hallucination, striving to make it go away.

'Sally. Good evening.'

'You?' Still not understanding why he was there, stepping out so he wouldn't step in. 'You?' she said.

'In town for the night. Thought I'd . . . look in on you. See how you were handling your loss,' Sleiman the sleaze said, and the wind or Mummy slammed her door, locked her out.

She looked at it, pushed at the door, then she turned on a stockinged heel and walked down to Number 4, where she knocked on Lyn's door. He was two steps behind her.

'I'm going out,' she said, but her shoeless feet gave up her lie. He smiled at her feet, looked at the long legs and short skirt, sucking seed as she knocked again.

Lyn wasn't answering her door and the sleaze wasn't moving. Too close, she could smell him, smell the hospital on him. 'Lyn. Lyn, are you there?'

'Altered plans?' His teeth escaped for a moment. 'You wouldn't take pity on a . . . a hometown guy stuck in the city for the night. A drink? A show?'

'What do you think?' she said and she ran upstairs, checking over her shoulder to see if he had followed.

How did he know where I live? Lived. Look, no keys, Sall old gal. She waited at the top of the stairs for five minutes, then she knocked on the bikie's door. He wasn't home, or he wasn't opening his door. She knocked on Numbers 15 and 13, knowing the Asian woman was in there. She could hear the machine. Twelve was vacant, but she gave it a quick rap, then she walked down and tried the old gay guy in 6, the flat beneath her own – any port in a storm. Closed port.

'God!'

Out on the street, she searched for the maroon Volvo, but the sleaze had given up and gone. She glanced up at her window, wide open, and out of reach except via the drainpipe. It ran up the wall a bare half-metre from her window. In jeans she could have done it but she wasn't wearing jeans. Head back, she measured the distance. She'd been able to climb like a monkey once, been able to scale a lamppost. There were struts holding the pipe and two windowsills below her own. She could do it, but not with cars driving by. Have to wait until dark.

Can't stand out here for two hours. Can't go for a walk in pantihose either. Sit on the stairs, wait for someone to come home, she thought.

A glance behind then. Leafy trees hid her from the houses on the other side of Bollinger Street and car drivers didn't look up. Only walkers to see her. She placed her foot on a strut and climbed, got a foot on the first windowsill, then reached higher. Her knees gripping the drainpipe, she dragged herself up. Couldn't reach the gay guy's sill, though; she was out of climbing condition.

Have to find a pay phone, ring a locksmith. Look, no money, Sall old gal. The thought gained her an extra half-metre, and at full stretch she got the fingers of her left hand on the windowsill.

'I can. I must, and I will,' she said.

'You're not dressed for it, De Rooster. You need a catsuit and balaclava.'

She didn't need to look down to identify that voice. 'Nick off.'

'I know the guy in 6. Nothing worth knocking off in his flat. His last boyfriend took the lot when he cleared out.'

She tried to slide down slowly, decently, but her knees lost their grip and she slipped, ripping her pantihose from knee to toe and landing in a heap at his feet. Up fast, her skirt slapped down, shirt pulled down, she explained. 'My door blew shut.'

'Yeah? That's what we all say.'

'Stop being a smartarse for five minutes. Can you pick a lock?'

He slapped his pockets. 'I haven't got my skeleton keys on me. I was planning to spend the night in, De Rooster.'

'Can I use your mobile phone then, to call a locksmith? Please. I'll pay for the call when I get inside.'

But he was looking at the pipe, then climbing it, and making it look easy. Tall people in trousers had an unfair advantage. She watched him hit her flyscreen, knock it in. And he was in. She wouldn't be sleeping with that window open again.

Upstairs, he waited at her door. 'Step into my parlour, said the spider to the fly.'

'You've done that before,' she accused, pushing by him.

'Only a couple of nights a week these days. I've cut my habit down since I met you, De Rooster. You've been a great influence on me. An exercise in self-control.' He left her flat and walked across to his own door.

'Thanks.'

'Just call me the White Knight,' he said, and he laughed.

best friends

Ross drove to Melbourne on the last Saturday in February. He'd sold the stored furniture at an auction, most of it. The rest he had on his ute tray.

'I tried bidding up the dining room setting and ended up with it.'

'I don't want it!' Her eyes were wide, her voice high as they looked around the flat.

'No. No. I've got used to having it around,' he said.

She made coffee and toasted sandwiches for lunch, no home baking, no lemon meringue pies. 'How much did they offer, Ross?'

'Nowhere near its value. I got seventy-five for that old fridge, though, and a hundred and twenty for the dryer. A hundred and seventy for the washing machine. Should have got more for that. It was hardly used.' He was walking the small space, a giant bear on a chain. 'I decided to keep the television and microwave; got used to having them in the kitchen. Them and the dining room suite will cover the funeral costs.'

'It's me you're talking to. The television is five years old and that suite is fifty-year-old junk and it's cluttering up your lounge room. Sell it for what you can get.'

'It's an antique. I like it.'

'It's just old.'

He'd cleaned out her mother's pension account, told the banking Sleiman he needed it for the funeral; he'd closed the insurance account at the National Bank before her mother had died. There had been three hundred and seventy dollars left in that one. His eyes watching her for reaction, he handed her a cheque for the total.

She glanced at it then waved it away. 'Don't be ridiculous,' she said.

'It's yours. Most of it is from her pension. She was in hospital for months.'

'What did you pay for the funeral?' He shook his head and she looked again at the figures written on the cheque: $3500. Ross's signature was there too. So it was in his account. It was just another piece of paper – unless she cashed it. Plenty more paper in the bottom of her bag.

He was wearing the maroon shirt she'd bought him for Christmas and it suited him, as she'd known it would. Maybe he'd lost a bit of weight in the six weeks since the funeral, or bought a larger size in jeans. Farmer Bertram, all dressed up for his day in the city. He had good eyes, Mrs Bertram's, soft and brown. Every time she looked at his eyes she could see Mrs Bertram. Those eyes watched her every mouthful. She knew he was still hoping to fatten her up, still wanting to get her home where he thought she belonged. His hand kept touching. Touching, then pulling away. He touched her hair that now sat on her shoulders.

'I like your hair better like that. You look more like you used to,' he said. 'You've put on a bit of weight too, haven't you?'

'I'm still taking Sleiman's pills when I need them. They turn off my brain and make me hungry.'

'You should have been on them years ago. You look better than you've looked in months.'

Ross had parked out front. She helped unload the carton of ornaments, the photographs, the white chest of drawers he'd refused to let go for four dollars, the battered bookshelf that had raised a two-dollar bid.

'I thought it wasn't worth selling them. We'll make room, love.'

And he did. He moved the bed, placed the drawers on its left and the bookshelf on its right; they fitted perfectly and were supported by the window wall, which was to the good; those old shelves had always needed any support they could get.

'Okay.' He rubbed his hands, pleased with his labour.

'I liked it bare,' she said, lining the ornaments up on the sink, giving them a fast spray with Mr Muscle. A scrub then with a toothbrush and a dunk into hot water made sudsy with dish-washing detergent, and years of dust and grime dissolved away like magic.

The ornaments looked new. Some of them looked new. The goose girl was placed on the bookshelf beside the Shane boy and his dog. They knew they belonged together. She put china mummy and daddy on the chest of drawers, allowing them a brief kiss first. Have to buy some pale-pink nail polish and touch up china mummy's neck, she thought. The glue had gone brown. It looked as if she'd tried to cut her throat.

I never marked my throat. My throat was my fortune.

It was clear. In her head it was as clear as day.

'Only thing you didn't mark,' she replied, and Ross looked up from the bookshelf he was hammering with the heel of her boot because she didn't own a hammer.

'What?'

She shrugged, climbed onto a chair and lifted the elephant and his turbanned rider up to the top of her kitchen cupboard where they could roam with the black wolf and the eagle. She placed the boy with the hiatus elbow on the window ledge. Maybe she'd make him a new elbow with modelling clay, let the poor kid finally eat his apple.

Slowly the room filled with ornaments and the bare beige walls no longer looked so bare. Her books had been tossed into the bottom of her wardrobe. Stacked neatly on a lower shelf, many books became few.

The bare hook over her bed had claimed the framed wedding photograph of her mother, and Grandma found a hook in the bathroom, positioned so she could stare down at Sally every time she sat on the loo.

I hope you are ashamed of yourself.

'Look on her as a laxative, Mummy. She's got a face like a prune.'

'Are you talking to me, love?'

'No.' Back in the main room she found Ross looking at the photograph of her father. She took it from his hands, wanting to place it face down in a drawer. Instead she wiped the dust away with a damp cloth and for once looked at his face. Memory of her father was a dark shape against orange fire. But his hair, and that jaw. The shape of his face –

She stood staring at it until Ross took it from her and placed it on the second shelf. Slowly she unwrapped the boys. Beautiful little boys, all three dressed in navy and white sailor suits, even Nicky. Fat little Nicky with his wide eyes. It must have been taken just before the accident because that was how she remembered him, those eyes, his clinging little arms, his hands that had grasped at her pigtails. And Robby, the serious. And Shane, the silly sausage, dark and fine like Daddy. Tears prickled as she stood her brothers safe beside Daddy.

Why could she look at them now, when she had been unable to for twenty years? Had she forgiven them at last?

Or forgiven herself?

Bits and pieces everywhere, and all gleaming clean. The flat looked different, it smelt different. It smelt of Mr Muscle and dishwashing detergent.

'It looks like someone might live here, love.'

'Sally De Rooze, almost thirty, still hauling around Grandma's worthless junk.' She sat on the bed, looking at her possessions. The boy and his dog, bought at the Queen Vic market, had gone over to the other side to become number thirteen. She'd have to buy another one, make it fourteen. She loved fourteen, that first year of sweet sanity.

'I'm going out tonight to a karaoke bar,' she said.

'That's okay.' He stood too quickly, bumping the bookshelves. They rocked and the goose girl rocked, but his big hands grabbed, saved.

Pity overwhelmed her. In the past she believed he had felt pity for her, but she'd never pitied him – except when his mother had died. Pity for him had trapped her once.

He looked down at the voluptuous china lady with the cat, chip off the old cat's nose. 'I thought . . . I thought, while I was down here I might have a look around the Sunday markets, love.'

'Stay if you like. We're family, Ross.'

'Right. Righto, love.' He glanced at the bed and thought of the other guy. She wouldn't be bringing him home tonight. He'd damn near driven himself mad these last months imagining her sleeping with another bloke. Maybe she didn't sleep with him. He took a deep breath, let it out slow. It had been a long time since they'd spent the night together and he'd planned his night in town. He'd asked old Charlie to feed his dogs and chooks, and he'd bought his pyjamas and a clean shirt. Left them in the ute, though.

He walked downstairs fast, his smile growing. He put on his steering lock, picked up his old sports bag and ran back, taking the stairs two at a time. They were family, all right. She was his wife, just going through the eleven-year itch, and she only had one bed, and tonight he'd be in it.

It was near eight, Sally in the bathroom dressing for her date, Ross attempting to tune the television to pick up Channel 2, when they heard the door. Ross downed his tools, eager to get a look at the opposition.

'Tell him I won't be a minute, but for God's sake, don't let him in. We'll never get him out,' Sally called.

We'll never get him out? Ross drew himself up to his full height, sucked his chest back where it ought to be and opened the door. He looked out, then down, and he smiled.

'Oh, there you are, mate. She won't be a tick.' A second glance and he turned away fast, left the kid standing at the open door and returned to the television. His smile grew wide, wider. What the hell had he been worrying about? It was just a bit of a kid out there.

'Don't lock yourself out,' she said as she was leaving. 'The key is on the bench.'

'Have a good time.' He craned his neck to see how she greeted the kid with the bug on his jaw. He didn't get a kiss. She walked past him, her high heels tap-tapping on concrete.

Ross straightened. God, but he was relieved. 'Only a bit of a kid,' he said, rubbing his palms together, trying to wipe the grin from his face. 'Phew,' he said, at the window now, looking down at a small red car backing out to the street. He saw Sally wave. She'd known he'd be there, watching. He waved back, feeling good now, feeling great, feeling hungry. Bread, butter, cheese and lettuce in the fridge. He didn't need to go out for dinner. He found frozen yoghurt, bananas, a tin of sliced peaches.

'No worries,' he said.

going places

Sally barely glanced at the pipsqueak, but she noticed the mole on his jaw. No bandaid covering it tonight, it wriggled when he spoke, and before they turned into Toorak Road his mole was dancing.

They drove around St Kilda for half an hour looking for a park. Sally saw car parks, she offered to pay, but he was a determined little sod. They got a free park eventually, which left them a half-kilometre walk back to the club.

Inside, the lighting was dim. He found his way out back to the karaoke bar, and she followed where he led. For half an hour she managed not to look at him, but after a drink he was almost on her lap, his face in her face, checking out the menu of songs. He was going to get up and sing tonight.

Noise was currently being made on stage by a raucous female wearing a shiny green skirt split to the crotch and a gold vest open to the waist – not a lot left to the imagination, but her voice needed all the help it could get.

'This is ear abuse,' Sally yelled.

'I'm better than her, babe.'

'So is Ross's rooster.'

'What?'

'Nothing.' She emptied her glass.

'I used to be in the school band. I play guitar, keyboard. You name it, I can play it. My flat is full of equipment, two guitars.' She'd started him up again, so she let him go while her mind and her eyes went elsewhere.

Two fast glasses of wine hit the spot so she ordered a third, and a scotch and Coke for the cocky little bugger. 'I used to play the guitar a bit at school,' she said. 'Used to know most of the chords.'

'More to playing guitar than a few chords, babe.'

'You may be right, smartarse.'

'I ought to know. I studied it from when I was eight years old.'

How had she got herself into this? How was she going to get out of it? Go to the loo, then find a phone and call a taxi, that's how. Her eyes looked past her date to the ladies room; there was a guy seated in front of it, and from the rear he looked like Matt. He was with a blonde. His wife? She stared, willing him to turn around.

The pipsqueak became aware that he'd lost her attention. 'Did you see how I got the most sales on Thursday? I can't put a foot wrong with Ratsus.' The drink had moved him, encouraged him to move his chair against her own; it had given his mouth less control. She wiped her face, her ear, moved her chair and stared at the back of the dark head.

It was Matt for sure, and the wine and the company was making her want what she didn't want to want, what she hadn't wanted since Christmas Eve. She willed him to turn, to see her, to leave his blonde and save her from purgatory.

'I reckon she's a bull dyke,' Pipsqueak said.

'Who?'

'Ratsus. She's got to be. She said to me on Friday –'

'I don't care what she said to you. Will you give my ears a break for five minutes, and stop spitting all over me?' The man who had to be Matt didn't like the entertainment. He stood, turned around, and he was as ugly as a bag full of monkeys.

'It's not him,' she said.

'Not who?' His nose was in her face again, a long nose. Thin. Awful hair, lank and rusty blond.

She eyed the nose and the mole on his jaw that looked like a cockroach. Every house she'd ever lived in had resident cockroaches. She'd declared war on them, stomped them, listened to the crack. She wanted to stomp this one too, get it out of her face. She watched it crawl under his chin. Crawl back up again.

He smiled, pleased her interest was again centred on him. The cockroach stretched, stood up on its back legs and preened. Good pickings in the dark tonight, it thought, and she laughed because she knew how to handle insects.

Matt had no blemishes, no scars. Gold-dust skin. Smooth, long fine legs. Her black swan. Beautiful, serene black swan. Want travelled through her as she thought of Matt but stared at a cockroach, hypnotising it with her eye.

It cowered. 'What do you reckon, babe?' it said. 'I'm getting cold feet.'

'Drink up, I reckon.' Another drink might kill that old weak want in her belly. She ordered two more.

'I've been thinking of selling my old one. Thought I might put an ad on the noticeboard at work.'

'Your old what?' she yelled. There was a guy sucking up to the mike now and he had a voice like a working bullock.

'Guitar.'

'How much do you want for it?'

This was a new twist. He wanted her, but he wanted top dollar for his guitar too. What did he want more? She saw his eyes weigh up the scales; he found a balance. Spoke it.

'Sold. Bring it to work on payday.'

'That's without a case. Someone knocked off the case once when I was busking, took it and my money and jumped a tram.'

'What?'

'Someone knocked off the case. It's got no case.'

'I've got my own,' she yelled. Mine now to tie me down, like the goose girl is mine. The photographs.

The working bullock moved off and an elderly woman was having her moment of glory. Maybe she'd been good once, but she'd left her run too late. The pipsqueak was on about his school band, so she tuned out. What a cocky little bugger. But he no longer wanted to get up and sing. Still planning to grab a taxi home to Ross, she escaped to the loo and tossed down a don't-care pill. It changed her mind. She was going to force him up there, make him put up or shut up. And she wanted to hear 'Runaway Girl'. Hadn't heard it in years.

Again she moved her chair. They'd almost completed a circle. What was his name, anyway? She'd heard it in the tearoom. D for Davey? Donny?

Minutes later, she heard it. Dennis Roach. He cowered. Not so Cocky Roach now, and she laughed as she watched his mole drink from his glass. Dennis didn't suit him. Cocky did. What were names, anyway? What use naming a baby Amanda and having it grow up to look like a Maude, a Christopher to look like a Norm? Names were confusing. Only Matt was perfect. And Ross. Their names suited them well.

Sally De Rooze. It sounded like a stage name.

'Dennis Roach?'

'You're being paged,' she said.

He kept his head low. 'Can't,' he said. 'I can't, babe. Those last two were good.'

'I love ''Runaway Girl''. I bought the tape when I was nineteen and wore it out. Get up there and sing it for me, you chicken.'

'No. No, I shouldn't have let you talk me into that one. It's got too much range for me. You shouldn't have talked me into that one.'

'Squawk-squawk,' she said and she flapped her elbows. 'I've got the range.'

And she stood, because she wanted to hear that song. She emptied her glass in a long swallow and emptied his scotch and Coke too. She shrugged, smoothed down her skirt and walked in a near straight line to the stage; she grasped the mike for support and looked out at the tables, at the expectant faces. Her skirt was short, her make-up intact; they didn't mind looking at her.

Crow with a sore throat. That's what Mummy used to say. Stop that noise, it's grating on my nerves. That's what Mummy used to say. Shane would have been the singer. That's what Mummy used to say.

But Mummy was dead.

Shit. What a bloody idiot. She licked her lips as she glanced at the screen, at the mike. She'd never used a mike and didn't need the words on the screen. She knew 'Runaway Girl'. She'd sung it a thousand times, sung it in the paddocks to Ross's sheep. She'd almost broken up with him that first time over this song.

Then the music began.

'Shit,' she said, and the mike amplified her word.

Laughter. Flock of faces.

She stepped back, repeating the word. That bloody mike! How close was too close? She swallowed, closed her eyes and thought of Ross's fat lambs on their way to the slaughterhouse, and she opened her mouth and sang to them:

Little runaway girl,
Keep on running till you get to the place where you want to be.
Take the mountains in your stride, cross the rivers swift and wide –

She brought the house down.

She brought the house down! They clapped her and wanted more, but she ran back to the table, sobered. Cocky wouldn't let her sit down and hide. He made her get up and sing 'Wind

Beneath My Wings'. And she'd always loved that one too, so she sucked up to the mike pretending she was Bette Midler, and gave it everything she had.

It was like . . . like finally . . . It was like. God only knew what it was like.

'Jesus, you're good, babe. You're something else. Jesus! What are you doing flogging stuff on bloody telephones?'

Something else. That's what it was like. Like she had been someone else. Like she'd finally come together. Here in this place, in front of these people, someone had swept up all the bits of her from all of the old floors in all of the houses and –

Pow!

Her atoms had flung themselves back together as she'd opened her mouth and let it rip.

'Pow!'

'You and me together, babe. We could go places.'

She looked at him then, looked at his mole and she laughed. 'Let's go places, babe,' she said, and they headed off in search of his car. She sang as they walked, sang 'Wind Beneath My Wings', but to him, altering the words to suit.

They couldn't find the street where he'd left his car, and she was away in some crazy, hazy laughing wonderland and no help at all. He was laughing with her, until he found his car with a parking ticket under the wiper. *Residents only.*

'I'll pay half,' she said. 'Sorry, babe. But I'm not really sorry because it was worth every cent of it. I'll pay the lot.'

'Thanks, babe,' he said.

He walked her to her door and he wanted in that door, but she laughed again.

'You're just the wind beneath my wings, so be a wind and blow, babe,' she said. But she kissed his cheek, gave him a Bertram hug. He was just a kid, just a kid full up with dreams.

Dreams were contagious.

the utility

Blustery north winds were blowing around Lakeside at midday, trapped there by the hills. It had the dust flying in the paddocks, and the sticky bushflies sheltering indoors, looking for moisture. Ross was supplying it. On his back beneath the ute, sweat trickled, prickled. The ute's tail shaft had vibrated all the way home from Melbourne, but it was Tuesday before he'd found the time to look at it. He was up to his elbows in grease, undoing the final U-bolt, and the dogs started their 'some bugger is coming' bark.

Minutes later he heard the car. 'Who the hell wants me now?' he said.

He heard the car doors slam as he eased the tail shaft down, then he whistled the dogs, who came at a run to the shed and proceeded to crouch down lower than their top dog, still flat out beneath the ute.

'Mr Bertram?' The voice spoke to a pair of size-twelve boots.

'That's me.' Boots, followed by greasy overalls and a grin, slid out, but the grin disappeared as he looked into the light where two cops stood, shoulder to shoulder.

'What's happened?' he said, on his feet, his vibrating tail shaft forgotten.

'We believe you may be able to assist us with our inquiries into the death of Helen Lee, Mr Bertram.'

'Who?'

'At approximately 8.45 p.m. on Sunday evening, Helen Lee was struck by a vehicle in Bollinger Street, South Yarra. We believe you may have been in the vicinity at the time.'

Ross eyeballed them, first the tall guy, then the little bloke with the notebook. He swallowed, wiped a greasy hand across his mouth, tasted grease and spat as the smaller cop looked across to the ute.

'I didn't hit anyone,' he said reaching for his cigarettes, looking at the packet, then at his black hands. Slowly he picked up an old T-shirt from the floor and wiped at the grease.

'We believe that you left Bollinger Street at approximately 8.45 p.m. on Sunday evening.'

'It was a bit after 8.30. I got home here around 10.30. I used the Bolte Bridge and it took me half an hour less coming home than what it took me to get there. Who was she?'

'Her parents live at 18 Bollinger Street, Mr Bertram.'

He stared at the duo, suddenly knowing why they were there. 'You mean that little kid. That little Asian kid. Helen?' The tall cop nodded. 'Oh, Jesus. We were only talking to them that afternoon. We were fixing Sally's door and these two cute little kids came out. Oh Jesus. That bastard of a city.'

They were waiting for more but Ross closed his mouth and looked down at his dogs, tears stinging his eyes, his head shaking, denying, denying that bastard of a city.

'Did you notice any other vehicles in the street at the time you were leaving, Mr Bertram?'

'I wouldn't know where to start, would I? There were cars everywhere.'

'Where was your vehicle parked?'

'On the street. On the right-hand side, about two spaces back from the drive.' He tossed his butt to the earth, ground it in and lit another. 'A couple of cars drove in, a couple drove out. There was an old bloke delivering junk mail – or something.'

'Can you give us a description?'

'Who looks at junk-mail deliverers, or their junk? I didn't take any notice.'

'Old, you said. Tall? Short?'

'He looked . . . I dunno.' Ross hunted a fly, watched it land on the smaller cop's ear. 'He looked small, but I'm inclined to think anyone under six foot is a genetic dwarf.' The smaller cop didn't like that. He swatted the fly and spent some time identifing its corpse.

'Did you get an idea of his age, Mr Bertram?'

'He wasn't young.' Ross blew smoke. 'Sixty-odd, I'd say, but he drove a racy little car.'

'Any idea of the make?'

'It was a Honda, one of those sporty little two-door jobs. A 97–98 model, black, Honda Prelude.'

'Delivering junk mail, Mr Bertram?'

'I don't know. I'm just trying to help you. He was hanging around the letterboxes. How would I know what he was doing?' He waited, but they weren't saying anything. 'You don't think of what you're seeing in Melbourne, because you're seeing too much. I mean, you don't wander around thinking, I'd better take note of this, someone is going to commit a crime. He was at the letterboxes when I walked past with my bag, then I saw him open his car door as I drove away. He wouldn't have done it.'

'Where was he parked, Mr Bertram?'

'Down from my ute. There was a white van in front of me and a little Asian guy loading something into it when I left.' He patted Rusty's head, then Fred pushed in, expecting his due. Ross gave him a pat while the lemon meringue pie he'd eaten for morning tea rose to his throat. He swallowed it, his mind flitting back to Saturday night and that bed. He swallowed again, coughed and turned away.

'We believe the vehicle would have been damaged, Mr Bertram. Would you mind if we –?'

'Oh, Christ, man! Come off the grass! As if I'd run over a little kid and not stop.' Ross looked at his grease-stained hands, and at a knuckle newly scraped. He walked to the door, looked out at the Matthews' farm, and thought of home-baked pie. 'Bloody Melbourne,' he said. 'She won't be getting me back there in a hurry. She goes down there to find herself. Find herself!' He walked to the utility and flung the doors wide, dropped the tail gate. 'I haven't cleaned it for six months. Any blood you see on it is sheep's blood. I'm going in to have a shower. If you want to talk, come up to the house.'

'Bloody find herself,' he muttered as he walked away from the two men, the dogs at his heels. 'She's found something. Dunno what it bloody was. Shit. That bastard of a city.'

on the edge

Melbourne had pulled a day straight from hell's oven. The shadeless roof was deserted. Smokers might brave the wind and rain, but they ran from this flesh-baking heat, escaping to the shade twelve floors below.

Cocky Roach's workstation had sat vacant for most of that morning, but within minutes of his arrival, the entire crew knew why he'd been late. He was still at it when they walked to the tearoom.

The police had questioned Sally on Monday evening; she'd known the reason for Cocky's absence. She hadn't seen him on Sunday night; he'd knocked at her door. Forewarned is forearmed – she'd seen his car, which must have been seconds before Helen Lee had walked downstairs with her bundle of tracksuits, as she'd been doing, twice a week, since Sally had moved in. Cocky had watched her fly through the air. He'd seen her fall.

'Like a rag doll,' he said for the umpteenth time. 'She looked like a rag doll.'

Varicose wasn't eating. 'I let Tania ride her bike to school today. I knew I shouldn't have.' Fear in her voice. Fear in her eyes as she looked at her watch. 'I think I might go home. I told her to ride on the footpath but children don't listen these days.'

No-one in the tearoom listened to her either, but Pimples was staring at her breasts. Sue was eating melon. Sally wasn't hungry. Today she wanted to close up, shut down. Didn't want to think of the dark-eyed little girl from Number 13. Didn't want to think.

Her eyes roamed across the table to Pimples. Like a gangly shadow he always wandered in behind old coot Ron, wandered out behind him; there, but not there. He was half a metre taller than Ron, but he let the old coot push him around – stinging old wasp, feeding on a crippled spider.

She stared at the blood and at the great boil-like pimple on his neck. He caught her eye, blushed, and his finger moved to his neck. Old coot Ron belted his elbow.

What was with those two?

Pimples picked up his apple, picked at a pimple on its red skin.

All of that height, cowered by an overbearing old coot with stinking feet.

What was his name? She'd worked with him for almost ten months and didn't know his name. Had she heard it? Colin Carbuncle? Wally Wimp?

She shivered, and Cocky's arm behind her chair fell to her shoulder, squeezed. He was crowding her; everyone had to know they were a twosome, that they'd shared some high drama at the weekend.

'I'm pretty certain it was the car I saw driving off that got her,' he said. This was stuff straight out of *Blue Heelers*. Cocky had his listeners on the edge of their seats. 'It was black, or that real dark green, and going like a bat out of hell.'

Famous eyewitness Cocky. He'd got his face on television last night. Was there anything he hadn't done?

'The cops'll be crawling all over your place again tonight,

babe. You might be better off staying with me for a few days.'

Eyes stared. This was something new. Another romance blooming in the workplace? Toy boy Norm had got off with married Red. She'd left her husband to set up house with a ratty moustache. He'd left his wife and the kids.

Ron took the floor. He started his favourite recitation on Asians and Aborigines, and an argumentative greenie told him that Australia was part of Asia and they had more right to be here than the white man.

'And where would bloody Australia be if it hadn't been for the white man?'

'A fucking sight better off with one less of them,' Sue said.

'Stop it. Stop it, all of you. A little girl is dead and you don't care.'

'Not my bloody fault, is it,' Ron said.

Varicose rose to her aching legs and left for the toilets. Then they were all up and looking at their watches as they wandered back to staff the phones, to sell the unsaleable to those who didn't want to buy it. Pimples gangling in behind, always behind, but head and shoulders taller than the rest, he stood out in the crowd.

And the great grey hulk bore down on him, a man o'war under full sail. And she did it. She blasted him out of the water. 'You no good for me. Go home, watch video. I have no place here for you,' she said. 'You go now.'

Pimples' face became a mottled puce. He gangled, looked at Ron. Cringed.

'Useless little bastard.' Ron's dentures click-clacked.

No words of defence. Pimples walked.

'You coming back late. Everyone. You thinking this office is for fun here. No.' Ratsus's finger stabbed the air. 'You wanting to work or you not wanting work. Is not material to me. Yes, but my job is material. You not doing you job then I losing my job. Or right? Ratsus Sydney are doing two times what we doing last week. We lose the big client because you are all lazy.'

Sally watched Pimples' back disappear behind a partition, watched his head walk off alone. No more jackhammer finger breaking through the concrete scabs. No more big, staring baby blues.

Then the argumentative greenie got the chop. Ratsus, still weeding her patch, caught Varicose attempting to creep back to her station. Too big to creep, too visible in her black, wide as Ratsus but not as tall.

'You too. You, the big one. You go. All lazy people. Australia is full of the lazy people. You watching video too. Be happy.'

Varicose drew herself up to her full height and her rounded chin lifted. 'My name is Joyce Rogers, and I was going home anyway, and I can't afford to own a video on what you pay me,' she said, joining the greenie at the lifts.

Ratsus gulped air for the next burst. 'In Australia you having it good for too long. In Australia you –'

Pimples wasn't waiting at the lifts. Where had he gone?

'In Australia you are not understanding of what the working ethic is about. You –'

'Oh, for Christ's sake! If you don't like the pee in our pool, then no-one is forcing you to swim in it.'

Heads turned to face Sally. Jesus! Had she said that?

Old coot Ron's dentures dropped, hobbling a tongue that wanted to buy in; he always had his say, but jobs were not easy for a man over seventy to come by, and bejesus, didn't he know it.

The spaceless space grew silent. Shuffling feet stilled. Ratsus was silent, her mouth jammed open. Air sucked in for the next burst had no place to go. Sally watched the trapped air swell behind the old queen rat's eyeballs as they sought, found Sally.

'You it is who talk the ratsus racism to me? You, who I have give to the hundred opportunity.'

Faces turned away, disassociating themselves from Sally's mad mouth, and from her truth, truth she'd heard spoken a hundred times in the tearoom, in the coffee shop, in the toilets, on the roof. Old Ron's head was down. Even he knew that truth must be hidden behind beetroot sandwiches and tearoom doors.

'You spit on opportunity. You are lazy ratsus. Always late. Always with excuse. My poor mother is sick.' She'd grown huge and the bodies crammed into this space heard her power, knew her power. She sucked more air.

The space around Sally was widening. Sue fiddled with her hair. Christmas green all gone. Shock of red with flecks of purple today.

'Rat's arse,' Sally corrected. She walked to the whiteboard and wrote the words there, in red, underlining them, a tutor instructing her class. 'The – rat's – arse. What he sits on. And this job is rat shit, which is associated with the rat's arse, and I'm sick of shovelling it.' She walked back to her station and picked up her bag.

The hulk was ready to explode, transistors glowing, electricity flashing, she stared at the whiteboard.

Rat's arse? Rodent? Dirty black thing with flea? So it was no more the ratsus. So now it was the rat's bum? Trapped air given a lead, rolled. It found a breach and escaped in a long drawn-out squeal. She tensed her huge buttocks, tried to hold it in, only extending the length of the squeak-squawk. Then, in front of a hundred eyes, she deflated.

Confused by her diminishing size, she click-clicked away fast to her rat pad, but she got the last word. 'You ... you going from my office. Out! Now! Go!'

Sally was already walking.

Sue caught her eye, winked, waved. Poor Sue, granddaughter of a Collins Street specialist, daughter of a barrister, not good enough for her professional family. Didn't finish university, did she? Poor dropout Sue, pushing her failure up her family's nose with her nose ring. Working day and night to pay off the bank, trying to do the impossible.

But the banks were like Queen Ratsus. They demanded the impossible, and if you couldn't give it to them willingly, they took it, took your house. Sue knew. Spiked red and purple hair, a tattoo and nose ring were her armour against this grab-all society. But armour rusted away. She'd go under, just to keep her house. She'd let her hair go back to common mouse and she'd go back to uni so her father would pay out the mortgage. If you can't beat them, join them.

Varicose and the greenie had taken the lift down. Not a sign of Pimples. Sally glanced at the corridor leading to the toilets. Maybe he'd walked down.

She looked into the dark cavern of stairs. Smell of musty dust, smell of mice, and sort of ... homey. 'Hello,' she yelled. Hollow, like the houses and flats she had emptied; her words bounced back. She shrugged, and her hand reached into her pocket and came out with her smokes. Just one more on the roof, just for old times' sake, just to show the hard old bitch that one of her mice would leave when it was good and ready.

Up the concrete steps then, over the butts and the grime, up, up to the roof, just to say goodbye to the view, to wave goodbye to the beetle people and the matchbox cars.

flying away

He was up there. He was standing on the concrete ledge and he wasn't picking his pimples either; his arms were spread wide. A gangly aeroplane, poised for take-off.

He swayed when he heard the door, and Sally's mouth opened, a scream wanting to get out; she held it back, her throat muscles closing around it as she continued forward, clenched fingers crushing the cigarette packet.

She had mentally stood on that ledge a thousand times. She knew that place intimately. So easy to jump. No use changing your mind halfway down. No bungee-rope doctor to pull you back, pump your stomach, sew up slashed wrists, not if you jumped.

Had to say something. What would a social worker say?

'The condemned man always gets a last smoke.' She was no social worker and he didn't accept her offer, which was to the good because she couldn't find her lighter and her cigarettes were bent. Then she found it, straightened a smoke, lit it and sucked, her eyes never leaving him. 'I lost my job too. Varico – a couple of others got the shove.'

He was deaf, or already gone from this world, her words were not reaching him. She glanced back at the stairs. No help down there, so she edged a step closer, and two more, and she was at the ledge. A fast glance down. No tree below, no awning to catch him, just a brightly wrapped snack bar on wheels, beetles tumbling out, more beetles queuing to get on.

'What if you land on someone?' she said. He didn't hear her. 'Think of the poor coot who'd have to clean up the mess,' she said. Had to say something but shouldn't have said that. What did people say? What did they do in suicide situations?

He wiped at his nose with his wrist and it wasn't the right thing to do on a ledge. Her cigarette fell to the concrete and her hand reached out to grab a leg. Couldn't reach. But he regained his balance and her hand blindly snatched and straightened a second cigarette as she stepped closer. Not that she could do much if she did grab one of his legs. She'd go over with him, give them two for the price of one.

Smoke drifted by him; he turned his head. 'Smoking makes me dizzy now.'

He could talk! But dizzy wasn't good on a narrow ledge. The hand holding the cigarette dropped to her side as her heart rate hit two thousand revs a minute, on idle, and she looked at the sky for help. Black clouds rolling in from the bay. Rain coming to wash this heat away. Thunder in the distance.

He swayed to the left, or was it the clouds, or was she swaying? 'My grandfather hates my guts. I got dumped on him when I was five. All I ever get at home is what a moll my mother was. I'm going to do it,' he said.

'Not in front of me, thanks. I've already watched my father and three little brothers die. What's your name?'

He glanced at her. His feet were too big, the ledge too narrow, the wind growing, blowing, wanting to snatch him, sweep him away.

'Sit down,' she ordered. 'You're making me dizzy.' She didn't have the right tone to command obedience. Ross's dogs knew that.

'Bloody old Razakenowskie bitch. I make enough sales.'

'Razakenowskie? I call her Ratsus. What's your name, I said?'

'You want to sell it to the newspapers? Get on television like that cocky little dickhead.'

'I just asked your name. People do it every day.'

'Who cares?'

'I care.' Mrs Bertram had said that to her once, and it had worked too; it wasn't working for him.

'You're like everyone else. You're full of it.'

'Stop feeling sorry for yourself and get down.'

'What would you know about anything? People like you have got it all.'

'That's me, born under a lucky star.' She looked at the clouds and at the lightning like fireworks over the bay. A beautiful city from up here. You could see the big picture from this roof – and she wanted it. 'That's me,' she said. 'I've got everything, and what I haven't got, I'm going to get.' Then she began speaking of her father and the boys. Didn't know why. It just seemed like the right thing to do at the time.

She spoke of her mother, and the families she'd lived with, and once she began she couldn't find a place to stop, because she was remembering stuff she hadn't thought about in twenty years.

It got him sitting down, his long legs straddling the ledge, his big red-rimmed baby blues staring at her. Maybe he was just waiting to hear the end of the story before he flew, so she didn't let it end. She sucked more smoke, and told him how her own mother hadn't liked her, even before the accident, because she'd been her father's girl. And how one night her father had stood her on the kitchen table and got her to sing a song for Grandma and Papa, and how Mummy had thrown a screaming fit and they'd had to call the doctor.

She spoke of the night her father died, and how she'd sat on the wet grass and watched the car burn. She poured it all out and, right or wrong, it got him off the ledge, got him standing by her side, looking sorry for her, or still sorry for himself but asking if he could have that cigarette, please, and he'd pay her back later.

Later was good. It was very good. She gave him the crushed packet and lighter.

'You probably read that in a horror novel,' he said, bent smoke in his mouth.

'I don't read horror. I lived it. But now I'm into fantasy.'

He lit up with shaking hands, and he stood there smoking, still holding her packet and lighter, so he couldn't pick his pimples. 'I'm not going home,' he said.

'Living with a miserable grandfather might be better than living with a nutcase mother.' She told him about the purse full of pills, and the psychiatric hospitals, and how her mother had blamed her for the accident. How she'd wake her up in the night to say, 'You killed them.' And how, one night, her mother had mixed her a glass of chocolate milk with half a packet of pills in it.

'And you're the first person I've ever told about that. And it's true.'

This wasn't the time or the place to feel good, but somehow, as she had poured it out on him, something dark was lifting from her shoulders. All of her life she'd covered up for her mother. She'd lied to welfare ladies, lied to the schools and Mrs Bertram. She'd burned Marian's death certificate her mother had obtained just to deface. No more cover-up. She was dobbing, and it felt so right.

He handed back her cigarettes, and his hands empty, he picked a pimple. A crater filled, spilled. 'I'm still not going home. That miserable old bugger won't let me live this down.'

'Don't tell him. There are plenty of jobs in call centres.'

He looked at her. 'Don't tell him? He bloody knows, doesn't he!'

And suddenly she knew too, knew why he hung around old Ron. 'Not miserable old bugger Ron?' she said.

'He's my grandfather.'

'Shiiiiit! I'd jump if I were you.'

'I'll have another smoke first. I'll pay you back.'

She gave him another bent smoke and leaned with him, staring down at the movement below as thunder rolled, moving in on them. No rain yet, but the earth felt cleansed.

'Did you ever hear that song kids used to sing at school? A man fell out of an aeroplane at forty thousand feet,' he said, flicking ash to the wind.

'And he ain't gunna fly no more.'

'They scraped him off the tarmac like a blob of strawberry jam.'

'Raspberry jam,' she said.

'Strawberry.'

'Raspberry.'

'We used to sing strawberry. You made me think of it when you said about someone cleaning up the mess.'

'I always knew I should have been a social worker.'

A half-smile lifted one side of his lips. Maybe she'd talked him down, actually saved a life today. And maybe he hadn't been planning to jump anyway. But it didn't matter. She felt good.

'I'm Michael,' he said.

'Want to go down for a coffee?'

'Dunno what I want. I've been thinking I might give Joyce a call. She's got a bungalow to rent. She's only asking fifty bucks a week for it.'

'Joyce who?'

'Joyce Rogers.' His large hands cupped the air fifty centimetres from his chest, then he blushed one of his better maroons.

symbol of love

Downstairs Sally watched him wander off to find a phone. She went into the coffee shop; he wasn't the only one who didn't want to go home.

Few customers around at this time, a male reading in the corner, a deaf couple talking with their hands, cigarettes adding emphasis. Sally sipped hot coffee and lit up while her mind wandered back to Saturday night and Ross.

She'd slept with him by default that first time, slept with him because his mother had died. Slept with him by default again on Saturday night.

She'd been on such a crazy high when she'd come home from the karaoke bar, up there somewhere, straddling the moon, dreaming dreams again. Hadn't dreamed those dreams in years, if ever.

'Oh, Ross,' she'd said when he'd opened her door. 'I am so happy I'm going to burst.' She'd bear hugged him and danced him to the kitchenette. 'I've never been this happy in my life.' Wrong thing to say. She'd known it as soon as the words were out of her mouth.

'Me too, love. I've missed you like you wouldn't believe.' And he'd kissed her.

No way out of it after that. She'd looked for a way out. They'd had coffee. She'd tried to explain her happiness, but he'd never listened. She'd told him about getting up on stage and singing 'Runaway Girl'.

He hadn't liked that song ten years ago. 'Good for you, love,' he'd said, his head on her pillows, uninterested in her triumph but smiling a lot and waiting for her to put the light out, get into that bed.

Gold dust, moondust all around her on Saturday night and no place else for her overflow of happiness to go.

So she'd . . . she'd made love to him.

'Who's that sleeping in my bed?' she'd said, and she'd jumped him.

'What are you up to? Put the light out, love.'

'Don't you move. I've got you covered,' she'd said. 'If you want to come down to the big bad city and sleep in Goldilocks' bed, then you take what you get and like it, Ross Bear.'

He'd liked it. He'd really liked it. No complaints at all, but he hadn't been the same man on Sunday morning, hardly game to look at her.

They'd gone out to the Wantirna Trash-and-Treasure market and he'd bought a tonne of old tools, and she'd found a dusty ornament and named it number fourteen. It was a leprechaun man with long boots and a jaunty hat, and she got him for one dollar. The end of his walking stick had been broken, which made him fit in with the rest of the motley crew. She'd found a stick in the car park, sawed it to length with a kitchen knife, glued it into place, then applied half a dozen coats of brown nail polish; from a distance you couldn't even see the repair.

On Sunday afternoon Ross had removed her sticking front door and cut a centimetre from its base with a blunt saw, also purchased at the market. The bikie walked from his room as they were sawing.

'Got the demolition squad in there, De Rooster?' he'd said.

She'd glanced through his open door. His flat was empty. No bed. No table. No chair. Just the same beige carpet on the same shaped floor as her own. Just the same walls, the same kitchen bench.

'Moving out at last?' she'd said.

'Don't get your hopes up.'

'What is there if not hope?'

He'd walked downstairs, then turned. 'And stop sticking junk in my letterbox.'

'Stop parking in my space, then.'

'He's black,' Ross said when the bikie was out of hearing range. 'What are you doing, talking to him like that?'

'How am I supposed to talk to him?'

'What's he do? Does he work?'

'I don't know. This is the city. You don't ask a person's occupation when you meet them on the stairs. He probably deals drugs or something. I saw him out at the casino one night.'

The old Bertram disapproval had reared its head. 'I don't know what's got into you lately, Sally. You've changed.'

She ordered a second coffee and sat on. Better to stay away from the flats. She didn't want to meet the little Asian guy on the stairs, hear the unsighted mother's terrible keening wail.

No job to go to tomorrow either. Just one of the unemployed again.

No more Ratsus, though. No more Monday pep talks. No more telephones. She'd look around for a shop job. Plenty of those, plenty of waitress work, sandwich hands. She'd get something. Underpaid, but money hadn't been a problem lately. Her Christmas Club thousand was in the bank, intact. Ross's cheque was still in the bottom of her bag, probably intact. Her rent was paid and her petrol tank full, and she now bought her cigarettes by the carton from a discount place, cut the price per pack by seven cents.

The thought of cigarettes had her reaching for her packet, and she lit up. It was catching. The reader in the corner lit up, then the deaf couple, stilling their chatter long enough to join in. Sally frowned as a hugely pregnant woman opened the door and stepped into the haze. Quick to pick up the scent she hugged her stomach as she backed out again.

Backed into Matt.

'Oh shit!'

He was apologising, then opening the door. He was coming in here. She moaned and cowered low in her chair. Her face shielded by her hand, she watched him walk to the counter.

He ordered coffee while Sally stared at his back. She hadn't seen him since the day in the lift with Sue, and she didn't want to see him. She was buying Cocky's old guitar on Thursday and on Sunday they were going places. She was free.

But the back of his head, the shape of his ears, the collar of his shirt. His shoulders, not broad, but broad enough.

He's not going to turn around, she thought. She drew on her cigarette and blew the smoke high. Let him smell smoke, buy takeaway coffee, and go. Make him go. She forced more smoke in his direction.

But the woman was putting a pastry on a plate. He'd sit down. He'd see her.

She glanced at the rear of the shop. No toilet. No back exit. Just the kitchen. She couldn't run through the kitchen. She mashed her cigarette and took a don't-care pill from her handbag, swallowing it with hot coffee. It caught in her throat. She gulped more hot coffee and it burned all the way down.

Then he turned around. Looked at her table. Walked to her table.

'So,' he said. 'So, look who's here.'

'So,' she replied. Hands beneath the table, fingers gripping the table leg, strove to draw strength from inanimate wood as she willed the tiny pill to get her together, to make her strong enough to tell him where to go.

'So here we are,' he said. Their relationship had not been based on conversation.

'So here I am, and there you are too.' Sally kept playing the game. She could keep it up as long as him, but her stomach felt weak and was still burning from the gulped coffee. And the pill wasn't dissolving fast enough, wasn't getting into her blood and saying 'I don't care' fast enough.

She cared. She still cared. He was so beautiful. Why the hell did he have to come in here today?

'Do you mind?'

'Yes,' she said, 'I mind. Plenty of vacant tables.'

He moved the ashtray, placed his coffee and pastry down, but remained standing while his hand went to his pocket and withdrew a small parcel. He offered it. 'I knew I'd see you today. I woke up knowing it. When I walked out of the office I knew where I'd find you. A late Merry Christmas, Sall.'

Liar. She was always on the twelfth floor at this time. He'd probably bought the present for his wife, or his office girl. She looked at the door, reached for her coffee. He wasn't going to buy his way back onto her bed, fridge, table, with his two-bit present. She was going to be all right. Her stomach had settled. Maybe the pill was kicking in. She sipped, uninterested, and he placed the gift beside her saucer, stooped, kissed her cheek.

'That's desperate stuff. This is a public place, Matt,' she said, wiping her cheek with the back of her hand. But he was seated now. Paid for his seat with that kiss.

'Desperation breeds desperate measures.' He took her hand. Just his touch. Electric. And his eyes: sad, pleading. His half-smile, his lifted eyebrow.

How do you kill love? How do you kill it stone-dead?

'How did you know I'd be down here? I'm never down here at this time.'

'Mental telepathy. I told you we didn't need telephones.'

He's left his wife, she thought, and hope crawled. Hope rose to her throat, choking her, then disappointment followed on hope's heels. She didn't want to go back. She wanted to go forward. Her and little Cocky Roach and their guitars. That's what she wanted. There would be no more circles in her life. No more breaking up and going back. That's what she'd done with Ross, and she wasn't going to do it any more.

Keep on running till you get to the place –

Straight ahead. Straight down the middle. No more Jim Beam to buy, she was going to have her front tooth capped next week and pay it off. That's what she wanted. That's what she'd do.

But stupid bloody hope and the don't-care pill got their heads together.

He has left her. He must have. He's got her to agree to a settlement. He said all along that, given time, he would get her to agree.

Don't do this. Stand up. Run for your life.

She picked up her bag, slipped the strap over her shoulder, then two women walked in and eyed Matt as if he was something God only makes once before throwing away the mould, because He's made something too good to be true.

Far too good to be true.

In her head she knew that; it was only her brainless heart she had to control.

'Open it, Sall.' Again he offered the gift. 'I saw it, and I knew it was you.'

'What is it? A used bus ticket to Hallam? A pizza voucher? Sorry. The price has gone up.'

'On the advice of your new financial adviser?' He smiled, and her heart full of hope rolled over.

Don't do this.

Catch a moonbeam, catch a star, hold it high and you'll see far –

But she was doing it, and the two women were still staring, and so was the deaf couple. They watched her lift the sticky tape. Peel back the paper. Purple and gold, colours of royalty. They watched her remove a small grey suede pouch with a gold drawstring. Watched her pull the drawstring open. Upend the pouch.

And a ring fell into her palm. It was a golden heart, set with a single diamond.

'Oh, my God, Matt! My God! It's beautiful!'

'So are you, and I can't function without you in my life. I can't get through a day, a night, without wanting you.' He touched her face, stroked it with long fingers, then he lifted her pointed chin, made her look at him.

He'd bought her an engagement ring and the stone was huge. She looked at it, at him. Wasn't this what she'd wanted? Wanted. Wasn't he what she'd wanted?

'God, Matt.' The ring must have cost him a fortune, and she'd pushed him, she'd nagged him to leave his wife. 'God.' It slipped too easily onto her engagement finger. Of course it was too big. She had kid's hands. But it fitted the second finger of her right hand.

He ate his pastry, drank his coffee, then he stood. 'I've got an appointment,' he said. 'Tonight?'

She nodded, picked up the suede pouch, the purple and gold paper, folded it and dropped it in her bag as she stood. 'Dinner. We'll go somewhere to celebrate, Matt.'

'I don't want to share you with the crowd, Sall.'

His ring was on her finger. His ring. He and the don't-care pill were engaged. The don't-care pill nodded.

He stayed with her on the bed while their watches tick-ticked and 9.30 was lost, and the clock ticked on. She thought he'd stay the night, but he couldn't, or wouldn't.

Then he was gone and the flat was empty.

She walked to the bathroom, found the half-pack of contraceptive pills she'd been taking since her night with Ross. As she lifted the glass of water to her mouth, the light caught her ring, making the colours bounce. She slipped it off and placed it on her engagement finger, squeezing her fingers together to keep the stone upright.

He hadn't mentioned his wife, and she hadn't asked if he'd left her. Hadn't wanted to know the answer, that's why.

But he loves me. He needs me. He said it tonight, over and over.

She looked at the ring again. Even if he hasn't left his wife, that ring, that rock, was his promise that he was going to. No man would buy that diamond just for the sake of a few hours in bed.

A wide, empty bed now. What would it be like waking up next to Matt? Would he be grumpy? Happy? Soon she'd know. Where would they live? The hand wearing his ring was beneath her cheek; she could feel it. Sharp.

So she slept.

But like Matt, the ring slipped off in the night. Sally found it gouging into her hip when the alarm woke her, and she remembered she had nowhere to go. She tolerated the alarm and the discomfort of sharp, tolerated it for minutes before her hand killed the alarm and sought the cause of sharp. And she found it, found the ring she had forgotten in the night, and by the light of a new day she loved it anew. She slid it onto her engagement finger, adding a small bandaid later, just to keep it safe.

It brought her luck too: she found a job that day, working three nights a week at the Riverdale Hotel, waiting on tables. She'd done it before at a Lakeside pub. The guy wanted her to start immediately, but today was Wednesday and Wednesdays had always belonged to Matt. He'd said he'd be there at six.

He arrived near seven and he drank a fast Jim Beam as he glanced around the flat.

'You're nesting. I preferred your cardboard cubbyhouse,' he said, then he picked up the photograph of her father and stared at it. 'Who is he?'

'My father. He died when I was eight.'

'Interesting,' he said. 'Very, very interesting. Freud might have written a paper on this one, Sall.'

'Wasn't he that dirty-minded old weirdo who could read sex into inkblots?'

'You have a way of reducing the complicated to basics. I love your lack of complications, kiddo, your little cubbyhouse.'

She didn't tell him she'd left her job at Phonepross, or about her new job, or what she was planning to do with little Cocky on Sunday. Didn't tell him she was buying a guitar either. What had they spoken about?

Nothing.

On Thursday afternoon she rode up to the twelfth floor for the last time and she picked up her last pay from Ratsus. A portion of it handed to Cocky, she took delivery of her second-hand guitar.

It looked as good as the one her mother had smashed, if a little worn. Worn in, and it fitted in the old case. Made to measure.

But what use was a guitar in a closed case? She took it out and sat cross-legged on the floor, nursing it a while. Years had passed since she'd played. She couldn't remember one chord. Then the ring and bandaid got in the way, so she peeled off the bandaid, slipped the ring from her finger, closed her eyes and allowed her ears to remember. They did.

Later she began humming the old songs. And it was coming, it was coming back. She sang then, quietly at first, aware that the walls were thin, then she forgot the walls.

Her fingertips were raw when she put the guitar away, but she soaked them in salty water.

That's what her mother used to do.

'Thanks, Mummy.'

nightingale with a broken heart

march 2000

Matt was on his back, sleeping. He frowned, his eyes fluttered. Strange to see him like this, not a god, just a man with a little snore. He seemed younger than when she'd met him in September. Or maybe she had grown older.

They'd spoken of birthdays tonight, his and hers. He'd said that they'd go out somewhere special for a joint celebration. He'd turned thirty-four in February. He'd spoken about his sister too, thirteen months his senior.

She sighed, more at peace with herself tonight. They would marry, and she would meet his family. She could imagine Chari as dark, like Matt, stunningly beautiful. And his grandfather, he'd be Matt with grey hair. His parents she couldn't see – or his wife.

Eleven-thirty and he slept on. She knew she should wake him, and knew if she did, he'd get up and go home to the faceless void that haunted her life. Wife. Bitch.

She didn't wake him.

It was close to twelve when he turned to her clock. 'You shouldn't have let me sleep, Sall.'

'Why not?'

No reply. He was up, in the shower. He never left with the scent of love on him. Why not? He didn't share Bitch's bed. She didn't cook for him, clean for him, so why wash up for her?

Sally leant against the bathroom door, watching him wash. 'Why me, Matt?'

'You're part of me, kiddo.'

She smiled, watching the water splash onto her floor. He always made a mess of her bathroom. 'Is Chari married?'

'No.'

'Does she live with your parents?'

'She has her own establishment. I'll take you to visit her one day.'

'I'd like that. Does she live with a guy?'

'She's got a lot of close friends, Sall, but she sleeps alone.'

'Tell me about your parents, Matt.'

'Daddy is a retired army man, and Mummy digs Jehovah, and Gramps has lost his onions and doesn't know where to find them.'

'Do they like your wife?'

'No.'

'Will they like me?'

'No.' He used the last of her shampoo and he laughed, tossing the plastic bottle at her. She picked it up, hoping there was a squeeze left in it; she wanted to wash her hair in the morning.

'Who do you see when you look at me, Matt?'

He stepped from the shower and towelled his hair, then he took her wrist and checked the time. 'I see midnight, kiddo, and I've got to get home.'

Home. Why did he have to call that house home? Why couldn't he say, I have to leave? I have to fly, Sall?

Home.

Busy days now, busy nights. What was home, other than a place to park the car and put your pillow? Busy weeks, and Sundays no longer days of rest, of sleeping until noon. Not these days. Her Sundays were crazy working days, and the money she made on Sundays had a different feel to it.

It was after five on a Sunday afternoon in mid-March when she lifted her guitar from the boot. Her handbag, heavy with coins, dragging her shoulder down, as she walked to her letterbox, sunburned, windblown, higher than high, and not a pill, not one glass of wine to lift her up there.

The Harley was parked in one of the front bays, the bikie polishing his chrome. She ignored him, retrieved her junk mail, which she redeposited in the garbage bin.

'What's wrong with my letterbox today?' he said.

'Don't worry about it, there'll be more tomorrow.' She tossed the words over her shoulder.

'You've been sprung, De Rooster.'

'What?' She'd lent him a cup of milk one night, left the chain on her door and passed the milk through the gap. He'd changed a flat tyre for her one morning, but that didn't mean she was on speaking terms with him.

'You've been sprung. My sister sells junk down at the Esplanade. I was down there this afternoon. Saw you singing up a storm in your mad hat.'

'You didn't?' Now she swung around to face him. 'Say you didn't recognise me. Please say it.'

'I could say it. It wouldn't alter the fact that I did. I was going to give you a stir but threw you a dollar instead.'

'How could you recognise me? Cocky promised me that no-one would.'

'I've heard you before, haven't I? The haunting tones of a nightingale with a broken heart flooding the barren halls at midnight.'

'Smartarse,' she said, taking a cigarette from her pocket, leaning her guitar against the concrete wall while she hunted for her lighter amid the coins.

'Don't you read the warnings on the packets?' He walked to

the concrete wall, leaned with her guitar.

'We've all got to do what we've all got to do.'

'How long have you been doing it?'

'Since I was eleven.'

'Singing?'

'Smoking. The kid on the guitar talked me into busking a few weeks back,' she said around the cigarette, her hand still searching for a lighter. It was hours since she'd had a smoke. She was gasping for one, but he snatched it from her mouth.

A reflex grab to reclaim it. Cigarettes cost money, and she wasn't into wasting them. He caught her hand, and she jerked it free. Didn't get the cigarette, and Matt's ring slipped off, tinkling as it fell on the concrete.

'Who the hell do you think you are?' she said. 'Just who the hell?'

'I know who I am, De Rooster. Not too certain about you.' He picked up the ring, glanced at it, held it to the sun before handing it back. 'No harm done.'

'And no thanks to you.' The ring reclaimed, slipped onto her finger, she picked up her guitar.

'Who is the cheapskate?' She tossed him a look of disdain and walked towards the entrance. 'Not Mr Smooth with the classy wheels and Italian suits,' he said, following her to the door. 'It's not a diamond, De Rooster.'

'What would you know about anything?'

'You'd be surprised what I know. My sister's husband has got a jewellery shop in Sydney. They made me work there for my keep for a while. The capitalists.'

'Bloody bull in a china shop.'

He laughed. 'Yeah. It was a bit like that, but it still doesn't make Mr Smooth's zircon a diamond, and with a voice like yours, you don't need second-rate.'

A voice like yours? She glanced at him, looking for derision, finding none. Long hair, black as a crow's wing in the sun. No smart reply she could make to that one, so she lit a cigarette and walked fast up the stairs. No more crow with a sore throat. Now a nightingale with a broken heart.

Still a bird.

That night she looked at her ring beneath the bathroom light. It was a diamond. It had to be. What would a bikie know? It was a diamond, and a big one. Symbol of Matt's love. His promise to marry her – as they might say in Mills and Boon.

But she read a second-hand Stephen King that night. Read it in one greedy gulp, and when she put it down at 2 a.m., she dreamed of the ring. It had turned her hand as black as the bikie's, and when she looked at the diamond, she could see a bleeding rose thorn in its centre and she couldn't dig it out.

She woke up prickling, and she ate breakfast prickling, the phone book open. She was going to take her ring to Cash Converters, see what they offered for it.

Lots of Cash Converters, and one at Forest Hill, which was close to East Burwood, or so Varicose – Joyce Rogers – had said. Joyce with her bungalow for fifty dollars a week.

Flipping through the phone book, thinking of rings and pimples and grandfathers and Mummy, she found herself staring at a column of Rogers; her fingernail tracked down to the J's. Only two in East Burwood; she chose the top one and dialled. Why not?

J Rogers picked up the phone. A female 'Hello.'

'Would I be speaking to Joyce Rogers? Ex-Phonepross.'

'Yes?'

'It's Sally from the tearoom.'

'How sweet of you to call,' Joyce said.

It took a minute of polite conversation before she got to the point. 'This is probably a very silly question, but ... but did Michael, you know, the pimply guy who got the boot ... did he ever contact you about your bungalow?'

'I'll get him for you.'

'I don't want to talk to him –'

'He's in the kitchen. We were talking about you last week. We never did know your other name.'

We? Pimples and Varicose?

Fifteen minutes later, phone down, she was still uncertain of how it had happened, but Joyce Rogers had somehow made the swift transition from big woman with bungalow to lunch date at twelve at Forest Hill Chase.

The guy at Cash Converters barely glanced at Sally's diamond.

'Zircon,' he said. 'We don't touch them.'

She didn't want to touch it either. She escaped. Fast. Ran across the road and entered the shopping centre, seeing the field of grey mushroom tables Joyce had described. A multitude of eaters, but not twelve yet, too early for Joyce. She sat a moment while her heartbeat steadied, her eyes staring at that ring that was turning her mood, if not her hand, black, then she sprang to her feet and rode the escalator up. What would a guy in the second-hand junk business know?

Jewellers on this level and plenty of them, windows glittering. She chose one and walked in, head high.

The jeweller smiled his smile saved for the young and the beautiful. She flashed an answering smile. 'I want to have it made smaller. It is a diamond, isn't it?' she said, offering the ring.

'Nope,' he replied, and his smile shrank to the size saved for those wasting his diamond-studded time.

'Are you certain?'

One brief glance through his eyeglass and he was certain. 'Zirconia.' She held out her hand and from a height he dropped the ring into her palm.

Smartarse bikie. Cheap ratsus Matt.

The ring held in her palm, she walked to another glittering window. Display of zircons there. Lots of them, and cheap. The heart was on show, big and bold and brash. Half-price, the sign said: $79.

Just a bauble. Just a gewgaw for a fool.

Lunch with Joyce was a baked potato that would have fed Sally for a week when she was a kid. She snapped the plastic knife trying to get into it. Joyce managed, but she had a mother's gentle hand.

'I went with Mike to get his things and old Ron hardly said boo. But you should have heard his wife!'

Melburnians, packed like assorted olives in a jar, only thin skins keeping them apart, but prick the skin and allow the juices to mix, and what did you find? Just lonely people, eager for friends. Here she was having lunch with a woman she'd known for almost a year but barely spoken a word to. Here she was discussing Mike, who a month ago had pimples instead of a name. She glanced at Joyce's breasts. Michael had always been obsessed by those breasts.

'It's nice having a man about the place. I mean, the lawns were up to my knees.'

Sally looked at her fake diamond as her plastic fork attempted to excavate the potato. Nice having a man around the place? Not so nice any more. It used to be nicer. When Matt had given her the ring, she'd believed it meant total commitment, total trust.

Total bloody fool. She'd sold her first true independence for a bit of fancy glass.

happy birthday

The trees in Bollinger Street were already turning gold; heat was slowly moving away from the city. Summer long gone but, to Sally, it would only slip into its annual coffin when March ended and took daylight-saving with it. She mourned the loss of that extra hour of light. Mourned another birthday too. All year she'd been counting down to the end of March to her birthday.

Thirty. Halfway to sixty.

The world turned too quickly. The year 2000, such a big deal for so long, was just another year. Now Australians had Olympics mania, but few, other than the rich and famous and those who had friends in high places, had managed to get worthwhile tickets. Sally wasn't rich or famous and her friends were all on the ground floor, struggling to make ends meet. She struggled along with them. Only April's rent to pay, which would take her up to end-of-lease May, then maybe she'd move into Joyce's bungalow. Michael wasn't using it.

She hadn't spoken to Ross in weeks. Out busking every Sunday with Cocky, temping at call centres all day Saturday and some weekdays, playing waitress three nights a week. Perhaps he called while she was out. Perhaps he didn't. She'd shocked the pants off him back in February. Literally.

It was late when she emptied her letterbox on Wednesday evening, and she was tired. Eight hours spent plugged into a telephone, trying to sell advertising space. She hadn't sold any. Didn't believe in the product. The boss lady had told her not to bother coming back. A Queen Ratsus in the making, not as big, no accent, but as tough.

Advertising space. Who wanted to buy it? Who looked at ads anyway, who sat avidly through television commercials – and junk mail? Did anyone ever open it?

She yawned, felt her left breast, then her right. Painful. Her back was aching too, and her neck. Symptom of thirty. She hoped.

A glance through her junk mail revealed a small padded envelope, a free sample of something. She turned it, felt it. No stamps, no address, no advertising. A small post-pack someone had hand delivered.

Number 14 got the junk mail; she kept the padded envelope and the phone bill, opening the bill as she walked to the stairs. It wasn't a big one. No phone calls to Lakeside to swell it these days. Lots of calls to Sue and Joyce, a few to Cocky.

Six weeks and she'd be gone from this place. May to May. The year of Sally De Rooze, almost gone. So fast, and so slow. The bloodiest and the best year of her life.

She checked her watch. Plenty of time; Matt rarely arrived before seven. Time for a shower and a glass or two of wine. Have to get in the mood to entertain him. Have to paint a smile on her face, pretend she didn't care that they weren't going out for her birthday. Pretend she didn't care that she wouldn't even see him on her birthday.

'Laugh and the world laughs with you, Sall old gal.'

Key in her door. Bag on the fridge. Wine in a glass, cigarette in her mouth and she tried to gain entrance to the envelope with her long fingernails. They made little impression. Too well-sealed with sticky tape, she had to cut her way into the envelope with scissors, and when she did, a tissue-wrapped brooch slid free.

Gold, with a stone that looked like a ruby. An oval cut. She stared at it. Who would have put something like that in her box? She turned the brooch in her hand, held it against the sleeve of her black sweater, and a ghost walked over her grave.

'Pretty,' she whispered, her hand searching for a card or note. Nothing. Tissue paper and her name on the envelope, written in small block letters. SALLY. No mistake about who it was meant for. But who would have placed it in her box?

An hour later, the brooch still in her hand, she stood by the window watching the car lights approach and drive on by. No Matt. Maybe he'd arrived early and dropped off the present. Picked it up at the two-dollar shop.

But it hadn't come from a two-dollar shop. She knew that. The stone had a fire trapped within it, and the intricate gold-work looked old, worn. She studied the brooch, examined the fastener. It had been bent by years of use. And the loop at the top that a chain might be threaded through. A worn loop, almost worn through, needle thin. Someone had used this brooch as a pendant.

She showered, watched at the window until nine. Matt didn't come and he didn't call, so she went to bed, asleep when her head hit the pillow. And Thursday came too soon and she woke up thirty, and thirty felt nauseous and achy old, and people didn't get cancer simultaneously in two breasts, but she checked each side for lumps, just in case.

She was still in bed when the phone rang. She snatched it up, ready for war.

'Was last night a payback, Matt?' she said.

'It's me, love. Happy birthday.'

'Oh, Ross. I'm sorry. Thanks. I'm sorry, I thought it was –'

'I know. It's okay. So, how's it going down there?'

'I don't know. So, how's Lakeside?'

'A bit of a madhouse. Old Charlie's wife took off for Queensland and he's gone after her. She's been at him for years to give up work and buy a caravan. Might have got sick of waiting for him, I think.'

Then she heard a child's laughter in the background. And she heard 'Shush.' A woman's voice.

'Got visitors?' she asked.

A breath. A long, true silence. A cough. 'Carol. Carol and the kids.'

'Carol who?'

'Your old schoolmate. Carol from Geelong.'

'Carol Rigg!'

'Murphy.'

'What's she doing there?' Stupid question. Very stupid – 8.15 a.m. and Carol Rigg at the farm, hours away from Geelong? She swallowed hard, dug deep for a not-so-stupid comment. Wide awake now. 'So you've . . . you've stopped fighting the women off with big sticks, have you?'

'I wore out my old cricket bat on you, love.' She raised a laugh. 'Yeah, well how's it going down there? How's little Matt going?'

'What?'

'Matt. That's his name, isn't it? The little bloke with the bug on his jaw?'

'Oh, he's great. I'm great. Life's great.' Silence. 'So. So, say g'day to Carol for me. I'd better let you go. Thanks for the call.'

'Right. Carol says happy birthday and have a good day.'

'I will. Tell her thanks.'

'You come up some time and bring Matt. There's always a bed here for you. Always will be. You know that. Bye, love.'

She hung up, but stood unmoving, her bare feet stuck to the floor.

Carol bloody Rigg! She got my house, now she's got my old boyfriend. Carol bloody Rigg. Statue still, she stared at the phone and beyond the phone into a world that was darkening.

'Ring me, Matt. You know it's my birthday.'

For an hour she waited, then she went back to bed, reading and dozing until she had to get up and go to the Riverdale pub, wait on tables, and every plate she served reminded her of Ross – and bloody Carol Rigg.

That night the fire-dream returned.

Yellow balloon, dipping, diving beneath the clouds. Sally reaching, reaching high. Almost. Almost there. Almost in her hands.

Then Daddy, running away from her. Smoky, misty Daddy, leaving behind him a road of fire. Sally, all grown up, trying to follow him, or run away from something.

Legs couldn't run. Daddy all gone.

And a big black beast behind her, snarling.

She woke, heart pounding, on her knees again, on the bed, her hands reaching out for the beige wall.

Gasping for air she scrambled to her feet and found the window, where she stood counting while her heartbeat slowed. Dark out, but morning dark. Today. What was today? Thirty plus one day. Interview-in-Carlton day.

Gotta go, Sally. Got to get up, get dressed, get out there. Can't slop food in a pub for the rest of your life.

Why not? At least my customers want what I serve.

She made coffee at seven and it didn't taste right, but she sipped it while flipping through the phone book to the M's, looking for the Marsdens. Not too many, easy to check. But knowing silent Matt, he'd have a silent number.

Marsden, MT 17 Charlton Grove, Hallam. Right on centre page. Matthew Thomas; that was his name. She checked the Marsdens again. No other MT in Hallam. It could have been him. Probably wasn't. Might have been. Why hadn't she looked him up before?

Because you can't call him, because he still lives with his wife. You got sucked in by a zircon, Sall old gal. Go back to bed. Crawl beneath the blankets and hide. You're thirty years old and you've still got nothing but a room full of junk, and that's all you'll ever have, and you'll haul it around on your back until the day you die.

Black beast from her dream, still behind her, coming to get her, to drag her down. But she had her guitar, and it wasn't junk, and she had Sue.

Sue would be on the train to work.

Joyce. I'll wait until nine. I'll call her at nine and I'll go out there for lunch, check out her bungalow.

Joyce wasn't answering her phone at nine, or at 9.30, or at ten.

Nobody home. Nobody for little Sally.

Frightened little animal, little chameleon wanting to hide in the dark, hide from something she didn't want to know. Wanting to suck her thumb and hide until the black beast gobbled her up for breakfast.

Chameleon. That's what Matt had called her on Monday night. Chameleon.

'So change your colour,' he'd said.

It had started out badly. Rain battering her window, he'd come to her door, his shirt wet, his hair dripping. She'd handed him a towel.

'Tonight reminds me of that first night, Sall, the rain thundering down around us. I was sitting in the car, wondering what I'd find beneath your black overcoat,' he'd said.

'What if I hadn't asked you in for a drink? Would you have pursued me?' She'd been twisting the ring on her finger, wanting to accuse him – or throw it at his head. But he'd never said it was a diamond. Never asked her to marry him.

'You did invite me in, and I knew you would. I can climb into your mind, kiddo. If you were lost, I could find you.'

'Yeah,' she said. 'And what did you find under my overcoat, Matt?'

'It was like unwrapping a birthday gift, expecting the usual socks, but finding what you'd wanted for half of your life. A chameleon kid.'

'A lizard?'

'So change your colour. Play the whore for me tonight, kiddo. I've got money to spend and I want the works.'

He liked to play sex games. They'd had fun some nights. He'd sit on the bed and call her number on his mobile, and ask for the little blonde who worked at Phone-a-pro. They'd had some crazy conversations; done some crazy things.

'Sorry, she's left town, Matt, and didn't leave her number.'

'You forget. I picked you up on a street corner, and you said you needed a hit. Said you'd do anything to get it.'

'I conned you. I've been taken down once too often, so I rob my clients these days.'

He'd tried to take what he wanted, but he'd been too rough; she'd kicked him, the heel of her boot connecting with his inner thigh. It hurt him – and she didn't care.

No way back after that. No plans made for her birthday. Nothing.

The relationship had gone wrong.

'How am I going to explain that bruise?' he'd said.

'To your wife? I suggest you keep your pants on – or turn the light off when you sleep with her, Matty.'

'You like to call the shots these days, don't you?'

'I just want honesty.' She'd looked at the fake ring, almost told him that she knew it was fake. Not worth the effort.

No rote 'Love you, Sall'. Just those eyes, angry, then home to the wife to explain his bruise. And if he had been honest about his living arrangements in Hallam, how the hell was she going to see his inner thigh?

Sally had spent hours imagining his home, his wife. She'd tried to force the mental image of a nagging, overweight blonde, sitting on her bum, eating chocolates. She'd tried to imagine Matt mowing the lawns on Sundays.

Daddy had mowed the lawns. Daddy in his short shorts, Sally not far away. It was weird, but every time she tried to imagine Matt's garden, she saw her old garden in Geelong, saw her father working there.

She glanced at her father's photograph, and he smiled at her. She picked it up, looked at the lock of dark hair falling over his brow, and at the shape of his face. Daddy in his suits. Daddy with his briefcase. Daddy with melted chocolate frogs in his pocket.

You're spoiling her, Bren.

How do you spoil a little girl with chocolate frogs, Glen?

The memory had her searching through the photographs found in her mother's handbag. It had her standing close to the window, lifting a small black negative to the light. Just a puzzle in black and white. Woman with dark hair and face, light dress, light trees and black sky. Life in reverse. There was one of three women, all with dark hair and faces, and some structure behind them. Light bars against the dark. She took up another. Same bars, different angle and a lone woman's figure before this one.

It was a house frame! And that was a roof shape at the edge of the negative!

It was the Geelong house, and that was Raelene's roof. The Masons had moved into Carter Street six months before Mummy and Daddy.

Her search continued, but faster now. Seven negatives had been slipped back into their envelope when she found the one of a man holding a little girl's hand. Her heart leapt to her throat. She wanted it to be of her father, wanted, wanted, wanted it to be her father holding her hand. But she knew it wasn't. Even with the dark and light reversed, she knew the clothing was wrong, the shape of the male was wrong.

She scattered the old snapshots onto the table then. The one of the man and child, faces scribbled out with red biro, was not among them. Ross had packed them up that day in Lakeside; he'd deemed photographs with red-biro faces junk. Easy for some to toss away junk.

Again she looked at the negative. Was it Mummy and her father, or had it been taken on the same day as the ones of that house frame? Was it Sally and old Papa? She placed it to the side and picked up another. Two women seated. Then one of a woman with a small boy in her arms. Mummy and Shane? She searched the scattered photographs until she found the negative's perfect match. Grandma and Shane. Had there been a matching shot of Sally and Papa?

The negatives were probably too old to have printed, the surfaces worn by years of rubbing against mates. But it might be worth a try. With a shrug she slid the single negative into a clean envelope and placed it into her bag, then she dressed in her op-shop gear, picked up her guitar and her crazy hat, and left the flat.

The photography shop on Toorak Road couldn't print the old negative on the spot. It would have to be sent away, the woman said. She didn't like its condition either. 'We can't guarantee it.'

'I'm not looking for guarantees. Enlarge it, please. A ten by eight.'

The woman attempted to explain the problems associated with enlargement, but Sally waved her hand and returned to her car.

Keys in her purse, old brooch beside them; she hadn't wanted to leave it in the flat. As she removed her keys, the brooch pin became entangled in the bunch and the glass ruby glanced at the sunlight, near blinding her. She stood beside her car, tilting her purse, watching the stone catch the rays. It was magic.

There was a jeweller a few shops up. She looked towards it. Why not? Been there, done that before, why not make a fool of herself one more time?

He had a barred door, barred windows too, but she pushed his door wide and walked to the small rear counter, placing the brooch down. He came from behind a wall, distrustful, half-pirate, with his one eye.

'Is that stone real?' she said.

'It's very old!' His voice was old. He looked at her through his eyeglass, then applied it to the brooch. 'It's a beautiful stone.' Again she was examined under magnification. 'A family heirloom?' Her op-shop gear didn't go with family heirlooms.

'My grandmother died recently,' she said, knowing he thought it was stolen.

'You're looking to sell it?'

'No! I said I wanted to know if it's real.' Want to get out of here too.

'If you should change your mind . . .' He wasn't handing it back.

'Thank you for . . . for your time.' She took the brooch from his hand, pinned it on her bodice and got away.

So, it wasn't Matt who had placed that padded envelope in her letterbox.

But who?

The bikie! Had he stolen it, dropped it in her letterbox for safekeeping? He knew he could scale her drainpipe to get it back. She looked over her shoulder. That jeweller was probably on the phone to the cops, giving them a description of her op-shop gear.

She went home and changed into black slacks and sweater, then she and her guitar caught the tram to the city. All afternoon she stood in the Bourke Street Mall, singing the songs she loved, not the ones Cocky liked. She had a crowd around her at lunch-time and she didn't have to share her coins either.

No-one recognised her. Street busker. Matt's prostitute. A waitress. Junk collector? Home wrecker. Nightingale with a broken heart. Bikie's safety-deposit box.

reality

april 2000

A black Honda Prelude was parked in Bollinger Street when she left the flats on Sunday morning; it had been there for an hour last night too. Probably a plain-clothes cop, or an insurance investigator with his video camera – it was a nice little car, though.

As she drove out to the street, she tried to see the cop behind the windows. Couldn't see much at all, but she mounted the kerb trying, and probably buckled her front wheel. The steering had a wobbly feel to it as she headed for Toorak Road.

The Honda moved off too. He was watching her. She'd hoped he might have been after the bikie. It tracked her to St Kilda, and all the way she watched it in the rear-view mirror, and all the way her steering wheel felt queer. But she got a park, and the Honda didn't.

She hadn't seen Matt since Monday night, and as she took her guitar from the boot, she began writing a different scenario for her tail. Matt's wife had hired a private detective to follow her, and that was the reason Matt had stayed away on Wednesday. His wife had seen the bruise on his thigh and put two and two together.

Sally smiled, and wondered why, but it was a funny image, Matt cowering down before this overweight blond wife.

Poor Matt.

Until Christmas she had seen him as faultless. But he wasn't. He came to her flat empty-handed. Never bought wine, or the Jim Beam he liked to drink with ginger ale. When they ate together he left her with the washing-up. He used her expensive shampoo as if it was water and he wasted her toilet paper, swallowed her Panadols. He'd promised to take her out for her birthday, but he hadn't. He'd never taken her out.

Little Cocky spent half of his life pleading to take her out.

There had been months when she'd lived on Matt's Mondays and Wednesdays. These days she managed to slot them between the Sundays she spent with Cocky.

He was waiting on their corner of the Esplanade, revved up and ready to go, his guitar case primed with his own coins.

They played their guitars and they sang, they did requests and had a ball until the weather changed and an old guy tossed an envelope into the case. Cocky snatched it, as the wind tried to steal it away.

'I've had enough. Let's go to the pub, babe. Do the split there while we have a drink.'

He was a pint-sized pain in the bum, but brilliant on the guitar and he had a good feel for harmony. They did well on their corner, not many notes but plenty of coins. Today there was a note – when Cocky opened the envelope they saw green.

'Jesus, babe! Somebody appreciates us,' he said.

'It was an old guy in a suit. He probably wanted your body.'

'Nice to know someone does.'

They cashed the note, split it and the coins, and he was still nagging. 'Come on, babe. It's too early to go home.'

'I'm old enough to be your mother,' she said.

'You get into it young in the country, eh?'

'I'm thirty,' she said. 'I was thirty on Thursday.'

'Well, don't tell anyone and they won't know. How about it,

then? Dinner and back to my place, and we'll tape those songs.'

'See you next Sunday, babe.'

Like he said, it was too early to go home.

Home?

What made a home? Possessions? People? When Daddy and the boys had been alive, she'd known the meaning of home. Her mind far away, she drove down Dandenong Road, thought of Joyce and turned left into Blackburn Road, thought of Sue and turned right onto the South Eastern Freeway.

So many cars, all going to someplace, but no PI in his black Honda tailing her.

Once I knew the way to get back home again,
Once there was a place where I could be . . .

She sang as she drove, enjoying the sound of her voice against the rhythm of a motor that now suggested its own new rhythms. Her mother used to write songs, and it wasn't hard. You just let the words flow, let the pain pour out in words, so she sang on, altering a line from time to time, finding the rhymes, then returning to the beginning to sing the line again.

Once I knew the way to get back home again,
Once there was a place where I could be,
Now there is a world of strangers in the street
and loneliness my new reality.

Gather up days, the scattered memories,
Toss them all away, and set me free,
Let me search the world until I find the place,
For somewhere there is a place for me.

Her foot growing heavy on the accelerator, she sang, past Springvale Road and on, faster now, faster. She was going to go to Sue's to borrow a book, but she passed Sue's exit and drove on by Dandenong. Freedom driving, no traffic lights dictating.

Then the sign. Hallam. She had found her direction. She was going to Hallam, to Charlton Grove, just to see what she might see.

The Melway map-book, her knowledgeable friend, was on her passenger seat. She opened it at the traffic lights and let it guide her down a road she should have taken months ago. She found Charlton Grove. She found MT Marsden's street. And later she found the house. Was it the place Matt flew to when he drove away from Bollinger Street? It was no black swan's nest on a dark river bank, but a mansion with a wide garage beneath.

Her car parked across the road, two houses down, she put on her flower-power hat and her owl sunglasses, and she looked at a leadlight front door, at trees that had found time to grow tall, at the manicured lawns. She scanned the windows. No movement behind the expensive curtains.

There were pot plants on the porch. Why didn't the wife come out, water her plants? Why didn't Mr Marsden come out, turn on the sprinkling system?

Not a movement. Not a sound.

Then the perennial junk-mail deliverer walked by, dropping off her bundles from a child's stroller, and a neighbour and her dog appeared from behind a security door. They checked their letterbox, walked next door and stole the bundle from MT Marsden's box.

Junk-mail thieves in Hallam? And bad-mannered dogs. It leaked on the letterbox while the neighbour leafed through her collection. The dog treed a cat, then, satisfied with himself, he raked MT Marsden's manicured lawn with all four paws, sending the turf flying behind him. Together they sprayed the pot plants. Sally liked that bad-mannered dog, but he scuttled off for home, the neighbour following on his heels.

At 7.15, a four-wheel drive turned into the street. It slowed before the Marsdens' drive, and the big, brown garage door opened. The vehicle drove in. Matt. It must be Matt. Even an inanimate door could not deny him entrance.

Sliding low in her seat, she hid as the vehicle's lights flooded the garage and the dark blue station wagon waiting there. She knew that wagon.

Then he stepped down from the four-wheel drive, and he turned on the lights. Her heart thumping in her breast, she held her breath, afraid now, afraid he'd turn, see her.

He didn't turn.

But she saw three small boys tumble out of the four-wheel drive – tumble out running.

Boys?

Three boys?

Her mind quivered. Stilled. Slipped a track. She went skidding off into a time warp.

Nicky and Robby and Shane with their little boy laughter, their little boy feet on concrete, their high little voices. Her eyes staring at the well-lit scene were not taking it in. They were watching an old scene, in negative.

Daddy. Tall and slim and beautiful. The dark hair, the long legs. She was watching Daddy unload the cases when they'd come home from their holiday to Echuca. They'd been on the paddleboats and they were all sunburned.

They hadn't died. They'd grown up in another place.

Shane. A big boy. And laughing, not screaming. And Robby, the quiet one, not so quiet tonight. And Nicky. No more thistle-down hair.

She didn't see the woman.

Until she heard her.

Heard the voice that jarred her back into the now.

'Run in and get the mail from Mrs Bryant, Troy.'

Sally closed her eyes, covered her ears, and her stomach tried to lose the sandwich and the Diet Coke she'd had for lunch. Dry-retching, her mind was blank, until slowly she lifted her eyes to the woman and to an altered scene.

And she saw Matt's bitch.

Not a bitch, though. Just a wife. Just a young mother. Dark as Matt. Long, straight hair, slim as Matt, wearing jeans like Matt; they were two black swans, perfectly matched and mated for life.

And they had three little boys.

Matt had three little boys.

She wanted to run. Had to run from what she'd done. Had to get away. Couldn't get away. He'd see her car. He'd know her car. Know her numberplate. Not many old yellow Datsuns left on the roads these days. She had to sit and control her mind and her stomach until he went inside. Just sit and wait it out.

And cry. Cry for what she'd done, and for Matt's lies. Cry for his beautiful boys. Cry for the fool she'd been. Just cry.

The neighbour and her dog were out again and the dog treed the cat again while the neighbour walked to the fence, not trusting a small boy with her pile of stolen junk mail. The street was breathing now, moving because Matt and his wife had returned. Lights came on behind Sally's car. She cowered there and wept as she heard Matt's voice.

Loved that voice once.

Hated that lying bastard.

'Everyone inside. It's late. Quick. We're going to ring up for a pizza. Come on. Inside, I said.'

The smallest one came from up a tree, the cat looped over his shoulder, and Sally remembered a cat who had purred, who had kissed, as this cat kissed. Soft, sweet-scented ginger cat. For a time it had replaced Teddy. Then they'd packed up and left it to starve.

Matt took the mail. One hand on her shoulder, he guided his wife away from the neighbour. Control freak. Do it his way. Always had to do it his way, whether you liked it or not. He picked up the smallest boy and the cat. His boy. His cat.

'You said I was your family, Matt. You said you'd find me if I was lost. I'm lost. Find me,' she wept.

He didn't find her, didn't even look her way. He had his family at his side and he walked them to his front door, shepherding in the boys. And when they were all inside, together, he closed the door on Sally, turned off the lights on Sally, locked her out. Left Sally in the dark to cry alone.

She had to get away. Drive away. How to drive when she couldn't see to drive, that was the problem. She had to do it, though, had to think her way out of this. Had to pretend until she got home. Had to get home, lock her door. Hide.

Bloody fool. Bloody pitiful clown. She'd seen him in the lift that day and she'd known him. She'd loved him in another lifetime. Loved him, or someone who had looked very much like him.

But she made it home – or back to the flats. Her car space was bare. She ran up the stairs, ran for her bathroom and emptied her stomach into the toilet bowl, then sat in the dark, holding the photograph of Daddy to her breast, crying and cursing herself for a fool.

It was close to ten when she walked down for her guitar. Cold out, but there was warmth in the varnished wood, and comfort in the sad strumming, and later, comfort in the sound of her voice as she let the pain come out in words.

Across the small landing two doors were open.

'Who is she?' the guy from Number 15 asked, his stereo turned off a while.

'Something you won't often hear around this place,' the bikie said.

'What's her name? Have I heard of her?'

'De Rooze. Sally.' He didn't want to talk. He wanted to listen.

The melody rising and falling they stood on, the long, slim blond guy wearing bottle-top glasses and the dark-skinned bikie in black jeans.

And the song drew a third tenant to the hall, a tiny Asian

woman. The bikie nodded to her, and she nodded, listening for a moment before closing her door.

'She's brilliant,' the blond guy said as he returned to his unit.

Only the bikie stood on.

Strings plucked. She was feeling for a rhythm, then that voice again; the nightingale, singing her little broken heart out tonight.

I found a lover who'd love me completely
We'd walk together through sunshine and rain
We'd build a dream that would go on forever
At my side he would always remain.

I asked my lover to wed me in Maytime
Confetti of leaves touched with ruby and gold
He was the one I had searched for for a lifetime
But my lover is not mine to hold.

Autumn winds blow scented with rain
Winter whispering out there again
The seasons go but here I remain
Alone, all alone with my pain.

Take me away winds, carry me over
sky and the ocean, don't let me see
I am the jester, clown of the weeping
I am the fool. Laugh at me.

On Monday morning when the little yellow Datsun drove again to the freeway, the bikie tailed it to the Dandenong exit, staying just far enough behind. He had to pick up a car at his sister's place and fit a new exhaust pipe.

Her husband was in Timor, but he'd be home in May, his tour of duty ended. He could look after his own car come May.

doughnuts and coffee

She was calm now. Tears all cried and dried. She was thinking rationally this morning. It was remotely possible that Matt and his wife had been babysitting, still putting on a show for friends and neighbours. She had to go back and see those boys by daylight. Then she'd know. Then she could move on.

His house was alive this morning, windows open, cat on the letterbox taking the sun. Fat cat. She heard the children's voices, and they were like the other voices in that other street, the street like this one, but not as rich. Her beautiful home, beautiful then. Worn out now by Carol Rigg.

She didn't want it back. Didn't want Ross back either. Carol Rigg would be good for him, and he'd be good with her kids too. Three ready-made farm labourers. And he'd end up with his six. Carol was built to bear babies. Good wide hips. And she'd fit into Lakeside, always say and do the right thing, never embarrass. A worthy Mrs Bertram.

It was 8.40 when she saw the boys walk from their door, saw a mother tuck in a small shirt, then walk with her beautiful sons right by the old yellow Datsun, and across the road, around the corner. A young mother and her handsome little boys, walking safe in the sun.

They all looked like Matt. Slim little-boy necks. Dark, shiny heads; smart, well-pressed uniforms. Sally followed them in her car, watched them enter the school grounds where they became lost in the crush of other uniforms. She found her way around the block, returning in time to see Matt's garage door open.

His blue station wagon was not there today. She hadn't expected it to be. Today was Monday, Sally the fool's day, bit of fluff on the side day. He'd be on the fourth floor selling dreams to retirees, but he'd be knocking on Sally's door tonight.

She'd been conned by a memory. She'd seen what she'd wanted to see in Matt.

The four-wheel drive backed out and Sally watched the magic door close, then the big car drove away and she followed it to a shopping centre in Endeavour Hills. Sue's ex lived in Endeavour Hills. Why was she always lost in Sue country? But she had her Melway. They could find their way anywhere, her and her Melway. They'd find their way back.

Her car parked two spaces up from the four-wheel drive, she followed its driver, saw her meet and greet another woman. They looked at jackets in an expensive boutique, they looked at shoes and the friend tried on white sandals. She didn't buy. The friends ordered coffee and a doughnut each at the coffee shop, then stood talking. Sally stood close by, listening to their conversation.

'The weather was perfect. Dad took the boys camping on Friday night, and they loved it.'

'How's your mum?'

'She'll have to take it easy for a while. Can't drive for a month, which is frustrating her, but she was delighted to see us. It's been months since we've got away.'

They paid for their coffee and doughnuts, and Sally ordered the same. A table beside theirs was vacant. She claimed it and sat with her back to them, chair legs almost touching. Then the conversation turned to Matt, and Sally listened to every word.

'Got the biggest boy back at work?'

'He couldn't wait to get back, and to tell you the truth, I couldn't wait to get him back. I thought a break from work would be good for him. I don't know what's wrong with him lately, Jan. He can't turn off.'

Sally chewed on her thumbnail, frowned.

'He spent most of the time checking the market, or on his mobile to Jeff. Sell this. Buy that. He didn't even go camping with Dad and the boys.'

'Did you get to see his parents?'

'No. I just wanted to get home, and he'd prefer to go there by himself. He was like a kid with a new toy this morning. He was going back to work.'

'Matt the workaholic.'

'Maybe. Honest to God, I think sometimes that he's playing around. He's different lately, Jan.'

A rowdy trio claimed the next table. Sally sat on, hearing snippets of conversations about charities, families and pregnancies. She picked at the hole in her doughnut, slid it on her ring finger. It was about as real as Matt's diamond, and as greasy as his love.

As she drained her coffee cup and stood to leave, the trio's forks became busy and their mouths found better things to do. Again she listened.

'His parents are something else. His father looks at Troy as if he'd like to put him in uniform, teach him some discipline; his mother would prefer us to leg-rope the lot of them to a verandah post and give them a Bible. I haven't been to see them in months. Matt usually goes up on Sundays, stays over some nights. Or he says he does.'

He certainly doesn't stay with me, Sally thought.

'His mother never did like me. Chari and I did ballet together, so Mum and Matt's mother knew each other. I was about nine or ten at the time.' She laughed. 'Love at first sight.'

They were preparing to leave. Sally watched the friends walk out of sight, then she and her friend, the Melway, found their way back to the freeway, where the inward-bound traffic was heavy.

On the city side of Blackburn Road the oil light began to glow. She moved into the left lane, seeking an exit. But when the fuel gauge showed empty, she still had another twenty-odd kilometres before it ran dry, and she wanted to get home. Probably had enough oil to get her home. Ross had checked it, topped it up when he was down in February.

February.

'Checking Carol's now. Fixing her car now. I should have it serviced, buy new tyres, see what's wrong with the steering.'

She had plenty of money in the bank since Ross's birthday call. She'd claimed his cheque. It had been a little crumpled, a wee bit soiled, but the bank accepted it. Carol Rigg could have Ross; she wasn't going to buy new curtains with Mummy's legacy.

The motor began to labour. Sally bore down on the accelerator but the car continued to lose power. She changed gear, smelt heat, smelt burning oil.

And the motor stopped, the car rolling to a halt. With the wheels' final slow revolution she tried to guide them towards the emergency lane. Didn't make it all the way, and the cars behind her beeped, bunched, then roared away, roared by the poor little yellow Datsun 120Y, passed away on the side of the freeway. Dead as a doorknob.

Ross had given her the car. He'd kept it on the road. She'd never learned how to check the oil and water. Never put air in her tyres. Didn't know how. She'd gone from being Mummy's little watchdog to Ross's bed and hadn't grown in between.

But it wasn't Ross's fault. She'd stopped growing nice and straight and tall when Daddy had died. Too many years stagnating in Mummy's pool of sludge. Too many nights hiding with Mummy beneath the bed, afraid of the bogyman. Too many years of watching. Watching. Always watching Mummy.

Count when she goes to the bathroom. Listen to the wee hitting the water. Listen for the paper rustle, listen for the cistern flush.

Hide her pills under your mattress, and don't let her see where you hide them, dole them out to her, two by two.

Throw the sharp knives away so there is nothing for her to cut herself with, and nothing to cut the tomatoes with either.

Too much time spent between a rock and a hard place, Sall old gal. You grew stunted. But you're out now. You can live in the sun now. So the first days of full-on heat might burn, but they won't kill you.

'They won't kill me,' she screamed at the thousand motorists roaring by, bunching, cursing her car and her, but not offering to help push it off the freeway. She turned her lights on, flashed her turning signal and tried to push the car off to the side.

Useless. Not strong enough. She had the build of a twelve-year-old kid. She looked left, right. There would be an emergency phone somewhere. Which way, that was the question. Back in the car she tried once more to start the motor. 'Deader than a doorknob.'

A motorbike pulled in behind her. Maybe a helpful cop. She turned, but the sun on the chrome was in her eyes. She looked at the helmet, and down. Saw the long black hair beneath the helmet. And what the hell was he doing here? And where were all the cops when you needed them?

She watched him prop his bike before walking to her passenger-side window. Slow to reach across, she wound it down an inch or three.

'What are you doing here?' she said.

'It's a free freeway. What are you doing here?'

'I'm out of oil.'

'You're also blocking the traffic. Let your handbrake off.' He pushed the little car into the emergency lane. So easy for him. He sniffed at the air and shook his head. The smell of burnt oil had grown stronger. 'You've done it this time, De Rooster. Pull your bonnet.'

She pulled the lever and stepped from the car to peer with him into the maze of pipes and metal. 'What's that smell?'

'Smells like a buggered motor to me. Are you in the RACV?'

She was. Ross had joined her up when she'd left Lakeside. Bloody Ross. He'd paid for that too.

The bikie offered her his phone, but she didn't know how to use it, so she handed him her keys. He made the call.

'They're sending a tow truck for you.'

'Did you tell them I was just out of oil?'

'Your motor is red hot. I'd say you've seized it, De Rooster.'

She opened the passenger-side door and leaned against the seat, and she thanked him, but he didn't get on his bike. He walked off to the grass and sat down.

'You don't have to wait.'

'Sunshine, green grass. Sit down and relax. You're like a grasshopper on an ant hill. It could take an hour for them to get here.'

Too hot in the car, she walked to the grass, found a sprinkling of shade three metres from him and she sat.

They spoke of the traffic first, then of mobile phones, and they waited. He took a call and she reached for her cigarettes while he spoke to his mobile friend. And the cars zoomed on by. He moved into her shady space and offered her a stick of chewing gum, and he showed her how to use a mobile. She called Phonepross and asked if they had any raffle books for sale, please, then hung up fast, handed back the phone. They spoke about the country then and green grass, and about nothing in particular and everything in general.

'How long have you had your bike?'

'It's not a bike, it's a Harley. I've had this one for two years. I got my first *bike* when I was eighteen. Went around Australia on it. I had a couple in between.'

He'd been everywhere: Alice Springs, Birdsville, Tasmania.

The tow truck killed their conversation. It picked up the little car, dragged it up to the truck tray with rattling chains. She heard its groan, and she groaned with it.

The driver was ready to leave and she didn't want to go with him. He wasn't offering a lift anyway.

'It looks as if I walk,' she said.

'No animals and pedestrians on the freeway.' The bikie pointed to the sign. 'You'd better get on.'

'On that thing? I'll hop and cop the animal fine, thanks.'

'Get on and stop playing hard to get.'

'Of all the places that you might be today, how come you were here?'

'I'm the White Knight. I spend my life saving damsels in distress.' He offered her the helmet, and she eyed it, and him, and his bike.

'I used to think you were a criminal – a jewellery thief.'

'I used to think you were a feisty little bantam, so don't turn chicken on me.' Again he offered the helmet.

She mounted the pillion, pleased she was wearing jeans. He placed the helmet on her head and adjusted the strap, then he was almost sitting on her and the motor roared beneath her and the bike wanted to go.

'Ever been on one of these?' he yelled.

'I never got my pushbike licence. Santa wouldn't give me one.'

'What?'

'Santa Claus. I asked him for a bike one year and he gave me a plastic doll.'

'You were lucky to get a doll. The old bugger always gave me school shoes and jeans. Hang on to me.'

'I'm as ready as I'll ever be.' She leaned back and clung to the pillion seat.

'Hang on to me or I'll lose you on the first bend.'

'I can think of worse fates,' she yelled.

'Arms around me or we don't budge, De Rooster. Come on.

Give me a thrill. My colour doesn't rub off. I found that out when I was five.'

Her hands crept to his shirt and he grabbed them, wrapped them around him. 'Now, hang on.'

The roar of untamed power, the primal lunge, then the air sharp in her face, and his hair, wind-whipped, blinding her. She hung on. Tight. Tighter.

This was flying. No windows to lock her in. This was freedom. No seatbelt to hold her prisoner. They couldn't talk. They had to yell, and she yelled, the sun and the wind and his hair in her face as they passed cars and caught up with the tow truck before it turned off the freeway to make its way to an RACV-approved repairer in Warrigal Road.

The motor stilled and it was over, her feet were back on the ground and she didn't want it to be over. She wanted to fly.

The mechanic, approved or not, didn't have a good bedside manner. He tried to turn the engine over with a greasy spanner applied to the crankshaft pulley. It wouldn't turn. 'She's had it. Cost you big bucks to fix her and the old girl isn't worth it.'

'I can pay. How many big bucks?'

'Have to rebuild your motor. You're looking at two thousand, with labour. Give or take a few bucks.' He kicked a tyre. 'They wouldn't pass a roadworthy in a pink fit. Set you back another four hundred. You could buy the whole car for two hundred. You're nearly out of rego, too.'

'I've got another ten days.'

'She's wrecker material, De Rooster. Face it.'

Sally looked towards Lakeside. Too long since Ross had been to Melbourne. He'd checked her tyres and radiator, poured in enough oil to run a battleship for a week. She walked around the car while the approved repairer stood back, wiping his hands on his overalls. She opened the bruised door, picked up her knowledgeable friend and a box of tissues. Then she opened the boot. And found the plastic container of oil Ross had bought at the market. It was still half full.

'Shit,' she said.

The approved repairer walked to the boot, took the container of oil, weighing it, his eyes accusing her. He was a car doctor, called in too late, and the necessary medicine had been at hand to save the old girl's life.

'Worth nothing now,' he said. 'They're good little cars, these. They go till they drop.' Died in harness of neglect, his words said, and she wanted to cry for her little car and her neglect. Why hadn't she learnt anything?

'Why don't you ring the RSPCA, mate, report her for Datsun abuse?'

'I should have looked in the boot. I should have –'

'No weeping over spilt oil, De Rooster. Should-have-beens don't count for much in this world. They're the ifs and the buts of life. Kiss her goodbye, pay up and let's go. I've got to get to work.'

'Work? You?'

'I'm a blackjack dealer at the casino.'

'Still a thief. You probably rob the poor gamblers blind.'

'I've got an old bugger robbing me blind at the moment. He's got to be counting cards but he's so cute I hate to dob him in.'

She paid for the car funeral with Visa, then they rode away, rode away home and when they got there, he parked in her bay and laughed about it. 'The winner in the parking stakes.'

'A worthy winner.' She bowed low to his Harley.

'The old girl was junk, De Rooster. Dangerous.'

'She went.'

'Can you buy another one?' He walked with her to the stairs, and up the stairs, one step to her two.

'I can afford some more junk, I suppose. I don't know. I haven't thought that far yet. I haven't thought. Your bike blew my mind. I might . . . might get on a plane and fly away, or buy a bike – a Harley.' She shrugged. 'Thanks. Thanks for the ride. Thanks for your phone, thanks for . . . for being there. Just thanks.'

'I wouldn't have missed it for quids. I'm going to frame this shirt. It's got your handprints on it.'

That afternoon she sat fondling the goose girl while the television played. She didn't shower, didn't get ready to entertain Matt. She wasn't thinking about Matt or his wife or his boys. She was thinking of her ride in the wind.

'I was flying free on the eagle's back. I was flying free there for a while.'

in the blood

Walter spent a lot of time following her little car around, or just watching her at her window. Not much he could do about it, though. Stirring up old emotions caused more harm than good. He'd learnt that much, but it hadn't stopped him wanting what he wanted.

He'd been shopping today, bought a few necessities and a few non-necessities. He delved into a plastic bag and withdrew a shirt. A nice one, too. He'd picked it up cheap, and a pair of jeans, not so cheap. They were for his youngest boy to wear home. He'd finally agreed to go home when they let him out. He'd picked up a couple of nice ornaments for his daughters-in-law. Nothing for the oldest boys, though. Have to get them something.

'Not long now. A few more weeks, Walter, and the waiting will be over.'

It might be a relief to hit those roads, to put Melbourne behind him again. He liked driving. A lot of his years had been spent on the roads. A retired sales rep, he'd sold men's suits all over the western district.

That's when he'd found the photographs, three of them, still in their frames. He preferred the small one. It was in the glove box. He'd almost left it sitting on the television when he'd checked out of the motel this morning.

Tonight he'd be sleeping at Richmond again. He'd got himself a ground floor room on the east side, two doors from the bathroom. It was cheap, and good enough, and impersonal too. And close to her. He'd wait it out there.

He looked at the photograph in the fading light, making his own mental adjustments to the features, removed the bows from the long hair but retained the smile and the eyes. Even an artist couldn't have improved on those.

'Essence of innocence,' he said. 'The little love of my life.' He thought of that day in Ballarat; he'd seen her walking down the street and he'd known her. Should have spoken to her that day, but he'd followed her home. Hadn't done him much good. Done him less good making that phone call. One of your better mistakes, Walter. It was like she'd been sitting there waiting for me. And probably had been. Probably been warned.

Go home to your bloody wife and stay out of my life, she'd said.

'Hell hath no fury like a woman betrayed.' His black-rimmed glasses removed, his fingers rubbed his eyes, kept rubbing.

His mother used to do that, take off her glasses and rub her eyes. If she'd lived a few more years, things might have turned out differently. At eighteen a boy wasn't meant to live alone. He hadn't either, not for long. He'd met and married Elaine in three months. She'd been too old for him, or he'd been too young for her. Bad days. Bad years, those.

His mind moved back to his boyhood. Slower, safer years. Back then a twelve-year old could put his bike on the train to Heidelberg on Sundays and ride out to the Yarra, sit by it in safety, catch a bag of fish and take them home for his mother to toss in flour and fry up for dinner.

He smiled, his dark eyes staring at the window but seeing

beyond it to the past, seeing Mother and little Wally in a slum villa. Dark, narrow rooms. Smell of mould, stink of poverty in that old house. The smell of the old place in Richmond reminded him of slum villa.

Gone now, of course. A whole row of those little houses had been ripped down and high-rise flats built on the site. Maybe some of the mould had lived on to creep up those towering walls.

He could still see that old street in his mind's eye, still see his mother at the wash trough. A hard worker, a religious little woman, wed to a gambler. At nine, Wally had sworn on the Bible that he'd never touch liquor and never gamble. He'd pretty much kept one promise – only because he didn't like the taste of beer and hadn't been able to afford spirits.

'It's in the blood, Mother. Blame the wild O'Leary blood.'

No finer woman ever born than his mother, parsimonious but fine. She hadn't wanted her boy to grow up, and she'd had her way. He hadn't grown much. Small feet. Small hands, not good for anything at fifteen, so they'd set him up behind a menswear counter. His occupation had given him a lifelong interest in his appearance.

His gaze concentrated now on the slim slits of light at the window where the little one had separated the blinds and was peering through. Then the blind was hitched high, and her hands cupped the glass. Such a little dot of a girl. You'd swear she was looking for him, sitting up there waiting for him to walk down that drive and up those stairs.

'Lordy me,' he sighed, his hand raking at his curls, attempting to claw out his need, dig through his scalp and alter his yesterdays. But they were all in there, set fast in time and there was no going back. He knew it. Didn't like it.

She moved away, but his eyes didn't leave that rectangle of light. Three minutes, five. Where was she? Was she coming down? Would he have the guts to face her if she did?

No.

But there she was, back at that window again.

He placed the old photograph back in the glove box and reached for his ignition key as a blue station wagon pulled in behind him. He'd seen it before, knew who owned it too. He watched the boyfriend lock his car and pick up his briefcase, walk down the drive and disappear. Walter turned his key and listened to his motor's purr.

'Some you win and some you lose, Walter, and you've lost this little one.'

Sally looked at Matt seated at her table, a glass of wine in his hand; she was all out of Jim Beam and she wouldn't be buying any more.

'Where did you get to on Wednesday, Matt?' Her voice would not give her away and if her smile was false, he didn't notice. She was still wearing her jeans and her face was clean of makeup.

'A business trip, Sall. I couldn't contact you. It came up on the Monday night and I had to fly to Sydney. Spent the week in conference and hardly came up for air.'

And she had him.

She smiled, stepping away when he reached for her. The kitchen bench between them, she told him that her car had died on the South Eastern Freeway.

'No great loss, kiddo.' So sure of himself, he poured another glass of wine from the cask.

Then she told him where she had been before her car died and he flinched.

'You make such beautiful little boys, Matt. I played Mary's lamb today. I followed them to school, which was against the rules. I know that.' He swallowed a gulp of wine and he turned his back, looked out the window. She waited, ready for another lie.

Nothing.

'You didn't go on a business trip. You took the family away

for a holiday to Mildura.' Now he faced her. She stepped back again.

Silence.

Stereo playing next door.

Silence.

Breathing.

'You're a liar, Matt.' His lips remained closed, his long finger brushing his hair back from his brow. So like her father, but not like him at all. Not those eyes. Not that mouth. 'I had coffee with your wife today. We compared diamond rings and spoke about our favourite charities.'

That got a reaction. He caught her wrist and his fingers crushed it. His voice when it came was a whisper. 'Stay away from my family. Do you hear me? Stay away from my family.'

'I thought I was your family, Matty. You said that I was all you had, Matty. Wife and mother, sister, lover, playmate, friend. The only one you needed, Matty.' She tugged her wrist free and rubbed it. 'Get out of my sight, you liar.'

He left, and left her shaking, left her nauseated. But for once she had been in control. For once she'd said what she'd wanted to say and she'd said it well. He was out of her life.

She took a don't-care pill from her pack and swallowed it with wine. It killed the pain, killed the anger, didn't kill her need to cry. Always crying these days.

good luck charm

Interview at Myer day. Too sick to go; but she went. Caught a tram. Found a seat beside a woman who had a newspaper. And it was on the front page – they'd got the hit-and-run killer!

Hard to read on a moving tram when another was turning the pages.

Fourteen-year-old youth . . . Driving his mother's car . . . She had seen the damage . . . Hadn't reported it.

Sally moved closer, but the woman turned the page. Photograph of a pretty teenager shooting up. Why? How could anyone stick needles dipped in poison in themselves?

Victoria will get five safe injecting rooms this year

Stop the world, I want to get off, she thought. Then the woman and her newspaper got off, and Sally continued on to her interview.

A sad week, sad television, sad Sally; and in Number 13, the Asian family mourned anew.

Cruel old Melbourne, it took what it would and gave no apology. Helen Lee, her life stolen by a fool of a boy. And Carla Miller. Her murderer was still free, still out there biding his time. Every week someone died violently. Kids overdosing, babies used as punching bags, families murdered in their beds.

But Melbourne gives back too, Sally thought. It held out its arms to me like some weird old relative, far too distant to recall the bond of blood, but eager to claim me, and to offer its all. It tested me, but didn't blame, didn't disapprove. You're good enough as you are for me, Sally De Rooze, it said, but you'd better grow up fast if you want to share my world.

Sally sang her own sad song on Sunday. 'I am a Jester', she'd named it. Cocky said it was brilliant. A hit. They did it again later, sang it together, and it sounded like a hit.

'You and me, babe. We've got the world at our feet. We're going to be big.'

He could write music. Was there anything he couldn't do? He said he'd put her song on paper, just like Mummy had put her songs on paper, and that night Sally didn't want to be alone, so they sat late at his flat, getting all of the squiggles and dots in the right places and it looked ... looked like music when it was done. Sort of permanent.

She had made something. She had created.

But Sunday ended at midnight. Monday came again, and at 6.15 in the evening she heard that familiar knock on her door.

How did he have the nerve to come back?

She wouldn't open the door. Five times he knocked, and she stood, heart pounding, waiting for him to give up and go away. Her phone rang.

Please, God, let it be Cocky.

Please, God, let it be Sue.

She picked it up, though some ancient wisdom warned her not to.

'I'm sorry, kiddo. Don't hang up on me,' he said.

She hung up. And she shook and cried a fool's tears because she knew now. She'd been a pill-popping fool back in February, and she'd stopped denying it, stopped making excuses and started counting weeks.

She was pregnant. She was pregnant and she had to do something about it.

At ten she took her packet of don't-care pills from her bag and popped one, popped two into her palm, needing strong medicine to turn off her tears. For minutes she stood looking at the twin pills, thinking of Sleiman, thinking of her mother and the glass of chocolate milk.

Once upon a time she'd recognised bad medicine when she'd seen it. She'd been smart back then. Pills wouldn't fix anything. They wouldn't make a pregnancy go away. Her hand turned, dropped the pills into the toilet, and she stood there popping more from their bubble pack, listening to their small plop-plop-plop as they hit the water.

'Dose yourself up on reality. Gulp it down, and keep it down,' she whispered.

Sleep didn't come for her until daylight, then Myer woke her at 9.15. They wanted her in for a second interview. Could she come in this afternoon?

Her stomach had gone mad; coffee tasted bad, cigarettes tasted worse. Three outfits were tried and discarded on her bed before she settled on her black suit. The skirt was long, the jacket fitted but it needed colour. Her face needed colour. She took the old brooch from her purse and pinned it to her lapel and she stared at its reflection in the mirror as her fingers touched.

'Pretty,' she whispered.

The woman conducting the interview commented on it.

'My good luck charm,' Sally replied, and deep within she knew those words had been spoken before. Someone, somewhere, had said those words before.

It's my good luck charm.

Too many interviews behind her, she'd learnt how to give the right answers, and she had the job too. Until they sat her before a computer.

She could type. She could do thirty words a minute, but she didn't have a clue what to do with a modern computer. It had Windows 98; totally different from the one she'd learnt on in Lakeside, it had a mouse. She'd only used the keys before, and this thing was a speed freak; it wouldn't respond to keys.

She tried the mouse. Stupid name for a piece of computer. She'd trapped mice, cleaned up their dirt, attempted to feed them to her cat once, but she'd never tried to find her way around a computer by clicking on a mouse's haunches. The cursor shot every which way. It seemed logical to turn it around, to point the mouse head in the right direction, let it see where it was going. That wasn't right either. She couldn't click.

The woman's mouth was still smiling but her eyes had lost their interest. 'Thank you,' she said. 'We'll be in touch, Sally.' About as genuine as a bowl of plastic peanuts.

Why couldn't anyone tell the truth? Sorry, Sall, with those computer skills we can offer you a job cleaning the toilets. So easy. Why hadn't Matt told her the truth that first night? Sorry, Sall. I've got a wife and three sons.

She could have walked away from him, just like she was walking away from the job. She didn't want to work on a computer. She wanted to sing. Cocky was trying to get them into a bar. And he'd do it. He had more push than a used car salesman.

Wandering aimlessly through the departments, she looked at shoes, at books and nail polish – considered palming one. The pale pink. A perfect match for the china lady's throat. She used to be good at palming nail polish. At one of the homes, nicking stuff had been an initiation rite, and why not? Her hand ready to slip the small bottle into her pocket, she saw a little leprechaun watching her.

A reflex step back, a reflex dropping of the polish, but when she looked again he was gone, disappeared in a puff of smoke.

Like somewhere else. Old hallucination.

Out to the street then. Air out there. Lightheaded, her legs jelly snakes, she sat a while watching a busker toss balls. She tossed him a coin before walking on.

Her two-hour tram ticket was still valid, and she found a seat. She didn't see him get on, didn't see him until he sat beside her. Wide mouth, woolly head – old leprechaun, but no hallucination.

'A beautiful brooch,' he said, eyeing it. Her hand reached up, covered it. 'And no doubt very precious, my dear.'

The high-pitched voice was like a breeze in her mind. The tram swayed and she swayed against him, memory whispering in her ears, nausea crawling in her stomach. Then she recognised him. He was the guy who had spoken to her at the tram stop in Toorak Road, way back in September, the guy with the brown suitcase. He was the old guy who had tossed the envelope into the guitar case.

No empty seats. She couldn't stand all the way home or she'd fall down. She turned her face to the window, urging the tram on.

'It's Sally, isn't it?'

Her head left the rest of her behind as she swung around to face him. Dark eyes behind black-rimmed glasses, hand adjusting the glasses. His features were shimmering, changing.

She stood, pulled the cord and left the tram.

He didn't follow her.

Walking fast then, her hand unconsciously fingering the brooch. *My good luck charm. My good luck charm.*

By the time the next tram groaned to a halt her two-hour ticket was no longer valid, but it carried her to her stop. She was walking past the photography shop when she remembered the negative. Couldn't find the slip of paper, but the woman behind the counter brought out a bright envelope and slowly slipped the black-and-white print from it, apologising for its poor quality.

He who expects nothing is never disappointed.

'God!'

It was on the counter before her, and there she was. Little Sally with her knickers hanging. Little blonde head, shy smile. She looked like Robby, the serious. And she looked like Sally too.

'The negative was damaged, and the original shot was poorly focused.'

'It's beautiful!' Her eyes were filling, blurring. She caught the tears with her index fingers, and the woman stopped apologising. 'It's beautiful.'

She bought a frame that matched Daddy and the boys' frames, almost, and it cost more than the print, but the woman fitted it, convinced that her customer was mad when she didn't want it wrapped, when she left the shop weeping, the photograph held to her breast.

milk and dragons

That evening, the television on and selling hard, Sally sat at the table, staring at the child she'd been, and drinking wine. Couldn't stop crying lately, and didn't know why she was doing it. Everything made her cry. Even stupid television shows.

'Fly to Bali for six nights,' the announcer on the television crowed. 'Only seven hundred and ninety-nine dollars.'

Bali. It made her cry again. Made her think of Ross and their planned honeymoon. Made her think of February and the night she'd made love to him. Made her think of Matt, who had made love to her three nights later.

Made her think.

So she poured more wine to turn off thinking.

Tomorrow she'd find out where you went to get an abortion.

And perhaps kill a tiny Nicky with his thistledown hair.

The thought got the tears really dripping. It was lucky she'd had the out-of-focus photograph framed because the glass was wet. Maybe she needed a cigarette. Maybe her brain was in nicotine withdrawal, but cigarettes didn't taste the same lately, and she couldn't find any anyway.

She emptied her bag onto the table, sipping wine as she sorted through the last year of her life.

Scrap of purple and gold wrapping paper. She crumpled it and tossed it to the floor, glancing at the ring she still wore. Should toss it too, but her hand looked bare without it. She found the packet of condoms, never opened, and old supermarket receipts, and a packet of disintegrating chewing gum stuck to a phone bill. She'd meant to pay that.

She glanced at her bankbook. Enough in there to murder a little Nicky – or buy an old car, or a ticket to fly. It was placed in the zip compartment, safe, and her glass was empty again.

All control lost, her hands dragged the wine cask close and it knocked the salt shaker to its side, spilling a small trail of white onto the table. She pinched a pinch, flicked it over her left shoulder to ward off bad luck. Mrs Bertram had done that, and Mrs Mason. She picked up the pepper, stared at it, then placed it on the opposite side of the table, and she named them Ross and Matt, raising her glass to both.

'Eeny, meeny, miney, mo, catch a tiger by the toe. If he hollers, let him go. Eeny, meeny, miney, mo.'

Ross won, so she tried it again, slowing the game, pointing her glass to each in turn, spilling wine, but no more tears. Ross, salt of the earth, the winner.

'Eeny. Meeny. Miney. Mo. Catch a tiger by the toe. If he hollers, let him go. Eeny, meeny, miney, mo.' She finished fast. 'Each, peach, pear, plum, out-goes-old-Tom-Thumb.'

Matt, hot black pepper, lost.

The salt and pepper left eyeing each other from opposite ends of the table, she picked up her new photograph, and her finger touched the child's face and wandered across to the hand, and up to the man who held the hand.

Then someone knocked at her door.

Just a little knock, not Matt's possessive rat-a-tat-tat. Not Cocky's cocky rap-rap. It was more like Sleiman the sleaze's rat-atat-tat tat-tat.

Funny the way people knocked on doors. Sue didn't knock at all. She belted the door and yelled, 'Let me in. I smell men.'

And again. An apologetic little tat-tat-tat. Then the voice. 'Have you got a drop of spare milk, De Rooster? I need a coffee.'

'Drink it black,' she yelled. 'Whoops! Black people are allowed to say white, but white people aren't allowed to say black,' she told the child in the photograph. 'Political correctness happened while you were lost, baby.'

'Just enough for one cup, De Rooster. I'll say please.'

She stood then, and wiped at her face, her nose, with her hands, then with difficulty made it to the door. Hadn't put on the safety chain. It swung open as she weaved her way to the fridge.

'Just a drop.' Her head swung around, almost swung her off her feet. He'd followed her in. 'Been hitting the happy juice?' he said, picking up the wine cask.

'Not so's you'd notice.' She sniffed and took it from his hand, lifting it high. It felt lighter than when she'd poured her first glass.

'I'll have a coffee if you're offering,' he said.

'I wasn't offering. I was weighing it.' She found a serviette and blew her nose.

He looked bigger up close – like a car in a showroom always looks bigger than when it's in a yard. She eyed him, up and down. He was inches taller than Matt, heavier too. He filled the small space between bed and kitchen.

Bedsitters were bad, bed waiting there, ready for use. She ran her fingers through her hair, wishing she hadn't tossed down so much wine. Didn't want to turn her back to fill the jug, so she filled it side on, splashing water on herself and the floor. It took a while to find the right holes to plug it in, turn it on. She opened the tin of coffee, one eye on her visitor, then she noticed the fridge door hanging open and she slammed it. It rocked.

'Buy a fridge and you won't have to keep borrowing my milk.'

'I meant to get some on my way home, De Rooster.'

'Only wimps drink their coffee with milk anyway.'

'You drink yours black, I take it?'

'Because we owned the least-used thirty-year-old fridge in existence. And we still got seventy-five dollars for it – which proves it, doesn't it?'

He stood there, taking in the swollen eyes and papers strewn on the floor, the wine cask and the single glass. 'What have you been celebrating?'

'Birth. How much coffee?'

'A round teaspoon. Two sugars.'

She glanced at her wineglass, then took out a second mug, added coffee, and placed two slices of bread in the toaster. Black coffee and toast might soak up some of the wine. A stupid move, opening the door.

Silence. Only the hum of the traffic, the sound of the wind. What do you say to a big black bikie in a bedsitter at midnight? He wasn't saying anything. Just standing there, filling up the space.

But ... but he'd scaled a drainpipe for her. He'd changed a tyre, and she'd ridden on his bike, hadn't she? She'd left her handprints on his shirt, for Christ's sake.

Not in a bedroom.

She eyed him as the toast popped, then she took her sharp knife from the drawer, using it to spread butter thick. It didn't do it very well. She added peanut butter with the point. Had to dip it often. Dip and wipe. Dip and wipe, and the jar fell over. He caught it, then held it steady while she dipped and wiped some more.

'You're a patriot,' he said.

'What?' She looked where he pointed, at the jar. Its label was an Australian flag behind a familiar smiling face. 'No. I've just got tastebuds. He uses salt and gives the plastic peanuts a miss. It's all I can eat these days. Anyway,' she said. 'Anyway, why aren't you out dealing drugs or cards or something?'

'I'm working a day shift until May.'

'Everything hinges on May.' She offered a slice of uncut toast, no plate, but he took it and demolished it, so she made more, safe with the bench between them and the knife on the sink. The toaster was good too. Hot. It would singe his long hair if he tried anything.

Another slice down and he wasn't trying anything, but he wasn't going back to his flat either. She knew he didn't like smoke, so she edged her way by him to the wardrobe where she searched her jacket pockets and struck gold. She lit the cigarette on her gas ring, singed her hair, but it didn't smoke him out. He'd made himself comfortable on her kitchen bench.

'Why did you come to Melbourne?' she asked.

'To know what it looked like. Why did you come?'

'To find room to bloom, but Melbourne is a forcing ground. Like . . . like at those hothouse nurseries; they get all the African violets – I didn't say African because – Oh, shut up.'

'I didn't say a word, De Rooster.'

'No. That's the trouble. Anyway, what I'm trying to say is, they get all of those flowers blooming for Mother's Day, and you buy them, take them home and give them to her, and a week later they're dead. All forced out. That's me. All forced out.' She glanced at the long black-clad legs and at the boots. Big. 'You can sit on a chair. That's what they're for.'

'I broke the habit a while back.'

He made the second cups of coffee and he sat on her floor, his back against the bench. His boots were too close so she moved to the side of the bed nearest the door. It was still open.

He spoke about the casino, said he'd worked at casinos in Launceston and Darwin, that he'd done a short stint in Perth.

'Have *they* got dragons?'

'Dragons?'

'You know. That fire dance. It's that Sean Connery dragon, from *Dragonheart*. The casino has got him and his family imprisoned in a cave beneath the Yarra, and between dusk and dawn a cruel dragon master whips them awake, every hour on the hour, just to say, you killed 'em.'

'Killed who?'

'Everybody. Let them out before you go.'

'I'll slip them a hacksaw in a cake.'

'They don't eat cake. Give them some bolt cutters. Set them free to fly.'

They talked for an hour, about *Dragonheart* and the casino, and she told him that pokie machines saw her coming, that the noise they made turned into hysterical laughter as soon as she sat down in front of one, so she didn't sit down any more.

'But I love the magic of that place. I can stand for hours watching the water dance, and I walk up and down that staircase and I feel like someone else, like the someone else I always wanted to be.' She looked up and caught his eye. 'That's why it works. It offers ordinary little people magic so the fat cats can fleece them.'

'You weren't born to be a cynic, De Rooster.'

It was after one when he stood and washed his mug, returned the milk to the fridge. He found space there for her cask of wine too, then he wiped the bench. A house-trained bikie with no furniture?

He looked at her new photograph before he left.

'See. I was right. There are stars in those eyes.' Then he frowned, took the photograph to the light. 'I know him,' he said.

She walked to the light and leant close, looking at the face of the male. Too wrapped in looking at the Sally child, she'd barely glanced at the out-of-focus male. Didn't know him.

'Stick a pair of black-rimmed glasses on him, De Rooster, give him grey hair, and he's the little bugger who's counting cards, robbing my table blind. I'll swear it's him.'

on the right track

may 2000

Beautiful April had led into May with its warm, clear days and moonlit nights, and the rich smell of autumn. It was in the air of Bollinger Street, that ancient earthy scent of decay as Melbourne's leaves fell to feed the buds of a new beginning.

Sally felt so pregnant and well. She was going to have this baby. It was going to be a little girl who looked like the one in the photograph, and she was going to raise it the way a little girl should be raised.

Seated by the window, her hands busy crocheting a white layette, her mind visualising the arms that would fit these miniature sleeves, she hadn't seen the black Honda stop out front. But she saw him.

Her chair pushed back, she stood, watching the little leprechaun walk to the letterboxes, a white envelope in his hand. She watched him stand a moment, glance up, then over his shoulder before he delivered his mail. Quickly then, he walked back towards the road. Fast little steps.

It was the walk. It was the way he turned his head. The way he looked over his shoulder, his hand raised in a half-salute.

Her crocheting tossed down, she was out the door, the white wool catching beneath her high heel, tailing her. She shook it loose at the stairs and ran, her door left wide open. The Honda was completing its careful three-point turn when she ran out to Bollinger Street, and into its pathway.

The driver braked and she walked to his window. 'I know who you are.' Glass between them, dark glass, and she slapped at the glass between them, hitting out at the one behind glass. 'You're Papa. You're Papa O'Leary.'

The rustle of autumn all around. Skittering, scattering leaves chatting on the footpath, playing on the road. Tiny tumblers, chuckling as they raced headlong into the mulch of winter.

She was in his arms. Didn't know how, or who had made the first move, or how she'd got him out of the car, but she was holding someone of her own, being held by someone of her own and she was bawling like a baby, holding on too tight. He was so little and too skinny to hold so tight, and her tears or her arms were going to break him.

Black-rimmed glasses knocked askew. Navy-blue eyes, like her own, swimming. Little hands, like her own, patting.

She was talking. He was talking. They were standing on the road, saying little words, silly rushing words. And 'sorry'. He said it and she said it, and then they said it together. And a car beeped them, so they told the car sorry and moved to the kerb.

Do you remember, he said, and she said no, and they couldn't stand on the kerb all day.

'Come inside, Papa.'

He shook his head. 'I left you a letter, little one. I've tried to explain.'

'I don't need a letter. That's just an excuse for you to disappear again, and I won't let you.'

He wiped tears from her face with the palms of his hands. 'You don't know me. Read my letter. Don't make a decision now that you might regret tomorrow.'

'You come inside and have a coffee then, and you let me get

to know you – or I'll rip up your letter and throw it in the rubbish.' She wiped at her dripping nose with her wrist, searched for a tissue in her pocket and blew her nose. 'I don't care who you are or what you've done or haven't done. All I know is, I belong to someone. I haven't got anyone else.'

He blew his own nose while overhead leaves chattered impatiently, eager for their turn to fall and join the play.

He looked at the trees, then towards Toorak Road. 'There's a little coffee shop just down the way. They make a nice vanilla slice.'

She lifted her head then, wiped her nose with her fist, and she sniffed and pointed her finger. 'When they were building that Geelong house. Vanilla slices. You brought vanilla slices in a white paper bag and Grandma put a red checked tablecloth on the grass. See, I do know you. I do remember you.'

They sat long over their coffee, two cups, and she read his letter, all the while remembering more of this little man who had been in the car with Grandma when Sally was three and Shane was two and there was no Robby or Nicky. Grandma with the *pretty* always on her lapel. Papa singing nursery rhymes. Sally coveting that *pretty* on Grandma's coat. He had remembered. He'd given her the gold and ruby brooch for her birthday.

His letter was all apology. Two of a kind, Walter O'Leary and Sally De Rooze, always apologising for being alive. Two of a kind. Just like Mummy had always said. Both suffocated by guilt and rejection, they'd run away to find air enough to breathe.

His handwriting, like her own, was small, an apology in itself.

The brooch is a family heirloom, our good luck charm. Wear it always, my dear. It has been in the family since 1785. Some of your ancestors were a little wild, a little to the left of the law. The brooch was stolen from a fine English house, or so the story goes. And five brothers fought for five days over it. The youngest won it and gave it to his sweetheart as a wedding gift. My old Dada gave it to my mother. I gave it to your grandmother, Elaine, on our wedding day, then to Marian, my second wife. Your mother never forgave me for that.

You must never blame her. What I did to my two daughters was unforgivable. The brooch should have gone to Bernice, then to your mother, and so to you. It is now with its rightful owner.

He'd written that he'd been at her mother's funeral, and they spoke of that day while they ordered a second coffee and vanilla slice. She told him she'd seen him seated on a toadstool, that he'd looked like a little leprechaun, then he'd disappeared.

He spoke of his two married sons, Craig and Glen. Since Marian had died, he'd been living in a caravan behind his oldest boy's house.

For my size, I inherited a large portion of the family's wild streak, as did my youngest, Dean. He has spent the last twelve months in a corrections centre. His mother died while we were in Melbourne for his trial in May. He blamed himself for her death, and has tried to cut himself off from his family, but tomorrow I am taking him home.

Melbourne was no good for him, and not so good for me either. I have what could be termed an obsessive personality. I do nothing by half measures. When I gamble, I do little else. I need the stability of my oldest boys to keep me on the straight and narrow. They are Marian's true sons.

'You play blackjack. Down at the casino,' she said.

'I followed you there one night, and I won seven thousand on the roulette wheel. It was my undoing. I'd given most of it back then, after Christmas, I took away enough to buy my little car.'

'Did you ever own a green car?'

'The old Holden. I've had it since '74. Two hundred and fifty thousand miles on the clock and it's never had the head off,' he said proudly. 'I'll give it to my boy when I get him home.'

Your forgiveness I do not ask for. I deserted you when your need was greatest. So much I could have, should have done, for you. I did try in those early years. Many times I begged your mother to allow me to raise you with my boys. She refused to see me, to speak to me.

For years I kept track of you by your letters to your little friend, Raelene. The Masons were very understanding, but each time I found you, your mother took you away again. Then you stopped writing to Raelene and I lost you for years.

In May, when Marian died, I received a condolence card from Glenda and I was able to read the postmark on the envelope. I saw her twice in Lakeside. She told me that you had no desire to see me, but I saw your address on the refrigerator, and I have this obsession with numbers. Flat 11/ 18 Bollinger.

My dear little girl, it saddens me to write these words, and I write them only because I am leaving in the morning and I won't be coming back. I can understand that you want nothing to do with me, and I write this not to change your mind, or in defence of my neglect, but to make you know that I do love you, that I have never stopped loving you and your mother.

I do not ask for your forgiveness, but to leave Melbourne and lose contact with you again – this I cannot do.

If one day you can find it within your heart to forgive the unforgivable, then at least you will know where I am.

My love to you always, Papa O'Leary.

'I forgive,' she said and she folded his letter, placed it in her bag. 'So what's to forgive, and I still like vanilla slices.'

count his claws

Her high heels rang on the concrete stairs and her heart sang. No purse, no keys, luckily she'd been wearing shoes when she'd run from the flat. And she'd left her television on, and her door wide open, and thank God it hadn't blown shut.

She hit the light switch, then cursed the light fitting that ate globes like a kid eating Easter eggs. No use calling the agent about it; instead, she bought her seventy-five watt globes in half dozen lots.

The bathroom light was on. She pushed the door wide, and by its borrowed light, snibbed her safety chain and opened the slats of the venetian blind. The street lamp sent its light through to paint stripes on the floor, bench and wall.

'Subdued lighting,' she said. 'Some people pay a fortune for it.'

A strange, still night, but it had been a strange day. She'd stepped out of her old world and into fantasy. Old Papa, what a funny little man. What was it about blood that led to total acceptance? He had three sons, two married and living in Gladstone, Queensland. Sally De Rooze was no longer the last survivor of her clan; she had a whole nest of relatives.

She looked at the bundle of white wool on the table as she dragged a chair close to the high cupboard over the stove; then she walked back to the table, picking up the near completed jacket. The wool that had followed her to the door had been rewound. Someone had been here.

Quickly she stepped up to the chair, reaching for her light globe stash, wanting light now.

And she heard the toilet flush, and the words, 'You need a few extra inches, kiddo.'

She snatched the globe, knocked two others onto the stove and jumped to the floor. 'What are –'

'Just passing. Thought I'd drop in and use the facilities.' He reached for the chair, but she held it before her.

'Most people wait for an invitation.'

'Since when have we been most people?' He picked up the near completed baby jacket. 'You have hidden talents. What else are you hiding, Sall?'

She looked at the give-away white thing, watched him toss it to the table. 'You know where the door is.'

'No drink? Just for old times' sake.' He offered his endearing shrug, his lifted eyebrow and half-smile, but long contact with infection built immunity. 'I've missed this place like you wouldn't believe, Sall.'

'Go home to your boys. They're probably missing you.'

The slatted light from the street lamp lit his face, his shirt. Striped Matt. Segmented Matt. She wanted him gone.

'A drink. One drink and I'll go. Promise.' The space between the table and the bench was slim. No way around him.

'It's over, Matt.'

'It's not over until I say it's over, Sall, and it doesn't need to be over. She's left me. Packed up and gone home to Daddy.'

'I'm sorry, but that's your problem.'

'No,' he said thoughtfully. 'No. It's your problem.' He snatched the chair from her and tossed it across the room, and when she tried to go past him, he smiled. Then he punched her, low in the stomach.

She had seen the smile. She hadn't seen his closed fist that stole her breath and her pride away. As she doubled over, grasping the table for support, he calmly walked to the television and turned the volume high.

Her lungs howled for air; her mouth opened, trying to give them what they needed while she stared at him, stared without recognition. He grasped her hair, lifted her, then aimed a second blow at her baby. As she fell forward he caught her arm and tossed her to the bed.

Blood in her head, the pain of his fist growing. It swallowed her. Too late she tried to scream. No air. Only vomit rose to her throat.

This was nightmare time. Screams had always become lost in the nightmare time; refused exit, they had seeped away unscreamed. Her eyes not understanding stared at the venetian blind now creating cage bars of light behind something dark and cruel, some spitting nightmare beast she couldn't run from.

'Planning to hit me with a maintenance order somewhere down the track, Sall? Was that your little game?'

My baby. My baby. Little Sally, born new, born into love. Stay with me, baby. Got a Papa for you. Got uncles to love you. Hold onto me. It's just another nightmare. We can count it away. Count our fingers. Ten and ten more. Twenty. Count the bad dream away. Count our toes. Ten and ten more. I'll breathe for you, baby. I'll push the pain down for you, baby. Count the bars of the city beast's cage. Count his claws. Count his teeth. We'll count him away. Just stay with me, baby.

He stood looking down at the short grey skirt, dragged high, and at the slim thigh, the knee. And his loins stirred.

His hand reached for his zip, slid it down.

'Just one more for the road, kiddo. What do you say?'

She didn't say no. Curled up, waiting for it, on that bed he knew so well, knees to her chin, the white of her briefs just visible. Child-like. Charity child. His to do with as he would.

He laughed as his hand reached for her knee. It played there, slid higher.

The present was separating from the past. She couldn't keep the numbers marching in line. Couldn't ride the pain anymore. Wanted the past and the safe old nightmares back.

But an ambulance or cops were outside her window, screaming off to some new emergency. People out there, all going about their business. Old gay guy downstairs with his new partner. Not home as often these days.

Outside that door there were people. Outside that door. Had to gather enough air to scream. Someone might hear it.

But the television was loud and her scream too small. No scream at all. Barely a whisper.

'Bastard.' Wasted air.

His smile vanished. The word grated, spoiled his game. This one had possessed no venom. She'd been laughter for a while – his own little whore in fantasy land. Always ready for him – a playful child in a woman's body. But not tonight. Couldn't have her tonight, so he slapped her mouth, reinforcing his control.

'Keep it nice, kiddo.'

Pain had become an ocean's waves, gathering way down in the deep black then washing in to swamp her. But ebbing. She waited for the ebb-tides, found their rhythm and learned to ride the waves, sucking air deep when the tide ebbed.

Rap-a-tap-tap.

Had she heard it? But no time to wonder, she was wallowing in the swamp of pain and it sucked her mind down, trying to drain the last of her will away.

Then what would be left of her? What would be left of her Sally baby?

Had to count. Keep on counting. Not lose her place. Not lose her one chance. If chance came.

Two hundred and seven. Two hundred and eight.

Concentrate on the bars of light and on the beast who had looked like Matt. Watch that half-face.

This is what happened when you traced a black beast to his lair and exposed him.

Shouldn't have gone to Hallam.

Shouldn't have left the baby's jacket on the table.

Funny how an entire life can become one long 'shouldn't have'.

Shouldn't have left the door open.

Shouldn't have –

Knuckles against the door now. Hard. 'De Rooster. Turn that bloody television down.'

This time she heard him.

And the black beast heard him. He turned his face, and she saw the camouflage stripes on his hide. Big bad wolf in borrowed clothing, come to gobble her up. But he stepped back, and her face turned to follow him, looked past him to the television.

Raucous thing on its red plastic box, marking time. How much time had gone? How much time to the next ebb-tide? Television commercial clusters, three minutes long. She'd counted them once, then counted the five minutes of sitcom, complete with canned laughter, slotted in between the important business of selling.

What if we promised to watch twelve minutes of commercials? Would they give us the fifteen minutes of sitcom unbroken? Would anyone keep their promise?

Probably not.

She sucked air, waiting for the lull between laughter and commercial, and for the ebb-tide. Soon they would intersect. Only let it be soon or she'd die of pain.

Wouldn't die. Couldn't die. No name waiting ready on a tombstone for Sally Ann De Rooze. Three fat, stupid cherubs keeping watch over the boys.

Shane would have hated them. He would have wanted a Superman stone. Mummy might have wanted to share a grave with Daddy, but Sally had never wanted to share those cherubs.

Too many places she hadn't seen. Too many songs she wanted to sing.

Silence. The television had taken a breath and he was leaning over the bed.

She screamed as she uncoiled and lashed out at him with her high heels. Got him hard. Got him good. Caught him unready, unsteady. He lost his balance, and she screamed out the pain that swamped her as she kicked him again, then she rolled from the bed, hit the floor, rolled, and crouched against the window wall, ready to spring.

Fists pounding the door now.

'Help me!' she screamed. Loud. High. Long. A singer's scream.

The bikie was outside the door. Always around when she needed him; she had to hang on for just a little longer. Long enough to let him in.

Pushing up, her back to the wall, her left hand reaching out for support rocked the old bookshelves. Ornaments tumbled, and on the television an audience laughed from its can while the door of Number 11 shuddered in its frame.

One hand on the floor, her fingers searched, feeling old, familiar shapes.

The black beast stood between door and window, frowning now. This wasn't the way he'd planned it, because he hadn't planned it. Just driving by, thought he'd drop in. Not a smart move.

He'd always been smart. Smart at school. Smart at home. He'd talked his way out of trouble more times than he could recall. Twelve that first time and he'd had to talk hard.

'He could sell ice to an Eskimo,' old Gramps had said.

'Innocent as a little angel,' his mother, the holy bitch, had replied.

'Cunning as a bloody fox.' Lieutenant Marsden had known. 'Whip-smart little bastard.'

Whip smart?

Whipped smart.

He smiled. He'd talk his way out of this one too. So she'd fallen. Climbed on the chair to get a new globe and fallen. He'd dial 000. Had to think smart now, think fast. Who'd believe that dumb little bitch if he got his story in first? No-one. He'd popped in to give her some financial advice, found her on the floor.

But why had he closed the front door?

He stepped back, thinking on that one as his hand searched beneath his shirt for blood. The kicking little alley cat bitch had hurt him. He'd have more bruises to explain at home.

One of the boys must have done it when they were playing. Or he'd walked into that tree in the back yard. Have to prune it this year.

He'd been good these past months. Home early. Football with the boys. But good had always been a bore. He looked from the phone to the crouched form before the window, and he saw her right hand rise.

Saw the haze of white. And pink.

He frowned as the goose girl struck him. Struck him between eye and ear. Head to the side, he looked with interest at china fallen to the floor, and he looked at his knees as they began to fold. He swayed, and his eyes didn't understand.

Had to get home. Hadn't meant to be so late. Had to play the good boy.

Then he fell to the side, silently. Hit the edge of the bed, silently. His legs were not listening, not obeying his command to get away, live to play another day.

And he fell, still not understanding. To the floor.

While the television played on.

Blood was crawling like a blind black worm into the cave of his ear, then changing its mind, altering its course down to the collar of his business shirt. The shaft of light from the bathroom created its own piece of modern art on her biege carpet. A polished shoe, a light sock, a black-clad leg amid the shards of china. Lustrous light on the goose's bill. Goose girl's hand empty, her basket of eggs flung away. And where was her pink and gold hat?

No time to look for it now. Had to get by that shaft of light, get to the door, and there was only one way to go.

Should have got a bigger flat, Sall old girl.

She was crawling across the bed when the door burst open and a blur came through, shoulder first. Trod on the black beast, tripped on the black beast and sprawled to the floor.

'Jesus H Christ, De Rooster!'

She looked at the long hair, and at the dark face and the wide eyes, and at the shattered goose girl, and she gasped in air, moaned it out as pain gripped her womb, squeezed it.

Hot that first dragging rush of blood, but she made it to the bathroom, leaving a trail of red pearls to bead the white tiled floor. She made it to the toilet seat.

Little Sally baby all gone away down the toilet bowl.

Better for it.

Cramps rolling in, rolling over her. Couldn't move if she wanted to and she didn't want to, so she stared at the red on white, stared too long.

'Are you all right in there?'

Was anyone ever all right? She considered saying, I'm okay, but couldn't find a lull in the pain to place it. He came to the door when she didn't reply, and stood there, face turned, his hair like clean black silk beneath the light. But he saw the blood, and he stepped away to use his mobile phone.

Should have closed the bathroom door.

Should have done a lot of things and shouldn't have done a lot more.

Empty now.

Emptied.

Little crocheted jacket, almost done, tiny booties not begun. On the floor.

Too weak to stand. To weak to sit. The naked globe was weaving circles overhead, so she stopped looking up and looked down. Down at the hand, still wearing the ring. A glass bauble. Gewgaw for a fool.

It slipped off easily but it left its mark behind. Light against the dark.

Banded.

Branded.

She'd seen him and she'd wanted him. She'd set her trap for a black swan, but caught a black wolf by the tail.

Got bitten. Got bitten bad.

Eyes staring at the golden heart, stone-cold in the palm of her hand. Television silent now. Only the bikie talking to his mobile phone.

Her legs spread and with a slight turn of her hand the ring dropped into the bloody bowl, tinkling as it fell. She reached around and flushed the toilet.

Couldn't stand. She tried to. She wadded toilet paper to hold the bleeding, lots of paper. Used the last of the roll. She inched up her briefs to hold the paper, first one side, then the other, but when she tried to stand she fell to her knees, and all the while the room was dancing.

The bikie came back to the door. A worried face didn't suit him. 'The ambulance is on its way, De Rooster.'

'Shut the door.'

He walked to her, stood before her. 'I've seen it all before. I've got a bunch of sisters.'

Friend? Neighbour? Their relationship had been hard built, its foundations in insults and humour. No humour in this scene. Her hand pushing him away, she tried to stand, to straighten her skirt, but she fell against him. He lifted her so easily.

'I can –'

'You're only a bantamweight,' he said, and he placed her on the bed, and when she wanted to sit, he eased her back. 'Head down. Let the blood get to your brain.' He brushed her hair from her face and his dark hand felt cool. It stilled the ceiling's waltz. It took away some of the pain.

She turned to the clock. Only 7.55. How can you live a thousand years in moments? A glance at the television for verification. Cartoon faces with no voice trying to sell her Tetleys Tea. She preferred coffee, black coffee.

He had drawn the quilt over her, and now he stood between her and that dark thing on the floor. She lifted her head, looking past him to the flinch of an expensive black shoe.

'Relax and keep your head down. The ambulance won't be long.'

He had a good face. Strong. And warm, honest eyes; she could see right through them, see right on down to his soul. There were no words she could say to him, but she had to say something. Never been lost for a few smart words, not for her bikie, right from the days of their fight over the parking bay and those notes she'd Blu-Tacked to his Harley. She was just Sally with him, and no apology. A feisty little bantam, he'd called her. De Rooster, he'd called her.

'He'll be okay. He's coming around.'

'Better aim . . . with a . . . with a cricket ball,' she said.

black and white

She'd packed her old case, she'd cleaned out her drawers and wardrobe. She'd wrapped the ornaments again, wrapped them well in newspaper. No goose girl to wrap first this time. She'd always wrapped that one first. The bikie had locked up her flat on the night the ambulance came. He'd picked up the scattered china and tossed it in the garbage bin.

But she'd wrapped the lady with the broken neck and the boy with the hiatus elbow, the elephant and his red-turbanned rider, chip off the old turban. They were all packed up again in their supermarket carton, ready for the little Asian guy with the white kombi van who'd offered to move her junk out to Joyce and Mike's bungalow, in East Burwood.

So much she'd accumulated in only a year. The battered old chest of drawers, the bookshelves, empty now. She glanced at the bed, second-hand when she'd purchased it from the *Trading Post*. She hated that bed. Its bloodstained quilt and pink quilt cover had been tossed in the rubbish bin.

She'd outgrown pink.

Her long black overcoat lay with a pile of discards in the

corner. She picked it up, shook it, smelt it, then pushed it quickly into a bag earmarked for the op shop. It reminded her of time best forgotten. She hadn't charged Matt. His wife and sons had enough problems.

She sighed, shrugged, then worked on. All of the cartons had been labelled, all of the bags; experienced packer, Sally De Rooze. The three 8×10 photographs were in a separate bag. They'd go with her in the taxi.

At noon, a bag of rubbish in each hand, she was heading out the door when the bikie walked from his unit, his bedroll and backpack over one shoulder.

'What are you doing lifting stuff, De Rooster? Give it here.'

'Go on, flaunt your muscles again,' she said.

'If you've got 'em, flaunt 'em, I say.'

He took the bags, and she leaned against the wall. 'You're still heading off today?'

'Flying north with the birds. Got a sister in Brisbane I'll stay with for a while. Another winter in Melbourne and I'll lose my suntan.' He laughed, his teeth so white.

'Half your luck,' she said.

She didn't want to see him go. Who else did she have to talk with about everything and nothing?

'You decided not to take a new lease?'

'New lease? Here!' Her voice was high. 'No way known to mankind.'

'Where are you going?'

'To Joyce and Mike. For a while. I've got to get a decent job, buy another car.'

'You've got to sing, De Rooster.'

'Yeah. I'll get back to that soon.'

'You'd better.' He placed his load down and offered his hand. She took it, pumped it hard, and he didn't want to release her hand so he pumped it again. They laughed a while then grew quiet. 'I'd like to say that it's been nice knowing you, but you're turning me into a nervous wreck.'

'Thanks.'

His backpack and bedroll over a shoulder, her rubbish bags over the other, he moved towards the stairs.

'Bye.' She lifted a hand.

Two steps away, he turned. 'Dare to dream, De Rooster. Dream big, and you'll make it big. I've got faith in you.'

'I will.'

And the bags were down again. 'No you won't. Once I'm not around to stir you, you'll take some dead-end job to pay your rent and end up in the suburbs with five kids.'

She shrugged. 'Worse fates, I suppose.'

'Not much worse.' His head was down, but his eyes, those big, soft eyes, were watching her face for a reaction as he said, 'Pack a bag and fly with me.'

'Too much junk to fly, Monk. I'm earthbound.'

He turned to the stairs, then changed his mind, walked to her door, peered through. 'And that's all it is. A nest of bloody junk. I don't believe in furniture.'

'Yeah. I've noticed that.'

'It ties your dreams to the ground, De Rooster.'

'I've been hauling mine around for so long now, I don't know how to stop.'

'Easy. Give it to the Salvos.' Light words but no smile, just those eyes, and a hand fiddling with his watchband. Not his habit.

'That's the distilled essence of my best dreams.' She looked at the window, and at the clouds flying free. Misty morning all gone now, sunny afternoon coming. Winter was on its way to Melbourne but it hadn't arrived yet.

She sighed, wanting to fly. 'I love your bike, Monk. I love the air blowing free in my face and no seatbelts to hold me down. I do.'

'I love your fight and your fire, De Rooster. Not much of you, but what there is is gutsy stuff.' He drew a breath, then a finger reached out and brushed her cheek. 'Dust,' he said. 'The . . . the true fact of the matter is, I can't see myself riding off into the sunset and leaving you behind. Pick up your bag. Come on.'

'God,' she said. 'God.' She looked at the carton of newspaper-wrapped ornaments, and at the bed, at the chest of drawers. 'I've got a grandpa in Queensland, and three half ... sort of uncles, younger than me.'

'So we'll visit them, beg a space on their floor.'

She shrugged.

'No strings, De Rooster, just freedom and living, talking and singing, and maybe you'll get to like my colour.'

'I like it. It suits your face.' Her thumb went to her mouth; she chewed a moment on a long strong nail. 'You're ... are you serious?'

'Me? Serious? No. I've just got used to having you around.'

'You wouldn't have room on your bike for my guitar.'

'It's part of the deal. You're going to sing for your supper, or my name isn't what it is.'

'What is it, anyway? Your Christian name.'

'Arthur George – but tell anyone and, *phutt*, you're dead.'

'I prefer Monk.' She picked up her guitar. 'It's big.'

'So we'll buy a trailer.' He took the guitar. 'I've got a sister in Dubbo. We'll camp there tonight.'

'Sister in Dubbo, sister in Brisbane, sister in Dandenong, sister down on the Esplanade. How many sisters have you got?'

'Nine of the buggers,' he said. 'I'll tell you about the rest of them on the way.'

She looked at her battered case and her zip-bag of important bits, shaking her head, but laughing as her eyes continued to scan the bedsitter, seeing what he could see – aged and battered junk.

No goose girl here. She'd grown up and left the carton full of rejects.

And wasn't it about time?

epilogue

'... I could see you in the distance, so I planted my foot and the old Datsun flew.'

'Did you catch me?' Monk asked.

'Yeah.'

'Was I on the Harley?'

'Yeah. And then so was I, and the dream changed; it wandered off to Lakeside and we were having a picnic in Ross's top paddock.' She picked up the pages of newsprint, blotting one with a tissue before glancing again at the photograph of Kermit and at the words below it.

It was a good interview. She had to admit that. It didn't sound like Lakeside Sally, or the one who had sold the unsaleable at Phonepross. In it she was Sally De Rooze, with partner, *Ajie* Moncton. The reporter had called him AG during the interview. Confused reporter. Monk refused to admit to his given names.

Thank God for him. Thank God for the years that had passed. Thank God that the past was just that.

A glance then at the frock spread ready on the motel bed. A few hours yet before she'd need to dress and put on her make-up, step outside the door. But he'd be with her, and he'd be standing offstage, as he always did.

The dress would give her confidence too. It was long and black and glittery. She loved it. She'd bought it yesterday, at Myer – hadn't even asked the price. Money to waste was still new to her, but she had an image to maintain these days. No more flowery hats and op-shop gear for Sally De Rooze. She'd left them behind with her junk and bad memories.

Monk's phone rang at five. He spoke of family for a while, spoke of sisters and nephews. 'Butch,' he said as he placed his phone back in his belt. 'She's at the airport now. Mum and Cassidy have just flown in.'

'Good. Sue and Cocky said they'd be there. I rang Ross and got Carol. Their baby is overdue but, baby or not, you wouldn't catch Ross inside a casino.' She looked out the window towards Lakeside and shook her head. Hadn't been back there. May not ever go back there. 'It's a boy. Isn't it a bit weird, Monk – I mean, wanting to know the sex of your baby before it's born? I wouldn't want to know.'

'Are you planning something, De Rooster?'

'I suppose we ought to have one some day. We'll have to give Papa's brooch to someone.'

'You're talking house here. You're talking furniture!'

'Some day. Maybe when I'm forty. That's a fashionable age to start a family these days.' She smiled as she watched him brush his hair. She loved that hair, loved its length, loved his strength and his honesty, loved his family. Her family now. She'd have three sisters-in-law in the crowd, and Mum, his mum, fat and cuddly.

'How are you wearing the brooch tonight?'

'On the long chain around my neck. It will look good against the black.' She always wore it on stage. Papa was so proud of her, and her young uncles thought she was 'big time'.

Her mind wandering, her eyes turned towards the window where a skywriter was painting his white message on the blue.

GOO

Baby talk? Was the big clock in the sky trying to tell her something? She pushed her chair back and stood, watching the forming of a perfect *D*.

What a clever pilot. How did he do it? She couldn't see the plane, just the fine lines of white and the occasional glint of sun on metal as the plane turned. She saw the straight line of an *L* and tried to outguess the skywriter.

Then it formed a *U* and a *C*, a *K*.

Just a message for one of the three million Melburnians. Not for her, but she could steal it for herself if she wanted to; the plane and the rest of its message were out of view.

GOOD LUCK.

'Monk. Come here. Melbourne knows I'm back in town.'

He came to stand with her at the window, and together they looked up at the smoky, white words painted in the sky.

She placed her arm around his waist, and his hand slipped over her shoulder. For five minutes they stood that way, their eyes concentrated on the letters, now elongating, plumping into drifting clouds, blurring. And when the last smudge of white had moved away from their window, he kissed her. 'Okay. That's enough slacking off for one day. You wanted to run through some of your songs again, didn't you?'

'I should. That second one, Monk. I'm not certain of the words yet.'

'You're sure you want to do that one?'

'Don't you like it?'

'What do you think, De Rooster?'

'I think you like it. I think you like it a lot, but you're bashful.'

He winked at her and took a small CD player from the cluttered bench, loaded it and found the second song. She didn't play her guitar these days, not on stage. She left the backing to the professionals.

Her foot picked up the rhythm while she drained her coffee mug, then she sang. Sang to him. Sang for him.

He fills my world with fantasy
There is no fence to hold me
My realm the sky, the air, the sea
While his broad arms enfold me.

I swing on the rim of the rainbow
I steal moondust to tint the dawn sky
I fill up my pockets with embryo stars
Stole from my true lover's eye.

He gave to me Aladdin's lamp
And polish-cloth so fine
And now I have my wishes three
He's mine, forever mine.

So I swing on the rim of the rainbow
Stealing moondust to tint a dawn sky
And I fill all my pockets with embryo stars
Stole from my true lover's eye
Stole from my true lover's eye.